Clemence Dane was [...] in 1888. She took he[...] Clements Dane (whi[...] during the Second W[...] and Ireland, and studying under the Tombs and France, she adopted a second name; Diane Cortis, and hit the London stage. Four years later she started writing, first novels – *Regiment of Women*, *First the Blade* and *Legend* – and later plays and screenplays. In 1945 she won an Oscar for her film *Perfect Strangers*. Other films she wrote starred major Hollywood names such as Greta Garbo, Katherine Hepburn, Vivien Leigh and Laurence Olivier. She also remained an accomplished artist all her life – her portrait of Nöel Coward hangs today in the National Portrait Gallery. He was a regular visitor to her home where, he recalled, her rooms were always crammed with friends who included Joyce Grenfell, David Niven, Richard Adinsell and Mary Martin. She proved to be the inspiration behind Nöel Coward's most famous character, Madame Arcati in *Blithe Spirit*. In 1941 she was made President of The Society of Women Journalists, and was created a CBE in 1953. She died in 1965.

Alison Hennegan, the series editor of *Lesbian Landmarks*, read English at Girton College, Cambridge. From 1977 until its closure in 1983 she was Literary Editor and Assistant Features Editor at *Gay News*. She went on to become Editor of the Women's Press Bookclub 1984–1991 and in 1992 launched the specialist feminist Open Letters Bookclub.

LESBIAN LANDMARKS

Lesbian writing is booming today – from the most rigorous of scholarly studies to the softest of soft-centre fiction – with special lesbian sections in many bookshops, crammed with volumes from the tiniest lesbian presses and the biggest publishing giants. In the midst of such plenty, it's easy to forget that it was not always so . . . .

Lesbian Landmarks is an exciting new series of reprints which illuminates the rich and eventful history of lesbian writing.

Their politics as varied as their prose and poetry, their ideas on gender as diverse as the genres in which they express them, the writers reprinted here span centuries, castes and cultures. Some were celebrated in their lifetimes but are now forgotten; others were silenced and exiled.

Amongst these authors you will find remarkable innovators in style and content. You may also find women whose far-distant attitudes and assumptions perplex or even anger you. But all of them, in their different ways, engaged in the long struggle to articulate and explore ways of living and loving that have, over the centuries, been variously misrepresented, feared, pathologized and outlawed.

The world these authors knew was often a world apart from ours; yet however unlikely it may sometimes seem, each of these books has helped to make possible today's frequently very different, confidently open lesbian writing. These, in short, are Lesbian Landmarks.

Clemence
Dane

Regiment of Women

Introduction by Alison Hennegan

The monstruous empire of cruell woman we knowe to be the onlie occasion of all these miseries: and yet with silence we passe the time as thogh the mater did nothinge appertein to us.

JOHN KNOX — *First Blast of the Trumpet against the Monstrous Regiment of Women*

To E. A.

Here's Our Book
As it grew.
But it's Your Book!
For, but for you,
Who'd look
At My Book?
C. D.

Published by VIRAGO PRESS Limited February 1995
20 Vauxhall Bridge Road, London SW1V 2SA

First published by Heinemann 1917, reprinted 1966

Copyright © Winifred Ashton 1917
Introduction copyright © Alison Hennegan 1995

*A CIP catalogue record for this book
is available from the British Library.*

Printed and bound in Great Britain by
Cox & Wyman Ltd, Reading, Berkshire

INTRODUCTION

The cold night air was like wine to her. After all, for an insignificant spinster, she had a fair share of power – real power – not the mere authority of kings and policemen. Her mind, not her office, ruled a hundred other minds, and in one heart, at least, a shrug of her shoulders had toppled God off his throne; and the vacant seat was hers, to fill or flout as she chose.

That is Clare Hartill in one of her many moments of dubious triumph, exulting in the terrifying power which her dangerously flawed but almost irresistible personality gives her over one small community of souls. Her kingdom is a girls' school in the ancient English provincial town of Utterbridge, in the early years of the twentieth century; in it she exercises a particularly female tyranny, that 'monstrous regiment [rule] of women', against which John Knox, the Scottish Calvinist, had inveighed some three centuries before.

Clare Hartill, as the discerning reader should already have realized, is *not* a safe role model for the younger lesbian. She herself would be the first to agree with her enemies' verdict, that 'she hated responsibility, though she loved authority'. She finds it harder to acknowledge that her seemingly insatiable hunger for power over female hearts and minds hides an even greater hunger for love – and terror of the vulnerability love brings. As desperate to inspire love as she is to protect herself from the pain of loving, Clare's ceaseless bid for emotional domination shapes and mars many lives, from the teachers she goaded as a girl, and her adolescent classmates, to her present day pupils and fellow teachers. A thoroughly bad lot, obviously, and her creator, Clemence Dane, weighed in with gusto to lay bare the horror of her anti–heroine's twisted emotions and perverted mind. Except that it didn't really work out that way. For the enormous paradox of the book, planned as one of the great Awful Warnings of anti–lesbian literature, is that in it we have one of the most fascinatingly complex and subtly observed psychological portraits of a particular sort of homosexual woman. She's not one we

v

want to boast about or claim eagerly as our own, but she *is* utterly credible, even (dare we whisper it?) recognizable, and made so by the depth of knowledgeable engagement which Dane seems to bring to her subject.

Dane recognizes Clare's fascination and writes as one who has herself responded to such a woman. This, her first and extremely successful novel, was not her only treatment of lesbian themes. Two years later, in 1919, her second novel, *Legend*, described the network of intense emotions which link a group of women united (and sometimes bitterly divided) in their adoration of the now dead Madala Grey. Almost a decade later, she was still pondering the topic, in an essay called 'A Problem in Education', printed in her collection, *The Women's Side* (1926). The 'Problem' referred to is 'emotional attachments between members of the same sex' and in the essay Dane returns once more to the danger of intensely charged relationships between girls and their female teachers. Her target is, yet again, the 'morbid and selfish woman [who may] amuse herself and gratify her love of excitement by playing on this tendency to exaggerated hero–worship in the children and mistresses under her care.' Then she makes a foray into autobiography:

> Such women do exist. It is to be hoped that they are rare; but they do exist. I have myself come across such types and I have been told, not by hysterical school-girls but by sober headmistresses of many years experience, stories enough of such women. I quote one of them –
>
> 'I have known at least four of these vampire women in my own experience, and have heard of many others. Two belong to my school and college days, the other two to my days as headmistress, and both have been sent packing. I am responsible for over eighty boarders, so you may imagine I feel pretty strongly about this sort of love–making.'

Clare (herself denounced as a vampire by Elsbeth Loveday, the angry aunt of Alwynne Durand, the woman Clare loves) stands as the fictional archetype of a woman increasingly feared early in this century: the spinster teacher, against whom an intensifying campaign was waged during the 1920s and 1930s, culminating in unsuccessful but vehemently argued efforts to outlaw unmarried women from the profession.

That particular battle was just one in a larger war waged over girls' education. It had already been raging for at least fifty years when Dane first published *Regiment of Women*, and the novel engages with most of its key conflicts. Chief amongst them was a fundamental question: are girls best educated in a single–sex institution, such as Miss Marsham's where Clare is Deputy Headmistress, or in a co–educational school, such as Dene Compton which Alwynne comes to know late in the book, when convalescing after a bad bout of influenza and too much Clare? Underlying that debate was a basic assumption, sometimes only implied, often explicitly and hysterically stated, that single–sex education was 'unnatural', 'unhealthy' and dangerous, co–education 'natural', 'healthy' and safe (and not only for the individual girl but also, and rather more importantly for 'the nation' and 'the race'). Within that broad, overarching concern were two further sources of conflict. One was a battle over the true end and purpose of educating girls: was it to prepare them for marriage and motherhood (on the basis that to educate a woman means educating a family and that marriage as an institution has most chance of surviving if men are mated with women who are rational, adult companions rather than eternal children, empty–headed and as much in need of governance as their own unlucky offspring, cursed with such a vapid mother)? Or was the function of girls' education to produce women capable of achieving and rejoicing in new freedoms of economic, intellectual and psychological independence, in a world where women's perceived worth and own self-esteem was not determined by their status as daughters, wives and mothers? The second conflict entailed a bitter tussle for female authority in the larger world beyond the home – specifically in girls' schools and colleges. Were women capable of governing themselves wisely – as Headteachers and mistresses – and were they fit to have unsupervised charge of the female young who were their pupils; or must female government always result in truly 'monstrous regiment'?

Such debates admit no easy answers; in Clare Hartill both advocates and enemies of women's educational rule would find their finest hopes and their worst fears exemplified. For Dane, though in theory Clare's intransigent enemy, is during most of the book honest and intelligent enough to recognize – indeed to praise – Clare's many real strengths and virtues. Moreover, Dane also sees and shows us that Clare, almost alone of those Utterbridge schoolmistresses whom we come to know, believes passionately in the life of the mind and in the transforming power of education which, in its best and widest sense, far transcends the petty narrownesses of school life. As Dane unambiguously informs us, early in the book:

There are women today, old girls of the school, who owe Clare Hartill the best things of their lives, their wide knowledge, their original ideals, their hopeful futures and happy memories: to whom she was inspiration incarnate.

The tragedy of Clare's life and of the book is that in her insatiable quest for power, exercised through her dealings with colleagues and especially pupils, she permits herself to pervert and corrupt a vision of education which she, more fully than her fellow-teachers, glimpses and pursues. All too often her own egoism comes between the vision and its attainment. Clare, in her benigner aspects, is a brilliantly gifted teacher, capable of taking infinite pains for pupils who merit it and revealing unexpected depths of patience, tact and tenderness in her efforts to help girls achieve a best which often astonishes them. But Clare at her demon worst is cold and contemptuous, a creature of sudden boredoms and quixotic rejections. She can exalt her constantly changing favourites to the heavens with a smile and plunge them into the depths with a frown, as she does often, simply, it seems, for the pleasure of proving she can. Yet Clare herself is not fully in control of her own capricious exercise of power, as two characters in this novel have particular and painful cause to know – Louise Denny, a pupil, and Alwynne Durand, a very junior colleague. Both love Clare deeply. Clare warns each of them on various occasions that loving her is dangerous. Neither believes her, both are indeed rejected by her, and each one responds by seeking her own version of escape.

Clare foresees neither flight, nor the loss and danger each will bring her. Louise's chosen method of escape threatens the school with scandal, and Clare with public disgrace. Alwynne's inflicts a more private devastation. As Dane herself had observed early in the novel, 'It was her misfortune not to realize that, for all her Olympian poses, she had come to love Alwynne deeply and enduringly'. That Alwynne loves *her*, 'with all the discrimination of a fine mind, and all the ardour of an affectionate child', Clare is swift to recognize: 'Here was no question of a fleeting devotion that must end as schooldays ended. Here was love for Clare at last, a widow's cruse to last her for all time' – provided, that is, that she understands the value of what is being so freely offered, respects the giver and does not abuse the gift. All of which would constitute a remarkable reform of Clare's character after some thirty–six years of unbridled egoism.

As readers we need not be unduly surprised that we see no such miraculous transformation. We might, however, reasonably expect that at this point the novel would become a cautionary tale lamenting the waste created when one self–destructive woman wantonly engineers her own personal defeat and deservedly loses the love she held too cheap (as Red does in another Lesbian Landmark written some forty–five years later, Han Suyin's *Winter Love*). But Dane's underlying concerns make such a novel an impossibility. Although in Clare she has created a fully convincing, three-dimensional character, she then, in a manner which does violence to the subtlety and honesty of her own intelligence, insists on placing her in a novel whose moral and political agenda can function in only two dimensions. Dane is concerned to establish two interdependent hypotheses: that heterosexuality is morally superior to homo-sexuality; and that therefore co–education is superior to single–sex schooling. To further those arguments Clare must be reduced in the novel's moral scheme to a symbol of 'unnatural passions', of the monstrous regiment of women, and of the necessary and inevitable connections between the two.

Clare thus becomes evil incarnate, a figure more recognizable from an earlier, and mainly French, tradition of fictional lesbians, larger than life and twice as horrible. She is, in that sense, a rather dated and melodramatic creation, a *femme fatale* of the old school, evoking that familiar figure, the lesbian vampire, and inspiring that familiar fear, unappeasable lesbian desire: 'I tell you, Clare Hartill, you'll die of hunger in the end', predicts Elsbeth Loveday in the novel's closing pages.

Yet melodrama, which might appear an anachronistic embar-rassment in a novel tackling such boldly 'modern' and controversial themes, is in fact most cunningly enlisted as Dane's ally. It is not just that characters behave melodramatically or find themselves enmeshed in melodramatic events. The prose itself is constantly overcharged with dramatic intensity, particularly at moments when female characters wrestle with conflicts and dilemmas caused by their powerful emotions – horror, desire, fear, rage, need and love – for other women (often but not always Clare). The prose can become as agitated as the women themselves, and its very ferment indicts Clare as the main cause of turmoil. Sometimes the prose reproduces the tones of denunciatory rhetoric more appropriate to the courtroom than the schoolroom, becoming in effect a speech for the prosecution – and, once again, it is Clare who's in the dock.

But Clare, as many of the first reviewers noted in 1917, will not be reduced to a symbol. One of the things which gives the book its enduring power and fascination is the almighty battle waged between Dane and a fictional character so fully realized that she perpetually threatens to break through the artificially imposed constraints within which Dane is determined to conduct the moral argument. As the book progresses, it becomes clear that Dane can 'win' the moral argument only by rigging the odds against Clare. The more sceptical reader may also begin to wonder whether Dane must battle so mightily because she herself finds Clare dangerously seductive.

An unlikely degree of muddle, we might think, for an author whose anti-lesbian moral purpose seems so clear. But muddle about sex was, we know from a host of Clemence Dane's long-suffering friends, one of her most abiding characteristics. Her conversation was constantly littered with sexual *doubles entendres* of which she herself seemed completely unaware. In his autobiography, *Life's Rich Pageant*, Arthur Marshall maintains that:

> The physical side of life had passed her by, together with the words, slang and otherwise, that accompany it. She had no idea at all why people laughed, or tried tactfully to conceal laughter, as time and time again she settled for an unfortunate word or phrase .... She never cottoned on to the fact that the name 'John Thomas' had a hidden significance and she was heard one day expatiating about the different sides to a person's nature: 'Yes, every man has three John Thomases – the John Thomas he keeps to himself, the John Thomas he shares with his friends, and the John Thomas he shows to the world'. 'Of course, Winifred' people said, when they could speak.

It's funny, and Arthur Marshall tells it beautifully, but it's also rather disquieting. In Marshall's account (much abridged here) Dane's behaviour seems compulsive rather than genuinely unaware. The 'physical side' of life may have passed her by, but in *Regiment of Women* its language is everywhere, from the description of Alwynne's response to Clare's distress, when 'All her love for Clare rose within her, overflowed her like a warm tide', to Clare's characteristic reaction to any interesting new girl: 'Egoism aroused her curiosity, her suspicion of hidden lands, virgin, ripe for exploration'. In the light of Marshall's 'John Thomas' anecdote, we may also ponder Dane's infelicitous choice of name for the 'hero' whose mission is to claim Alwynne for heterosexuality: he's called Roger. He's also a gardener, which is why, perhaps, he's so anxious to persuade Alwynne, convalescing from her near-breakdown, to 'show him all the weeds that were choking her before he could set about uprooting them and planting good seed in their stead'. Oh, as Arthur Marshall would say, *dear!*

If, however, we set anecdotal evidence such as Marshall's aside for the moment and look at Dane's prose by itself, will we still read it as the product of a sexually inexperienced author unwittingly making risibly inept choices of words and metaphors? Or might we see instead a language which embodies intuitive forms of half-knowledge whereby its author articulates, through imagery and metaphor, what she usually cannot say directly? Such a reading goes a long way to explain the otherwise inexplicable contradiction between Dane's supposed ineptitude in sexual matters and the apparent sexual sophistication of much of her language. It might also explain why she can render so deftly the intricate shades and nuances of the lesbian emotions she supposedly rejects, but fails abysmally when she comes to depict the frank and open heterosexuality she supposedly endorses.

Dane's pressing need is to prove the innate naturalness of heterosexuality. And to do so she must establish, to her own satisfaction at least, that passionate relations between women are at best immature and temporary (the last gasp of emotions perfectly proper, and indeed 'natural', to adolescent girlhood), and at worst, pathological and manipulative, destructive of health and sanity. To make Clare a monster best fits her purpose. In effect she constructs the book on a foundation of glaring illogic, and produces a series of false syllogisms, those rhetorical devices beloved by mediaeval philosophers. Her most important one goes like this:

Clare Hartill is a lesbian
Clare Hartill is a monster
Therefore all lesbians are monsters

But she also slips in an important subsidiary:

Alwynne and Clare are both women
Alwynne and Clare cannot conduct an equal and adult relationship
Therefore an equal and adult relationship is impossible between women.

(Quite easy, isn't it, once you get the hang of it – and terribly useful.)

One of the most important effects of this curious logic is to undermine any pro–lesbian arguments voiced by characters within the book. Clare, for instance, questions the supremacy of marriage in terms perfectly familiar and acceptable to any feminist; Alwynne insists, in the teeth of family opposition, that she and Clare can adequately fulfil each other's emotional needs. But this is a book which cannot afford to give them a fair hearing. Instead, its author determinedly plans a victory for the forces of heterosexuality, engineered by Elsbeth Loveday, Alwynne's aunt, and Roger Lumsden, Alwynne's thirty-year-old cousin recently returned to England.

Alwynne's marriage to any man would gladden Elsbeth's heart. She has precious little reason to love Clare, and would rejoice in her defeat. But in Roger Lumsden she has a gratifyingly perfect candidate – not just *any* man, but the son of the man she herself loved and lost.

Fastidious readers will inevitably have recoiled from much of Clare's emotional mess. But they should feel positively queasy at the compulsory nature of the heterosexuality now imposed by Dane, ably abetted by Elsbeth and Roger. Clare's (ab)uses of Alwynne are obvious; Elsbeth's may be less so for the unwary reader, but they are quite as manipulative and at least as perverted. In Elsbeth's version of the future, so much 'healthier', so much more 'natural' than the one Alwynne has envisaged sharing with Clare, Alwynne is to bear for Roger the children Elsbeth never bore for his father. Her children, once borne, will, by Roger's decree, be cared for by Elsbeth, since, as he and Elsbeth both so often agree, 'Alwynne is *such* a child'. In this unholy equation Alwynne becomes a surrogate twice over: once as the wife and mother Elsbeth never was; and again, as a surrogate child to Elsbeth and Roger who share so many anxious 'parental' consultations about their beloved, but essentially infantile, Alwynne. If this is a 'victory' for natural, normal, healthy heterosexuality it is a victory at least as flawed as the 'moral failure' of lesbianism, so vigorously denounced throughout the book.

Dane herself seems more than a little uncertain in her handling of that victory. Certainly her prose suffers, and so too does her usually fine ear for dialogue and tone. When she does eventually present a courtship scene between Alwynne and Roger, she even lapses into hideously arch attempts at drawing–room comedy. The humour here is painfully strained, very different from the dry wit, sardonic irony, and pithy one–liners scattered through the novel. The predominant note here is one of jarring coyness and a fluttering whimsy which even allocates speaking parts to a bedful of tulips. The effect is embarrassingly inept, but also revealing. Now, when Dane has at last triumphantly procured a 'proper' (heterosexual) love scene for Alwynne, she can bring to it nothing of the passion and directness which have characterized Alwynne's exchanges with Clare. It is, in fact, a very uncomfortable, most 'unnatural' love scene, with both parties addressing the tulips rather than each other.

Unsatisfactory as Dane's resolution of her plot may be, *Regiment of Women* established a pattern and a cast of characters which would exert a powerful influence over lesbian fiction for the next half-century. Versions of Clare the Vampire, Alwynne the Innocent, Elsbeth the Guardian Angel and Roger the Redeemer appear in various permutations in novels such as Naomi Royde-Smith's *The Tortoise-Shell Cat* (1925), Rosalind Lehmann's *Dusty Answer* (1927), Radcliffe Hall's *The Well of Loneliness* (1928), Molly Keane's *Devoted Ladies* (1934) and Dorothy Baker's *Trio* (1943). That the anti-Fascist German novelist, Christa Winsloe, writing a very different sort of lesbian novel in the early 1930s, was also influenced by the book seems clear from internal evidence. Various minor characters mirror those in Dane's novel: Winsloe, too, makes one of her central characters a most powerfully charismatic teacher, albeit a benign version of Clare; and, most important of all, one of Clare's pupils shares the same fate as Winsloe's young heroine, Manuela. (Winsloe's novel, *The Child Manuela*, on which the film *Schoolgirls in Uniform* is based, has already been published in the Lesbian Landmarks series.) Writing fifteen years after Dane, Winsloe presents a vision of the world in which love between women offers the only hope of redemption.

For Alwynne, redemption is to come, however unconvincingly, from heterosexuality, while Clare is condemned to a hell of loneliness. Or is she? Characteristically Dane's closing paragraphs are, like the rest of the novel, full of ambiguity. Clare, alone, has spent a sleepless night: she has 'reviewed her life as she remembered it, thought by thought, word by word, action by action. Faces rose about her, whispering reminders, forgotten faces of the many who had loved her . . . .' Each face prompts painful memories, poses unpleasant questions which Clare can no longer evade. *Why* is she now alone? 'What had happened? What had Clare done or left undone? She realized grimly that of this at least she might be sure – it had been her own doing . . . .' The book draws to a close with Clare facing, for the first time, the truth about herself. What she will do with her knowledge, how and whether it will change her, we cannot know. But the last lines of the novel suggest the prognosis may yet be favourable:

When the dawn came, she was still sitting there, thinking –
thinking.

Alison Hennegan, Cambridge 1994

CHAPTER I

THE school secretary pattered down the long corridor and turned into a class-room.

The room was a big one. There were old-fashioned casement windows and distempered walls; the modern desks, ranged in double rows, were small and shallow, scarred, and incredibly inky. In the window-seats stood an over-populous fish-bowl, two trays of silkworms, and a row of experimental jam-pots. There were pictures on the walls—*The Infant Samuel* was paired with *Cherry Ripe*, and Alfred, in the costume of Robin Hood, conscientiously ignored a neat row of halfpenny buns. The form was obviously a low one.

Through the opening door came the hive-like hum of a school at work, but the room was empty, save for a mistress sitting at the raised desk, idle, hands folded, ominously patient. A thin woman, undeveloped, sallow-skinned, with a sensitive mouth, and eyes that were bold and shining.

They narrowed curiously at sight of the new-comer, but she was greeted with sufficient courtesy.

" Yes, Miss Vigers ? "

Henrietta Vigers was spare, precise, with pale, twitching eyes and a high voice. Her manner was self-sufficient, her speech deliberate and unnecessarily correct : her effect was the colourless obstinacy of an elderly mule. She stared about her inquisitively.

" Miss Hartill, I am looking for Milly Fiske. Her mother has telephoned—— Where is the class ? I can't be mistaken. It's a quarter to one. You take the Lower Third from twelve-fifteen, don't you ? "

" Yes," said Clare Hartill.

" Well, but—where is it ? " The secretary frowned suspiciously. She was instinctively hostile to what she did not understand.

" I don't know," said Clare sweetly.

Henrietta gaped. Clare, justly annoyed as she was, could not but be grateful to the occasion for providing her with amusement. She enjoyed baiting Henrietta.

"I should have thought you could tell me. Don't you control the time-table? I only know "—her anger rose again—"that I have been waiting here since a quarter past twelve. I have waited quite long enough, I think. I am going home. Perhaps you will be good enough to enquire into the matter."

"But haven't you been to look for them?" began Henrietta perplexedly.

"No," said Clare. "I don't, you know. I expect people to come to me. And I don't like wasting my time." Then, with a change of tone, "Really, Miss Vigers, I don't know whose fault it is, but it has no business to happen. The class knows perfectly well that it is due here. You must see that I can't run about looking for it."

"Of course, of course!" Henrietta was taken aback. "But I assure you that it's nothing to do with me. I have re-arranged nothing. Let me see—who takes them before you?"

Clare shrugged her shoulders.

"How should I know? I hardly have time for my own classes——"

Henrietta broke in excitedly.

"It's Miss Durand! I might have known. Miss Durand, naturally. Miss Hartill, I will see to the matter at once. It shall not happen again. I will speak to Miss Marsham. I might have known."

"Miss Durand?" Clare's annoyance vanished. She looked interested and a trifle amused. "That tall girl with the yellow hair? I've heard about her. I haven't spoken to her yet, but the children approve, don't they?" She laughed pointedly and Henrietta flushed. "I rather like the look of her."

"Do you?" Henrietta smiled sourly. "I can't agree. A most unsuitable person. Miss Marsham engaged her without consulting me—or you either, I suppose? The niece or daughter or something, of an old mistress. I wonder you didn't hear—but of course you were away the first fortnight. A terrible young woman—boisterous—undignified—a bad influence on the children!"

Clare's eyes narrowed again.

" Are you sure ? The junior classes are working quite as well as usual—better indeed. I've been surprised. Of course, to-day——"

" To-day is an example. She has detained them, I suppose. It has happened before—five minutes here—ten there—every one is complaining. Really—I shall speak to Miss Marsham."

" Of course, if that's the case, you had better," said Clare, rather impatiently, as she moved towards the door. She regretted the impulse that had induced her to explain matters to Miss Vigers. If it did not suit her dignity to go in search of her errant pupils, still less did it accord with a complaint to the fidgety secretary. She should have managed the affair for herself. However—it could not be helped. . . . Henrietta Vigers was looking important. . . . Henrietta Vigers would enjoy baiting the new-comer—what was her name—Durand ? Miss Durand would submit, she supposed. Henrietta was a petty tyrant to the younger mistresses, and Clare Hartill was very much aware of the fact. But the younger mistresses did not interest her; she was no more than idly contemptuous of their flabbiness. Why on earth had none of them appealed to the head mistress ? But the new assistant was a spirited-looking creature. . . . Clare had noticed her keen nostrils—nothing sheepish there. . . . And Henrietta disliked her—distinctly a point in her favour. . . . Clare suspected that trouble might yet arise. . . . She paused uncertainly. Even now she might herself interfere. . . . But Miss Durand had certainly had no right to detain Clare's class. . . . It was gross carelessness, if not impertinence. . . . Let her fight it out with Miss Vigers. . . . Nevertheless—she wished her luck. . . .

With another glance at her watch, and a cool little nod. to her colleague, she left the class-room, and was shortly setting out for her walk home.

Henrietta looked after her with an angry shrug.

For the hundredth time she assured herself that she was submitting positively for the last time to the dictates of Clare Hartill; that such usurpation was not to be borne. . . . Who, after all, had been Authority's right hand for the last twenty years ? Certainly not Clare Hartill. . . . Why, she could recall Clare's first term, a bare eight years ago ! She had disliked her less in those days; had respected her as a woman who knew her business. . . . The school had been going through a lean year, with Miss Marsham, the head mistress, seriously ill; with a weak staff, and girls growing riotous and indolent. So lean a year, indeed, that Henrietta, left in charge, had one day taken a train and her troubles to Bournemouth, and poured them out to Authority's bath-chair. And Edith Marsham, the old war-horse, had frowned and nodded, and chuckled, and sent her home again, no wiser than she came. But a letter had come for her later, and the bearer had been a quiet, any-aged woman with disquieting eyes. They had summed Henrietta up, and Henrietta had resented it. The new assistant, given, according to instructions, a free hand, had gone about her business, asking no advice. But there had certainly followed a peaceful six months. Then had come speech-day and Henrietta's world had turned upside down. She had not known such a speech-day for years. Complacent parents had listened to amazingly efficient performances—the guest of honour had enjoyed herself with obvious, naïve surprise: there had been the bomb-shell of the lists. Henrietta had nothing to do with the examinations, but she knew such a standard had not been reached for many a long term. And the head mistress, restored and rubicund, had alluded to her, Henrietta's, vice-regency in a neat little speech. She had received felicitations, and was beginning, albeit confusedly, to persuade herself that the stirring of the pie had been indeed due to her own forefinger, when the guests left, and she had that disturbing little interview with her principal.

Edith Marsham had greeted her vigorously. She was still in her prime then, old as she was. She had another six years before senility, striking late, struck heavily.

" Well—what do you think of her, eh ? I hope you were a good girl—did as she told you ? "

Henrietta had flushed, resenting it that Miss Marsham, cer-tainly a head mistress of forty years' standing, should, as she aged, treat her staff more and more as if it were but a degree removed from the Upper Sixth. The younger women might like it, but it did not accord with Henrietta's notions of her own dignity. She was devoutly thankful that Miss Marsham reserved her freedom for private interviews; had, in public at least, the grand manner. Yet she had a respect for her; knew her dimly for a notable dame, who could have coerced a recalcitrant cabinet as easily as she bullied the school staff.

She had rubbed her hands together, shrewd eyes a-twinkle.

" I knew what I was doing ! How long have you been with me, Henrietta ? Twelve years, eh ? Ah, well, it's longer ago than that. Let me see—she's twenty-eight now, Clare Hartill—and she left me at sixteen. A responsibility, a great responsibility. An orphan—too much money. A difficult child—I spent a lot of time on her, and prayer too, my dear. Well, I don't regret it now. When I met her at Bournemouth that day—oh, I wasn't pleased with you, Henrietta ! It has taken me forty years to build up my school, and I can't be ill two months, but—— Well, I made up my mind. I found her at a loose end. I talked to her. She'll take plain speaking from me. I told her she'd had enough of operas and art schools, and literary societies (she's been running round Europe for the last ten years). I told her my difficulty—I told her to come back to me and do a little honest work. Of course she wouldn't hear of it."

" Then how did you persuade Miss Hartill ? "

But Henrietta, raising prim brows, had but drawn a chuckle from the old woman.

" How many types of school-girl have you met, Henrietta ? Here, under me ? "

Henrietta fidgeted. The question was an offence. It was not in her department. She had no note of it in her memorandum books.

" Really—I can hardly tell you—blondes and brunettes, do you mean ? No two girls are quite the same, are they ? "

But Miss Marsham had not attended.

" Just two—that's my experience. The girl from whom you get work by telling her you are sure she can do it—and the girl from whom you get work by telling her you are sure she can't. You'll soon find out which I told Clare Hartill. And now, understand this, Henrietta. There are to be no dissensions. I want Clare Hartill to stay. If she gets engrossed in the work, she will. She won't interfere with you, you'll find. She's too lazy. Get on with her if you can."

But Henrietta had not got on with her, had resented fiercely Miss Marsham's preferential treatment of the new-comer. That Miss Marsham was obviously wise in her generation did not appease her *amour propre*. She knew that where she had failed, Clare had been uncannily successful. Yet Clare was not aggressively efficient : indeed it was a grievance that she was so apparently casual, so gracefully indifferent. But, as if it were a matter of course, she did whatever she set out to do so much better, so much more graphically than it had ever been done before, that inevitably she attracted disciples. But Henrietta's grievance went deeper. She denied her any vestige of personal charm, and at the same time insisted fiercely that she was an unscrupulous woman, in that she used her personal charm to accomplish her aims : her aims, in Henrietta's eyes, being the ousting of the secretary from her position of trust and possible succession to the headship. Henrietta did not realize that it was herself, far more than Clare, who was jeopardizing that position. Though there was no system of prefecture among the staff, she had come to consider herself responsible for the junior mistresses, encouraging them to bring complaints to her, rather than to the head of the school. Old Miss Marsham, little as she liked relaxing her hold on the reins, dreaded, as old age must, the tussle that would inevitably follow any insistence on her prerogatives, and had acquiesced ; yet with reservations. Had one of the younger mistresses rebelled and carried her grievance to the higher court, Miss Vigers' eyes might have been opened ; but as yet no one had challenged her self-assumed supremacy. Clare, who might have done so, cared little who supervised the boarders or was supreme in the matter of time-table and commissariat. Her interest lay in the actual work, in the characters and possibilities of the workers. There she brooked no interference, and Henrietta attempted little, for when she did she was neatly and completely routed.

But the more chary Henrietta grew of interfering with Clare's activities, the more she realized that it was her duty (she would not have said pleasure) to supervise the younger women. She had a gift that was almost genius of appearing among them at awkward moments. If a child were proving refractory and victory hanging in the balance, Miss Vigers would surely choose that moment to knock at the class-room door, and, politely refusing to inconvenience the embarrassed novice, wait, all-observant, until the scene ended, before explaining her errand. Later in the day the young mistress would be button-holed, and the i's and t's of her errors of judgment dotted and crossed. Those who would not submit to tutelage she contrived to render so uncomfortable that, sooner or later, they retired in favour of temperaments more sheeplike or more thick-skinned.

To Alwynne Durand, at present under grave suspicion of

tampering with Clare Hartill's literature class, she had been from the first inimical. She had been engaged without Henrietta's sanction; she was young, and pretty, and already ridiculously popular. And there was the affair of the nickname. Alwynne had certainly looked out of place at the mistresses' table, on the day of her arrival, with her yellow hair and green gown—'like a daffodil stuck into a bunch of everlastings,' as an early adorer had described her. The phrase had appealed and spread, and within a week she was 'Daffy' to the school; but her popularity among her colleagues had not been heightened by rumours of the collective nickname the contrast with their junior had evoked. Her obvious shyness and desire to please were, however, sufficiently disarming, and her first days had not been made too difficult for her by any save Henrietta. But Henrietta was sure she was incompetent—called to witness her joyous, casual manner, her unorthodox methods, her way of submerging the mistress in the fellow-creature. She had labelled her undisciplined—which Alwynne certainly was—lax and undignified; had prophesied that she would be unable to maintain order; had been annoyed to find that, inspiring neither fear nor awe, she was yet quite capable of making herself respected. Alwynne's jolliness never seemed to expose her to familiarities, ready as she was to join in the laugh against herself when, new to the ways of the school, she outraged Media, or reduced Persia to hysterical giggles. She was soon reckoned up by the shrewd children as 'mad, but a perfect dear,' and she managed to make her governance so enjoyable that it would have been considered bad form, as well as bad policy, to make her unconventionality an excuse for ragging. She had, indeed, easily assimilated the school atmosphere. She was humble and anxious to learn, had no notions of her own importance. But she was quick-tempered, and though she could be meek and grateful to experience backed by good manners, she reared at patronage. Inevitably she made mistakes, the mistakes of her age and temperament, but common sense and good humour saved her from any serious blunders.

Miss Vigers had, nevertheless, noted each insignificant slip, and carried the tale, less insignificant in bulk, in her mind, ready to produce at a favourable opportunity.

And now the opportunity had arisen. Miss Hartill had delivered Miss Durand into her hand. Miss Hartill, she was glad to note, had not shown any interest in the new-comer. . . .

Miss Hartill had a way of taking any one young and attractive under her protection. . . . That it was with Miss Hartill that the girl had come into conflict, however, did away with any need of caution. . . . Miss Durand needed putting in her place. . . . Henrietta, in all speed, would reconduct her thither.

CHAPTER II

Miss Vigers hurried along to the Upper Third class-room. She straightened her jersey, and patted her netted hair as she went, much in the manner of a countryman squaring for a fight, opened the door, after a tap so rudimentary as to be inaudible to those within, and entered aggressively, the light of battle in her eye.

To her amazement and annoyance her entry was entirely unnoticed. The entire class had deserted its desks and was clustered round the rostrum, where Alwynne Durand, looking flushed and excited and prettier than a school-mistress had any business to be, was talking fast and eagerly. She had a little stick in her hand which she was using as a conductor's baton, emphasizing with it the points of the story she was evidently telling. A map and some portraits were pinned to the blackboard beside her, and the children's heads were grouped, three and four together, over pictures apparently taken from the open portfolio lying before her on the desk. But their eyes were on Miss Durand, and the varying yet intent attitudes gave the collective effect of an audience at a melodrama. They were obviously and breathlessly interested, and the occasional quick crackle of question and answer merely accentuated the tension. Once, as Alwynne paused a moment, her stick hovering uncertainly over the map, a child, with a little wriggle of impatience, piped up—

" We'll find it afterwards. Oh, go on, Miss Durand ! Please, go on ! "

And Alwynne, equally absorbed, went on and the class hung upon her words.

The listener was outraged. Children were to be allowed to give orders—to leave their places—to be obviously and hugely enjoying themselves—in school hours—and the whole pack of them due elsewhere ! She had never witnessed so disgraceful a scene.

9

Her dry precision shivered at Alwynne's coruscating adjectives. (It is not to be denied that Alwynne, at that period of her career, was lax and lavish in speech, altogether too fond of conceits and superlatives.) She cut aridly into the lecture.

"Miss Durand! Are you aware of the time?"

Alwynne jumped, and the class jumped with her.

It was curious to watch that which but a moment before had been one absorbed, collective personality suddenly disintegrating into Lotties and Maries and Sylvias, shy, curious, impish or indifferent, after their kind. Miss Vigers's presence intimidated : each peeping personality retired, snail-like, into its schoolgirl shell. With a curious yet distinct consciousness of guilt, they edged away from the two women, huddling sheepishly together, watching and waiting, inimical to the disturber of their enjoyment, but distinctly doubtful as to whether 'Daffy,' in the encounter that they knew quite well was imminent, would be able to hold her own.

But Miss Durand was self-possessed. She looked down at Miss Vigers from her high seat and gave a natural little laugh.

"Oh, Miss Vigers! How you startled me!"

"I'm sorry. I have been endeavouring to attract your attention for some moments. Are you aware of the time?"

Alwynne glanced at the clock. The hands stood at an impossible hour.

"There!" she remarked penitently, "it's stopped again!"

She smiled at the class, all ears and interest.

"One of you children will just have to remind me. Helen? No, you do the chalks already. Millicent!" She singled out a dreamy child, who was taking surreptitious advantage of the interruption to pore over the pictures that had slid from the desk to the floor of the rostrum.

"Milly! Your head's a sieve too! Will you undertake to remind me? Each time I have to be reminded—in goes a penny to the mission—and each time you forget to remind me, you do the same. It'll do us both good! And if we both forget— the rest of the class must pull us up."

The little girl nodded, serious and important.

Alwynne turned to Henrietta.

"Excuse me, Miss Vigers, were you wanting to speak to me? I'm afraid we're in rather a muddle. Children—pick up those pictures : at least—Helen and Milly ! Go back to your desks, the rest of you." And then, to Henrietta again, " I suppose the gong will go in a minute ? "

She was being courteous, but she was implying quite clearly that she considered the interruption of her lesson unnecessary.

Henrietta's eyes snapped.

" The twelve-fifteen gong went a long time ago, Miss Durand. It's nearly one. Miss Hartill wishes to know what has happened to her class."

" My hat ! " murmured Alwynne, appalled.

It was the most rudimentary murmur—a mere movement of the lips; but Henrietta caught it. Justifiably, she detested slang. She stiffened yet more, but Alwynne was continuing with deprecating gestures.

" This is dreadful ! I'm awfully sorry, Miss Vigers, but, you know, we never heard the gong ! Not a sound ! Are you sure it rang ? " (This to Henrietta, who never slackened her supervision of the relays of prefects responsible for the ever-punctual gong. But Alwynne had no eye for detail.) She continued agitatedly, unconscious of offence—

" But of course I must go and explain to Miss Hartill at once. Children—get your things together, and go straight to the Lower Second. I'll come with you. Miss Vigers, I am so sorry—it was entirely my fault, of course, but we none of us heard the gong."

But as she spoke, and the girls, attentive and curious, obediently gathered up their belongings and filed into the passage, the gong, audible enough to any one less absorbed than Alwynne and her class had been, boomed for its last time that morning, the prolonged boom that was the signal for the day-girls to go home. The children dispersed hurriedly, and Alwynne was left alone with Henrietta.

Alwynne was grave—distinctly distressed.

" I must go and explain to Miss Hartill at once," she repeated, making for the door.

" You needn't trouble yourself," Henrietta called after her. " Miss Hartill went home half-an-hour ago."

The irrepressible note of gratification in her voice startled Alwynne. She turned and faced her.

" I don't understand ! You said she was waiting."

" When I left her, she had been waiting over half-an-hour. She told me that she should do so no longer. Miss Hartill is not accustomed to be kept waiting while the junior mistresses amuse themselves."

Alwynne raised her eyebrows and regarded her carefully.

"Did Miss Hartill ask you to tell me that? Are you her messenger?" she asked blandly.

The last sentence had enlightened her, at any rate, as to Miss Vigers's personal attitude to herself. She was perfectly aware that she had been guilty of gross carelessness; that, if Miss Hartill chose, she could make it a serious matter for her; but for the moment her apprehensive regrets, as well as her profound sense of the apology due to the formidable Miss Hartill, were shrivelled in the white heat of her anger at the tone Henrietta Vigers was permitting herself. She was as much hurt as horrified by the revelation of an antipathy she had been unconscious of exciting; it was her first experience of gratuitous ill-will. She rebelled hotly, incapable of analysing her emotion, indifferent to the probable consequences of a defiance of the older woman, but passionately resolved that she would not allow any one alive to be rude to her.

And Henrietta, amazed at the veiled rebuke of her manner, also lost her temper.

"Miss Hartill and I were overwhelmed by such an occurrence. Do you realize what you are doing, Miss Durand? You keep the children away from their lesson—you alter the school time-table to suit your convenience—without a remark, or warning, or apology."

"I've told you already that I didn't hear the gong," interrupted Alwynne, between courtesy and impatience. She was trying hard to control herself.

"That is nonsense. Everybody hears the gong. You didn't choose to hear it, I suppose. Anyhow, I feel it my duty to tell you that such behaviour will not be tolerated, Miss Durand, in this, or any school. It is not your place to make innovations. I was horrified just now when I came in. The class-room littered about with pictures and papers—the children not in their places—allowed to interrupt and argue. I never heard of such a thing."

Alwynne's chin went up.

"Excuse me, Miss Vigers, but I hardly see that it is your business to criticize my way of teaching."

"I am speaking to you for your own good," said Henrietta.

"That is kind of you; but if you speak to me in such a tone, you cannot expect me to listen."

Henrietta hesitated.

" Miss Durand, you are new to the school——"

" That gives you no right to be rude to me ! "

Henrietta took a step towards her.

" Rude ? And you ? I consider you insolent. Ever since you came to the school you have been impossible. You go your own way, teach in your own way——"

" I do as I'm told," said Alwynne sharply.

" In your own way. You neither ask nor take advice——"

" At any rate, Miss Marsham is satisfied with me—she told me so last week." She felt it undignified to be justifying herself, but she feared that silent contempt would be lost on Miss Vigers. Also, such an attitude was not easy to Alwynne; she had a tongue; when she was angry, the brutal effectiveness of Billingsgate must always tempt her.

Henrietta countered coldly—

" I am sorry that I shall be obliged to undeceive her; that is, unless you apologize——"

" To Miss Hartill ? Certainly ! I intend to. I hope I know when I'm in the wrong."

" To me——"

" To you ? " cried Alwynne, with a little high-pitched laugh. " If you will tell me what for ? "

" In Miss Marsham's absence I take her place," began Henrietta.

" Miss Hartill, I was told, did that."

" You are mistaken. The younger mistresses come to me for orders."

" I shall be the exception, then. I am not a housemaid. Will you let me get to my desk, please, Miss Vigers ? I want my books."

She brushed past Henrietta, cheeks flaming, chin in air, and opened her desk.

The secretary, for all her anger, hesitated uncertainly. She was unused to opposition, and had been accustomed to allow herself a greater licence of speech than she knew. Alwynne's instant resentment, for all its crude young insolence, was, she realized, to some extent justified. She had, she knew, exceeded her powers, but she had not stopped to consider whether Alwynne would know that she had done so, or, knowing, have the courage to act upon that knowledge. She had been staggered by the girl's swift counter-attack and was soon wishing that she had left her alone; but she had gone too far to retreat with dignity; also, she had by no means regained control of her temper.

"I can only report you to Miss Marsham," she remarked lamely, to Alwynne's back.

Alwynne turned.

"You needn't trouble. If Miss Hartill doesn't, I shall go to her myself."

"You?" said Henrietta uneasily.

"Why," cried Alwynne, flaming out at her, "d'you think I'm afraid of you? D'you think I am going to stand this sort of thing? I know I was careless, and I'm sorry. I'm going straight down to Miss Hartill to tell her so. And if she slangs me—it's all right. And if Miss Marsham slangs me—it's all right. She's the head of the school. But I won't be slanged by you. You are rude and interfering and I shall tell Miss Marsham so."

Shaking with indignation, she slammed down the lid of her desk: and with her head held high, and a dignity that a friendly word would have dissolved into tears, walked out of the class-room.

CHAPTER III

ALWYNNE DURAND was quite aware that she was an arrant
coward. The cronies of her not remote school-days would
have exclaimed at the label, have cited this or that memorable
audacity in confutation, but Alwynne herself knew better.
When her impulsiveness had jockeyed her into an uncomfortable situation, pure pride could always be trusted to sustain
her, straighten her shoulders and sharpen her wits; but she
triumphed with shaking knees. Alwynne, touchy with the
touchiness of eighteen, was bound to fling down her glove before
a Henrietta Vigers, and be ostentatiously ready to face cornet,
flute, harp, sackbut, psaltery, and all kinds of music. But
Alwynne, half-an-hour later, on her way to Miss Hartill and
her overdue apology, was bound also to be feeling more like a
naughty schoolgirl than a mistress of six weeks' standing has
any business to feel, to be uneasily wondering what she should
say, how she should say it, and why on earth she had been
fool enough to get herself into the mess.

If it had been any one but Miss Hartill, with whom she had
not exchanged five words, but whom she had heard discussed,
nevertheless, from every conceivable and inconceivable point
of view, with that accompanying profusion of anecdote of
which only schoolgirl memory, so traditional as well as personal,
is capable.

Miss Marsham, she had been given to understand, might be
head mistress, but Miss Hartill was Miss Hartill. Alwynne,
accustomed as she was to the cults of a boarding-school, had
ended by growing exceedingly curious. Yet when Miss Hartill
had returned, a week or two late, to her post, Alwynne could
not, as she phrased it, for the life of her see what all the fuss
was about. Miss Hartill was ordinary enough. Alwynne had
looked up one morning, from an obscure corner of the Common-
room, at the sound of a clicking latch, had had an impression
of a tall woman, harshly outlined by the white panelled door,

against which she leaned lazily as she quizzed the roomful of women. Alwynne told herself that she was not at all impressed. . . . This the Miss Hartill of a hundred legends? This the Olympian to whom three-fourths of the school said its prayers? Who had split the staff into an enthusiastic majority and a minority that concealed its dislike? Queer! Alwynne, shrugging her shoulders over the intricacies of a school's enthusiasms, had leaned back in her chair to watch, between amusement and contempt, the commotion that had broken out. There was a babble of welcome, a cross-fire of question and answer. And then, over the heads of the little group that had gathered about the door, a pair of keen, roving eyes had settled on herself, coolly appraising. Alwynne had been annoyed with herself for flushing under the stare. She had a swift impression of being summed up, all raw and youthful and ambitious as she was, her attitude of unwilling curiosity detected, expected even. There had been a flicker of a smile, amused, faintly insolent. . . .

But it had all been merest impression. Miss Hartill, who had been, indeed, surrounded, inaccessible, from the instant of her entrance until the prayer bell rang, did not look her way a second time. But the impression had remained, and Alwynne, obscure in her newness and her corner, found herself reconsidering this Miss Hartill, more roused than she would confess. If she were not the Hypatia-Helen of the class-rooms, she was none the less a personality! Whether Alwynne would like her was another matter.

Alwynne, in the next few days, had not come into direct contact with Miss Hartill. She had noticed, however, a certain stirring of the school atmosphere, a something of briskness and tension that affected her pleasantly. The children, she supposed, were getting into their stride. . . . But she began to see that the classes chiefly affected were the classes with which Miss Hartill had most to do, that the mistresses, too, were working with unusual energy, and that Miss Vigers was less in evidence than heretofore; that, in short, Miss Hartill's return was making a difference. Insensibly she slipped into the fashion of being slightly in awe of her—was daily and undeniably relieved that her work had as yet escaped the swift eyes and lazy criticism. But she was also aware that she would be distinctly gratified if Miss Hartill should at any time express satisfaction with her and her efforts. Miss Hartill was certainly interesting. She had wondered if she should ever get to know her; had hoped so.

And now Napoleon Buonaparte and a stopped clock had between them managed the business for her effectually. She was going to know Miss Hartill—a justifiably, and, according to Miss Vigers, excessively indignant Miss Hartill. She looked forward without enthusiasm to that acquaintance. She did not know what she should say to Miss Hartill. . . . But Miss Hartill would do the talking, she imagined. . . . She was extremely sorry for herself as she knocked at Miss Hartill's door.

The maid left her stranded in the hall, and she waited, uncomfortably conscious of voices in the next room.

"Brand? But I don't know any—— Drand! Oh, Durand! What an extraordinary time to—— All right Bagot. No. Lunch as usual."

The maid slipped across the hall again to her kitchen as Miss Hartill came forward, polite, unsmiling. She did not offer her hand, but stood waiting for Alwynne to deliver herself of her errand.

But Alwynne was embarrassed. The exordium she had so carefully prepared during her walk was eluding her. It had been easy to arrange the conversation beforehand, but Miss Hartill in the flesh was disconcerting. She jumbled her opening sentences, flushed, floundered, and was silent. Ensued a pause.

Clare surveyed her visitor quizzically, enjoying her discomfort. Alwynne was at her prettiest at a disadvantage. She had an air of shedding eight of her eighteen years, of recognizing in her opponent a long-lost nurse.

Clare repressed a chuckle.

"Try again, Miss Durand," she said solemnly.

"I came," said Alwynne blankly. "You see, I came——" She paused again.

"Yes, I think I see that," said Clare, as one enlightened.

Alwynne eyed her dubiously. There might or might not have been a twinkle in her colleague's eye. She took heart of grace and began again.

"Miss Hartill, I'm awfully sorry! It was me—I, I mean, I kept the girls. I didn't hear the gong. Really and truly I didn't. Honestly, it was an accident. I thought I ought to come and apologize. Truly, I'm most awfully sorry, quite apart from avoiding getting into a row. Because I've got into that already."

Clare's lips twitched. Alwynne was built on generous lines. She had a good carriage, could enter a room effectively. Clare had not been unaware of her secure manner. Her present collapse was the more amusing. Clare was beginning to guess that what Miss Durand did, she did wholeheartedly.

" I expect you're simply wild with me. Miss Vigers said you would be," said Alwynne hopelessly.

" Miss Vigers ought to know," said Clare.

There was another pause.

" I'm frightfully sorry," said Alwynne suggestively.

" Are you, Miss Durand ? "

" I mean, apart from upsetting you, I'm so savage with myself. One doesn't exactly enjoy making a fool of oneself, does one, Miss Hartill ? You know how it feels. And it's my first post, and I did mean to do it well, and I've only been here six weeks, and I'm in a row with three people already."

" How—three ? " said Clare with interest.

" Well—there's you——"

" I think we're settling that," said Clare, with her sudden smile.

" Are we ? " Alwynne looked up so warily that Clare laughed outright.

" But the other two, Miss Durand—the other two ? This grows interesting."

" Well, you see," Alwynne expanded, " I had an awful row with Miss Vigers—and she's sure to tell Miss Marsham. I suppose I was rude, but she did make me so mad. I don't see that it was her business to come and slang me before my class."

" My class," corrected Clare.

" I wouldn't have minded you," said Alwynne, lifting ingenuous eyes.

" I'm flattered," murmured Clare.

" Well—you would have understood," said Alwynne with conviction. " But Miss Vigers—— I ask you, Miss Hartill, what would be the use of talking about Napoleon to Miss Vigers ? "

" I give it up," said Clare promptly.

" There you are ! " Alwynne waved her hand triumphantly.

" But, excuse me "—Clare was elaborately respectful—" has Napoleon any traceable connection with the kidnapping of my class ? "

" Oh, I thought I explained." Alwynne plunged into her story. " You see, I was giving them Elocution—they're learning the *Incident in the French Camp*—you know ? "

Clare nodded.

" Well, I thought they were rather more wooden than usual, and I found out that they knew practically nothing about Napoleon ! Marengo—Talleyrand—never heard of 'em ! Waterloo, and that he behaved badly to his wife—that's all they knew ! "

" The English in a nutshell ! " murmured Clare.

" So, of course, I told them all about him, and his life, and tit-bits like the Sèvres tea-things, and Madame Sans-gêne. They loved it. And I was showing them pictures and I suppose we got absorbed. You can't help it with Napoleon, somehow. Oh, Miss Hartill, doesn't it seem crazy, though, to keep those children at Latin exercises, and the exports of Lower Tooting, and Bills of Attainder in the reign of Queen Anne, before they know about things like Napoleon, and Homer, and the Panama Canal ? Wouldn't you rather know about the life of Buddha than the war of Jenkins's ear ? Not that I ever got to the Georges myself ! Oh, it makes me so wild ! It's like stuffing them with pea-nuts, when one has got a basket of peaches on one's arm. It isn't education ! It's goose-cramming ! I can't explain properly what I mean. I expect you think I'm a fool ! "

" An enthusiast. It's much the same," said Clare absently. " You'll get over it." Then, with a twinkle : " Reform's an excellent thing, of course—but why annex my class to experiment with ? "

Alwynne defervesced.

There was an unhappy pause.

" You know, I'm most awfully sorry," said Alwynne at last, as one making a brilliant and original contribution to the discussion.

A piercing shriek from the kitchen interrupted them. Alwynne jumped, but Clare was undisturbed.

" It's only Bagot. She's always having accidents. But she's an excellent cook. After all, what's a shilling's worth of crockery a week compared with a good cook ? But to return to Napoleon and the Lower Third——"

" You don't think she's hurt herself ? " Alwynne ventured to interrupt. " She did squeal."

Clare looked suddenly concerned.

" I hope not. I haven't had lunch yet."

She went to the kitchen door, reappearing with a slightly harried air.

"Miss Durand, I wish you'd come here a minute. She's cut her hand. Oh, lavishly! Most careless! What is one to do? I suppose one must bandage it?"

Her tone of helpless disgust was so genuine that Alwynne was inclined to laugh. So there were circumstances that could be too much even for Miss Hartill! How reassuring! And how it warmed the cockles of one's heart to her! Her lips twitched mischievously as she looked from the disconcerted mistress to the sniffing maid, but she lost no time in stripping off her gloves and setting to work, issuing orders the while that Clare obeyed with a meekness that surprised herself.

"Linen, please, Miss Hartill, or old rags! It's rather a bad cut." Then, to the maid, "How on earth did you do it? A tin-opener? No, no, Miss Hartill! a duster's no good. An old handkerchief or something." She was achieving complicated effects with a fork and a knotted scarf as she spoke, and Clare, obediently tearing linen into strips, considered her critically. The girl was capable then, as well as amusing. . . . That tourniquet might not be professional, but it was at least effective. . . . The bleeding was stopping. . . . Very good of her to toil over Bagot's unappetizing hand. . . . Clare marvelled at her unconcern, for she was dainty enough in her own person to please even Clare's fastidious eye. Clare supposed that it was a good thing that some people had the nursing instinct. . . . She thanked her stars that she herself had not. . . .

Alwynne, unconscious of scrutiny, put in her final safety-pin, settled the sling and stepped back at last, surveying her handiwork with some pride.

"It'll want a stitch, though. She'd better go to the doctor, I think," she said decisively. "Shall I come with you?" This to the maid, complacently the centre of attention.

But the maid preferred to fetch her mother. "Her mother lived quite close, miss. If Miss 'Artill could get on——"

"She can't do any cooking with that hand," said Alwynne to Clare, more in decision than appeal, and Clare acquiescing, she fetched hat and coat, manipulated hat-pins, and bundled the girl forth.

She returned to the kitchen to find Miss Hartill, skirts clutched high, eyeing the crowded table with distaste, and prodding with a toasting-fork at the half-prepared meal.

"Isn't it disgusting? How these people bleed! I can't stand a mess! Really, I'm very much obliged to you, Miss

Durand, for seeing to Bagot. I'm no good at that sort of thing. I hate touching people. You don't think it was a bad cut, though?"

"It must have hurt! She won't be able to use her hand for a day or two."

Clare rubbed her nose peevishly. She had a comical air of resenting the necessity for concerning herself with her own domestic arrangements.

"Well, what am I to do? And I loathe charwomen. She might at least have got lunch first!"

"The meat's cooked, anyhow," said Alwynne hopefully, drawing forth a congealing dishful.

Clare shivered.

"Take it away! It's all over Bagot."

"I don't think it is," Alwynne examined it cautiously.

Clare gave her short laugh.

"Anyhow, it doesn't appeal any more. Never mind, Miss Durand, I shall manage—I mustn't keep you."

Alwynne disregarded the hint. She seemed preoccupied.

"There aren't any eggs, I suppose," she ventured diffidently.

Clare flung out vague hands.

"Heaven knows! It's Bagot's business. Why?"

"Because," Alwynne had crossed the room and was struggling with a stiff cupboard door, "Elsbeth says I'm a fool at cooking (Elsbeth's my aunt, you know), but I can make omelets——" The door gave suddenly and Alwynne fell forward into the dark pantry. There was a clatter as of scattered bread-pans. She soon emerged, however, floury but serene.

"Yes! There are some! It wouldn't take ten minutes, Miss Hartill. That is—if——" she sought delicately for a tactful phrase: "if you would perhaps like to go away and read. If any one stands about and watches—you know what I mean——"

"Are you proposing to cook my lunch?" Clare demanded.

"Of course, if you don't like omelets," said Alwynne demurely.

Clare laughed outright.

"I do—I do. All right, Miss Durand, I'm too hungry to refuse. But I see through it, you know. It's to cry quits!"

Alwynne broke in indignantly—

"It isn't! It's the *amende honorable*—at least, if it doesn't scorch."

"All right, I accept it!" Clare pacified her; then, as she left the kitchen, "Miss Durand?"

" Yes, Miss Hartill ? "

" Are you going to make one for Miss Vigers ? "

Alwynne's face fell.

" I'd forgotten Miss Vigers."

Clare twinkled.

" Perhaps—if it doesn't scorch—I'll see what I can do,"
she promised her.

The lunch was a success. Alwynne, dishing up, had her hat
ordered off her head, and was soon sharing the omelet and
marvelling at herself for being where she was, and Clare, for
her part, found herself enjoying her visitor as much as her meal.

Clare Hartill led a sufficiently solitary life. She was a woman
of feverish friendships and sudden ruptures. Always the
cleverest and most restless of her circle, she usually found her
affinities as unable to satisfy her demands on their intellect as
on their emotions. Disillusionment would be swift and final :
Clare never forgave a bore. Gradually it came to pass that intercourse she so carefully fostered with her elder pupils became
her absorbing and satisfying interest. She plumed herself on
her independence of social amenities, did not guess, would not
have admitted, that her pleasure in a chance table companion
had its flavour of pathos. It was enough to acknowledge to
herself that Alwynne Durand, with her enthusiasms, her inco-
herencies, and her capacities had certainly caught her difficult
fancy. She liked the girl's manner; its compound of shyness
and audacity, deference and independence pleased her sophisticated taste. She found her racy and original, and, in the exertion of drawing her out, was herself at her best. A brilliant
talker, she chose to listen, and soon heard all there was to hear
of Alwynne's short history; of her mother's sister, Elsbeth
Loveday (Clare pricked up her ears at the name), who had
reared her from babyhood; of her schooldays; her crude young
likes and dislikes; her hero-worships and passionate, vague
ambitions. Clare knew it all by heart, had heard the tale from
more pairs of lips than she could remember, for more years
than she cared to count. But Alwynne, nevertheless, told it in
a way of her own that appealed to Clare and interested her anew.
She told herself that the girl was worth cultivating; and what
with apt comments, apter silences, and the half-finished phrases
and abrupt noddings of perfect comprehension, contrived to
make Alwynne think her the most sympathetic person she had
ever had the fortune to meet. Indeed, they pleased each other

so well that when Alwynne, towards tea-time, made an unwilling move, Clare was as unwilling, for her part, to let her go.

"It was certainly a most excellent omelet," she said, as she sped her from the door. "I suppose you won't come and cook me another to-night?"

Alwynne took her at her word.

"I will! Of course I will! Would you like me to, really? I will! I'd love to!"

Clare laughed.

"Oh, I was only in fun. Whatever would your aunt say?"

"She wouldn't mind," began Alwynne eagerly.

Clare temporized.

"But your work? Haven't you any work?"

Alwynne overwhelmed her.

"That's all right! It isn't much! I'll sit up. I wish you'd let me. I would love to. You must have some one to cook your supper for you, mustn't you?"

"Well, of course, if you'd really like to——" Clare hesitated between jest and earnest.

But Alwynne was wholly in earnest.

"I'll come. Thank you very much indeed," said Alwynne, eyes sparkling.

CHAPTER IV

In the months that followed the eating of the omelet, Alwynne would have agreed that the cynic who said that ' an entirely successful love-affair can only be achieved by foundlings ' should have included friendship in his dictum. For relations . . . well, everybody knew what everybody meant when relations were mentioned in that particular tone; and Elsbeth, dearest of maiden aunts, was nevertheless at times aggressively a relation : privileged to wet-blanket enthusiasms.

Elsbeth made, indeed, no stand against the alliance that had sprung mushroom-like into existence; was courteous, in her sweet silent fashion, to Clare Hartill at their occasional meetings; but she remained subtly uninterested. But when, again, had that suppressed and self-effacing personality shown interest in any living thing save Alwynne herself ?

Alwynne, shrugging her shoulders, and ignoring, as youth must, the affectionate prevision that had lapped her all her life, supposed that she must not expect too much of poor, dear Elsbeth. . . . (It was characteristic of their relationship that she never called her guardian ' Aunt.') Elsbeth, darling Elsbeth—but a little limited, perhaps ? Hardly to be expected that she should appreciate a Miss Hartill. . . .

Elsbeth, though Alwynne never guessed it, quite understood what went on in her niece's mind : was resigned to it. She knew that she was not a clever woman. She had been too much occupied, all her life, in smoothing the way for other people, to have had leisure for her own cultivation, physical or mental. Her two years of teaching, in the uncertificated 'eighties, had but served to reveal to herself her ingrained incapacity for government. She had never forgotten the humiliation of those months when Clare Hartill, a pitiless fourteen-year-old, had headed one successful revolt after another against her. It had been an episode; with the advent of Alwynne she had returned to domesticity; but the experience had intensified her innate lack of self-esteem. There were times when she seriously debated whether, in bringing up her orphaned niece, she were indulging herself at the expense of her duty. She knew quite well, and rejoiced shamefacedly in the knowledge, that Alwynne, her beautiful, brilliant, headstrong girl, could twist the old aunt round her little finger. And that, of course, could not be good for Alwynne.

Alwynne was, to do her justice, extremely fond of her aunt. Till the advent of Clare Hartill, Elsbeth had been the pole-star of her world. All the more disconcerting of Elsbeth, receiver of confidences, therefore, to be so entirely uninterested in the comet that was deflecting Alwynne from her accustomed orbit.

She wondered occasionally what her aunt's history had been. Elsbeth was reticent : never a woman of reminiscences. Her relations were distant ones, whom she rarely mentioned and apparently more rarely missed. Alwynne was the more surprised one breakfast, when, retailing the school's latest scandal, she was interrupted by an exclamation of pleasure.

"Alwynne! The Lumsdens are coming back!" Elsbeth rustled foreign paper delightedly.

Alwynne wrinkled her brows.

"The Lumsdens? Oh—those cousins of yours?"

"Yes. The youngest, Rosemary, only died last year. Don't you remember? They've lived abroad for years on account of her health, and her son Roger always went out to her for his holidays."

"Roger? Is that the velveteen boy in the big album?"

Elsbeth laughed.

"He must be thirty by now. The estate went to him. It was let, you know, and the Great House at Dene—to a school, I believe. They had lost money. And Rosemary was always extravagant. Roger went to America for a time. But still he's well enough off. He came home when his mother died last year, and now, it seems, he's taken a house close to their old home, and settled down as a market-gardener. The Lumsdens are to come and keep house for him. He's very fond of his aunts, I know. Well! To think of seeing Jean and Alicia again after all these years. They want us to come and stay when they've settled down."

"You'll enjoy that?" Alwynne eyed her aunt curiously. Elsbeth's pale cheeks were pink, her faded eyes dreamy. Her unconscious hand was rapping out its tune upon the table-

cloth—the only symptom of excitement that Elsbeth ever
showed. " Were you fond of them ? Why haven't you ever
been to see them, Elsbeth ? "

" Time flies. And I certainly can't afford to gad about the
Riviera. And there was you, you know. Besides——" she
hesitated.

" Besides what ? "

Elsbeth did not seem to hear.

" You'll like Dene, Alwynne. Oh, yes, I know it well. I
used to stay with them—before the Great House was let. Years
ago. And Roger—I hope you'll get on with Roger. I haven't
seen him since he was five. A jolly little fellow. And from
what Alicia says——"

But Alwynne would not take any interest in Roger. He had
a snub nose in the photograph; and besides, she hated men.
So dull. As Clare said—— Indeed, she wasn't always quoting
Clare ! She didn't always set up Clare's judgment against
Elsbeth's ! Elsbeth needn't get huffy ! She would like to go
down to Dene very much, if Elsbeth wanted to, some time or
other.

But when the holidays came and the formal invitation,
Alwynne was less amenable.

Why couldn't Elsbeth go alone ? Elsbeth couldn't expect
her to go and stay with utter strangers. She hated strangers.
Besides, there was Clare. (It was ' Clare ' and ' Alwynne '
by that time.) She and Clare had planned out every day of
the holidays. Everything fixed. She really couldn't ask Clare
to upset all her arrangements. It wouldn't be fair. Awfully
sorry, of course, but why couldn't Alwynne's dear Elsbeth go
by herself ? She, Alwynne, could keep house. Oh, perfectly
well ! She wasn't a fool ! She wouldn't dream of spoiling
Elsbeth's holiday, but Elsbeth must see that there was no
need for Alwynne to share it.

But Elsbeth was unusually obstinate. Elsbeth, it appeared,
wanted Alwynne with her; wanted to show Alwynne to these
old friends; wanted to show these old friends to Alwynne;
wouldn't enjoy the visit without Alwynne at her elbow; refused
utterly to be convinced of unreasonableness. Alwynne would
enjoy the change, the country—didn't Alwynne love the country ?
—and if she herself, and Alicia, and Jean, were not of Alwynne's
generation, there was always Roger ! By all accounts Roger
was very nice ; witness the aunts who adored him.

Alwynne snorted.

She argued the matter mercilessly, length, breadth, depth and back again, and ended, as Elsbeth knew she would, by getting her own way. But Elsbeth did not go to Dene by herself. There she was mulish. Go visiting and leave the housekeeping to Alwynne's tender mercies? Heaven forbid! There was more in housekeeping than dusting a bedroom, making peppermint creams, or wasting four eggs on an omelet.

So Alwynne spent her pleasant holidays in and out of Clare Hartill's pocket and Elsbeth stayed at home. But Elsbeth had learned her lesson. It was many a long day before she again suggested a visit to Dene.

CHAPTER V

ONE of Alwynne's duties was the conduct of a small 'extra' class, consisting of girls, who, for reasons of stupidity, ill-health or defective grounding, fell too far below the average of knowledge in their respective classes. She devoted certain afternoons in the week to coaching them, and was considered to be unusually successful in her methods. She could be extremely patient, and had quaint and unorthodox ways of insinuating facts into her pupils' minds. As she told Elsbeth, she invented their memories for them. She was sufficiently imaginative to realize their difficulties, yet sufficiently young to dream of developing, in due course, all her lame ducks into swans. She was intensely interested in hearing how her coaching had succeeded; her pleasure at an amended place in class was so genuine, her disappointment at a collapse so comically real, yet so devoid of contempt, so tinged with conviction that it was anybody's fault but the culprit's, that either attitude was an incentive to real effort. Like Clare, she did not suffer fools gladly, but unlike Clare, she had not the moral courage to be ruthless. Stupidity seemed as terrible to her as physical deformity; she treated it with the same touch of motherliness, the same instinctive desire to spare it realization of its own unsightliness.

Her rather lovable cowardice brought a mixed reward; she stifled in sick-rooms, yet invalids liked her well; she was frankly envious of Clare's circle of brilliant girls and as inevitably surrounded by inarticulate adorers, who bored her mightily, but whose clumsy affection she was too kind-hearted to suppress.

It had been well for Alwynne, however, that her following was of the duller portion of the school. This Clare could endure, could countenance; such boy-bishopry could not affect her own sovereignty, and her subject's consequence increased her own. But to see Alwynne swaying, however unconsciously, minds of a finer type, would not have been easy for Clare. She had grown very fond of Alwynne; but the sentiment was proprietary; she could derive no pleasure from her that was not personal, and, in its most literal sense, selfish. She was un-maternal to the core. She could not see her human property admired by others with any sensation but that of a double jealousy; she was subtly angered that Alwynne could attract, yet was caught herself in the net of those attractions, and unable to endure to watch them spread for any but herself.

Alwynne, quite unconscious of the trait, had at first done herself harm by her unfeigned interest in Clare's circle. It took the elder woman some suspicious weeks to realize that Alwynne lacked completely her own *dompteuse* instinct, her craving for power; that she was as innocent of knowledge of her own charm as unwedded Eve; that her impulse to Clare was an impulse of the freshest, sweetest hero-worship; but the realiza-tion came at last, and Clare opened her hungry heart to her, and, warmed by Alwynne's affection, wondered that she had hesitated so long.

Alwynne never guessed that she had been doubted. Clare was proud of her genuine skill as a character reader—had been a little pleased to give Alwynne proof of her penetration when occasion arose; and Alwynne, less trained, less critical, thought her omniscient, and never dreamed that the motives of her obscurest actions, the sources of her most veiled references were not plain to Clare. Secure of comprehension, she went her way : any one in whom Clare was interested must needs attract her : so she took pains to become intimate with Clare's adorers, from a very real sympathy with their appreciation of Clare, whom she no more grudged to them than a priestess would grudge the unveiling of her goddess to the initiate. She received their confidences, learned their secrets, fanned the flame of their enthusiasms. Too lately a schoolgirl herself, too innocent and ignorant to dream of danger, she did her loyal utmost in furtherance of the cult, measuring the artificial and unbalanced emotions she encountered by the rule of her own saner affection, and, in her desire to see her friend appreciated, in all good faith utilized her degree of authority to encourage what an older woman would have recognized and combated as incipient hysteria.

Gradually she became, through her frank sympathy, com-bined with her slightly indeterminate official position, the intermediary, the interpreter of Clare to the feverish school. Clare herself, her initial distrust over, found this useful. She could afford to be moody, erratic, whimsical; to be extravagant in her praises and reproofs; to deteriorate, at times, into a caricature of her own bizarre personality, with the comfortable assurance that there was ever a magician in her wake to steady her tottering shrines, mix oil with her vitriol, and prove her pinchbeck gold.

Fatal, this relaxation of effort, to a woman of Clare's type. Love of some sort was vital to her. Of this her surface personality was dimly, ashamedly aware, and would, if challenged, have frigidly denied; but the whole of her larger self knew its need, and saw to it that that need was satisfied. Clare, unconscious, had taught Clare, conscious, that there must be effort—constant, straining effort at cultivation of all her alluring qualities, at concealment of all in her that could repulse—effort that all appearances of complete success must never allow her to relax. She knew well the evanescent character of a schoolgirl's affection; so well that when her pupils left the school she seldom tried to retain her hold upon them. Their letters would come thick as autumn leaves at first; she rarely answered, or after long intervals; and the letters dwindled and ceased. She knew that, in the nature of things, it must be so, and had no wish to prolong the farewells.

Also, her interest in her correspondents usually died first; to sustain it required their physical nearness. But every new year filled the gaps left by the old, stimulated Clare to fresh exertion.

So the lean years went by. Then came vehement Alwynne —no schoolgirl—yet more youthful and ingenuous than any mistress had right to be, loving with all the discrimination of a fine mind, and all the ardour of an affectionate child. Here was no question of a fleeting devotion that must end as the schooldays ended. Here was love for Clare at last, a widow's cruse to last her for all time. Clare thanked the gods of her unbelief, and, relaxing all effort, settled herself to enjoy to the full the cushioning sense of security; the mock despot of their pleasant, earlier intercourse becoming, as she bound Alwynne ever more closely to her, albeit unconsciously, a very real tyrant indeed.

Yet she had no intention of weakening her hold on any lesser member of her coterie. Alwynne was too ingenuous, too obviously subject through her own free impulse, to entirely satisfy: Clare's love of power had its morbid moments, when a struggling victim, head averted, pleased her. There was never, among the new-comers, a child, self-absorbed, nonchalant or rebellious, who passed a term unmolested by Miss Hartill. Egoism aroused her curiosity, her suspicion of hidden lands, virgin, ripe for exploration; indifference piqued her; a flung gauntlet she welcomed with frank amusement. She had been a rebel in her own time, and had ever a thrill of sympathy for the mutinies she relentlessly crushed. War, personal war, delighted her; she was a mistress of tactics, and the certainty of eventual victory gave zest to her campaigns. She did not realize that the strain upon her childish opponents was very great. The finer, the more sensitive the character, the more complete the eventual defeat, the more permanent its effects. Clare was pitiless after victory : not till then did she examine into the nature thus enslaved, seldom did she find it worth the trouble of the skirmish. In most cases she gave semi-liberty; enough of smiles to keep the children feverishly at work to please her (the average of achievement in her classes was astounding), and enough of indifference to prevent them from becoming a nuisance. To the few that pleased her fastidious taste, she gave of her best, lavishly, as she had given to Alwynne. There are women to-day, old girls of the school, who owe Clare Hartill the best things of their lives, their wide knowledge, their original ideals, their hopeful futures and happy memories : to whom she was inspiration incarnate. The Clare they remember is not the Clare that Elsbeth knew, that Alwynne learned to know, that Clare herself, one bitter night, faced and blanched at. But which of them had knowledge of the true Clare, who shall say?

In Clare's favourite class was a certain Louise Denny. She was thirteen—nearly three years below the average of the class in age. How far beyond it in all else, not even Clare realized.

Clare had discovered her, as she phrased it, in the limbo of the Lower Third. She had been paying one of her surprise visits to the afternoon 'extra' needlework classes (the possibility of her occasional appearance, book in hand, was responsible for the school's un-English proficiency in hemming, darning and kindred mysteries), to read aloud to the children carefully edited excerpts from Poe's *Tales*, had forgotten her copy and had been shyly offered another, private property from Louise Denny's desk. Thereon must Alwynne, for a week or two, resign perforce her Lower Third literature classes to Clare, intent on her blue rose. Louise's compositions had been read—Clare and Alwynne spent a long evening over them, weighing, comparing, discussing. Clare could be exquisitely tender, could keep all-patient vigil over an unfolding mind, provided that the calyx concealed a rare enough blossom. Louise was encouraged, her shyness swept aside, her ideas developed, her knowledge tested; she was fed too, cautiously, on richer and richer food—stray evening lectures, picture galleries with Alwynne, headiest of cicerones; the freedom of the library and long talks with Clare. Finally Clare, bearing down all opposition, transplanted her to the Lower Fifth, containing at that time some brilliantly clever girls. Louise justified her by speedily capturing, and doggedly retaining, the highest place in the class.

Clare was delighted. Her critics—there were some mistresses who vaguely disapproved of the experiment—were refuted, and the class, already needing no spur, outdoing itself in its efforts to compete with the intruder, swept the board at an important public examination.

On the morning of the announcement of results, Clare entered her form-room radiant. It was a low, many-windowed room, with desks ranged single-file along the walls. The class being a small one, the girls were accustomed to sit for their lessons at a large oval table at the upper end of the room. Beside the passage door-way, there was a smaller one, that led into the studio, and was never used by the children. Clare, however, would sometimes enter by it, but so seldom that they invariably forgot to keep watch. Clare enjoyed the occasional view she thus obtained of her unconscious and relaxed subjects, and the piquancy of their uncensored conversation; she enjoyed still more the sudden hush, the crisp thrill, that ran through their groups, when they became aware of her, observant in the doorway.

On the morning in question she had watched them for some little while. Before each girl lay her open exercise-book and school edition of Browning. They were deep in discussion of their work, very eager upon some question. By the empty chair at the head of the table sat Marion Hughes, blonde and placid, a rounded elbow on her neatly written theme, that her neighbour was trying to pull away, to compare with her own well-inked manuscript. This neighbour, one Agatha Middleton, was dark, gaunt, with restless eyes and a restless tongue. She

was old for her fifteen years, and had been original until she
discovered the fact, and that her originality appealed to Miss
Hartill. Since then she had sedulously imitated her own
mannerisms, and was rapidly degenerating into an eccentric.
The law of opposites had decreed that the sedate Marion should
be her bosom friend. They went up the school together, an
incongruous, yet well-suited pair, for they were so unlike that
there could be no rivalry. Marion was alternately amused and
dazzled by the pyrotechnic Agatha. Agatha's respect for
Marion's common sense was pleasantly tempered by a conviction of superior mental agility. Finally, they were united
by their common devotion to their form-mistress. Whether it
would have occurred to Marion, unprompted, to admire Miss
Hartill, is uncertain. Her affections were domestic and calm.
But adoration was in the air, and she had not sufficient originality to be unfashionable. She was caught, too, in Agatha's
whirlwind emotions, and ended by worshipping Clare conscientiously and sincerely. Clare, on her side, respected her,
as she told Alwynne, for her " painstaking and intelligent
stupidity," and, recognizing a nature too worthy for neglect,
yet too lymphatic to be suitable for experiments, was uniformly
kind to her. Agatha, she had revelled in for six weeks, and had
since more or less ignored as a bore. Below the pair sat a
spectacled student, predestined to scholarships and a junior
mistress-ship; opposite, between giggling twins, a vivid little
Jewess, whose showy work was due to the same vanity that
tied her curls with giant bows, and over-corseted her matured
figure. At the foot of the oval, directly opposite Clare's vacant
chair, stood Louise, flushed and excited, chanting low-voicedly
a snatch of verse.

During a lull in the hubbub Marion called to her down the
table—

" How many pages ? "

Louise flushed. She was still a little in awe of these elders
whom she had outstripped. She rapidly counted the leaves of
her essay, and held up both hands, smiling shyly.

Marion exclaimed.

" Ten ? You marvel ! I only got to seven. I simply didn't
understand it. Whatever did you find to say ? "

Agatha fell upon the query.

" That's nothing ! I've done twenty-two ! " she cried
triumphantly, and turned to face the shower of comments.

"Miss Hartill will bless you. She said last time that you thought ink and ideas were synonyms."

"Agatha only writes three words to a line, anyway."

They liked her, but she was of the type whose imperiousness provokes snubs.

"Well, I thought I shouldn't get it done under forty—an essay on *The Dark Tower*. It's the beastliest yet. *The Ancient Mariner* was nothing to it. I've made an awful hash—didn't you?"

"I understood all right when she read it, and explained. It's so absurd not to let one take notes. I've been years at it. Fortunately she said we needn't learn it—Louise and I—with all our extra work." An unimaginative hockey captain fluttered her pages distractedly.

"Oh, but I have!" Louise looked up quickly.

"Why?" The hockey captain opened eyes and mouth.

"Oh, I rather wanted to."

The little Jewess giggled.

"'*Déjà?*'" she murmured. She did not love Clare.

Marion returned to the subject with her usual perseverance.

"Did you understand it, kid?"

Louise stammered a little.

"When she reads it, and when I say it aloud, I think I do. It was impossible to write it down."

"Let's see what you have put." Agatha, by a quick movement, possessed herself of Louise's exercise-book. Louise, shy and desperate, strove silently with her neighbours, who, curious, held her back, while Agatha, holding the book at arm's length, recited from it in a high mocking voice.

"*Childe Roland to the Dark Tower came*. Description! Description! Description! for three—five—seven pages! You've let yourself go, Louise. Ah, here we are—*The meaning of the poem*. Now we're getting to it. *Shakespeare and Browning may have known all the real history of Childe Roland; the reason of his quest, the secret of the horror of the Tower; but we are left in ignorance. That does not matter, for, as we read, the inner meaning of the terrible poem kills all curiosity. Shuddering we close the book, and pray to God that Childe Roland's journey may never be ours; that for our adventurous souls, knight-erranting through this queer life, there may never come a choice of ways, a turning from the pleasant highroad, to go upon a hideous journey; till, crossing the Plains of*

*Loneliness, Fear and Sorrow, we face the Hills of Madness, and
enter the Dark Tower of that Despair which is our soul's death.*
With capital letters galore ! What a sentence ! Here, shut up,
you spit-fire ! " Louise had wrenched herself free and flung
herself upon Agatha, in a white heat of anger.

" Give it me ! You've no right ! You've no right ! " she
gasped. Her shyness had gone, she was blazing with indignation.

Agatha, the book held teasingly out of reach, affected to
search for her place. Louise raised her clenched fist desperately.

A cool hand caught her wrist in a firm yet kindly grip. A
hush fell on the voluble group and Agatha collapsed into an
apologetic nonentity.

Clare, who had entered in her usual noiseless fashion, stood
a moment between the combatants, watching the effect of her
appearance. Her hand shifted to Louise's bony little shoulder ;
through the thin blouse she could feel the driven blood pulsing.
She did not move till she felt the child regaining comparative
calm, when, giving her a gentle push towards her place, she
walked slowly to the head of the table and seated herself. The
class watched her furtively. It was quite aware that all rules
of decorum had been transgressed—that pains and penalties
would be in order with any other mistress. But with Miss
Hartill there was always glorious uncertainty—and Miss Hartill
did not look annoyed. Little gestures began to break the
tension and Agatha, relieved, smiled a shade too broadly.
Instantly Clare closed with her.

She began blandly—

" Agatha, I thought you could read aloud better than that.
You are not doing your work justice. Pass me your essay."

" It's Louise's," said Agatha helplessly.

" Ah, I see. And you kindly read it to us for her ? It's a
pity you didn't understand what you read—but an excuse, of
course. Louise must not expect too much."

Agatha flung up her head angrily.

" Oh, I understood it all right. I thought it was silly."

" You did ? Read me your own."

" Now ? "

" Certainly."

Now Clare, as she corrected and commented upon the weekly
essays, did occasionally, if the mood took her, read extracts,
humorous chiefly, therefrom ; but it had never been customary
for a pupil to read her own work aloud. Agatha had the pioneer

spirit—but she was no fool. She comprehended that, with Clare inimical, she could climb no higher than the pillory. She fell back upon the tradition of the school.

" Oh, Miss Hartill—I can't ! "

" Why not ? "

" No one ever does——"

Clare waited.

Agatha protested redly, her fear of ridicule outweighing her fear of Clare.

" Miss Hartill, I simply couldn't. Before everybody—all this tosh—I mean all this stuff I wrote. It's a written essay. I couldn't make it sound right aloud."

Clare waited.

" It's not good enough, Miss Hartill. Honestly ! And we never have. You've never made us. I couldn't."

Clare waited.

Agatha twisted her hands uneasily. The schoolgirl shyness that is physical misery was upon her.

" I—don't want to, Miss Hartill. I can't. It's not fair to have one's stuff—to be laughed at—to be——" She subsided just in time.

The class sat, breathless, all eyes on Clare.

And Clare waited ; waited till defiance faded to unease—unease to helplessness, till the girl, overborne by the utter silence, gave way, and dropping her eyes to her exercise, fluttering its pages in angry embarrassment, finally, with a giggle of pure nervousness, embarked on the opening sentence.

Clare cut through the clustering adjectives.

" Stand up, please."

Resistance was over. She rose sullenly.

She had been proud of her essay, had worked at it sincerely, knew its periods by heart. But her pleasure in it was destroyed, as completely, she realized, as she had destroyed that of little Louise. More—for Louise had found a champion. That, she recognized jealously. Unjust ! Her essay was no worse, read soberly—yet she was forced to render it ridiculous. She read a couple of pages in hurried jerks, stumbling over the illegibilities of her own handwriting, baulked by Clare's interpolations. She heard her own voice, high-pitched and out of control, perverting her meaning, felt the laden sentences breaking up into chaos on her lips. In her flurry she pronounced familiar words amiss, Clare's calm voice carefully correcting. Once she heard a chuckle. Two pages . . . three . . . only that . . . she remembered that she had boasted of twenty . . . seventeen to be read yet and they were all laughing. To have to stand there . . . three pages . . . four. . . . "*But as Childe Roland turned round*——"

"Louder, please," said Clare.

"*But as Childe Roland turned round*——" and even Marion was laughing. . . . *Turned round to look once more back to the high road*——"

"And slower."

"*To the high road*——" She stopped suddenly, a lump in her throat.

"Go on, Agatha."

"To the high road——" The letters danced up and down mistily. "*To the high road where the cripple—where the cripple*—— Oh, Miss Hartill," she cried imploringly, "isn't it enough?"

It was surrender. Clare nodded.

"Yes, you may sit down now. Your essay, please: thank you. And now I'll read you, once more, what Louise has to say on the same subject. I dare say you'll find, Agatha, that you were almost as unfair to her essay, as you were to—your own." And she smiled her sudden dazzling smile. Agatha, against her will, smiled tremulously back.

Clare, with a glance at the little figure, huddling at the foot of the table, began to read. The essay, for all its schoolgirl slips and extravagance, was unusual. The thought embodied in it, though tinged with morbidity, striking and matured. Clare did it more than justice. Her beautiful voice made music of the crude sentences, revealed, embellished, glorified. Her own interest growing as she read, infected the class; she swept them along with her, mutually enthusiastic. She ended abruptly, her voice like the echoes of a deep bell.

Marion broke the little pause.

"I liked that," she said, as if surprised at herself.

"So did I," Clare was pleased.

She dipped her pen in red ink and initialled the foot of the essay.

"That was good work, Louise. Now, the others."

But Louise, shy and glowing, broke in—

"But it wasn't mine, Miss Hartill, not a bit."

Clare looked at her, half frowning.

" Not yours ?   Your handwriting—— ? "

" Oh, I wrote it. But you've made it different. I hadn't
meant it like that."

Clare raised a quizzical eyebrow.

" I have misinterpreted—— ? "

Louise was too much in earnest to be fluttered.

" I only mean—you made it sound so beautiful that it was
like listening to—to an organ. I didn't bother about the words
while you read. It was all colours and gold—like the things
in the Venetian room. You know. The meaning didn't
matter. But I did mean something, not half so good, of
course, only quite different.   Horrid and grizzly like the plain
he travelled through, Childe Roland. It ought to have sounded
harsh and starved, like rats pattering—what I meant—not
beautiful."

" I see." Clare was interested. She was quite aware that
she had used her magnificent voice to impress arbitrarily her
opinion of Louise's work upon the class. That Louise, impressionable as she knew her to be, should have yet detected the
trick, amused her greatly.

" So you think I didn't understand your essay ? "

Louise's shy laugh was very pleasant.

" Oh, Miss Hartill. I'm not so stupid. It's only that I can't
have got the—the—— "

" Atmosphere ! "   The girl in spectacles helped her.

" The atmosphere that I meant to ; so you put in a different
one to help it. And it did. But it wasn't what I meant."

Clare glanced at her inscrutably, and began to score the other
essays. She would get at Louise's meaning in her own way.
She skimmed a couple, Agatha, be it recorded, receiving the
coveted initials, before she spoke again.

" Didn't I tell you all to learn *Childe Roland*, too ? Ah, I
thought so. Begin, Marion, while I finish these. Two verses."

Her pen scratched on, as Marion's expressionless voice rose,
fell and finished. Agatha continued, jarringly dramatic. Two
more followed her. Then Clare put down her pen.

" ' For mark ! . . . . ' "

There was a warning undertone in Louise's colourless voice,
that crept across the room like a shadow. Clare lifted her head
and stared at her.

> " ' For mark ! no sooner was I fairly found
> Pledged to the plain, after a pace or two,
> Than, pausing to throw backward a last view
> O'er the safe road, 'twas gone; grey plain all round :
> Nothing but plain to the horizon's bound.
> I might go on; nought else remained to do.' "

There was horror in the whispering voice : the accents of one
bowed beneath intolerable burdens, sick with the knowledge
of nearing doom, gay with the flippancy of despair. Louise
was looking straight before her, vacant as a medium, her hands
lying laxly in her lap. Clare made a quick sign to her neighbour
to be silent, and the strained voice rose anew.

Clare listened perplexedly. She told herself that this was
sheer technique—some trick had been played, she was harbour-
ing some child actress of parts—only to be convinced of folly.
She knew all about Louise. Besides, she had heard the child
read aloud before. Good, clean, intelligent delivery. But
nothing like this—this was uncanny. Uncanny, yet magnificent. The artist in her settled down to enjoyment; yet she
was uneasy too.

> " ' And just as far as ever from the end ! ' "

The creeping voice toiled on across the haunted plain, growing
louder, clearer, nearer.

Vision was forced upon Clare, serene in her form-room, swift
and sudden vision. She not only heard, every sense responded.
At her feet lay the waste land of the poem, she smelt the dank
air, shrank from the clammy undergrowth, watched the bowed
figure of the wandering knight, stumbling forwards doggedly.
It was coming towards her, the outline blurred in the evening
mist, the face hidden. The voice was surely his ?

> " ' Not hear ? when noise was everywhere ! it tolled
> Increasing like a bell.' "

She heard it, alive with warning.

Nearer, ever nearer; the bowed form was at her very feet,
as the voice rose anew in despairing defiance.

> " ' To view the last of me——' "

The helmeted head was flung back; the voice echoed from
hill to hill—

> " ' I saw them and I knew them all. And yet
> Dauntless the slug-horn to my lips I set,
> And blew. Childe Roland to the Dark Tower came.' "

The figure fell, face upwards, at her feet. Clare tore at the visor with desperate hands, for at the last line, the strong voice had broken, quavering into the pitiful treble of a frightened child. The bars melted under her touch, as dream things will, and she was staring down at no bearded face, but at Louise. Louise herself, with blank, dead eyes in a broken, blood-flecked face. The dead mouth smiled.

"You see, that was what I meant, Miss Hartill. That atmosphere."

Clare roused herself with a start. Louise, rosily alive, and quivering with eagerness, was waiting for her comments. She got none.

"Begin again," said Clare mechanically, to the next girl.

The brightness died out of Louise's face, as she subsided in her seat. Clare, dazed as she was, saw it, and was touched. The child deserved praise—should not be punished for the vagaries of Clare's own phantasy. And the monkey could recite! She shook off the impression of that recital as best she could. Curious, the freaks of the imagination! She must tell Alwynne of the adventure—Alwynne, dreamer of dreams. . . . And Alwynne was interested in Louise; was coaching her. . . . Perhaps she was responsible . . . had coached her in that very poem? She hoped not . . . it would be interference. . . . She did not like interference. But no—that performance was entirely original, she felt sure. There was genius in the child—sheer genius . . . and but for Clare herself, she would yet be rotting undeveloped in the Lower Third. She was pleased with herself, pleased with Louise too; ready to tell her so, to see the child's face light up again delightedly; she was less attractive in repose. . . .

Clare's chance came.

It was the turn of the hockey captain to recite. She appealed to Clare.

"Oh, Miss Hartill! You said I needn't, Louise and I—because of all our extra work. Not the poem."

Clare considered.

"I remember. Very well. But, Louise?" She looked at her questioningly, half smiling. "When did you find the time?"

Louise laughed.

"I don't know, Miss Hartill. It found itself."

"Ah! And how much extra work have you, Louise?"

Louise reflected.

" All the afternoons, I think. And three evenings when I go to lectures. And, of course, gallery days, when I make up in the evenings."

" And homework ? "

" Oh, there's heaps of time at night always."

Clare smiled upon her class.

" Well, Lower Fifth—what do you think of it ? "

The class opened its mouth.

" Louise is moved up four forms. She's thirteen. She's top of the class and first in to-day's results. You hear what her extra work is. And she finds time to learn *Childe Roland*— optional. What do you think of it ? "

Agatha bit down her envy.

" It's pretty good," she said.

Clare's glance approved her.

" Yes. So I think. It's so good that I'm more than pleased. I'm—impressed. Rather proud of my youngest pupil. For next time you will learn——" And with one of her quick transitions, she began to dictate the homework.

The gong clanged as she finished. Alwynne's voice was heard in the passage, inquiring for Miss Hartill, and Clare hurried out. Followed a confused banging of books and desk-lids, a tangle of fragmentary remarks, and much trampling of boots on uncarpeted boards, as one after another followed her. Within five minutes the room was bare, save for Clare's forgotten satchel at the upper end of the big table, and Louise, motionless in her chair at the foot.

CHAPTER VI

LOUISE was tasting happiness.

Happiness was a new and absorbing experience to Louise. The only child of a former marriage, she had grown up among boisterous half-brothers with whom she had little fellowship. Her father, a driving, thriving merchant, was prouder of his second brood of apple-cheeked youngsters than of his first-born, who fitted into his scheme of life as ill as her mother had done. He had imagined himself in love with his first wife, had married her, piqued by her elusive ways, charmed by her pale, wood-sorrel beauty; and she, shy and unawakened, had taken his six feet of bone and muscle for outward and visible sign of the matured spiritual strength her nature needed. The disappointment was mutual as swift; it had taken no longer than the honeymoon to convince the one that he had burdened himself with a phantast, the other that she was tied to a philistine. For a year they shared bed and board, severed and inseparable as earth and moon; then the wife, having passed on to a daughter the heritage of a nature rare and impracticable as a sensitive plant, died and was forgotten.

The widower's speedy re-marriage proved an unqualified success. Indeed, the worthy man's after life was so uniformly and deservedly prosperous (he was as shrewd and industrious in his business as he was genial and domesticated in his home), that he might be forgiven if his affection for his eldest child were tepid; for, apart from her likeness to his first wife, she was, in existing, a constant reminder of the one mistake of a prosperous career. He was kind to her, however, in his fashion; gave her plenty of pocket-money (he was fond of giving); saw to it that she had a sufficiency of toys and sweets, though it piqued him that she had never been known to ask for any. Otherwise was content to leave her to his wife.

The second Mrs. Denny, kindly, capable and unimaginative as her husband, had her sense of duty to her step-daughter;

but she was too much occupied in bearing and rearing her own family, whose numbers were augmented with Victorian regularity, to consider more than the physical well-being of the child. Louise was well fed and warmly clad, her share was accorded her in the pleasures of the nursery. What more could a busy woman do ?

Louise, docile and reserved, was not unhappy. Until she went to school, however, her mental outlook resembled that of a person suffering from myopia. Her elders, her half-brothers, all the persons of her small world, were indefinite figures among whom she moved, confused and blundering. She knew of their existence, but to focus them seemed as impossible as to establish communication. She did not try over hard; she was sensitive to ridicule; it was easier to retire within her childish self, be her own confidante and questioner.

She had an intricate imagination and before she learned to read had created for herself a fantastically complete inner world, in which she moved, absorbed and satisfied. Indeed, her outward surroundings became at last so dangerously shadowy that her manner began to show how entire was her abstraction, and Mrs. Denny, sworn foe to ' sulks ' and ' moping,' saw fit to engage a governess as an antidote.

The governess, a colourless lady, achieved little, though she was useful in taking the little boys for walks. But she taught Louise to read, and thereafter the child herself assumed entire control of her own education.

The mother's books, velvety with dust that had sifted down upon them since the day, six years back, when they had been tumbled in piles on an attic floor by busy maids preparing for the advent of the second Mrs. Denny, were discovered, one rainy day, by a pinafored Siegfried, alert for treasure. Contented years were passed in consuming the trove.

Her mother's choice of books was so completely to her taste that they gave the lonely child her first experience of mental companionship; suggesting to her that there might be other intelligences in the world about her than the kindly, stolid folk who cherished her growing body and ignored her growing mind. She was almost startled at times to realize how completely this vague mother of hers would have understood her. Each new volume, fanciful or quizzical or gracious, seemed a direct gift from an invisible yet human personality, that concerned itself with her as no other had ever done; that was never

occupied with the dustiness of the attic, or a forgotten tea-hour,
but was astonishingly sensitive to the needs of a little soul,
struggling unaided to birth. The pile of books, to her hungry
affections, became the temple, the veritable dwelling-place of
her mother's spirit.

Seated on the sun-baked floor, book on knee, the noises of
the high road floating up to her, distance-dulled and soothing,
she would shake her thick hair across her face, and see through
its veil a melting, shifting shadow of a hand that helped to
turn her pages. The warm floor was a soft lap; the battered
trunk a shoulder that supported; the faint breeze a kiss upon
her lips. The fantastic qualities the mother had bequeathed,
recreated her in the mind of her child, bringing vague comfort
(who knows ?) alike to the dead and the living Louise.

Yet the impalpable intercourse, compact of make-believe and
yearnings, was, at its sweetest, no safe substitute for the human
companionships that were lacking in the life of Louise. Half
consciously she desired an elder sister, a friend, on whom to
lavish the stores of her ardent, reticent nature.

At twelve she was sent to school. At first it did little for her.
She was unaccustomed to companions of her own age and sex
and, quite simply, did not know how to make friends with
many who would have been willing enough, if she could have
contributed her share, the small change of joke and quarrel
and confidence, towards intimacy. But Louise was too inured
to the solitude of crowds to be troubled by her continued loneliness. She met the complaints of Mrs. Denny, that she made
no friends like other children, with a shrug of resignation. What
could she do ? She supposed that she was not nice enough;
people didn't like her.

Secretly her stepmother agreed. She was kind to Louise,
but she, too, did not like her. She found her irritating. Her
dreamy, absent manner, her very docility and absence of self-
assertion were annoying to a hearty woman who was braced
rather than distressed by an occasional battle of wills. She
thought her shyness foolish, doubted the sincerity of her humility,
and looked upon her shrinking from publicity, noise and rough
caresses, her love of books and solitude, as a morbid pose. Yet
she was a just woman and did not let the child guess at her
dislike, though she made no pretence of actual affection. She
knew perfectly well that Louise's mother (they had been schoolgirls together), had irritated her in exactly the same way.

Educationally, too, the first year at school affected Louise but slightly. Her brothers' governesses had done their best for the shy, intelligent girl, and her wide reading had trained, her awkwardness and childish appearance obscured, a personality in some respects dangerously matured. But her dreaminess and total ignorance of the routine of lesson-learning hampered her curiously; she learnt mechanically, using her brain but little for her easy tasks, and she was not considered particularly promising.

With Clare's intervention the world was changed for Louise; she had her first taste of active pleasure.

It is difficult to realize what an effect a woman of Clare's temperament must have had on the impressionable child. In her knowledge, her enthusiasms, her delicate intuition and her keen intellectual sympathy, she must have seemed the embodiment of all dreams, the fulfilment of every longing, the ideal made flesh. A wanderer in an alien land, homesick, hungry, for whom, after weary days, a queen descends from her throne, speaking his language, supplying his unvoiced wants, might feel something of the adoring gratitude that possessed Louise. She rejoiced in Clare as a vault-bred flower in sunlight.

On all human beings, child or adult, emotional adventure entails, sooner or later, physical exhaustion; the deeper, the more novel the experience, the greater the drain on the bodily strength. To Louise, involved in the first passionate experience of her short life, in an affection as violent and undisciplined as a child's must be, an affection in itself completely occupying her mind and exhausting her energies, the amount of work made necessary by the position to which Clare and her own ambition had assigned her, was more of a burden than either realized. Only Alwynne, sympathetic coach (for Louise had two years back work to condense and assimilate), guessed how great were the efforts the child was making. Clare, who always affected unconsciousness of her own effect on the ambitions of the children, had persuaded herself that Louise was entirely in her right place; and Louise herself was too young, and too feverishly happy, to consider the occasional headaches, fits of lassitude and nights cinematographed with dreams, as anything but irritating pebbles in her path to success—and Clare.

The weeks in her new class had been spread with happiness—a happiness that had grown like Elijah's cloud, till, on the day of the Browning lesson, as she listened to the beloved voice

making music of her halting sentences, to the words of praise,
of affection even, that followed, it stretched from horizon to
horizon.

As she sat in the deserted class-room, her neat packet of
sandwiches untasted in the satchel at her elbow, she re-lived
that golden hour, dwelling on its incidents as a miser counts
money. There was the stormy beginning; Agatha's mockery;
her own raging helplessness; Clare's entrance; the exquisite
thrill she had felt at her touch, that was not only gratitude
for championship. . . . Never before had Clare been so near
to her, so gentle, so protecting. . . . And afterwards, facing
Louise at the foot of the table, how beautiful she had been. . . .
Yet some of the girls could not see it. . . . They were fools.
. . . Her head had been framed in the small, square window,
so darkened and cobwebbed by crimson vines that only the
merest blur of white clouds and blue hills was visible. . . . She
had worn a gown of duller blue that lay in stiff folds : the bowl
of Christmas roses, that mirrored themselves on the dark, polished
table, had hidden the papers and the smeared ink-pot. Suddenly
Louise remembered some austere Dutch Madonnas over whom
delightful, but erratic Miss Durand had lingered, on their last
visit to a picture gallery. She called them beautiful. Louise,
with fascinated eyes sidling past a wallful of riotous Rubens,
to fix on the soap and gentian of a Sassoferato, had wondered
if Miss Durand were trying to be funny. She remembered, too,
how some of the younger girls, comparing favourites, had called
Miss Hartill ugly. She had raged loyally—yet, secretly, all but
agreed. With her child's love of pink and white prettiness she
had had no eyes for Clare's irregular features. But to-day something in Clare's pose had recalled the Dutch pictures, and in a
flash she had understood, and wondered at her blindness. Miss
Durand was right : the drawn, grey faces and rigid outlines
had beauty, had charm—the charm of her stern smile. . . .
The saints were hedged with lilies, and she, too, had had white
flowers before her, that filled the air with the smell of the marvellous Roman church at Westminster. . . . The painted ladies
were Madonnas—mothers—and Miss Hartill, too, had worn for
a moment their protective look, half fierce, half tender. . . .

Why was it ? What had made her so kind ? Not only to-day,
but always ? The girls feared her, some of them ; those that
she did not like talked of her temper and her tongue ; Rose
Levy hated her; even Agatha and Marion, and all of them,

were a little frightened, though they adored. . . . Louise was
never frightened. . . . How could one be frightened of some
one so kind and wonderful? She could say what she liked to
Miss Hartill, and be sure that she would understand. . . . It
was like being in the attic, talking aloud. . . . Mother would
have been like that. . . . If it could be. . . .

Louise, her chin in her doubled fists, launched out upon her
sea of make-believe.

If it could be. . . . If it were possible, that Mother—not
Mamma, cheery, obtuse Mamma of nursery and parlour—but
Mother, the shadow of the attic—had come back? All things
are possible to him that believeth: and Mr. Chesterton had
said there was no real reason why tulips should not grow on
oaks. . . . Heaps of people—all India—believed in reincarna-
tion, and there was *The Gateless Barrier* and *The Dead Leman*
for proof. . . . Might it not be?

The idea was intoxicating. She did not actually believe in
it, but she played with it, wistfully, letting her imagination
run riot. She wove fantastic variations on the themes ' why
not,' ' perhaps,' ' who knows.'

She was but thirteen and very lonely.

She was in far too exalted a mood to have an appetite for
her sandwiches, or time for the books beside her. She was
due for extra work with Alwynne at three, and the intervening
hour should have been used for preparation. Wasting her time
meant sitting up at night, as Louise was well aware, and a
tussle with Mrs. Denny, concerned for the waste of gas. But
for all that, she would not and could not rouse herself from the
trance of pleasure that was upon her. Her mind was contem-
plating Clare as a mystic contemplates his divinity; rapt in an
ecstasy of adoration, oblivious alike of place and time. She
did not hear the luncheon gong, or the gong for afternoon school,
or a door, opening and shutting behind her. Yet it did not
startle her, when, turning dreamily to a tap on her shoulder,
she found herself facing Miss Hartill herself. Miss Hartill should
have left the school before lunch, she knew, but it was all in order.
What could surprise one on this miraculous day? She did not
even rise, as etiquette demanded; but she smiled up at Clare
with an expression of welcoming delight that disarmed comment.

Clare, too, could ignore conventions. She was merely touched
and amused by the child's expression.

" Well, Louise? Very busy? "

Louise glanced vaguely at her books.

"Yes. I ought to be, I mean. I don't believe I've touched anything. I was thinking——"

"Two hours on end? Do you know the time? I heard Miss Durand clamouring for you just now." Clare looked mischievous. She could forgive forgetfulness of other people's classes.

Louise was serene.

"I'm sorry. I'm very sorry. I'd forgotten. I must go."

But she made no movement. She sat looking at Miss Hartill as if nothing else existed for her. The intent, fearless adoration in her eyes was very pleasant to Clare; novel, too, after the more sophisticated glances of the older girls.

With an odd little impulse of motherliness she picked up Louise's books, stacked them neatly and fitted them into the satchel. Louise watched her. Miss Hartill buckled the strap and handed her the bundle.

"There you are, Louise! Run along, my child, I'm afraid you'll get a scolding." She stooped to her, bright-eyed, laughing. "And what were you thinking of, Louise, for two long hours?"

"You," said Louise simply.

A touch of colour stole into Clare's thin cheeks. She took the small face between her hands and kissed it lightly.

"Silly child!" said Miss Hartill.

CHAPTER VII

ALWYNNE, drumming with her fingers on the window-sill, as she stood by Louise's desk, was distinctly annoyed. Louise, for the first time since she had known her, was late. It was, indeed, not one of her assigned classes; but she and Louise had found their hours together so insufficient for all the work that they were trying to make good, that Alwynne had good-naturedly arranged to give her a daily extra lesson. It bit into Alwynne's meagre free time; but she was fond of Louise; proud of her, too; and there was Clare ! Clare was so anxious for Louise's success. Clare had been so pleased with the plan. . . .

Perhaps it was natural that Alwynne, as she made the arrangement, forgot to consult Elsbeth. She told her about it afterwards, and Elsbeth praised her for her unselfishness, and was anxious lest she should be overtired. She did not remind Alwynne that she was alone all day; that she had been accustomed to look forward to the gay tea-hour, when Alwynne returned, full of news and nonsense. She resigned herself cheerfully to a solitary meal, and to keeping the muffins hot against Alwynne's uncertain homecoming.

The extra lessons had been a real boon to Louise, and she had grown attached to Alwynne and intimate with her. Alwynne's elder-sisterly attitude to the children she taught, although it horrified the older women, was seldom abused; it merely made her the recipient of quaint confidences, and gave her an insight into the characters of her pupils that was invaluable to girls and governess alike. To developing girls a confidante is a necessity. The present boarding-school system of education ousts the mother from that, her natural position; renders her, to the daughter steeped in an alien atmosphere, an outsider, lacking all understanding. Invaluable years pass before the artificial gulf that boarding-school creates between them, is spanned. And the substitute for the only form of sympathy and interest that is entirely untainted by selfish impulses is usually the chance

49

acquaintance, the neighbour of desk and bedroom; occasionally, very occasionally, for the girl's feverish admiration usually precludes sane acquaintanceship, a mistress of more than average insight. Such a mistress, Alwynne, in spite of, or perhaps because of, her youthful indiscretions of manner, was in a fair way to become.

And of all the children who had opened their affairs to her, none had experienced more completely the tonic effect of a kind heart and a sense of humour, than Louise.

She would come to her lesson, overtired from the strain of the morning classes, over-stimulated from the contact with Clare, over-hopeful or utterly depressed, as the mood took her. Alwynne's cheerful interest was balm to the child's over-wrought nerves. Alwynne let her spend a quarter of an hour or more in confiding the worries and excitements of the day, after which, Louise, curiously revived, contrived to get through an amazing amount of work. There was no doubt as to Louise's capacity for advanced work, but her state of mind affected her output; she was, as Alwynne once phrased it to Clare, ' like a violin—you had to tune her before she was fit for use.' And Alwynne's ' tuning ' had done more than she or Clare or even Louise herself had guessed, towards her success in her new class.

Bit by bit, Alwynne had heard all about Louise; the details of her meagre home-life; her attitude to the busy world of school, that frightened while it attracted her; her difficulties with her fellows; her delight in her work. Finally, there was Clare. Louise was very shy about Clare; inclined to scent mockery, to be on the defensive; but Alwynne's own matter-of-fact enthusiasm had its effect. Also Alwynne's interest, though it invited, never demanded confidences. It took Louise some time to realize that it arose from simple friendliness of soul; that there was neither curiosity nor pedagogic zeal behind it; that, though she was teased and laughed at, she was respected, and, out of school hours, treated as an equal; that she and her schoolgirl secrets were safe with Miss Durand. It was, indeed, in the light of after events, pathetic that Louise, dazzled by Clare's will-o'-the-wisp brilliance, never realized how close to her for a season the friend, the elder sister she had longed for, really stood. With the egoism of a child, and a child in love, she was humbly and passionately grateful for Clare's least sign of interest, yet accepted all the many little kindnesses that

Alwynne showed her, as a matter of course. She scarcely realized, absorbed as she was in Clare, that she was even fond of Miss Durand, yet she relied on her implicitly : and Alwynne, innocent of the jealous, acquisitive impulse that tainted Clare's intercourse with any girl who caught her fancy, was not at all disturbed or hurt by Louise's attitude. She looked after the child as she would have looked after a starving cat or a fugitive emperor, if they had come her way, as a matter of course, and as instinctively as she ate her dinner.

She was thinking of Louise, as she sat waiting, and a little curious as to what the child would say to her. She had heard all about the Browning lesson, at lunch, from Rose Levy, whose veiled, epigrammatic malice was usually amusing. Agatha had been on her other side, and she had anticipated equally amusing protests and contradictions and a highly coloured and totally different version. But Agatha had been unusually subdued that morning. Both had made it apparent, however, that Clare had been more than a little pleased with Louise.

But, however triumphant Louise's morning might have been, she had no business to be late now. What did she mean by keeping her waiting ? Twice had Alwynne been down to the preparation room, searching for her : she did not mean to be impertinent, of course, but it was, at least, casual. Alwynne, with easy, evanescent indignation, resolved to give Louise a taste of her tongue.

Here the child herself burst in upon her meditations, flushed to her glowing eyes, that were bright as if with drugs, excited as Alwynne had never yet guessed that she could be, charged with some indefinable quality as a live wire is charged with electricity. She stammered her apologies mechanically, sure of pardon, and, the formality complied with, was eager, touchingly eager for questions and the relief of communication.

But Alwynne, at nineteen, could not be expected to forego a legitimate grievance.

She read Louise a little lecture on punctuality and politeness, and settled at once to the work in hand. She said, with intention, that they must not waste any more time.

Louise submitted with her usual meekness, and did, Alwynne could see, do her utmost to apply herself to her work. But her answers were ludicrously vague and *mal à propos*, and she met Alwynne's comments, momentarily sharper, with an abstracted smile.

Suddenly Alwynne lost patience with her.

"I don't know what's the matter with you to-day, Louise," she said sharply. "I don't believe you've taken in a word of what I've said. If you can't take a little more trouble, I'd better go home."

Louise, obviously and pathetically jerked back to consciousness from some dreamer's Paradise, looked up at her with scared, apologetic eyes. The radiance dimmed slowly from her face. She made no answer, only put up her hand to her head, with a queer little gesture of helplessness.

"What's the matter with you?" demanded Alwynne, but already more gently. Her anger was always fleeting as a puff of smoke.

But Louise merely shrugged her shoulders and looked vaguely at her again. Then she returned to her work.

Alwynne, walking up and down the room, watched her intently as she bent over the Latin grammar. She was wrinkling her brows over a piece of prose that she had already construed at the previous lesson, and with an ease that had astonished Alwynne. She looked bewildered and put up her hand to her head again. Her efforts to recall her wandering thoughts were patent and almost physical in their intensity; her small hand hovered, contracting and relaxing, like a baby catching at butterflies.

Alwynne was puzzled by her. The child was sincere : but obviously something momentous had happened, and was still occupying her, to the exclusion of all else. Alwynne wished that she had been less hasty : she felt that she should not have checked her.

She stood a moment beside her, reading what she had written. It was scarcely legible, and made no sense. She put a hand on her shoulder—

"Louise, you are writing nonsense. What is it? Tell me what the matter is?"

Louise laid down her pen, gave her a quick, shy smile, hesitated uncertainly, then, to Alwynne's dismay, collapsed on the low desk in a fit of wild, hysterical crying.

Alwynne always shed the mistress in emergency.

She whipped her arms about the child, and, sitting down, gathered her into her lap. She felt how the little, thin body was wrenched and shaken by the sobs it did not attempt to control, but she said nothing, only held it comfortingly tight.

Slowly the paroxysm subsided, and the words came, jerky, fragmentary, faint. Alwynne bent close, to catch them.

Louise was so sorry . . . she was all right now . . . Miss Durand must think her crazy. No—no—nothing was wrong . . . it was the other way round . . . she was so happy that it frightened her . . . she was madly happy . . . she had been in heaven all day . . . it was too wonderful to tell any one about . . . even Miss Durand. . . . Miss Hartill—no one could ever know what Miss Hartill was. . . . She had been so good to her—so wonderful. . . . She had made Louise so happy that she was frightened . . . she couldn't believe it was possible to be so madly happy. . . . That was all. . . . Yes, it had made her cry—the pure happiness. . . . Wasn't it silly? Only she was so dreadfully tired. . . . It had hurt her head, trying to do the Latin—because she was so tired. . . . Yes, she had had headaches lately. . . . But she didn't care—it was worth it, to please Miss Hartill. . . . It was queer that being so happy should make her want to cry; it was comical, wasn't it?

She began to laugh as she spoke, with tears brimming over her lashes, and for a few moments was inclined to be hysterical again.

But Alwynne's firm grasp and calm voice were too much for Louise's will, weakened by emotion and fatigue; she was soon coaxed and hushed into quiet again, and after lying passively for a while in Alwynne's arms, fell into the sudden light sleep of utter exhaustion.

Alwynne, rocking her gently, sat on in the darkening room, without a thought of the passage of time; puzzling over the problem in her arms.

She was too ignorant and inexperienced to understand Louise's outburst, or to realize the dangerous strain that the child's sensibilities were undergoing; but the touch of the little figure, clinging, nestling to her, stirred her. She was vaguely aware that something—somehow—was amiss. Innocently she rejoiced that Clare was being kind to Louise, that the child was so happy and content; but the complaint of fatigue, the frequent headaches, troubled her. She would speak to Elsbeth. . . . Perhaps the child needed a tonic? Elsbeth would know. . . .

She glanced down. How different people looked asleep. . . . She had never before realized how young Louise was. What was she? Thirteen? But what a baby she looked, with her thin, child's shape and small, clutching hands. . . . It was the

long-lashed lids that did it, hiding the beautiful eyes that were
so much older, as she saw now, than the rest of Louise. With
her soul asleep, Louise looked ten, and a frail little ghost of ten,
at that.

Alwynne frowned. She supposed Clare Hartill realized how
young Louise was, was right in allowing her to work so hard?
But Clare knew all about girls, and what did she, Alwynne,
know? After all Louise had never flagged before. . . . It was
probably the usual end of term fatigue—and of course it was
necessarily an unusually stiff three months for her. . . . She
needed a holiday. . . . Next term would come more easily to
her, poor little impetuous Louise. . . . Alwynne realized that
she was growing fond of the child.

Suddenly she heard footsteps in the corridor, and her own name
in Clare's impatient accents. Louise, too, roused at the sound,
and, jerking herself upright, slid from Alwynne's lap to her feet,
as the door opened and the light was switched on with a snap.
Clare stood in the doorway.

Serenely Alwynne rose, smoothing the creases in her dress,
while with the other hand she steadied Louise, swaying and
blinking in the strong light. Clare's sharp eyes appreciated
her calm no less than the tear-stains on Louise's cheek; she
guessed distortedly at the situation. She bit her lip. She
found nothing to be annoyed at, yet she was not pleased.

"Alwynne! I've been hunting for you high and low. I
thought you were coming home to tea with me."

Alwynne beamed at her.

"Of course! And do you know, I forgot to tell Elsbeth.
Isn't it disgraceful? But I'm coming."

She turned to Louise.

"My dear, run along home, and get to bed early; you look
dreadfully tired. Doesn't she, Miss Hartill?"

But Clare was already in the passage.

Alwynne hurried after her, with a last cheerful nod, and
Louise heard the echo of their footsteps die away in the
distance.

Still dazed and heavy with sleep, her thoughts obscured and
chaotic, she sat down again stupidly at her desk in the alcove
of the window. She leaned her forehead against the cold pane
and looked out.

It was a wild night. The wind soughed and shrieked in the
bare trees : the rain tore past in gusts; the lamp-post at the

corner was mirrored in the wet pavement, like a moon on an oily sea.

Louise pushed open the casement. The wind lulled as she did so, and she lent out. The air, at least, was mild, and a faint back-wash of rain sprayed soothingly upon her hot cheeks and swollen eyes.

Slowly her thoughts shaped themselves. So the day was over—the happiest day she had ever had. . . . She thought God was very wonderful to have made such a woman as Miss Hartill. She sent Him a hasty little prayer of thanks. But she had been very foolish that afternoon. . . . She could not understand it now. . . . She hoped Miss Durand would not tell Miss Hartill. . . . Miss Hartill had been in a great hurry ! Was that why she had not said good-night to her ? But such a little word. She wondered why Miss Hartill had not said good-night to her. . . .

The front door below the window creaked and opened. Louise peered downwards. Miss Durand and Miss Hartill came down the steps, sheltering under one umbrella, talking. Their voices floated up.

" I hope you don't spoil her, Alwynne ? Yes, I know——" Alwynne was murmuring friendly adjectives. " But a mistress is in a peculiar position. You should not let yourself be too familiar——" A gust of wind and rain whirling down the road bore away the rest of the sentence.

Louise shut the window. She shivered a little as she gathered up her books.

Her happiest day was over.

CHAPTER VIII

A WEEK before Christmas Alwynne began to wonder how the day itself should be spent, or rather, if her plans for the spending would ever pass Elsbeth's censorship. She was doubtful. For the last two or three years Christmas had been to them a rock of collision.

"The pity of it!" thought Alwynne. Once it had been the event, the crowning glory, the very reason of the ending year. A year, indeed, had always presented itself to her in advance as a wide country through which she must make her way, to reach the hostel, Christmas, hidden in the mists of time, on its further border. She had the whole map of the land in her mind, curiously vivid and distinct. She had never consciously devised the picture; it had, from the first, presented itself complete and unalterable. She stood, on New Year's Day, at the entrance of a country lane which ran between uneven hedges through a varying countryside of fields and woods and heatherland. Each change in the surroundings represented a month, the smaller differences the weeks and days. She went down this winding lane as the days went by, in slow content. January was a silent expanse of high tableland, snow-bound to the horizon. Winding down hill through the sodden grassland of the bare February country, where she lighted on nothing but early parsnip fronds and sleepy celandine buds in the dripping wickery hedges, she passed at last into the wood of March, a wood of pollard hazels and greening oaks and bramble-guarded dingles, where the anemones grew, and the first primroses. She slipped and slithered in and out of mossy leaf-pits, and the briars clawed her hair and pinafore, as she robbed the primrose clumps with wet, reddened fingers. The wind shrieked overhead and wrestled wildly with the bare branches, but beyond there was blue sky and a drift of cloud. But, unawares, she would always head through the wood to where the trees grew thinner and dash out at last, through a mist of pale cuckoopint, into the cowslip field that was April.

56

The path ran on through May and June between fields of ox-eye daisies and garden roses, always down hill, till she tumbled into August, the deep hot valley. There she found the sea.

With September the road lifted steadily, growing stony and ever steeper. It wound on ahead of her like a silver thread through a brocade of red and gold and purple, that was heather and bracken and beech. But the beech blossoms could never be gathered; they fell apart into a shower of dull leaves, and left her with a branch of bare twigs in her hand. The briony berries that she twisted into wreaths stained her straw hat with their black, evil juice; even the manna-like old-man's-beard smelled sour and rotten. The decaying, witchlike beauty of the season tricked and frightened her; autumn was a hard hill to climb.

But far away, on the summit of that difficult hill, stood a house. An old house, gayly bricked, dressed in ivy, with a belfry from which carols rang out unceasingly. It was always night-time where it stood and cheerful lights were set in every window. Alwynne never saw the house till she had turned the bend of the road into November; then it faced her suddenly and she would wave to the distant windows with a thrill of excitement, and quicken her steps, with the goal of the journey in sight at last. There was yet a weary climb before it was reached; every day of December was a boulder, painfully be-clambered. But she would come to the gates at last, and tear up the frosty drive, from the shadow of whose shrubberies Jacob Marley peered and clanked at her and ghosts of Christmas turkeys gobbled horribly, to the open holly-hung doorway where Santa Claus, authentic in beard and dressing-gown, welcomed her with Elspeth's voice. Followed stay-at-home days of delirious merry-making, from which she awoke a week later, to find herself, her back to a closed door, a spent cracker in her hand, looking out again, eager and a little wistful, across the white untrodden plain of yet another January.

But ever the next Christmas beckoned her anew.

To Elsbeth, too, Christmas was the day of delights, and Alwynne the queen of it. To Elsbeth, too, the pleasure of it began many weeks earlier in the secret fashioning of quaint gifts and surprises, and the anticipation of the small niece's delight in them. Elsbeth would have cheerfully cut off one of her slim fingers if Alwynne had happened to covet it. The

childless woman loved Alwynne—the child in Alwynne she
worshipped.

But though the delight of actual motherhood was denied
Elsbeth, she was spared none of its chagrins.

Stooping for years to a child's level, she was cruelly shaken
when Alwynne, suddenly and inexplicably, as it always seems,
grew up. It took Elsbeth almost as many years to straighten
herself again. Years when Alwynne, in the arrogance of her
enterprising youth, thought that Elsbeth was sometimes awfully
childish. She supposed that she was growing old; she used not
to be like that. . . .

Thereafter, each Christmas, challenging comparison as it did
with the memory-mellowed charm of its forerunners, emphasized
the change that had taken place. Yearly the ideal Christmas
lured them to the old observances; yearly the reality satisfied
them less.

Elsbeth still sat up half the night on Christmas Eve, at work
upon the little tree. Alwynne still planned gorgeous and
laborious presents for her aunt. Elsbeth still filled a stocking
(out-size) with tip-toe secrecy, and Alwynne, at sixteen, still
ran across in her dressing-gown, and curled up on Elsbeth's
bed to unpack it.

But at sixteen one is too old and too young to be a child
any more. The tree was a fir-tree, pure and simple; the fairy
lights stank of tallow; and not even for the sake of a new bright
sixpence, would Alwynne, in the thick of a vegetarian fad,
devour a slice of the evil-coloured Christmas pudding.

Elsbeth, as she saw her old-time jokes and small surprises
that could no longer surprise, fall utterly flat, thought that
school had altered Alwynne altogether; that she was assuming
airs of maturity ridiculous in a child of her age, (" Sixteen?
She's a mere baby still," affirmed poor Elsbeth,) that she was
growing indifferent, superior, heartless. And Alwynne, trying
to appear amused, wondered why Christmas was so different
from what it used to be and wished heartily that Elsbeth would
not try to be skittish. It didn't suit her—made her seem
undignified. Each, longing for the old days, when the other
had conjured up so easily the true spirit of the festival, tried her
affectionate best to do so still; each, failing inevitably, inevitably
blamed the other. Neither realized, that Dan Christmas is the
god of very little children, and that where they are not, he, too,
does not linger.

But the last restless, unsatisfactory day had settled the matter for them finally. Alwynne had fidgeted through morning service, and pained her aunt, on the walk home, with her sceptical young comments; had omitted to kiss her under the mistletoe; had sat through the ceremonious meal, answering Elsbeth's cheerful pleasantries in monosyllables; and finally, after an unguarded remark, and the inevitable reproving comment, had flung out of the room in a fever of irritation. She came near thinking Elsbeth a foolish and intolerable old maid. And Elsbeth, sitting sadly over the fire all the lonely afternoon, puzzled meekly over Alwynne's hardness of heart, and cried a little, in pure longing, for the baby of a few years back, to whom she had been as God.

They were reconciled, of course, by tea-time. Alwynne, quieted by solitude, was soon bewildered at her own ill-humour, shocked at the sentiments she had been able to entertain, remorseful at hurting Elsbeth's feelings and spoiling her Christmas Day. They were able to send each other to bed happy again.

But they had no more snap-dragons and early stockings. The next Christmas, shorn of its splendours, was a strange day to them both, but, at least, a peaceful one, with Alwynne at her gentlest, and Elsbeth, forgiving her as best she could, for her long skirts and her seventeen years.

With the passing of yet another year, however, Alwynne's last scruple as to the sacrosanct privacy of Christmas celebrations vanished utterly. The ideal day, she saw at last, and clearly, should be neither a children's carnival, nor a symposium of relatives. (Alwynne knew of none but Elsbeth, but she dearly loved a phrase.) Christmas should be a time of social intercourse, of peace and goodwill towards men—the human race—neighbours and friends—not merely relations. . . . One should not shut oneself up. . . . It would be a sound idea, for instance, to ask some one to dinner. . . . A friend of Elsbeth's —or there was Clare! It would be very jolly if Clare could come to dinner. . . . Clare was delightful when she was in holiday mood; she could keep the table in a roar. . . . A little fun would do Elsbeth good. . . . Surely Elsbeth would enjoy having Clare to dinner?

She found herself, however, experiencing considerable diffidence in opening up the project to her aunt. Elsbeth, to whom the possibility of such a request had long ago presented itself, who could have told you by sheer intuition at what exact moment the idea occurred to her niece, gave her no help. Alwynne had contrived to put her in the position of appearing to approve Clare Hartill. Clare, she felt, had had something to do with that. She knew that it would be unwise to lose the advantage of her apparent tolerance; knew that Clare expected her to lose it by some impulsive expression of mistrust or dislike, and intended to utilize the lapse for her own ends. It would be easy for Clare to pose as the generous victim of unreasoning hostility. But Clare should not, she resolved, have the opportunity. She, Elsbeth, would never be so far lacking in cordiality as to give her any sort of handle. But Clare Hartill should not eat her Christmas dinner with them, vowed Elsbeth, for all that.

So for a couple of days, Alwynne, approaching Elsbeth from all possible angles, found no crack in her armour, and somewhat puzzled, but entirely unsuspicious, thought it hard that Elsbeth should be, at times, so curiously unresponsive. She would not have scrupled to ask her aunt outright to invite Clare, but she quite genuinely wished to find out first if Elsbeth would mind, and never guessed that the difficulty she found in opening the matter was the answer to that question.

The arrival of the turkey was her opportunity.

Sailing into the kitchen in search of raisins (the more maturely dignified Alwynne's deportment, the more likely her detection in some absurd child's habit or predilection), she found Elsbeth raging low-voiced, and the small maid gaping admiration over the brobdingnagian proportions of their Christmas dinner.

" Look at it, Alwynne ! What am I to do ? Twenty pounds ! And we shan't get through ten ! Really, it's too bad—I wrote so distinctly. It's impossible to return it—to Devonshire ! No time. It's the twenty-second already. How shall we ever get through it ? "

" We might get some one in to help us," began Alwynne delightedly. But Elsbeth, very busy all of a sudden, with basin and egg-beater, whisked and bustled her out of the kitchen.

Alwynne returned to the matter, however, later in the day.

" Elsbeth, we shall never manage that turkey alone."

" Of course, I must send some over to Mrs. Marpler," began Elsbeth hastily.

Mrs. Marpler was a charwoman. Alwynne contrived to make their succession of little maids adore her, but she and Mrs.

Marpler detested one another cordially. Mrs. Marpler's offences, according to Alwynne, were that she was torpid, inefficient, breathed heavily, smelled of cats, and, by the complicated and judicious recital of the authentic calamities which regularly befel her, lured from Elsbeth more than her share of the broken meats and old clothes of the establishment, perquisites which Alwynne, entirely incredulous, coveted for pet dependents of her own. Alwynne's offences, according to Mrs. Marpler, were, the aforementioned incredulity, her hostile influence on Miss Loveday, a certain crispness of manner and a tendency to open all windows in Mrs. Marpler's neighbourhood. The feud distressed Elsbeth, and Alwynne's diagnosis of Mrs. Marpler's character; for she liked to believe the best of every one. Alwynne forced her to agree, but secretly she sympathized with her feckless char-lady.

"Marpler has been out of work three weeks, and as poor Mrs. Marpler says, where their Christmas dinner is to come from——"

"How much extra did you pay her this week?" demanded Alwynne remorselessly. "And last week—and the week before—and the week before that? Of course he's out of work. Who wouldn't be?"

"My dear Alwynne, if you think they can buy a Christmas dinner on what I gave them——" retorted Elsbeth heatedly. "But it's absurd to argue with you. What do you know of what food costs?"

"Anyhow, Mrs. Baker, with six children——" began Alwynne, who also had been primed by a protégée. But she recollected that she did not wish to annoy Elsbeth at this juncture. Clare must take precedence of Mrs. Baker. "Well, you can send them the legs and the carcase," she conceded; "even then there will be more than we can possibly manage. Couldn't we ask some one to spend the day with us?"

"I hardly think," said Elsbeth, with a touch of severity, "that you would find any one. Most people like to keep Christmas with their Relations."

"Well, I haven't got any. But by all accounts I think I should hate 'em in the plural as much as I love 'em in the singular." She blew Elsbeth a kiss. "But if we could find some one—to help us eat up the turkey—and spend the evening—it would be rather jolly, don't you think? It was dullish last year, wasn't it?"

"Was it?" said Elsbeth, with careful brightness. "I'm sorry. I had thought you enjoyed it."

"Oh, why is she so touchy? I didn't mean anything," cried Alwynne within herself. And aloud—

"Oh, I only meant without a tree or anything specially Christmassy——"

"Alwynne," said Elsbeth, with scrupulous patience, "it was you who suggested not having one."

"I know, I know, I know, I know!" cried Alwynne, in a fever.

Elsbeth sighed.

Alwynne repented.

"Elsbeth darling, I didn't mean to be rude; I'm a beast. And I didn't mean it wasn't nice last year. I only meant—it would be—be a change to have some one—because of the turkey —and I thought, perhaps Clare——"

"Can't you exist for a day without seeing Clare Hartill?" asked Elsbeth, with a wry smile.

Alwynne dimpled.

"Not very well," she said.

Elsbeth stared at her plate. Alwynne edged her chair along the table, till she sat at Elsbeth's elbow. She slid an arm round her neck.

"Elsbeth! Elsbeth, dear! You're not cross, Elsbeth? It's a very big turkey. Do, Elsbeth!"

"Do what?"

"Ask Clare. You like her, don't you?"

No answer.

"Don't you, Elsbeth?" Alwynne's tone was a little anxious.

"Would you care if I didn't?" The pattern of her plate still interested Elsbeth. She was tracing its windings with her fork.

"You silly—it would just spoil everything. That's just it— I would like to get you two fond of each other, only with Clare so busy there's never a chance of your really getting acquainted."

"I knew Clare Hartill long before you did, Alwynne. I knew her as a schoolgirl."

"But not well—not as I know her."

"No, not as you know her."

"There you are," said Alwynne, with satisfaction. "That's why—you don't know her properly. Oh, Elsbeth, you must share all my good things, and Clare's the very best of them. Do let her come."

"She may be engaged; she probably is."

"Oh, no—Clare will be alone—I know, because——" she stopped herself.

Elsbeth questioned her with her eyes.

"Oh, nothing—only I happen to know," said Alwynne.

"Because?"

Alwynne shook her head mischievously.

"Oh, well, if you won't tell me——" began Elsbeth.

"Oh, I will, I will," cried Alwynne hastily.

"My dear, I don't want to know Miss Hartill's secrets, or yours either," said Elsbeth huffily. But to herself, "Why am I losing my temper over these silly trifles?"

"Elsbeth dear, it was nothing. Only Clare did ask me to spend Christmas Day with her."

"Well?" said Elsbeth jealously.

"What?" asked Alwynne's ingenuous eyes.

"Are you going?"

Alwynne nestled up to her, humming with careful flatness the final bars of *Home, sweet home.*

"Elsbeth, you old darling—I do believe you're jealous! Are you, Elsbeth? Are you?"

"Are you going?" repeated Elsbeth.

Alwynne was sobered by her tone.

"I'm going to spend my Christmas Day in my own home, with my own Elsbeth," she said, "and I think you needn't have asked me."

Elsbeth melted.

"My dear, I'm a silly old woman——"

"Yes, you tell me that once a week."

"One day you'll believe it. All right—you can ask your Miss Hartill—or shall I write?"

Alwynne hugged her.

"Elsbeth, you're an angel! I'll go round at once. Oh, it will be jolly."

"If she comes."

Alwynne turned, on the way to her bedroom. Elsbeth's intonation was peculiar.

"What do you mean?"

"I don't think she'll come, Alwynne."

"But I know she'll be alone——"

"Well, you go and ask her."

"But why do you say that—in that tone?"

"I may be wrong. But I've known her longer than you have. But run along and ask her."

"But why? Why?"

"Oh, don't bother me, child," cried Elsbeth impatiently. "Run along and ask her."

CHAPTER IX

" I HAD a letter from Louise yesterday," announced Clare.

She was curled up in a saddle-bag before the roaring golden fire, and was busy with paper and pencil. Alwynne, big with her as yet unissued invitation, sat cross-legged on the white bearskin at her feet. The floor was littered with papers and book-catalogues. At Christmas-time Clare ordered books as a housewife orders groceries, and she and Alwynne had spent a luxurious evening over her lists. The vivid flames lit up Clare's thin, lazy length, and turned the hand she held up against their heat into transparent carnelian. Her face was in shadow, but there were dancing specks of light in her sombre eyes that kept time with the leaping blaze. Clare was a sybarite over her fires. She would not endure coal or gas or stove—wood, and wood only, must be used; and she would pay any price for apple-wood, ostensibly for the quality of its flame, secretly for the mere pleasure of burning fuel with so pleasant a name; for she liked beautiful words as a child likes chocolate—a sober, acquisitive liking. She had, too, though she would not own it, a delight in destruction, costly destruction; she enjoyed the sensation of reckless power that it gave her. The trait might be morbid, but there was not a trace of pose in it; she could have enjoyed a Whittington bonfire, without needing a king to gasp applause. Yet she shivered nightly as she undressed in her cold bedroom, rather than commit the extravagance of an extra fire. She never realized the comicality of her contradictoriness, or even its existence in her character, though it qualified every act and impulse of her daily life. Her soul was, indeed, a hybrid, combining the temper of a Calvinist with the tastes of a Renascence bishop.

At the moment she was in gala mood. The autumn term was but four days dead, she had not had time to tire of holidays, though, within a week, she would be bored again, and restless for the heavy work under which she affected to groan. Her

chafing mind seldom allowed her indolent body much of the
peace it delighted in—was ever the American in lotus-land.
It was fidgeted at the moment by Alwynne's absorption in a
lavishly illustrated catalogue.

"Did you hear, Alwynne? A letter from Louise."

Alwynne's "Oh?" was absent. It was in the years of the
Rackham craze, and she had just discovered a reproduction of
the *Midsummer* Helen.

"Any message?" Clare knew how to prod Alwynne.

The girl glanced up amused but a little indignant.

"You've answered it already? Well! And the weeks I've
had to wait sometimes."

"This was such a charming letter," said Clare smoothly.
"It deserved an answer. She really has the quaintest style.
And Alwynne—never a blot or a flourish! It's a pleasure to
read."

Alwynne laughed ruefully. She would always squirm goodhumouredly under Clare's pin-pricks, with such amusement at
her own discomfiture that Clare never knew whether to fling
away her needle for good, or, for the mere experiment's sake,
to stab hard and savagely. At that stage of their intimacy,
Alwynne's guilelessness invariably charmed and disarmed her—
she knew that it would take a very crude display of cruelty to
make Alwynne believe that she was being hurt intentionally.
Clare was amused by the novel pedestal upon which she had
been placed; she was accustomed to the panoply of Minerva,
or the bow of Dian Huntress, but she had never before been
hailed as Bona Dea. It tickled her to be endowed with every
domestic virtue, to be loved, as Alwynne loved her, with the
secure and fearless affection of a daughter for a newly-discovered
and adorable young mother. She appreciated Alwynne's determination of their relationship, her nice sense of the difference
in age, her modesty in reserving any claim to an equality in their
friendship, her frank and affectionate admiration—yet, while it
pleased her, it could pique. Calm comradeship or surrendering
adoration she could cope with, but the subtle admixture of
such alien states of mind was puzzling. She had acquired a
lover with a sense of humour and she felt that she had
her hands full. Her imperious will would, in time, she knew,
eliminate either the lover or the humour—it annoyed her that
she was not as yet quite convinced that it would be the humour.
She intended to master Alwynne, but she realized that it would

be a question of time, that she would give her more trouble than the children to whom she was accustomed. Alwynne's utter unrealization of the fact that a trial of strength was in progress, was disconcerting : yet Clare, jaded and super-subtle, found her innocence endearing. Without relaxing in her purpose, she yet caught herself wondering if an ally were not better than a slave. But the desire for domination was never entirely shaken off, and Alwynne's free bearing was in itself an ever-present challenge. Clare loved her for it, but her pride was in arms. It was her misfortune not to realize that, for all her Olympian poses, she had come to love Alwynne deeply and enduringly.

Alwynne, meanwhile, laughing and pouting on the hearth, the firelight revealing every change of expression in her piquant face, was declining to be classed with Agatha Middleton; her handwriting might be bad, but it wasn't a beetle-track; anyhow, Queen Elizabeth had a vile fist—Clare admired Queen Elizabeth, didn't she ? She had always so much to say to Clare, that if she stopped to bother about handwriting—— ! Had Clare never got into a row for untidiness in her own young days ? Elsbeth had hinted. . . . But of course she reserved judgment till she had heard Clare's version ! She settled to attention and Clare, inveigled into reminiscences, found herself recounting quaint and forgotten incidents to her own credit and discredit, till, before the evening was over, Alwynne knew almost as much of Clare's schooldays as Clare did herself. She could never resist telling Alwynne stories, Alwynne was always so genuinely breathless with interest.

They returned to Louise at last, and Alwynne read the letter, chuckling over the odd phrases and dainty marginal drawings. She would have dearly liked to see Clare's answer. She was glad, for all her protests, that Clare had been moved to answer ; she knew so well the delight it would give Louise. The child would need cheering up. For, quite resignedly and by the way, Louise had mentioned that the Denny family had developed whooping-cough, and emigrated to Torquay, and she, in quarantine, though it was hoped she had escaped infection, was preparing for a solitary Christmas.

Alwynne looked up at Clare with wrinkled brows.

" Poor child ! But what can I do ? I haven't had whooping-cough, and Elsbeth is always so afraid of infection ; or else she could have come to us. I know Elsbeth wouldn't have minded."

" You are going to leave me to myself then ? You've quite made up your mind ? "

Alwynne's eyes lighted up.

" Oh, Clare, it's all right. You are coming ! At least—I mean—Elsbeth sends her kindest regards, and she would be so pleased if you will come to dinner with us on Christmas Day," she finished politely.

Clare laughed.

" It's very kind of your aunt."

" Yes, isn't it ? " said Alwynne, with ingenuous enthusiasm.

" I'm afraid I can't come, Alwynne."

Alwynne's face lengthened.

" Oh, Clare ! Why ever not ? "

Clare hesitated. She had no valid reason, save that she preferred the comfort of her own fireside and that she had intended Alwynne to come to her. Alwynne's regretful refusal when she first mooted the arrangement, she had not considered final, but this invitation upset her plans. Elsbeth's influence was opposing her. She hated opposition. Also she did not care for Elsbeth. It would not be amiss to make Elsbeth (not her dislike of Elsbeth) the reason for her refusal. It would have its effect on Alwynne sooner or later.

She considered Alwynne narrowly, as she answered—

" My dear, I had arranged to be at home, for one thing."

Alwynne looked hurt.

" Of course, if you don't care about it—" she began.

Clare rallied her.

" Be sensible, my child. It is most kind of Miss Loveday; but—wasn't it chiefly your doing, Alwynne ? Imagine her dismay if I accepted. A stranger in the gate ! On Christmas Day ! One must make allowances for little prejudices, you know."

" She'll be awfully disappointed," cried Alwynne, so eager for Clare that she believed it.

" Will she ? " Clare laughed pleasantly. " Every one doesn't wear your spectacles. What would she do with me, for a whole day ? "

" We shouldn't see her much," began Alwynne. " She spends most of her time in church. I go in the morning—(yes, I'm very good !) but I've drawn the line at turning out after lunch."

" They why shouldn't you come to me instead ? It would

be so much better. I shall be all alone, you know." Clare's
wistful intonation was not entirely artificial.

Alwynne was distressed.

" Oh, Clare, I'd love to—you know I'd love to—but how
could I ? Elsbeth would be dreadfully hurt. I couldn't leave
her alone on Christmas Day."

" But you can me ? "

" Clare, don't put it like that. You know I shall want to
be with you all the time. But Elsbeth's like my mother. It
would be beastly of me. You must put relations first at
Christmas-time, even if they're not first really."

She smiled at Clare, but she felt disloyal as she said it, and
hated herself. Yet wasn't it true ? Clare came first, though
Elsbeth must never guess it. Dear old Elsbeth was pretty
dense, thank goodness ! Where ignorance is bliss, etcetera !
Yet she, Alwynne, felt extraordinarily mean. . . .

Clare watched her jealously. She had set her heart on securing
Alwynne for Christmas Day, and had thought, ten minutes since,
with a secret, confident smile, that there would not be much
difficulty. And here was Alwynne holding out—refusing cate-
gorically ! It was incredible ! Yet she could not be angry :
Alwynne so obviously was longing to be with her. . . . Equally
obviously prepared to risk her displeasure (a heavy penalty
already, Clare guessed, to Alwynne), rather than ignore the
older claim. Clare thought that an affection that could be so
loyal to a tedious old maid was better worth deflecting than
many a more ardent, unscrupulous enthusiasm. Alwynne was
showing strength of character.

She persisted nevertheless—

" Well, it's a pity. I must eat my Christmas dinner alone,
I suppose."

" Oh, Clare, you might come to us," cried Alwynne. " I
can't see why you won't."

Clare shrugged her shoulders.

" If you can't see why, my dear Alwynne, there's no more to
be said."

Alwynne most certainly did not see; but Clare's delicately
reproachful tone convicted her, and incidentally Elsbeth, of
some failure in tact. She supposed she had blundered . . .
she often did. . . . But Elsbeth, at least, must be exonerated . . .
she did so want Clare to think well of Elsbeth. . . .

She perjured herself in hasty propitiation.

"Yes. Yes—I do see. I ought to have known, of course. Elsbeth was quite right. She said you wouldn't, all along."

"Oh?" Clare sat up. "Oh? Your aunt said that, did she?" She spoke with detachment, but inwardly she was alert, on guard. Elsbeth had suddenly become worth attention.

"Oh, yes." Alwynne's voice was rueful. "She was quite sure of it. She said I might ask you, with pleasure, if I didn't believe her—you see, she'd love you to come—but she didn't think you would."

"I wonder," said Clare, laughing naturally, "what made her say that?"

"She said she knew you better than I did," confided Alwynne, with one of her spurts of indignation. "As if——"

"Yes, it's rather unlikely, isn't it?" said Clare, with an intimate smile. "But you're not going?"

"I must. Look at the time! Elsbeth will be having fits!" Alwynne called from the hall where she was hastily slipping on her coat and hat.

Clare stood a moment—thinking.

So the duel had been with Elsbeth! So that negligible and mouse-like woman had been aware—all along . . . had prepared, with a thoroughness worthy of Clare herself, for the inevitable encounter . . . had worsted Clare completely. . . . It was amazing. . . . Clare was compelled to admiration. It was clear to her now that Elsbeth must have distrusted her from the beginning. It had been Elsbeth's doing, not hers, that their intercourse had been so slight. . . . Yet she had never restrained Alwynne; she had risked giving her her head. . . . She was subtle! This affair of the Christmas dinner for instance—Clare appreciated its cleverness. Elsbeth had not wanted her, Clare now saw clearly; had been anxious to avoid the intimacy that such an invitation would imply; equally anxious, surely, that Alwynne should not guess her uneasy jealousy: so she had risked the invitation, counting on her knowledge of Clare's character (Clare stamped with vexation —that the woman should have such a memory!) secure that Clare, unsuspicious of her motives, would, by refusing, do exactly as Elsbeth wished. It had been the neatest of gossamer traps—and Clare had walked straight into it. . . . She was furious. If Alwynne, maddeningly unsuspicious Alwynne, had but enlightened her earlier in the evening! Now she was caught, committed by her own decision of manner to the course

of action she most would have wished to avoid. . . . She could
not change her mind now without appearing foolishly vacillat-
ing. . . . It would not do. . . . She had been bluffed, successfully, gorgeously bluffed. . . . And Elsbeth was sitting at home
enjoying the situation . . . too sure of herself and Clare even
to be curious as to the outcome of it all. She knew. Clare
stamped again. Oh, but she would pay Elsbeth for this. . . .
The *casus belli* was infinitely trivial, but the campaign should
be Homeric. . . . And this preliminary engagement could not
affect the final issues. . . . She always won in the end. . . .
But, after all, Elsbeth could not be blamed, though she must
be crushed; Alwynne was worth fighting for! Elsbeth was a
fool. . . . If she had treated Clare decently, Clare might—
possibly—have shared Alwynne with her. . . . She believed
she would have had scruples. . . . Now they were dispelled.
. . . Alwynne, by fair means or foul, should be detached . . .
should become Clare's property . . . should be given up to no
living woman or man.

She followed Alwynne into the hall and lit the staircase candle.
She would see Alwynne out. She would have liked to keep
Alwynne with her for a month. She was a delightful companion; it was extraordinary how indispensable she made herself. Clare knew that her flat would strike her as a dreary place
to return to, when she had shut the door on Alwynne. She
would sit and read and feel restless and lonely. Yet she did not
allow herself to feel lonely as a rule; she scouted the weakness.
But Alwynne wound herself about you, thought Clare, and you
never knew, till she had gone, what a difference she made to you.

She wished she could keep Alwynne another couple of hours.
. . . But it was eleven already . . . her hold was not yet
strong enough to warrant innovations to which Elsbeth could
object. . . . Her time would come later. . . . How much later
would depend on whether it were affection that swayed Alwynne,
or only a sense of duty. . . . She believed, because she hoped,
that it was duty—a sense of duty was more easily suborned
than an affection. . . . For the present, however, Alwynne must
be allowed to do as she thought right. Clare knew when she was
beaten, and, with her capacity for wry admiration of virtues
that she had not the faintest intention of incorporating in her
own character, she was able to applaud Alwynne heartily.
Yet she did not intend to make victory easy to her.

They went down the flights of stairs silently, side by side.

Alwynne opened the entrance doors and stood a moment, fascinated.

" Look, Clare ! What a night ! "

The moon was full and flooded earth and sky with bright, cold light. The garden, roadway, roofs, trees and fences glittered like powdered diamonds, white with frost and moonshine. The silence was exquisite.

They stood awhile, enjoying it.

Suddenly Clare shivered. Alwynne became instantly and anxiously practical.

" Clare, what am I thinking of ? Go in at once—you'll catch a dreadful cold."

With unusual passivity Clare allowed herself to be hurried in. At the staircase Alwynne said good-bye, handing her her candle, and waiting till she should have passed out of sight. On the fourth step Clare hesitated, and turned—

" Alwynne—come to me for Christmas ? "

Alwynne flung out her hands.

" Clare ! I mustn't."

" Alwynne—come to me for Christmas ? "

" You know I mustn't ! You know you'd think me a pig if I did, now wouldn't you ? "

" I expect so."

" But I'll come in for a peep at you," cried Alwynne, brightening, " while Elsbeth's at afternoon service. I could do that. And to say Merry Christmas ! "

" Come to dinner ? "

" I can't."

" Then you needn't come at all." Clare turned away.

Alwynne caught her hand, as it leaned on the balustrade. In the other the candle shook a little.

" Lady Macbeth ! Dear Lady Macbeth ! Miss Hartill of the Upper Sixth, whom I'm scared to death of, really—you're behaving like a very naughty small child. Now, aren't you ? Honestly ? Oh, do turn round and crush me with a look for being impudent, and then tell me that I'm only doing what you really approve. I don't want to, Clare, but you know you hate selfishness."

Clare looked down at her.

" All right, Alwynne. You must do as you like."

" Say good-night to me," demanded Alwynne. " Nicely, Clare, very nicely ! It's Christmas-time."

Carefully Clare deposited her candlestick on the stair above. Leaning over the banisters, she put her arms round Alwynne and kissed her passionately and repeatedly.

" Good-night, my darling," said Clare.

Then, recoiling, she caught up her candlestick, and without another word or look, hurried up the stairs.

Alwynne walked home on air.

CHAPTER X

ELSBETH bore the news of Clare's defection with stoicism; but her motherly soul was disturbed by Alwynne's disappointment, though she could not stifle her pleasure in its cause. She felt, indeed, somewhat guilty, and was eager to atone by acquiescing in Alwynne's plan of visiting Clare while she went to church; and met her more than half way over the question of an altered tea-hour.

Alwynne, who from the first had been fretted, though but half consciously, by the faintly repellent manner assumed by each of the two women at mention of the other, was soothed by Elsbeth's advances. Elsbeth was a dear, after all : there was no one quite like Elsbeth. . . . For all her obstinacies and unreasonablenesses, she never really failed you. . . . She could be depended on to love you at your worst; you could quarrel with her with never a fear of real alienation. . . . Elsbeth might not be exciting, but she was as indispensable as food. . . . She was, after all, the starting-point and ultimate goal of all one's adventures. . . . Clare would lose some of her delightfulness, if there were no Elsbeth to whom to en-sky her. . . . Alwynne did not see what she wanted with a mother, so long as she had Elsbeth. . . . She had said so once to her aunt and had never guessed, as she was chidden for sacrilege against the picture over her bed, at the exquisite pleasure she had given.

After the little coolness of the past few days (her aunt's fault entirely, Alwynne knew, and so could be unruffled) Elsbeth's renewal of sympathetic interest was very soothing. Alwynne was glad to foster it by talking of Clare, and Clare, and nothing but Clare, for the rest of the week. In church on Christmas morning, poor Elsbeth, settling her spiritual accounts, begging forgiveness for uncharitable thoughts, and assuring her Maker that she wished Clare no evil, could yet sigh for the useful age of miracles, and patron saints, and devils, when a prayer in the right quarter could transport your enemy to inaccessible islands

74

of the Antipodes. She would have been magnanimous, have
bargained for every comfort—Eden's climate and hot and cold
water laid on—but the island must be definitely inaccessible and
Antipodean.

Clare, too, had spent her morning, if not in prayer, at least
in profound meditation. She felt stranded, and was wishing for
Alwynne, and anathematizing the superfluous and intriguing
aunt.

Clare made the mistake of all tortuous intelligences in being
unable to credit appearances. She was being, as usual, unjust
to Elsbeth, Alwynne, and the world at large. She could not believe
in simplicity combined with brains : a simple soul was necessarily
a simpleton in her eyes. Because her own words were ever two
edged, her meaning flavoured by reservations and implications,
she literally could not accept a speech as expressing no more and
no less than its plain dictionary meaning. With any one of
her own type of mind she was at her ease; her mistake lay in
not recognizing how rare that type was; in detecting subtleties
where none existed, and wasting hint, suggestion and innuendo
on minds that drove as heartily through them as an ox walks
through a spider's thread stretched from post to gatepost of
the meadow he means to enter.

Elsbeth, whom she had considered a negligible fool, had yesterday startled her into respect—not for the kindly and selfless
pleasure in Alwynne's pleasure, that had, for all her little jealous
anxieties, prompted the invitation to Clare, but for the totally
imaginary cunning with which, in Clare's eyes, it had invested
her. Alwynne's repetition of Elsbeth's remark had enlightened
Clare : enlightened her to qualities in Elsbeth which Elsbeth
herself would have been horrified to possess.

Clare saw, in the manner of the invitation, a gauntlet flung
down, the preliminaries to a conflict, with Alwynne herself for
prize ; and the first warning of an antagonist sufficiently like herself
to be considered dangerous, the more dangerous, indeed, for the
apparently uninteresting harmlessness that could mask a mind
in reality so scheming and so complex. She did not realize that
if she did finally close with Elsbeth, with the intention of robbing
her of Alwynne, she would have far more to fear from her simple,
affectionate goodness of heart than from any subtlety of intellect
with which Clare was choosing to invest her.

She wondered, as she frittered away the morning, how she
should best counter Elsbeth's attack. She would call, of course

—in state; it would be due; she would not be judged deficient in courtesies. Alwynne should be there (she would ensure that), and she, Clare, would be exceedingly charming, and very delicately emphasize the contrast between Elsbeth and herself. It would be quite easy, with Alwynne already biassed. Her eyes sparkled with anticipation. It would be amusing. She should enjoy routing Elsbeth.

And there was the case of Alwynne to be considered. She had been excessively nice to Alwynne lately, had, in fact, allowed her, for a moment, to see how necessary she was becoming to Clare. . . . That was a mistake. . . . One must never let people feel secure of their hold upon one. . . . That little speech of Alwynne's last night, mocking and tender—she had thrilled to it at the time—did it not, ever so faintly, shadow forth a readjustment of attitudes, sound a note of equality? That, though it had pleased her at the moment, must not be. . . . Alwynne must be checked. . . . It would not hurt her. . . . She was subdued as easily as a child, and as easily revived. . . . She never bore malice. Clare, who never forgot or forgave a pinprick, had often marvelled at her, could even now scarcely believe in the spontaneity of her good temper. But Alwynne, certainly, had been going too far lately; was absurdly popular in the school; could, Clare guessed, have annexed more than one of her own special worshippers, if she had chosen. Louise, she knew, confided in her : she thought with a double stab of jealousy of the scene she had witnessed but a few days since; of Louise, fresh from her commendations, from her kiss even (that rare impulse, regretted as soon as gratified), at rest in Alwynne's arms. She recalled Louise's startled look and Alwynne's contrasting serenity. She had not enquired what it all meant—that was not her way. But she had not forgotten it. Alwynne was hers. Louise was hers. But they had nothing to seek from one another! Alwynne, undoubtedly, as the elder, the dearer, required the check; not little Louise. Louise's letter had genuinely touched her—she thought she would go and see the child, spend her Christmas Day charitably, in amusing her. And if (in after-thought) Alwynne came round in the afternoon, and found her gone—it couldn't be helped! It wouldn't hurt Alwynne to be disappointed . . . It wouldn't hurt Alwynne to spend a day of undiluted Elsbeth. . . . And Louise would be so amusingly charmed to see Clare. . . . It was pleasant to please a child—a clever, appreciative child. . . . She would go round directly after lunch. . . . The maid should go home for the afternoon. . . . She laughed mischievously as she imagined the blankness of Alwynne's face, when she should be confronted by silence and a closed door. Poor, dear Alwynne ! Well, it wouldn't hurt her.

But Alwynne set out gaily on Christmas afternoon, and, first escorting Elsbeth to the lych-gate of her favourite church, walked on as quickly as her narrow fur-edged skirt would let her.

The clocks were striking three as she turned into Friar's Lane.

It was a cold, still day, and Alwynne shivered a little, and drew her furs closely about her, as she stood outside the door of Clare's flat. She had rung, but the maid was usually slow in answering.

The passage was damply cold. It would be all the jollier to toast oneself before one of Clare's imperial fires. . . . She wished the maid would hurry up. She waited a moment and then rang again.

There was no answer.

It struck her that the maid might have been given the afternoon off ; but it was funny that Clare did not hear.

She rang again. She could hear the bell tinging shrilly within, but there was no other sound save the tick of the solemn little grandmother on the inner side of the wall.

Suddenly it occurred to her that Clare might be dozing. Clare never slept in the afternoons, but she did occasionally doze in her chair for a few minutes. She denied that she did so as strenuously as people always and unaccountably do ; but Alwynne knew better. It always delighted her when Clare succumbed to drowsiness ; a good sleeper herself, she had been appalled by Clare's acquiescence in four wakeful nights out of seven, and after a casual description that Clare had once given her of the arid miseries of insomnia, ten minutes unexpected slumber did not give Clare herself more ease than it gave Alwynne.

The possibility of such an explanation of the silence, therefore, had to be considered respectfully : if Clare slept, far be it from Alwynne to wake her ! Yet she could not go away. . . . Clare, after that unlucky clash of wills, would be doubly hurt if Alwynne left without seeing her first. . . . But if Clare were asleep. . . .

Resignedly Alwynne sat herself down on Clare's doorstep to wait until a movement within should be the signal to ring again.

She was not annoyed ; she always had plenty to think about ; and it would be very pleasant, when Clare did at last open the door, to be received with open arms, and pitied, and scolded, and warmed. . . . It was certainly very cold. . . All the draughts of the town seemed to have their home on the staircase, and to come sliding and slithering and undulating past, like a brood of invisible snakes.

She shifted her position. The doorstep was icy. She got up, and placed her muff, her chinchilla muff (shades of Elsbeth! her beautiful, new chinchilla muff) on the whitened doorstep. Then she sat on it.

"Ah! That's better," murmured Alwynne appreciatively. She was grateful to Elsbeth for reminding her to wear her muff.

But it did not get any warmer, and the daylight was beginning to fade. She glanced at her watch—twenty minutes past three. Surely Clare was awake again now. But she would wait another five minutes. She watched the hands—marvelled at the interminable length of a minute, and was drifting off on her favourite speculation as to the essential unreality of time, when simultaneously the grandmother struck the half-hour and she sneezed. She jumped up horrified. A cold would mean a week's absence from Clare, and a restatement of Elsbeth's thesis 'of the advisability of wearing flannel petticoats and long-sleeved bodices.'

Also, half of her hoarded hour was gone. She rang again impatiently. No answer. Clare must be out. . . . Gone to the post? No, Alwynne had been waiting half-an-hour, she would have returned by now. . . . Impossible that Clare should be out on Christmas afternoon, when she had refused an invitation and was expecting Alwynne herself. . . . She rang; and waited; and rang again and again and yet again.

"If Clare has gone out——" cried Alwynne indignantly; and subjected the handle to a final series of vicious tugs. The bell within pealed and rocked and jarred, gave a last hysterical gurgle and was dumb. She had broken the bell. She had broken Clare Hartill's bell!

Alwynne looked round about her guiltily; she felt more like nine than nineteen. The flight of stairs was still empty and silent. No one had seen her come; no one would see her go. . . . If she went quietly away, and said nothing about it? For Clare would be annoyed. . . . She always got so annoyed over little things. . . . What a pity to have a fuss with Clare over such a little thing as a broken bell!

She crept on tip-toe down the stairs and out into the road. Then she paused.

Was she being mean? After all—there was no earthly use in telling Clare. . . . Clare would never let her pay for the mending.

. . . Yet naturally she would be annoyed to come back and find her bell broken. . . . She would think it was the milkman or the paper-boy. . . . Alwynne hoped they would not get into trouble. . . . Perhaps, after all, she had better tell Clare. Such an absurd thing to confess to, though—that she had been in such a temper that she had broken the bell! Clare would be sarcastic . . . Yet it was Clare's fault for being out. . . . That was unkind. . . . She would tell Clare so . . . she would write and tell her. . . She would write a note now, and tell her about the bell at the same time. . . . She retraced her steps, pulled out her note-book and pencil, and began to scribble—

Dear Clare—I'm awfully sorry but I'm afraid I've broken the bell. I couldn't make you hear. I thought you were asleep, but I suppose you are out. I must have rung too hard, but I didn't think you could be out. Heavily underlined. *I'm dreadfully sorry about the bell.*

She hesitated. If Clare would let her pay for a new one, she wouldn't feel so bad. . . . Yet how could she suggest it ? It would sound so crude. . . . If only Clare would not be angry. . . . Absurd to be feeling afraid of Clare—but then she had never done anything so stupid before. . . . Angry or not, Clare would never let her pay. . . . Yet should she suggest it ? She bit her pencil in distracted indecision, till the lead broke off between her teeth.

That settled it. The damp stump was barely capable of scoring an *Alwynne.*

She pinned the paper to the door with her only hatpin (a present of the forenoon) and reluctantly departed.

It was a pity that her best hat blew off twice into the mud.

Elsbeth was glad to get Alwynne back so early. Had Alwynne enjoyed herself ?

Alwynne sneezed as she answered.

Before the evening was over Alwynne reeked of eucalyptus.

CHAPTER XI

LOUISE was at the nursery window, staring out into the brown, bare garden. The sky was smooth and a dark yellow, the naked trees barred it like a tiger's hide. The gathering dusk had swallowed up the wind. Not a twig stirred, not a sparrow's chirp broke the thick stillness. Spellbound, the world awaited the imminent snow.

Louise, sitting motionless in the window-seat, with her little pink nose flattening itself against the panes in dreary expectation of a stray unlikely postman, looked, with her peaked, ivory face and dark, unwinking eyes, her colourless clothes, and the sprig of holly with never a scarlet berry pinned to her flat little chest, like the mood of the December day made flesh.

Clare, at least, thought so. Dispensing with the indifferent maid, she had found her own way to the nursery, and pushing open the unlatched door, stood an instant, appraising the child and her surroundings. She noted with distaste the remains of the barely tasted lunch, still encumbering the table, and impinging on the little pile of austere Christmas presents, so carefully arranged : the gloves and stockings and the prim Prayer Book a mere background for a dainty calendar that she recognized. She smiled, with a touch of irritation—did Alwynne ever forget any one, she wondered ? But it was not suitable for a mistress to send her pupils presents. . . . She wished she had thought of sending Louise something herself . . . something more original than that obviously over-prized calendar. . . . It was not much of a Christmas table, she thought . . . not much of a Christmas Day for a child. . . .

She marvelled that a well-furnished room could look so dreary. Louise's huddled pose, the neglected fire, the book crushed face downwards on the floor, combined to touch her. With her incurable feeling for the effective attitude, she remained straight and stiff in the shadows of the doorway, but her gesture was beautiful in its awkward tenderness as she stretched out her hand to the window.

80

" Merry Christmas, Louise ! "

For an instant the child was silent, rigid, incredulous : then came a whirl of petticoats and a flash of black legs. Louise, wild with excitement, dropped to the floor and dashed across the room.

" Oh, Miss Hartill ! Oh, Miss Hartill ! You ? "

" Well, are you pleased to see me ? "

" Please, won't you sit down ? " Louise, between delight and embarrassment, did curious things with the big arm-chair. " I can't believe it's you. And on Christmas Day ! Won't you please sit down ? Is the room too warm for you ? Will you take off your furs ? Would you like some tea ? I'll make up the fire—it's cold in here. Will you take this chair ? Oh, Miss Hartill ! It's like the Queen calling on one. I don't know what to do." She looked up at Clare, blushing. Her pleasure and excitement were pretty enough.

Clare laughed.

" I'll tell you what to do. Run and put on your coat and hat. Would you like to come and spend the rest of the day with me ? "

" With you ? " Louise's eyes opened. " But it's Christmas Day ? "

" Well ? "

" I shan't be in the way ? "

" I don't think so," said Clare coolly. " I'll send you home if you are."

She twinkled, but Louise was serious.

" You could do that, couldn't you ? " she remarked with relief. " Oh, Miss Hartill, you are good ! And I was hating my Christmas Day so. Won't you sit down while I get my things on ? "

" Hurry up ! " said Clare. And Louise fled to her bedroom.

Their walk back to Friar's Lane was a silent one. The snow was at last beginning to fall. Clare, half hypnotized by the steady silent motion, tramped forward, keeping time to some fragment of tune within her head. She was warmed by the pleasant consciousness of a kindly action performed, but its object, trotting beside her, was half forgotten.

Louise, very shy at encountering Miss Hartill unofficially, was far too timid to speak unless she were addressed. But she was perfectly happy; marvelling and rejoicing at her situation (Miss Hartill's guest, bound for her home !), overflowing with dog-like devotion to the Olympian who had actually remembered

her existence. She was glad of the silent walk. It gave her time
to realize her own happiness; to learn by heart that picture of
Clare, against the background of the empty nursery, to get her
every sentence by rote, and store all safely in her memory
before turning to the contemplation of the incredible adventure
upon which she was now embarking.

Clare, preceding Louise up the staircase, found Alwynne's
note awaiting her. She frowned as she read it and felt for her
latch-key. It was just like Alwynne to leave a note like that
for any one to read. . . . And the hatpin for any one to steal.
. . . She wished it had been stolen before it had scratched her
paint. . . . And the bell! It was really annoying of Alwynne!
It would cost her five shillings to put right. . . . She, Clare, was
not mean, but she did grudge money for that sort of thing. . . .
Really, Alwynne might offer to pay for it. . . . But that, of
course, would never occur to Alwynne. . . . She was altogether
too reckless about other people's belongings. . . . Her own
were her own affair. . . . But to break Clare's bell. . . . She
must have been quite comprehensively annoyed to have actually
broken it. . . . Clare laughed. She had had a sudden vision of
Alwynne's blank face and indignant pealings. Poor old Alwynne!
Well—it wouldn't hurt her. . . . If she were careful to let
Alwynne know to whom she had been sacrificed, Alwynne might
not be quite so partisan over Louise next term. . . . That
wouldn't be a bad thing. . . . She did not approve of intimacies
between the girls and the mistresses. . . . But she, Clare, would
make it up to both of them. . . . She would begin now, with
Louise. . . . She would devote herself to amusing Louise. . . .
She would give Louise the time of her life. . . . Louise would be
sure to tell Alwynne about it afterwards. . . .

CHAPTER XII

" What are you going to do with yourself all the holidays ? " asked Clare, with a touch of curiosity. Louise had slipped off her chair on to the soft hearthrug, and sat, hugging her knees and staring up at Clare.

" Read," she said briefly, and gave a little gurgle of anticipation.

" All day long ? "

" Oh, yes, Miss Hartill. I never get a chance in term time. There's such heaps to read. I'd like to live in a library."

" Yet a peep at the world outside beats all the books that were ever written."

" I wonder." Louise rubbed her chin meditatively against her knees before she delivered herself. " You know—I think the way things strike people is much more interesting than the things themselves. I like exploring people's minds. Do you know ? "

" I know," said Clare. She laughed mischievously. " You mean—that what you think I am, for instance, is much more interesting than what I really am."

Louise protested mutely. Her black eyes glowed.

" I daresay you're right, Louise. You wear pink spectacles, you see. I'm quite sure you would be appalled if any one took them off. I'm a horrid person really."

Louise looked puzzled; then the twinkle in Miss Hartill's eyes enlightened her. Miss Hartill was teasing. She laughed merrily.

Clare shook her head.

" It's quite true. I'm an egoist, Louise ! "

" It's not true," said Louise passionately. She was on guard in an instant, ready to justify Miss Hartill to herself and the world. It amused Clare to excite her.

" My good child—what do you know about it ? "

" Lots," said Louise, with a catch in her voice. " You're not ! You're not ! "

"I am." Clare leaned forward, much tickled. She could afford to attempt to disillusion Louise. . . . Louise would not believe her, but she could not say later that she had not been warned. But at the same time, Clare warmed her cold and cynical self in the pure flame of affection her self-criticism was fanning. "I am," she repeated. "Why do you think I came round to see you to-day?"

Louise looked up at her shyly, dwelling on her answer as if it gave her exquisite pleasure.

"Because—because you knew I was alone, and you hated me to be miserable on Christmas Day."

"You?" Clare's eyebrows lifted for a second, but a glance into the child's candid eyes dispelled the vague suspicion. . . . Louise and conceit were incompatible. She listened with a touch of compunction to the innocent answer.

"Not me specially, of course. Any one who was down. Only it happened to be me. I think you can't help being good to people: you're made that way." Her eyes were full of wondering admiration.

Clare was touched. She sighed as she answered—

"I wish I were. You shouldn't believe in people, Louise. I came round because—yes, you were a lonely scrap of a school-girl, certainly—but there were lots of other reasons. I wanted a walk and I wanted to be amused, and I wanted—and I wanted——" she moved restlessly in her chair. "All pure egoism, anyhow."

"But you came," said Louise.

"To please you, or to punish some one else? I don't know!"

Louise enjoyed her incomprehensibility. She stored up her remarks to puzzle over later. Yet she would ask questions if Miss Hartill were in a talking mood.

"Do I know them?" (She had an odd habit of using the plural when she wished to be discreet.) She wondered who had been punished, and why, and thrilled deliciously, as she did to a ghost story. She thought that it would be terrible to have offended Miss Hartill: yet immensely exciting. . . . She wondered if all her courage would go if Miss Hartill were angry? She had always despised poor Jeanne du Barri: but Miss Hartill raging would be harder to face than a mob. . . .

"What have they done?" asked Louise eagerly.

"They? It's your dear Miss Durand," said Clare, with a grim

smile. " I'm very angry with her, Louise. She's been behaving badly."

Louise's eyes widened : she looked alarmed and distressed.

" Oh, but Miss Hartill—she hasn't ! She couldn't ! What has she done ? "

" Shall I tell you ? " Clare leaned forward mysteriously.

Louise nodded breathlessly.

" She wouldn't copy me and be an egoist. And I wanted her to, rather badly, Louise. There, that's all ! You're none the wiser, are you ? Never mind, you will be, some day. Don't look so worried, you funny child."

" Why do you call yourself such names ? You're not an egoist ? You can't be," cried Louise desperately.

Clare laughed

" Can't I ? Most people are. It's not a synonym for murderess ! Stop frowning, child. Why, I don't believe you know what it means even. Do you know what an egoist is, Louise ? "

" Sir Willoughby Patterne ! " said Louise promptly.

Clare threw up her hands.

" What next ? I wish I'd had charge of you earlier. You shouldn't try so hard to say ' Humph,' little pig."

" I don't." Louise was indignant.

" Then what possesses you to steer your cockle-boat on to Meredith ? Well—what do you think of him ? What have you read ? "

" About all. He's queer. He's not Dickens or Scott, of course——" Her tone deprecated.

" Of course not," said Clare, with grave sympathy.

" But I like him. I liked Chloe. I liked the sisters—you know—' Fine Shades and Nice Feeling '——"

" Why ? " Clare shot it at her.

" I don't know. They made me laugh. They're awfully real people. And I liked that book where the two gentlemen drink wine. ' Veuve ' something."

" What on earth did you see in that ? " Clare was amused.

" I don't know. I just liked them. Of course, I adore Shagpat."

" That I understand. It's a fairy tale to you, isn't it ? "

" Not a proper one—only Arabian Nightsy."

" What's a proper one, Louise ? "

Louise hesitated.

" Well, heaps that one loves aren't. Grimm's and Hans

Andersen's aren't, or even *The Wondrous Isles*. And, of course, none of the Lang books. I hate those. You know, proper fairy stories aren't easy to get. You have to dig. You get bits out of the notes in the Waverley Novels, and there's *Kilmeny*, and *The Celtic Twilight*, and *The Lore of Proserpine*, and Lemprière. Do you believe in fairies, Miss Hartill? "

" It depends on the mood I'm in," said Clare seriously, "and the place. Elves and electric railways are incompatible."

Louise flung herself upon the axiom.

" Do you think so? Now I don't, Miss Hartill—I don't. If they are—they can stand railways. But you just believe in them literaturily——"

" Literally," Clare corrected.

" No, no—literaturily—just as a pretty piece of writing. You'll never see them if you think of them like that, Miss Hartill. The Greeks didn't—they just believed in Pan, and the Oreads, and the Dryads, and all those delicious people; and the consequence was that the country was simply crammed with them. You just read Lemprière! I wish I'd lived then. Miss Hartill, did you ever see a Good Person? "

" I'm afraid not, Louise. But I had a nurse who used to tell me about her grand-aunt : she was supposed to be a changeling."

Louise wriggled with delight.

" Oh, tell about her, Miss Hartill. What was she like? "

" Tiny and black, with a very white skin. They were a fair family. Nurse said they all disliked her, though she never did them any harm. She used to be out in the woods all day—and she ate strange food."

" What? "

" Fungi, and nettle-tops, and young bracken, and blackberries, my nurse said."

" Blackberries? "

" She was Irish; the Irish peasants won't touch blackberries, you know. We're just as bad, Louise. Heaps of fungi are delicious—wait till you've been in Germany. They know what's good : but, then, they won't touch rabbits, so there you are ! I expect my nurse's aunt thought us an odd lot, us humans."

" Was she really a fairy? " Louise was breathless.

" How do I know? A witch perhaps. I should think a young witch, by all accounts."

" What happened to her? "

" She was ' swept ' on her wedding-day."

" Crossing water ? "

" No. She was to marry an old farmer. She went into the woods at dawn to wash in dew, and gather bindweed for her wreath——" She paused dramatically, her eyes dancing with fun ; but Louise was wholly in earnest.

" Go on ! Oh, go on ! "

" She was never seen again."

" Oh, how lovely ! " Louise shivered ecstatically. " I wish I'd been her. What did her foster people do ? "

" What could they ? I think they were glad to be rid of her." (Clare suppressed a certain tall young gipsy, who had figured suspiciously in the original narrative.) " Fairy blood is ill to live with, Louise. I don't envy Mrs. Blake, or Mrs. Thomas Rhymer."

" No. But it's so difficult to live in two worlds at once."

" Shouldering the wise man's burden already ? "

" You get absent-minded, and forget—ink-stains, you know, and messages."

" I know," said Clare.

" You see, I have such a gorgeous world inside my head, Miss Hartill : I go there when I'm rather down, here. It's a sort of Garden of the Hesperides, and you are there, and Mother, and all my special friends."

" Who, for instance ? " Clare was curious ; it was the first she had heard of Louise with friends of her own.

" Well—Elizabeth Bennett, and the Little Women, and Garm, and Amadis of Gaul——"

" Oh—not real people ? " Clare was amused at herself for being relieved.

" Oh, but Miss Hartill—they are real." Louise was indignant. " Ever so much more than—oh, most people ! Look at Mrs. Bennett and Mamma ! Nobody will think of Mamma in a hundred years—but who'd ever forget Mrs. Bennett ? "

" Mrs Bennett in the Garden of the Hesperides, Louise ? " Clare began to chuckle. " I can't swallow that."

Louise pealed with laughter.

" You should have seen her the other day, with the dragon after her. She'd been trying to sneak some apples, because Bingley was coming to tea."

" Who came to the rescue ? "

" Oh, I did." Louise was revelling in her sympathetic listener. " I have to keep order, you know. She was awfully blown, though. Siegfried helped me."

" I wish I could get to fairyland as easily as you do."

Louise considered.

" I don't. My country is only in my head. Fairyland must be somewhere, mustn't it ? Do you know what I think, Miss Hartill ? "

" In patches, Louise."

Louise blushed.

" No, but seriously—don't laugh. You know you explained the fourth dimension to us the other day ? "

" That I'm sure I never did." Clare was lying back in her chair, her arms behind her head, smiling inscrutably.

" Oh, but, Miss Hartill——"

" Never, Louise ! "

" Oh, but honestly—I'm not contradicting you, of course— but you did. Last Thursday fortnight, in second lesson."

" I wish you were as accurate over all your dates, Louise ! Your History paper was not all that it should be."

" It's holidays, Miss Hartill ! But don't you remember ? "

" I explained to you that the fourth dimension was inex- plicable—a very different thing."

" *The Plattner Story* explains it—clearly." Louise's tone was distinctly reproachful.

" Oh no, it doesn't, Louise. Mr. Wells only deludes you into thinking it does."

" Well, anyhow, I think—don't you think that it's rather likely that fairyland is the fourth dimension ? It would all fit in so beautifully with all the old stories of enchantment and disappearances. Then there was another book I read about it. *The Inheritors*——"

" Have done, Louise ! You make me dizzy. Don't try to live exclusively on truffles. If you could continue to confine your attention to books you have some slight chance of under- standing, for the next few years, it would be an excellent thing. Neither Meredith nor the fourth dimension is meat for babes, you know."

" I like what I don't understand. It's the finding out is the fun." Louise looked mutinous.

" And having found out ? "

" Then I start on something else."

Clare considered her.

" Louise, I don't know if it's a compliment to either of us— but I believe we're very much alike."

Louise gave a child's delighted chuckle, but she showed no surprise.

"That's nice, Miss Hartill." She hesitated. "Miss Hartill, did you know my Mother?"

"Mrs. Denny?" Clare hesitated.

Louise gave an impatient gesture.

"Not Mamma. My very own Mother."

"No, my dear." Clare's voice was soft.

Louise sighed.

"No one does. There are no pictures. Father was angry when I asked about her once: and Miss Murgatroyd—she was our governess—she said I had no tact. I miss her, you know, though I don't remember her. I had a nurse: she told me a little. Mother had grey eyes too, you know," said Louise, gazing into Clare's. "I expect she was rather like you."

She watched Clare a little breathlessly. There was more of tenderness in her face than many who thought they knew Clare Hartill would have credited, but no hint of awakening memory, of the recognition the child sought. She went on—

"People never come back when they're dead, do they?" She had no idea of the longing in her voice.

"No, you poor baby!" Clare rose hastily and began to walk up and down the room, as her fashion was when she was stirred.

"Never?"

"'*Stieg je ein Freund Dir aus dem Grabe wieder?*'" murmured Clare.

"What, Miss Hartill?"

"Never, Louise."

Louise's thistledown fancies were scattered by her tone. Impossible to discredit any statement of Miss Hartill's. Yet she protested timidly.

"There was the Witch of Endor, Miss Hartill. Samuel, you know."

"Is that Meredith?" said Clare absently. Then she caught Louise's expression. "What's the matter?"

"But it's the Bible!" cried Louise horrified.

Clare sat down again and began to laugh pleasantly.

"What am I to do with you, Louise? Are you five or fifty? You want to discuss Meredith with me—(not that I shall let you, my child—don't think I approve of all this reading—I did it myself at your age, you see) and five minutes later you look at me round-eyed because I've forgotten my Joshua or my

Judges! Kings? I beg your pardon; Kings be it! Never mind, Louise. Tell me about the Witch of Endor."

"Only that she called up Samuel, I meant, from the dead."

Louise was evidently abstracted; she was picking her words.

"Don't you believe it, Miss Hartill, quite?"

"It's the Old Testament, after all," temporized Clare. She began to see Louise's difficulty. She had no beliefs herself; but she thought she would find out how fourteen handled the problem.

"Then the New is different? There was Dorcas, you know, and the widow's son. That is all true, Miss Hartill?"

Clare fenced.

"Many people think so."

"I want to know the truth," said Louise tensely. "I want to know what you think." She spoke as if the two things were synonymous.

Clare shook her head.

"I won't help you, Louise. You must find out for yourself. Leave it alone, if you're wise."

"How can I? I've been reading——"

"Ah?"

"The *Origin of Species*—and *We Two*."

Clare's gravity fled. She lay back shaking with laughter.

"Louise, you're delightful! Anything else?"

Louise pulled up her footstool to Clare's knee.

"Miss Hartill, I've been reading a play. It's horrible. I can't bear it, though it was thrilling to read——"

Clare interrupted—

"Where do you get all these books, Louise?"

"There are all Mother's, you know. Nobody else wants them. And then there's the Free Library."

Clare shuddered. She would sooner have drunk from the tin cup of a public fountain than have handled the greasy volumes of a public library.

"How can you?" she said disgustedly. "Dirt and dog-ears!"

Louise opened her eyes. She was too young to be squeamish.

"'A book's a book for a' that,'" she laughed. "How else am I to get hold of any—that I like?"

Clare jerked her head to the lined walls.

"Help yourself," she said.

Louise was radiant.

"May I? Oh, you are good! I will take such care. I'll cover them in brown paper."

She jumped up and, running across the room, flung herself on her knees before the wide shelves. Timidly, at first, but with growing forgetfulness of Clare, she pulled out here a volume and there a volume, handling them tenderly, yet barely opening each, so eager was she for fresh discoveries. She reminded Clare of *Alice* with the scented rushes. Clare was amused by her absorption, and a little touched. The child's attitude to books hinted at the solitariness of her life : she relaxed to them, greeting them as intimates and companions; there was a new appearance on her; she was obviously at home, welcomed by her friends; a very different person to the shy-eyed, prim little prodigy her school-fellows knew.

Clare, glancing at her now and then, sympathized benevolently, and left her to herself; she understood that side of the child; her remark to Louise about the resemblance between them had not been made at random; she was constantly detecting traits and tastes in her similar to her own. She was interested; she had thought herself unique. Their histories were not dissimilar; she, too, different as her environment had been, could look back on a lonely, self-absorbed childhood; she, too, had had forced and premature successes. They had not been empty ones, she reflected complacently; she had used those schoolgirl triumphs as stepping-stones. She doubted if Louise could do the same : there was something unpractical about Louise—a hint of the visionary in her air. She had at present none of Clare's passion for power and the incense of success. Clare, quite aware of her failing, aware that it was a failing and perversely proud of it, yet hoped that she should not see it sprouting in the character of Louise. She hated to see her own defects reproduced (ineffably vulgarized) in others; it jarred her pride. The discovery of the resemblance between herself and Louise amused and charmed her, as long as it was confined to the qualities that Clare admired; but if the girl began to reflect her faults, Clare knew that she should be irritated.

She considered these things as she sat and sewed. She was an exquisite needlewoman. The frieze of tapestry that ran round the low-ceilinged room was her own work. Alwynne had designed it—a history of the loves of Deirdre and Naismi some months before, when she and Clare had discovered Yeats together; and Clare had adapted the rough, clever sketches, working with her usual amazing speed. The foot-deep strips of needlework and painted silk, with their golden skies and dark foregrounds, along which the dim, rainbow figures moved, were just what Clare had wanted to complete her panelled room; for she was beauty-loving and house-proud, though her love of originality, or more correctly her tendency to be superior and aloof, often enticed her into bizarrerie. But the Deirdre frieze was as harmonious as it was unusual; and Clare, as she daily feasted her eyes on the rich, mellow colours, was only annoyed that the idea of it had been Alwynne's. That fact, though she would not own it, was able, though imperceptibly, to taint Clare's pleasure. She was quite unnecessarily scrupulous in mentioning Alwynne's share in the work to any one who admired it; but it piqued her to do so, none the less. If any one had told her that it piqued her she would have been extremely amused at the absurdity of the idea.

She was at the time working out a medallion of her own design, and growing interested, she soon forgot all about Louise, sitting Turkish fashion at the big book-case. The light had long since faded and the enormous fire, gilding walls and furniture, rendered the candles' steady light almost superfluous. Candle-light was another predilection of Clare's—there was neither electricity nor gas in her tiny, perfect flat. The tick of the clock in the hall and the flutter of turning pages alone broke the silence. Outside, the snow fell steadily.

Half-a-mile away Alwynne Durand, drumming on the window-pane, while her aunt dozed in her chair, thought incessantly of Clare, and was filled with restless longing to be with her. She tried to count the snowflakes till her brain reeled. She felt cold and dreary, but she would not rouse Elsbeth by making up the fire. She wished she had something new to read. She thought it the longest Christmas Day she had ever spent.

The neat maid, bringing in the tea-tray, roused Clare. She pushed aside her work and began to pour out; but Louise in her corner, made no sign.

Clare laughed.

" Louise, wake up! Don't you want any tea? "

Louise, as if the conversation had not ceased for an instant, scrambled to her feet and came to the table, a load of books in her arms, saying as she did so—

" I'll be awfully careful. May I take these, perhaps? "

Clare nodded.

" Presently. I'll look them over first. Muffins? "

She gave Louise a delightful meal and taught her to take

tea with a slice of lemon. She was particular, Louise noticed; some of the muffins were not toasted to her liking, and were instantly banished; she criticized the cakes and the flavouring of the dainty sandwiches; then she laughed wickedly at Louise for her round eyes.

" What's the matter, child ? "

" Nothing," said Louise, embarrassed.

" I believe you're shocked because I talked so much about food ? "

Louise blushed scarlet.

" I like eating, Louise."

" Yes—yes, of course," she concurred hastily.

Clare was entertained. She knew quite well that Louise, like all children, considered a display of interest in food, if not indelicate, at least extremely human. She knew, too, that in Louise's eyes she was too entirely compounded of ideals and noble qualities to be more than officially human. She enjoyed upsetting her ideas.

" If you come to actual values, I'd rather do without Shakespeare than Mrs. Beeton," she remarked blandly.

" Oh, Miss Hartill ! " Louise was protesting—suspecting a trap—ready to ripple into laughter. " You do say queer things."

" I ? "

" Yes. As if you meant that ! "

" But I do ! Eating's an art, Louise, like painting or writing. I had a pheasant last Sunday——" She gave the entire menu, and enlarged on the etceteras with enthusiasm.

Louise looked bewildered.

" I never thought you thought about that sort of thing," she remarked. " I thought you just didn't notice—I thought you would always be thinking of poetry and pictures——" She subsided, blushing.

Clare laughed at her pleasantly.

" I thought, I thought, I think, I thought ! What a lot of thoughts. I'm sorry, Louise ! Is all my star-dust gone ? "

Louise shook her head vigorously, but she was still embarrassed. She changed the subject with agility.

" I've read that ! "

" What ? "

" The star-dust book—but I've picked out two others of his. May I ? All these ? "

Clare ran her finger along the titles.

" Yes—yes—Fiona Mcleod—yes—*Peer Gynt*—yes, if you like, you won't understand it, or Yeats—but all right. No, not Nietzsche ! Not on any account, Louise."

Louise protested.

" Oh, why not, Miss Hartill ? I'm nearly fourteen."

" Are you really ? " said Clare, with respect.

" He looks so jolly—Old Testamenty——"

" He does, Louise ! That's his little way. But he's not for the Upper Fifth."

" He's in the Free Library," said Louise, with a twinkle. Clare turned.

" You can have all the books you want, if you come to me. But no more Free Library, Louise. You understand ? I don't wish it."

Louise tingled like a bather under a cold spray. She liked and disliked the autocratic tone.

Clare went on.

" I detest trash—and there's a good deal, even in a Carnegie collection. There's no need for you to dull your imagination on melodrama like—what was it ? "

" What, Miss Hartill ? "

" The play you began to tell me about—you thought it horrible, you said."

Louise opened her eyes.

" Miss Hartill, it wasn't melodrama—it was good stuff. That's why it worried me. It's by a Norwegian or a Dane or some one. *Pastor Sang* it's called."

" That ? I don't follow. I should have thought the theology would have bored you, but there's nothing horrible in it."

" It worried me. Oh, Miss Hartill, what does it all mean ? Darwin says, we just grew—doesn't he ? and that the Bible's all wrong. But you say that doesn't matter—it's just Old Testament ? And this play says—do you remember ? the wife is ill—and the husband, who cures people by praying—he can't cure her——"

" Well ? " said Clare impatiently.

" And he says, if the apostles did miracles, we ought to be able to—he kills his wife, trying. He can't, you see. But the point is, if he couldn't, with all his faith—could the apostles ? And if the apostles couldn't, could Christ Himself ? The miracles are just only a tale, perhaps ? "

"Perhaps," said Clare. "You're not clear, Louise, but I know what you mean."

"It frightened me, that play," said the child in a low voice. "If there were no miracles—and everything one reads makes one sure there weren't—why, then, the Bible's not true! Jesus was just a man! He didn't rise? Perhaps there isn't an afterwards? Perhaps there isn't God?"

"Perhaps," said Clare.

The child's eyes were wide and frightened. She put her hand timidly on Clare's knee.

"Miss Hartill—you believe in God?"

Clare looked at her, weighing her.

Louise spoke again; her voice had grown curiously apprehensive.

"Miss Hartill—you do believe in God?"

Clare shrugged her shoulders.

Louise stared at her appalled.

"If *you* don't believe in God——" she began slowly, and then stopped.

They sat a long while in silence.

Clare felt uncomfortable. She had not intended to express any opinion, to let her own attitude to religion appear. But Louise, with her sudden question, had forced one from her. After all, if Louise had begun to doubt and to inquire, no silence on Clare's part would stop her. . . . Every girl went through the phase—with Louise it had begun early, that was all. . . . Yet in her heart she knew that Louise, with her already overworked mind, should have been kept from the mental distress of religious doubt. . . . She knew that for some years she could have been so kept; that, as the mouth can eat what the body will not absorb, so, though her intelligence might have assimilated all the books she chose to read, her soul need not necessarily have been disturbed by them. Her acquired knowledge that the world is round need not have jostled her rule of thumb conviction that it is flat. Her interest in 'ologies and 'osophies could have lived comfortably enough with her child's belief in four angels round her head, for another two or three years— strengthening, maturing years.

Clare knew her power. At a soothing word from her, Louise would have shelved her speculations, or at least have continued them impersonally. Clare could have guaranteed God to her. But Clare had shrugged her shoulders, and Louise had grown white—and she had felt like a murderess. Do children really take their religion so seriously? . . . After all, what real difference could it make to Louise? . . . She, Clare, had been glad to be rid of her clogging and irrational beliefs. . . . Louise, too, when she recovered from the shock, would enjoy the sense of freedom and self-respect. . . . If Louise talked like a girl of eighteen she could not be expected to receive the careful handling you gave a child of twelve. . . . Anyhow, it was done now. . . .

Suddenly and persuasively she began to talk to Louise. She touched gently on the history, the growth and inevitable decay of all religions—the contrasting immutability of the underlying code of ethics, upon which they, one and all, were founded. She told her vivid little stories of the religious struggles of the centuries, had her breathless over the death of Socrates, nailed up for her anew the ninety-five theses to the Wittenberg church door. Exerting all her powers, all her knowledge, all her descriptive and dramatic skill, to charm away one child's distress, Clare was, for an hour, a woman transformed, sound and honey-sweet. Against all that happened later, she could at least put the one hour, when, remorsefully, she had given Louise of the best that was in her.

Incidentally, she delivered to her audience of one the most brilliant lecture of her career. Later she wrote down what she remembered of it, and it became the foundation for her monograph on religions that was to become a minor classic. Its success was immediate—that was typical of Clare—but she never wrote another line. That also was typical of Clare. It bored her to repeat a triumph.

She soon had Louise happy again : it was not in Louise to stick to the high-road of her own thoughts, with Miss Hartill opening gates to fairyland at every sentence. Clare kept her for the rest of the evening, and took her home at last, weighed down by her parcel of books, sleepy from the effects of excitement and happiness. She poured out her incoherent thanks as they waited on the doorstep of her home. There had never been such a Christmas—she had never had such a glorious time— she couldn't thank Miss Hartill properly if she talked till next Christmas came.

Clare, nodding and laughing, handed her over to the maid, and went home, not ill-pleased with her Christmas either. She thought of the child as she walked down the snowy, star-lighted streets, and wondered whimsically what she was doing at the moment. Would she say her prayers on her way to bed still, or had Clare's little, calculated shrug stopped that sort of thing for many a long day? She rather thought so. She shook off her uneasy sense of compunction and laughed aloud. The cold night air was like wine to her. After all, for an insignificant spinster, she had a fair share of power—real power—not the mere authority of kings and policemen. Her mind, not her office, ruled a hundred other minds, and in one heart, at least, a shrug of her shoulders had toppled God off His throne; and the vacant seat was hers, to fill or flout as she chose.

CHAPTER XIII

WITH the opening of the spring term began the final and most arduous preparations for the Easter examinations.

The school had been endowed, some years before, under the will of a former pupil, with a scholarship, a valuable one, ensuring not only the freedom of the school, but substantial help in the subsequent college career, that the winning of it entailed.

The rules were strict. The papers were set and corrected by persons chosen by the trustees of the bequest. The scholarship was open to the school, but no girl over seventeen might enter : and though an unsuccessful candidate might compete a second time, she must gain a percentage of marks in the first attempt. Total failure debarred her from making a second. This last rule limited, in effect, the entries to members of the Sixths and Fifths, for the scholarship was too valuable for a chance of it to be risked through insufficient training. The standard, too, was high, and the rules so strictly enforced that withheld the grant if it were not attained, that Miss Marsham was accustomed to make special arrangements for those competing. They were called the ' Scholarship Class,' and had certain privileges and a great amount of extra work. To most of them the particular privilege that compensated for six months drudgery was the fact that they were almost entirely under Miss Hartill's supervision. She considered their training her special task and spared neither time nor pains. She loved the business. She understood the art of rousing their excitement, pitting ambition against ambition. She worked them like slaves, weeding out remorselessly the useless members. Theoretically all had the right to enter; but none remained against Miss Hartill's wishes.

In spite of the work, the members of the Scholarship Class had an envied position in the school. Clare saw to that. Without attackable bias, she differentiated subtly between them and the majority. Each of the group was given to understand,

without words, impalpably, yet very definitely, that if Miss
Hartill, the inexorable, could have a preference, one had but
to look in the glass to find it; and that to outstrip the rest of
the class, to be listed an easy first, would be the most exquisite
justification that preference could have. And as the type of
girl who succumbed the most surely to Clare's witchcraft was
also usually of the type to whom intellectual work was in itself
attractive, it was not surprising if her favourite class were a
hot-bed of emulation and enthusiasm—enthusiasm that was
justified of its origin, for not even Henrietta Vigers denied that
Clare contributed her full share to the earning of the scholarship,
Miss Marsham, towards the end of the spring, was wont to
declare, with her usual kindly concern, that she was thankful
that the examination was not an annual affair. . . . Their good
Miss Hartill was too anxious, too conscientious. . . . Miss
Marsham must really forbid her to make herself ill. And, indeed,
when the class was a large one, Clare was as reckless of her own
strength as of that of her pupils, and suffered more from its
expenditure. Where they were responsible, each for herself,
Clare toiled early and late for them all. She fed them, moreover, from her own resources of energy, was entirely willing to
devitalize herself on their behalf. The strain once over, she
appeared slack, gaunt, debilitated. She had, however, her own
methods of recuperation. Her ends gained, she could take back
what she had given—take back more than ever she had given.
Moreover, the supply of child-life never slackened. Old scholars
might go—but ever the new ones came. Was it not Clare who
gave the school its latter-day reputation? By the end of the
summer term Clare would be once more in excellent condition.

When the promotion of Louise to the Upper School had
first been mooted, Miss Hartill had not forgotten that the
scholarship examination was once more drawing near. She
saw no reason why Louise should not compete. That Louise,
the whilom dullard of the Third, the youngest girl in the Upper
School, should snatch the prize from the expectants of the
Sixths and Fifths, would be an effective retort on Clare's critics,
would redound very pleasantly to Clare's credit.

If she let the opportunity pass, Louise must wait two years:
at thirteen it would be a triumph for Louise and Clare; at
fifteen there would be nothing notable in her success. And the
baby herself would be delighted. Clare was already sufficiently
taken with Louise to enjoy the anticipation of her delight.

She was quite aware that it would entail special efforts on her own part, as well as on the child's, and that she had a large class already on her hands, and in need of coaching. But there was always Alwynne. Alwynne was so reliable; she could safely leave Louise's routine work in Alwynne's hands. It remained to consult Louise and incidentally the parent Dennys.

Louise was awestruck, overwhelmed by the honour of being allowed to compete, absurdly and touchingly delighted. No doubt as to Louise's sentiments. No doubt as to the sincerity of her efforts. No doubt, until the spring term began, of the certainty of her success.

The spring term opened with Clare in Miss Marsham's carved seat at morning prayers. The school had grown accustomed to its head-mistress's occasional absence. Miss Marsham, who had for some time felt the strain of school routine too much for her advanced years, was only able to sustain the fiction of her unimpaired powers by taking holidays, as a morphineuse takes her drug, in ever-increasing doses. She was confident in the discretion alike of Clare Hartill and Henrietta Vigers, and, indeed, but for their efficiency, the school would have suffered more quickly than it actually did. Nevertheless, the absence of supreme authority had, though but slightly, the usual disintegrating effect. There was always, naturally, an increase of friction between the two women, especially when the absence of the directress occurred at the beginning of a term. There would be the usual agitations—problems of housing and classification. There would arrive parents to be interviewed and impressed, new girls to be gracefully and graciously welcomed. Clare (to whom Henrietta, for all her hostility, invariably turned in emergencies), showing delicately yet unmistakably that she considered herself unwarrantably hampered in her own work, would submit to being on show with an air of bored acquiescence, tempered with modest surprise at the necessity for her presence. It was sufficiently irritating to Henrietta, under strict, if indirect, orders to leave the decorative side of the vice-regency to her rival. She was quite aware of Clare's greater effectiveness. She did not believe that it weighed with Miss Marsham against her own solid qualities. She affected to despise it. Yet despising, she envied.

She was unjust to Clare, however, in believing the latter's reluctance entirely assumed. Clare enjoyed ruffling the susceptibilities of Henrietta, but she was none the less genuinely annoyed at being even partially withdrawn from her classes and was relieved when, at the end of a fortnight, Miss Marsham returned to her post. Clare had been forced to neglect her special work. Classes had been curtailed and interrupted, the many extra lessons postponed or turned over to Alwynne, whom more than any other mistress she had trained and could trust.

It was Alwynne who, reporting to her at the end of the first fortnight, had made her more than ever eager to be rid of her deputyship.

There were new girls in the Fifth in whom Alwynne was interested. One, at least, she prophesied, would be found to have stuff in her. It was a pity she was not in the Scholarship Class. . . . She was too good for the Lower Fifth. . . . Alwynne supposed it would be quite impossible to let her enter?

" At this time of day? Impossible! Do you realize that we've only another three months? "

" I don't suppose she'd want to, anyhow," said Alwynne. " She's a quaint person! Talk about independence! She informed me to-day that she shouldn't stay longer than half-term, unless she liked us."

" Oho! Young America!" Clare was alert. " I didn't know you referred to Cynthia Griffiths. I interviewed the parents last week. Immensely rich! She was demure enough, but I gathered even then that she ruled the roost. Her mother was quite tearful—implored me to keep her happy for three months anyhow, while they both indulged in a rest cure abroad. She seemed doubtful of our capacities. But she was not explicit."

" Cynthia is. I've heard the whole story while I tried to find out how much she knew. She's a new type. Her French and her German are perfect—and her clothes. Her bedroom is a pig-sty and she gets up when she chooses. I gather that she has reduced Miss Vigers to a nervous wreck already. Thank goodness I'm a visiting mistress! I wonder what the girls will make of her! "

" Or she of them."

" That won't be the question," surmised Alwynne shrewdly. " Clare, she has five schools behind her, American and foreign— and she's fifteen! We are an incident. I know. There were two Americans at my school."

" It remains to be seen." Clare's eyes narrowed. " Well, what else? "

Alwynne fidgeted.

" I'm glad you're taking over everything again. I prefer my small kids."

" Why ? "

" Easier to understand—and manage."

Clare looked amused.

" Been getting into difficulties ? Who's the problem ? Agatha ? "

" That wind-bag ! She only needs pricking to collapse," said Alwynne contemptuously. Then, with a frown : " I wish poor little Mademoiselle Charette would realize it. Have you ever seen a Lower Fifth French lesson ? But, of course, you haven't. It's a farce."

Clare frowned.

" If she can't keep order——"

" She can teach anyhow," said Alwynne quickly. " I was at the other end of the room once, working. I listened a little. It's only Agatha. Mademoiselle can tackle the others. She's effective in a delicate way ; but senseless, noisy rotting—it breaks her up. She loses her temper. Of course, it's funny to watch. But I hate that sort of thing. I did when I was a schoolgirl even, didn't you ? "

" I don't remember." But in the back of Clare's mind was a class-room and herself, contemptuously impertinent to a certain ineffective Miss Loveday.

Alwynne continued, frowning—

" Anyhow, I wish you'd do something."

Clare yawned.

" One mustn't interfere with other departments—unasked."

" Well, I ask you." Alwynne was in earnest.

" Why ? "

" I want you to."

" Why ? "

Alwynne blushed.

" Why this championship ? I didn't know you and Mademoi-selle Charette were such intimates ? "

" It's just because we aren't. I like her, but——"

" But what ? "

" Well—we had a row. You see— You won't tell, Clare ? " Clare smiled.

" She doesn't like you," blurted out Alwynne indignantly. " And I just want to show her how altogether wrong——"

" What a crime ! How did you find it out ? " Clare was amused.

"She was telling me about Agatha. And I said—why on earth didn't she complain to you? And she said—nothing on earth would induce her to. I said—I was sure you would be only too glad for her to ask you. And she said——" Alwynne paused dramatically: "She said—she hadn't the faintest doubt you would, and that I was a charming child, but that she happened to understand you. Then we had a row, of course."

Clare pealed with laughter.

"She's quite right, Alwynne. You are a charming child. So that is Mademoiselle Charette, is it? And I never guessed." She mused, a curious little smile on her lips.

"She's a dear, really," said Alwynne apologetically. "Only she's what Mrs. Marpler calls ' 'aughty.' I can't think why her knife's into you."

"Suppose——" Clare's eyes lit up, she showed the tip of her tongue—sure sign of mischief afloat. "Suppose I pull it out? What do you bet me, Alwynne?"

Alwynne laughed.

"I wish you would. I don't like it when people don't appreciate you. Anyhow, I wish you'd settle Agatha. You know, it's not doing the scholarship French any good. The class slacks. Mademoiselle is worried, I know."

Clare was serious at once.

"That must stop. The standard's too high for trifling. And one or two of them are weak as it is. Especially Louise. Isn't she? Don't you coach her for the grammar? How is her extra work getting on, by the way? Like a house on fire, I suppose?"

"Not altogether." Alwynne looked uneasy.

"What?" Clare looked incredulous.

"She's the problem," said Alwynne.

She had a piece of paper on the table before her and was drawing fantastic profiles as she spoke, sure sign of perturbation with Alwynne, as Clare knew.

"Well?" demanded Clare, after an interval.

Alwynne paused, pencil hovering over an empty eye-socket. She seemed nervous, opened her lips once or twice and closed them again.

"What's wrong?" Clare prompted her.

"Nothing's wrong exactly." Alwynne flushed uncomfortably. "After all, you've seen her in class. Her work is as good as usual?"

"I think so. Her last essay was a little exotic, by the bye,

not quite as natural—but you corrected them. I was so
busy."

"You don't think she's getting too keen, working too hard ? "
Alwynne's tone was tentative.

"Do you think so ? " Clare was thoroughly interested. She
was tickled at Alwynne's anxious tones. She always enjoyed
her occasional bursts of responsibility. But she was nevertheless intrigued by Alwynne's hints. She had certainly not given
her class its usual attention lately. To Louise she had scarcely
spoken unofficially since term began ; no opportunity had
occurred, and she had been too busy to make one. Louise had
returned a bundle of books to her on the opening day of the
term, and had been bidden to fetch herself as many more as she
chose. But Clare had been out when Louise had called. Clare,
to tell the truth, had not once given a thought to Louise since
Christmas Day. She had taken a trip to London with Alwynne
soon after. The two had enjoyed themselves. The holidays
had flown. But she had been glad to find her class radiantly
awaiting her. She had found it much as usual. Alwynne's
perturbation was the more intriguing.

"Do you think so ? " she repeated, with a lift of her eyebrows
that reduced Alwynne's status to that of a Kindergarten pupil
teacher. She enjoyed seeing her grow pink.

"Of course, it's no affair of mine," said Alwynne aggrievedly.
She went on with her drawing.

Clare swung herself on to the low table and sat, skirts a-sway,
gazing down at Alwynne's head, bent over its grotesques.
There was a curl at the nape of the neck that fascinated her.
It lay fine and shining like a baby's. She picked up a pencil
and ran it through the tendril. Alwynne jumped.

"Clare, leave me alone. You only think I'm impertinent."

"Does she want a finger in the pie, then ? " said Clare softly.
"Poor old Alwynne ! " The pencil continued its investigations.

Alwynne tried not to laugh. She could never resist Clare's
soft voice, as Clare very well knew.

"I don't ! I only thought——"

"That Louise—your precious Louise——"

"She's trying so awfully hard——"

"Yes ? "

"She's overdoing it. The work's not so good. She's too
keen, I think——"

"Yes ? "

" I think——"

" Yes, Alwynne ? "

" You won't be annoyed ? "

" That depends."

" Then I can't tell you."

" I think you can," said Clare levelly.

Alwynne was silent. Clare took the paper from her and examined it.

" You've a fantastic imagination, Alwynne. When did you dream those faces ? Well—and what do you think ? Be quick."

" I think she's growing too fond of you," said Alwynne desperately.

She faced Clare, red and apprehensive. She expected an outburst. But Clare never did what Alwynne expected her to do.

" Is that all ? Pooh ! " said Clare lightly and began to laugh. She swung backwards, her finger-tips crooked round the edge of the table, her neat shoes peeping and disappearing beneath her skirts as she rocked herself. She regarded Alwynne with sly amusement.

" So I've a bad influence, Alwynne ? Is that the idea ? "

Alwynne protested redly. Clare continued unheeding.

" Well, it's a novel one, anyhow. Could you indicate exactly how my blighting effect is produced ? Don't mind me, you know." Then, with a chuckle : " Oh, you delicious child ! "

Alwynne was silent.

" Tell me all about it, Alwynne dear ! " cooed Clare.

Alwynne shrugged her shoulders with a curiously helpless gesture.

" I can't," she said. " I thought I could—but I can't. You don't help me. I was worried over Louise. I thought—I think she alters. I think she gets a strained look. I know she thinks about you all the time. I thought—but, of course, if you see nothing, it's my fancy. There's nothing definite, I know. If you don't know what I mean——"

" I don't ! " said Clare shortly. " Do you know yourself ? "

" No ! " said Alwynne. She searched Clare's face wistfully. " I just thought perhaps—she was too fond of you—I can't put it differently. I'm a fool ! I wish I hadn't said anything."

" So do I," said Clare gravely.

" I didn't mean to interfere : it wasn't impertinence, Clare," said Alwynne, her cheeks flaming.

Clare hesitated. She was annoyed at Alwynne's unnecessary

display of insight, yet tickled by her penetration, not displeased
by the jealousy which, as it seemed to her, must be at the root
of the protest. Alwynne had evidently not forgotten her chilly
Christmas afternoon. . . . Louise, as obviously, had talked. . . .
There must have been some small degree of friction for Alwynne to
complain of Louise. . . . Curiously, it never occurred to Clare that
Alwynne's remarks hid no motive, that Alwynne was genuinely
anxious and meant exactly what she had said, or tried to say.
Possibly in Alwynne's simplicity lay her real attraction for Clare.
It made her as much a sphinx to Clare as Clare was to her.

As she stood before her, apprehensive of her displeasure,
obviously afraid that she had exceeded those bounds to their
intercourse that she, more than Clare, had laid down, yet withal,
a curiously dogged look upon her face, Clare was puzzled as to
her own wisest attitude. She was inclined to batter her into a
retractation; it would have relieved her own feelings. Clare
could not endure criticism. But she was not yet so sure of
Alwynne as to allow herself the relief of invective. She thought
that she might easily reserve her annoyance for Louise. It was
Louise, after all, who had exposed her to criticism. . . . And if
Alwynne chose to be jealous, it was at least a flattering display.
. . . She supposed she must placate Alwynne. . . . After all, fifty
Louises and her own dignity could not weigh against the posses-
sion of Alwynne. . . . She spoke slowly, choosing her words.

" As if I could think you impertinent ! But, my dear—I'm
older than you. Can't you trust me to understand my girls ?
After all, I devote my life to them, Alwynne." Clare's quiet
dignity was in itself a reproof.

" I know." Alwynne lifted distressed eyes. " I didn't mean
—I didn't imply—of course, you know best. I only thought——"

" That I took more notice of Louise than was wise ? "

" No, no ! " protested Alwynne unhappily.

Clare continued—

" If you think I'm to blame for encouraging a lonely child—
she has no mother, Alwynne—lending her a few books—asking
her to tea with me—because I felt rather sorry for her——"

" I didn't mean that——" Alwynne twisted her fingers
helplessly.

" Then what did you mean ? " Clare asked her. She had slipped
on to the floor, and was facing Alwynne, very tall and grave and
quiet. " Won't you tell me just exactly what you did mean ? "
She allowed a glimmer of displeasure to appear in her eyes.

And Alwynne, tongue-tied and cornered, had nothing whatever to say. She had been filled with vague uneasiness and had come to Clare to have it dispelled. The uneasiness was still there, formless yet insistent—but the only effect of her clumsy phrases was to hurt Clare's feelings. After all, was she not worrying herself unduly? Was she to know better than Clare? She had felt for some moments that she had made a fool of herself. There remained to capitulate. Her anxiety over Louise melted before the pain in Clare's eyes—the reproof of her manner.

"Would you like me to speak to Louise, before you?" went on Clare patiently. "Perhaps she could explain what it is that worries you——"

"No, no! for goodness' sake, Clare!" cried Alwynne, appalled. Then surrendering, "Clare—I didn't mean anything. I do see—I've been fussing—impertinent—whatever you like. I didn't mean any harm. Oh, let's stop talking about it, please."

"I'd rather you convinced yourself first," said Clare frigidly. "I don't want the subject re-opened once a week." Then relenting, "Poor old Alwynne! The trials of a deputy! Has she worried herself to death? But I'm back now. I think I can manage my class, Alwynne—as long as you stand by to give me a word of advice now and then."

Alwynne squirmed. Clare laughed tenderly.

"My dear—give Louise a little less attention. It won't hurt either of you. Are you going to let me feel neglected?" Then, with a change of tone. "Now we've had enough of this nonsense." She curled herself in her big chair. "Alwynne, there's a box of Fuller's in the cupboard, and an English Review. Don't you want to hear the new Masefield before you go home?"

And Alwynne's eyes grew big, and she forgot all about Louise, as Claire's 'loveliest voice' read out the rhyme of *The River*.

Yet Clare had a last word as she sent her home to Elsbeth.

"Sorry?" said Clare whimsically, as Alwynne bade her good-bye.

"I always was a fool," said Alwynne, and hugged her defiantly.

But Clare, for once, made no protest. She patted her ruffled hair as she listened to the noises of the departure.

"Too fond of me?" she said softly. "Too fond of me? Alwynne—what about you?"

But if Alwynne heard, she made no answer.

CHAPTER XIV

Miss Marsham was accustomed to recognize that it was the brief career of Cynthia Griffiths that first induced her to consider the question of her own retirement.

It is certain that the school was never again quite as it had been before her advent. The Cynthia Griffiths term remained a school date from which to reckon as the nation reckons from the Jubilee. In an American school Cynthia Griffiths must have been at least a disturbing element—in the staid English establishment, with its curious mixture of modern pedagogy and Early Victorian training, she was seismic.

With their usual adaptability, the new girls, as they accustomed themselves subduedly to the strange atmosphere, had found nothing to cavil at in the school arrangements. They had not thought it incongruous to come from Swedish exercises to prolonged and personal daily prayers, kneeling for ten minutes at a time while their head mistress wrestled with Deity. It might have bored girls of sixteen and eighteen to learn their daily Bible verse, and recite it alternately with the Kindergarten and Lower School, but it never occurred to them to protest, any more than they were likely to object to the little note-book which each girl carried, with its printed list of twenty-five possible crimes, and the dangling pencil wherewith, at tea-time, to mark herself innocent or guilty. The hundred and one rules that Edith Marsham had found useful in the youth of her seminary, forty years before, and that time had rendered obsolete, irritating, or merely unintelligible, were nevertheless endured with entire good nature by her successions of pupils. Alwynne and her contemporaries might fume in private and Clare shrug her shoulders in languid tolerance, but nobody thought it worth while to question directly the entire sufficiency of a bygone system to the needs of the new century's hockey-playing generations.

But a little leaven leaveneth the whole lump.

What, if you please, is an old lady to do? An old lady, declining on her pleasant seventies, owning sixty, not a day more, traditionally awe-inspiring and unapproachable, whose security lies in the legends that have grown up of the terrors of her eye and tongue, when Young America clamours at her intimidating door? Young America, calm-eyed, courteous, coaxing, squatting confidentially at the feet of Authority, demanding counsel and comfort. Useless for harried Authority to suggest consultation with equally harried assistants. Young America, with a charming smile and the prettiest of gestures, would rather talk it over quietly with Authority's self. Authority, who is the very twin of her dear old Grannie at home, will be sure to understand. Such fusses about nothing all day and every day! Can it be that Authority expects her to keep her old bureau tidy, when she's had a maid all her life? Young America will be married as soon as she quits Europe (follows a confidential sketch of the more promising of Young America's best boys), and have her own maid right on. Can Authority, as a matter of cold common-sense, see any use in bothering over cupboards for just three months or so? If so—right! Young America will worry along somehow, but it seemed kind of foolish, didn't it? Or could Young America hire a girl—like she did in Paris? Anyway it was rough luck on the lady in the glasses to get an apoplexy every day, as Authority might take it was the case at present. Another point—could Authority, surveying matters impartially, see any harm in running down town when she was out of candy? It only meant missing ten minutes French, and if there was one thing Young America (lapsing suddenly, with bedazing fluency, into that language) was sure of, it was French. These English-French classes meant well—but, her God! how they were slow! There had been—Young America confessed it with candid regret—some difficulties with the cute little mark-books. Young America had mislaid three in a fortnight. She just put them down, and they lay around awhile, and then they weren't there. Some of the ladies had been real annoyed. And once on the subject of mark-books, did Authority really mean that she was to chalk it up each time she was late for breakfast, or said ' Darn it,' or talked in class? Would, in her place, Authority be able to keep tally? Couldn't Young America just mark off the whole concern and be done with it? Young America apologized for worrying Authority with these quaint matters—but, on her honour, every lady in

the school seemed to have gone plumb crazy, about them. . . .
They just sat around and yapped at her. Young America was
genuinely scared. She had thought a heart-to-heart chat with
Authority ought to put things right. She would be real grateful
to Authority for fixing things. . . .

And so, with the odd curtsey she had learned among ' the
Dutchies,' as she called her German pensionat, and a hearty
kiss on either cheek, Young America, affable as ever, beamed
upon Authority and withdrew.

Authority felt as if it had been out in a high wind. Instinctively it clutched at its imposing head-dress. All was in place.
Authority lay back in its chair and gasped fishily.

But Miss Vigers, frenzied into confession of inability to deal
with the situation—got scant sympathy.

" What am I to do ? I hate troubling you—I am sure, though,
it's a relief to us all to have you back. Of course, if you had
been at home she would never have been admitted. . . . You
would have realized the unsuitability—but it was not my
decision. . . . Miss Hartill. . . . But what am I to do ? I flatter
myself I can control our English girls—but these Americans !
Open defiance, Miss Marsham ! Her room ! She refuses to
attend to it. She comes and goes when she chooses. She
treats me, positively, as an equal. Her influence is unspeakable !
It must be stopped ! Ten minutes late for breakfast—oh,
every day ! Once, I could excuse. And on the top of it all
to offer me chocolates ! I must ask you to punish her severely.
. . . Keep her in ? Miss Marsham, I did. . . . I sent her to
her room. Miss Marsham, will you believe me ? When I went
up to her later, she was fast asleep ! On the bed ! In the
day-time ! ! Without taking off the counterpane ! ! ! Miss
Marsham, I leave the matter to you ! "

She paused for the comments her tale deserved. But to
outraged Authority, it had called up a picture—an impudent
picture of Young America, curled kitten-fashion on its austere
white pallet—pink cheek on rounded arm, guileless eyes opening
sleepily under a sour and scandalized gaze.

Henrietta started. She could not believe her ears.

Benevolently—unmistakably—Authority had chuckled.

But the scandal was short-lived. Before the term was over :
before Henrietta had braced herself to her usual resource, a threat
of resignation, or Miss Marsham, hesitating between the devil
of her protesting subordinates and the deep sea of Young

America's unshakable conviction that in her directress she had an enthusiastic partisan, could allow her maid to suggest to her that she needed a change, the end had arrived.

Cynthia, as Alwynne had surmised, found ten weeks of an English private school more than enough for her; and an imperious telegram had summoned her docile parents.

She departed as she had come, in a joyous flurry. The school mourned, and the Common-room, in its relief, sped the parting guest with a cordiality that was almost effusive.

A remark of Henrietta's, as the mistresses sat over their coffee on the afternoon of Cynthia's departure, voiced the attitude of the majority to its late pupil.

" I'm thankful," Miss Vigers was unusually talkative, " deeply thankful that she's gone. An impossible young woman. Oh, no—you couldn't call her a girl. Would any girl—any English girl—conceivably behave as she has ? They have begun to imitate her, of course. That was to be expected. She demoralized the school. It will take me a month to get things straight. I have three children in bed to-day. Headaches ? Fiddlesticks ! Over-eating ! I suppose you heard that there was a midnight feast last night ? "

The Common-room opened its eyes.

" I'm not astonished. A farewell gathering, I suppose ? I'm sure it's not the first," said Clare, her eyes alight with amusement. " But go on. How did you find it out ? "

" Miss Marsham informed me of it," said Henrietta, with desperate calmness. " It appears that Cynthia asked her permission. Miss Marsham—er—contributed a cake. Seed ! "

Clare gurgled.

" This is priceless. Did she tell you ? I wonder she had the face."

Henrietta grew pink.

" No. Cynthia herself. She—er—offered me a slice. She had the impertinence—the entirely American impertinence— to come to my room—after midnight—to borrow a toothglass. To eat ices in. It appeared that they were short of receptacles."

" Ices ? " came the chorus.

" Her mother provided them, I believe. In a pail," said Henrietta stiffly.

" Did you lend the tooth-glass ? " asked Clare.

Henrietta coughed.

" It was difficult to refuse. She had bare feet. I did not wish her to catch cold."

Clare turned away abruptly. Her shoulders shook.

" I do not wish to be unjust. I do not think she was intentionally insubordinate." Henrietta fingered one of the tall pink roses that had appeared on her desk that morning. " I believe she meant well."

" She was a dear ! " said the little gym mistress.

" She was an impossible young woman," retorted Henrietta with spirit. " At the same time——"

" At the same time ? " Clare spoke with unusual friendliness.

" She certainly had a way with her," said Henrietta.

CHAPTER XV

Cynthia Griffiths had set a fashion.

Her kewpie hair-ribbons and abbreviated blouses were an unofficial uniform long after she had ceased, probably, to know that such articles of dress existed. Her slang phrases incorporated themselves in the school vocabulary. Her deeds of derring-do were imitated from afar. To have been on intimate terms with her would have been an impressive distinction, had not every member of the school been able to lay claim to it. For Cynthia's jolly temperament laughed at schoolgirl etiquette, could never be brought to realize the existence of caste and clique. She darted into their lives and out again, like a dragonfly through a cloud of gnats. It was not strange that her beauty, her prodigality, in conjunction with the all-excusing fact of her nationality, should have attracted the weather-cock enthusiasm of her companions; should have made her, short as her career had been, the rage.

Yet the one person on whom that career was to have a lasting influence was, to all appearance, the least affected by it.

Cynthia and Louise Denny were class-mates, for Clare, amused and interested by the new type, had, after all, arranged for Cynthia to join the Scholarship Class, though there could be no idea of her entering. She agreed with Alwynne that there was not much likelihood of Cynthia's sojourn being a long one. In the meantime, as she had explained to Miss Marsham, it was better to have the firebrand under her own eye. Miss Marsham agreed with alacrity, and contrasted Clare's calmly capable manner with the protests of Henrietta. She realized joyfully that Cynthia would not be permitted to appeal from any decision of Miss Hartill. She recalled, not for the first time, that in all Clare's years there had never come a crisis for which she had been found unprepared. Details of a campaign might finally reach the ears of Authority—there would be always birds of the air to carry the matter—but from Miss Hartill herself, no word;

113

if pressed, there would be a brief summary, a laughing comment, never an appeal for help. Miss Marsham had built up her
school by sheer force of personality. She was old now, grown
slack and easy, but instinctively she recognized a ruling spirit,
a kindred mind. One day she must choose her successor. . . .
She was rich. Her school need not fall to the highest bidder. . . .
There were Henrietta and Clare. Henrietta had scraped and
saved, she knew. . . . Henrietta was fond of trying on Authority's shoes. . . . Of Clare's wishes she was less sure. . . .
But Clare was a capable girl—a capable girl. . . . Clare had
never let any one worry her. . . .

She read Clare correctly. Clare had no intention of allowing
Cynthia Griffiths to lessen her prestige. But she had her own
method of solving the American problem. She treated her new
pupil with the easy good humour, the mocking friendliness of
an equal. She realized the impossibility of counteracting the
effects of a haphazard education, but recognizing equally the
inherent kindliness and lawlessness of the character, played on
both qualities in her management of the girl. Her classes were
not demoralized, but stimulated, by the newcomer's presence :
yet Clare had said nothing to Cynthia of rules and regulations.
But Miss Hartill's manner had certainly implied that while to
her, too, they were a folly and a weariness, after all it was easy
to conform. It saved trouble and pleased people. All conveyed without prejudice to the morals of her other pupils in a
shrug, and a twinkle, and a half-finished phrase.

Cynthia was charmed. Here was common-sense. For the
first time she felt herself at home. She appalled the classes by
her loud encomiums, her delighted discovery of qualities that it
was blasphemy to connect with Miss Hartill. For Cynthia,
with the pitiful shrewdness that her cosmopolitan years had
instilled, admired Clare for reasons that bewildered the worshippers. To them Clare moved through the school, apart,
Olympian, a goddess, condescending delightfully. To Cynthia,
accustomed to intrigue, she was obviously and admirably
Machiavellian. It amazed her that the English girls could not
perceive Miss Hartill's cleverness, that they should adore her
for qualities as foreign to her character as they were essentially
insipid, and be indignant at understanding and discriminating
praise.

But Cynthia was above all philosophical. She shrugged her
shoulders over the crazy crew, and reserved her comments for—

Louise. For in Louise, incredible as Alwynne Durand, for instance, would have thought it, she did find a listener—an antagonist, easily pricked into amusing indignation, into white-hot denials—nevertheless, a listener. Indeed, it was the attitude of Cynthia to Clare Hartill rather than her personal attraction that was responsible for Louise's departure from her original and sincere attitude of indifference to the advances of the popular American.

Louise was less in the foreground than she had been in the previous term. She had come back to school, less talkative, less brilliant, but working with a dogged persistence that had on Alwynne, at least, a depressing effect. But Alwynne, also, was seeing less of the girl. Cynthia Griffiths obstructed her view—Cynthia, taking one of her vociferous likings to a sufficiently unresponsive Louise. For the *rapprochement* was scarcely a normal, school-girl intimacy. Cynthia Griffiths had been intrigued by Louise's personality. She had been quick to grasp the importance of the child's position—to guess her there by reason of her brains and temperament. Yet to Cynthia, judging life, as she did, chiefly by exterior appearances, Louise, insignificant, timid, shadowy, was an incessant denial of her nevertheless recognizable influence in school politics. In the language of Cynthia, she was a dark horse. Cynthia was charmed —school life was dull—the mildest of mysteries was better than none. She would devote herself to deciphering a new type. This little English kid had undoubted influence with girl and mistress alike. Cynthia had intercepted glances between her and Miss Hartill, and Miss Durand too, that spoke of mutual understanding. Perhaps it was money—half the school in her pay? Or secret influences of the most sinister? Hypnotism, maybe? Cynthia Griffiths, fed on dime novels and magazine literature, was not ten minutes in concocting the hopefullest of mare's nests. She approached Louise between excitement and suspicion.

Cynthia was not scrupulous. She forced her way through the reserves and defences of the younger girl like a bumble-bee clawing and screwing and buzzing into the heart of a half-shut flower.

She found much to puzzle her, more to amuse, but nothing to justify her gorgeous suspicions. She confessed them one day to Louise, in a burst of confidence, and Louise was hugely delighted. Cynthia always delighted her. She liked her jolly

ways, and her sense of fun, and was quite convinced that she had
no sense of humour at all. The conviction saved her some
suffering. She was jealous, inevitably jealous, of the brilliant
new-comer, painfully alive to, exaggerating and writhing at
Clare's preoccupation with her; yet with the warped shrewdness
proper to her state of mind, she could calculate with painful
accuracy how long it would take Clare to tire of her new toy,
what qualities would soonest induce satiety. She guessed,
hoped, prayed, that Miss Hartill would discover, as she had done,
Cynthia's lack of conscious humour, the obtuseness that under-
lay her boisterous ease. She was not fine enough to hold Miss
Hartill long : she would grow too fond of Miss Hartill : would,
in the terrible craving to render up her whole soul, expose herself
in all her crudity. Louise did, for a while, soothe the jealousy,
the tearing, clawing beast in her breast, with that comfortable
conviction. That her reasoning was subconscious, that she was
unaware of the process of analysation and deduction that led to
her conclusions, is immaterial; she felt—and as she felt, she
acted; her reasons for her actions were sounder than she
dreamed.

She made mistakes often enough : her profound occupation
with Clare Hartill had induced a spiritual myopia; the rest of
the world was out of focus; and it was her initial misunder-
standing of Cynthia Griffiths that led to their curious, un-
affectionate alliance. In all Louise's ponderings, she had never
doubted but that Cynthia would, like the rest of the world, fall
down and worship at the shrine of Clare Hartill. Cynthia
Griffiths, amused spectator of an alien life, did nothing of the
kind. On Louise—amazed, fiercely incredulous, all-suspicious,
yet finally convinced of the inconceivable fact—it had a curious
effect. She should have been indignant, contemptuous of the
obtuse creature—as, indeed, in a sense, she was—but chiefly
she was conscious of a lifted weight—of an enormous and
hysterical gratitude.

Cynthia was a fool—a purblind philistine. But what relief
was in her folly, what immense security ! Jealousy could not
die out in Louise, but it entered on a new phase—became passive,
enduring resignedly inevitable pain. But its vigilance, its fierce
pugnacity was dead; for Cynthia—dear fool—did not care.
Pearls had been cast before Americans. Louise was ready
enough to be gracious to such exquisite insensibility. She
became friendly. She had guarded her secret jealously from the

world. She was ' keen ' on Miss Hartill, certainly, but so was half the school, at least. She was merely in the fashion. Insignificant and circumspect, giving no confidences, no one but Clare herself, and Alwynne Durand, guessed at the intensity of her affection. But with Cynthia Griffiths she was reckless. Ostrich-like, she trusted to the protection of her formal disclaimer, while with each new discussion, each half-confidence, she exposed herself and her feelings more completely.

And Cynthia, dropping her theories, began to be interested in the strange, vehement imp, with its alternating fits of frankness and reticence, wit and childishness, its big brain and its inexplicable yet obvious unhappiness. She affected Louise, was accustomed to pet and parade her, long before she had solved the problem of her character; indeed, it was not until she had confided to the child her plans for an early departure, that Louise relaxed her self-protective vigilance. She had begun, in her talks with Cynthia, to realize the relief and healing of self-expression. If Cynthia were going away to Paris, America, never to be seen again, what harm in talking—in saying for once what you felt? There was wry pleasure in it, and, oh, what harm?

Louise found an odd satisfaction in leading Cynthia—on her side, if you please, alert for evidence, the amateur detective still—to sit in judgment on Clare Hartill; would sit, horrified, thrilled, drinking in blasphemy. She would have allowed no other human being to impeach the smallest detail of Clare Hartill's conduct, but from Cynthia, though she raged hotly, she did allow, and in some queer fashion, enjoy it. She had, perhaps, a vague assurance that Cynthia, being a foreigner, could not be taken seriously.

So the pair discussed Clare Hartill from all possible angles till Louise occasionally forgot to keep up her elaborate pretence of indifference, to insist on its being understood that the discussion was rhadamanthine in its impersonality.

" Yes, I'm off soon," Cynthia had confided. They were sitting together in her cubicle. " All this is slow—slow. Ne' mind! Wait till this child gets going! " She stretched herself lazily, and flung back on her little white bed, arms behind her head. Louise studied her magnificent torso.

" Why did you come? " she demanded.

Cynthia laughed.

" Italy—France—Deutschland—I'd done everywhere but

England. Now comes a tour round the world—and so home.
I'm Californian, you know. I'll have great times then. You
don't live, over here. You're afraid of your own shadows.
Now an American girl——"

" How do you mean ? "

" Aren't you ? Always afraid of breaking rules ! Haven't
I asked you—haven't I begged you to come out with me one
day ? Oh, Louise, it would be great ! I saw a taxi-man yesterday, outside church, with the duckiest eyes ! Lunch somewhere,
and 'phone through for the new show at Daly's. An American
show ! Dandy ! Only taken you four years to transfer here !
Let's go, Louise ? We'd be back to supper."

Louise twinkled.

" Rot ! We'd be expelled."

Cynthia opened her china-blue eyes.

" For a little thing like that ? Why ? We wouldn't miss
a class. Besides, we'd say you asked me home to tea."

Louise looked distressed. Their ideas of veracity had clashed
before.

Cynthia, watching mischievously, giggled.

" Poor kid ! Doesn't it want to tell lies, then ? "

" You see—English people don't ! Of course, I know it's
different abroad," said Louise delicately.

" Haven't you ever, Louise ? "

Louise flushed crimson.

" You have ? " Cynthia was amused. " What was it, Louise ?
Oh, what was it ? Tell ! Oh, you needn't mind me—my average
is—well, quite average. What was it ? "

Louise's lips closed.

" I call you the limit, you know ! ' English people don't ! '
With a red-hot tarradiddle on your little white conscience all
the time. You're a good pupil, Louise ! "

Louise, blushing, turned suspiciously.

" What are you at now ? " she demanded.

" I was thinking of Clarissa." Cynthia smiled with intention.

" Clarissa who ? "

" Clare, kid ! Clare ! Sweet Clare ! Sugar-sweet Clare !
Our dear Dame Double ! "

" I wish you wouldn't talk like that," said Louise, in her
lowest voice. " You know I hate it."

" All right, honey ! " Cynthia rolled lazily on to her side and
pulled a box of chocolates from the shelf beside her.

The room was quiet for a while.

" Cynthia ? "

" Um ? "

" What did you mean just now ? "

" Have a candy ? "

" No, thanks ! "

Cynthia munched on.

" About Miss Hartill ? " Louise's tone was half defiant, half guilty. She felt disloyal in re-opening the subject. Yet Cynthia's hints rankled.

" I don't know ! Nothing, I guess."

" Oh, but you did mean something," said Louise uneasily.

" Maybe."

" Tell me."

" Want to know ? "

" Yes."

" Badly ? "

" It's not true, of course ! But I'd like to know."

Cynthia's eyes danced. She could be grave enough otherwise, but her eyes and her dimples could never be kept in order.

" Tell about the tarradiddle first, and I will."

But to Louise a lie was a lie and no joking matter. She fidgeted.

" If you must know—— "

" I must."

" Well—you know how Miss Hartill hates birthdays ? "

" Why ? "

" At least, school ones. You know, there's such a fuss at Miss Marsham's—a holiday, and presents, and all that. So Miss Hartill won't let hers be known."

" ' Splendid Isolation ' stunt."

" If you're going to be a hatefully unjust pig, I won't tell you."

" I apologize. Have a candy ? "

" Well, you know, Agatha found out that Miss Hartill was giving a party last week, and, of course, every one thought it was for hers. But it turned out it was Daffy's birthday ; Miss Hartill gave it for her. It was Agatha's fault. She was so dead certain about it."

" But what did it matter ? "

" Well, you see, I'd got some roses—— "

" Pale pink and yellow ? Beauties ? "

" Yes."

" Oho ! So that's where they came from. I did Dame Double an injustice. I thought it was a best boy." Cynthia gurgled.

" You saw them ? "

" I went to tea with her—it must have been that day—the eighth ? "

Louise nodded.

" A party ! Agatha is a coon. There was only Daffy there ! I wonder she didn't ask you."

Louise said nothing. Her face was expressionless.

" Mean old thing ! " Cynthia grew indignant as the situation dawned on her.

" She can't ask every one. There was no reason whatever to ask me." But Louise's voice had a suspicious quiver in it, which Cynthia, with unusual tact, ignored.

" Well—about the roses ? They were beauties, kid ! "

" Oh, I brought 'em round, going to school. I thought she'd started, but she hadn't. She opened the door. So there I was, stuck." Louise began to laugh. " I'd meant to leave them, just without any name."

" I see." Cynthia twinkled.

" She was rather—rather breakfasty, you know—and I got flustered and forgot to wish her ' many happy.' Wasn't it lucky ? I was thankful afterwards. I only said they were out of the greenhouse and I thought she'd like them. She did, too." Louise smiled to herself.

" Well ? "

" That's all."

" But where did the lie come in ? "

" Oh ! Oh—well—I'd bought them, you see. As if Mamma would let me pick flowers. Besides, we haven't even got a greenhouse. But I had five shillings at Christmas, and sixpence in the pudding—and sixpence a week pocket-money—and I never have anything to buy. I could well afford it," said Louise, with dignity.

" That's not a lie," said Cynthia, disappointed. " It's barely an—an evasion."

" I didn't mean to—evade. I was only afraid she'd be cross, and yet I couldn't resist getting them. Do you know the feeling, when you ache to give people things ? But it was a lie, of course."

" Oh, well ! You needn't mind. She tells plenty herself—acts them, at least——"

Louise caught her up.

" There !   That's it !   That's one of the things !   You're
always hinting things !   Why do you ?   I won't have it !   Of
course, I know you're only in fun, but if anybody heard you——"

" I'm not !   Oh, but it's no use talking !   You think she's
a god almighty.   What's the use of my telling you that she's
a conceited——"

" She's not ! "

" Oh, she's a right to be.   She'd be a peach if I had the
dressing of her——"

" She doesn't like American fashions.   We don't want her to.
We like her as she is."

" And she knows it—you bet your bottom dollar !   There's
not much she doesn't know.   Why, she simply lives for effect !
She's the most gorgeous hypocrite——"

" You're a beastly one yourself—you pretend you like
her——"

" But I do !   I admire her heaps !   But I understand her.
You don't.   She likes to be top dog.   She'll do anything for
that.   She likes to know every woman and child in the school
is a bit of putty, to knead into shape.   I know !   I've met her
sort before—only generally it was men they were after.   And
yet it bores her too——" parenthesized Cynthia shrewdly.
" That's why she likes me.   I don't care two pins for her tricks.
That stings her up a bit.   She'll be mighty bored when I go."

Louise listened, angry, yet fascinated.   It gave her a curious
pleasure to hear Miss Hartill belied.   She would hug herself
for her own superior discernment.   A phrase from a half-digested
story often recurred to her : ' One doesn't defend one's god !
One's god is a defence in himself.'   But Cynthia was going too
far—abandoning innuendo for direct assault.   She struck back.

" It's easy to say things.   Just saying doesn't make it so.
And if it did, I shouldn't believe it."

" Oh !   I can prove it."   Cynthia laughed.   " Have you
noticed the Charette comedy ? "

" Mademoiselle ?   Oh, she hates Miss Hartill.   But she's
French, of course."

" Does she just ?   H'm——! "

" Well, there was a French girl—she left last term—she told
Marion that Mademoiselle had said things to her about Miss
Hartill.   Agatha told me.   Agatha loathes Mademoiselle.   Of
course, Mademoiselle is rather down on her."

"I don't wonder. You know how Agatha hazes her in class."

"I can't stand Agatha." Louise shook herself. "Last French Grammar it was awful—sil'y, you know, not funny. One simply couldn't work. Mademoiselle kept her in. I suppose Agatha didn't like that. She's been a lamb since, anyway. About time too!"

"Shucks! It wasn't being kept in. It was Clarissa. Oh, my dear, it was fun! There was poor little Mademoiselle, storming away in her absurd English, and Agatha cheeking her for all she was worth."

"How did you hear?"

"Why, I was in the studio! Agatha didn't know we were there, of course. The glass doors were open. You know, Daffy gives me extra drawing. And just when Agatha was in full swing, and Mademoiselle speechless with rage, Miss Hartill turned up—wanted Daffy."

"Oh, go on!" Louise cried breathlessly.

"It really was funny, you know. Miss Hartill was talking to Daffy and the row going on next door—you couldn't help hearing—and suddenly Daffy said—Daffy had been fidgeting for some time—'Listen!' and Clarissa said, 'Oho-o'! You know her way, with about ten o's at the end; and Daffy said, 'There! Now do you believe me?' kind of crowing. And Miss Hartill, she just smiled, like a cat with cream, and said, 'All right, Alwynne! All right, my dear!' and went into the next room. Say, it was exciting! She didn't raise her voice, but she just let herself go, and in about two minutes Agatha came out like a ripe cheese—literally crawling. I wish she hadn't shut the door. I couldn't hear any more. I could see, of course, and you bet I watched out of the tail of my eye. Daffy never noticed me."

"What happened then?"

"Oh! They stood and talked, and Mademoiselle was scarlet and seemed to be pitching into Miss Hartill, as far as I could see, and Miss Hartill was letting her talk herself out, and sometimes she smiled and said something; that always started Mademoiselle off again. And at last Mademoiselle went and sat in one of the window-seats, and I couldn't see her face, but I imagined she was howling. French people always do. Clarissa went and patted her shoulder."

"She is a dear!" Loyally Louise bit back her instant jealousy.

"Oh, she was enjoying herself," said Cynthia coolly. "You should have seen her face. Sort of smiling at her own thoughts. Have you ever seen a spider smile?"

Louise disdained an answer.

"Nor have I! Have a candy? But I bet I know what it looks like."

"Well, what happened?" demanded Louise impatiently.

"Oh, it was annoying! Daffy came and sat down in my place, to correct. I couldn't see any more. Only when Miss Hartill came out (she didn't notice me, I was putting away the group), she said to Daffy, 'She's coming to tea on Friday.' And Daffy said, 'Clare, you're a wonder!' And Miss Hartill said, 'I didn't do it for her, Alwynne!' And Daffy got pink. Clarissa did look pleased with herself."

"Well, so she ought! Wouldn't you be—if you could make people happy?"

Cynthia threw up her hands. "Happy! Oh, Momma! Are you happy?"

Louise winced.

"Is Daffy? Mademoiselle? Any of you fools? Oh, it's no use talking! You won't believe me when I tell you that she's a cat. Yes, a pussy-cat, Louise! A silky, purring pussy-cat, pawing you, pat—pat—so softly, like kisses. But if you wriggle—my! Look out for claws! Have a candy?"

Louise gathered herself together. She came close to the bed, and leaning over the older girl, spoke—

"I don't understand what you're driving at—but you're wrong. It's you that's a fool. You misjudge her, utterly. You don't understand her—you're not fit to."

"Are you?" Cynthia laughed at her openly.

"Of course not. No one—Daffy does, of course. But us?— girls? Just because she's been heavenly to you, you take advantage, to watch her, to judge, to twist all she says and does. Why do you hate her so?"

"I don't." Cynthia pulled herself upright. "My dear, you're wrong there. I like her immensely. She's a real treat. But I don't worship her like you do."

"I don't! I—I just love her." Louise glowed.

Cynthia laughed jollily.

"Oh, well! You'll get over that. Wait till you get a best boy."

"If you think I'd look at any silly man, after knowing her——"

"My dear girl! Has it never occurred to you that you'll
marry some day?"

Louise shook her head.

"I've thought it all out. I could never love anybody as much
as I do Miss Hartill. I know I couldn't."

"But it's not the same! Falling in love with a man——"

"Love's love," said Louise with finality. "Where's the
difference?"

Cynthia sat up.

"Where's the difference? Where's the——?" She giggled.
But something in the quality of her laughter disturbed. Louise
frowned.

"I didn't say anything funny. You'll love your husband,
I suppose, that you're always talking about having—and I'll
stick to Miss Hartill. It's perfectly simple."

But Cynthia was still laughing. Louise grew irritable under
her amused glances, and would have turned away, but Cynthia
flung her arm about her.

"Stop! Don't you really know?"

"What?"

"The difference."

Cynthia's eyes shone oddly. Louise moved uneasily, disconcerted by their expression.

Cynthia continued.

"Hasn't any one told you? Why, with the books you've
read—— Haven't you read the Bible ever?"

"Of course!" Louise was indignant. "I've been right
through—four times."

"And you've never noticed? Good Lord! That's all I
read it for."

"I haven't an idea what you're driving at," said Louise.
Cynthia was making her thoroughly uncomfortable.

Cynthia was flushed, laughing, pure devilry in her eyes. Her
lips were pouted, her little teeth gleamed. She looked like a
child licking its lips over forbidden dainties. She had pulled
Louise into her lap and her voice had dropped to a whisper.

"Shall I tell you? Would you like to know? You ought
to—you're fourteen—it's absurd—not knowing about things—
shall I tell you?"

Louise fidgeted. Cynthia's manner had aroused her curiosity,
but none the less she was repelled. Why, she could not have
said. She hesitated, aroused, yet half frightened.

" I'll tell you," said Cynthia lusciously.

With a sudden effort Louise freed herself from the encircling arm. She edged away from the elder girl, stammering a little.

" I don't think I want to know anything. It's awfully sweet of you. I'd rather—I always ask Daffy things. Do you mind ? "

Cynthia, good-tempered as ever, laughed aloud.

" Lord, no ! But what a little saint ! Aren't you ever curious, Louise ? All right ! I won't tease. Have a candy ? "

And Louise, eating chocolates, was not long in forgetting the conversation and all the curious discomfort it had aroused. If a leaf had fallen on the white garment of her innocence—a leaf from the tree of the knowledge of good and evil—she had brushed it aside, all unconscious, before it could leave a stain.

CHAPTER XVI

THE spring term was nearly over, holidays and a trip to Italy deliciously near; yet Clare Hartill sat at breakfast and frowned over a neatly-written letter.

Clare Hartill did not encourage the re-entry of old friends into her life. She did not forget them. She would look back upon the far-off flaming intimacy with regret, would quote its pleasures to the friend of the hour with disconcerting enthusiasm; but she was never eager for the reappearance of any whose ways had once diverged from her own. Pleasant memories, if you will; but, in the flesh, old friends were tiresome. They claimed instant intimacy; were free-tongued, fond, familiar; could not realize that though they might choose to stand still, she, Clare, had grown out of their knowledge, beyond their fellowship. She, indeed, would find them terribly unaltered; older, glamourless, yet amazingly, humiliatingly the same. She would look at them furtively as she entertained them, and shudder at the lapse from taste that surely must have explained her former affection. She would be gracious, kind, yet inimitably distant, and would send them away at last, subdued, vaguely disquieted, loyal still, yet very sure that they would never trouble her again. Which was exactly what Clare Hartill intended. Yet she had her fits of remorse withal, her secret bitter railing at fate and her own nature, for that she could neither keep a friend nor live without one. Recovering, she would be complacent at having contrived, without loss of prestige, to rid herself of bores.

There was one fly in her ointment. Who knows not that fly, earnest and well-intentioned, which, when it is dug out with a hairpin, cleanses itself exhaustively and forthwith returns to the vaseline jar? Such a fly, optimistic and persistent, was the correspondent who invariably signed herself, ' Ever, dear Clare, your affectionate little friend, Olivia Pring. P.S. Do you remember . . . ? ' There would follow a reminiscence, at least twenty years old, that Clare never did remember.

Olivia Pring was a school-mate. There had been a term together in the Lower Third. For a few weeks she had been Clare's best friend and she never let Clare forget it. Clare, with removes and double removes, had disappeared speedily from Olivia's world, but she never quite shook off Olivia. Olivia, amiable, admiring, impervious to snubs, refused to be shaken off. She went her placid way, became a governess, and an expert in the more complicated forms of crochet. She wrote to Clare about twice a year—dull, affectionate letters. Clare, that involute character, amazed herself by invariably answering them. At long intervals Olivia would be passing through London, and would announce herself, if quite convenient, as intending to visit her dear Clare that afternoon. She would describe the lengthy tussle between herself and her employer, before she had wrested the requisite permission to stay the night—and did Clare remember the last visit but three, and the amusing evening they had had? And the letter was invariably delayed in the posting, and its arrival would precede that of Olivia by a bare half-hour. Olivia, growing ever fatter and more placid, would apologize breathlessly between broad smiles at the sight of Clare and recollections of the dear old days. And Clare, as one hypnotized, would go to her linen cupboard and give out sheets for the spare room. There would follow an evening of interminable small-talk for Clare, of sheer delight for Olivia Pring, who, consciously and conscientiously commonplace, enjoyed dear Clare's daring views as a youthful curate might enjoy, strictly as an onlooker, what he imagines to be the less respectable aspects of an evening in Paris.

And Clare would retire to bed at ten-fifteen and sleep as she had not slept for weeks. Olivia would be regretfully obliged to catch the eight-eleven, and would depart amid embraces. And Clare would order up a second breakfast and wonder why she stood it. Yet the pile of unused doileys in her linen cupboard increased yearly. A doiley was Olivia's invariable tribute, and arrived, intricate and unlovely, within a week of her visit.

Clare fingered her letter in quaint helplessness. She had a sleepless night behind her, and a big morning's work before, and her usual end-of-term headache. Olivia was arriving—she glanced at the hopelessly legible sheets—at three-fifty. No chance of mistake there. Clare decided that it was quite impossible for her to survive a seven hours' tête-à-tête with her affectionate friend Olivia Pring. If only Alwynne could help

her out. But Alwynne, she knew, was taking the skimmings
of the Sixths and Fifths to a suitable Shakespeare performance.
She had taken the pick of the classes herself the evening before.
No chance of Alwynne, then. And Cynthia! Alack for
Cynthia! who could have been trusted to amuse Olivia Pring
as much as Olivia Pring would have amused her—Cynthia must
be aboard ship by now. Clare, in regretful parenthesis, hoped
Cynthia would send a few compatriots to Utterbridge. . . .
Americans gave a fillip to one's duties. . . . Anyhow Alwynne
and Cynthia were out of the question.

There was Louise! She brightened. Louise, queer little
thing, was always amusing. . . . Louise would serve her turn.
. . . Louise would be so charmed to come. . . . Clare laughed
a little consciously. Perhaps she had neglected Louise a trifle
of late, perhaps it was not altogether fair of her. A happy thought
buffered the prick of her yawning conscience. It was Alwynne's
fault. . . . Alwynne, with her ridiculous, well-meaning objec-
tions. . . . She, Clare, had given in to them, for peace and quiet
sake. . . . And now, most probably, Louise was not too content
with life. . . . One knew what schoolgirls were. . . . Never
mind! Clare would be very nice to Louise this evening. . . .
Louise should enjoy herself, and, incidentally, preserve Clare
from expiring of boredom at poor Olivia's large, flat feet.

The invitation was given during the eleven o'clock break.
Clare would occasionally join the school in Big Hall, and share
its milk and biscuits. Often enough to make it any day's
delightful possibility, not often enough for it to be other than an
event. She would sit on the platform steps, watching the gay
promenaders below, informal, approachable, tossing the ball
to the daring few, hedged about, in turn, by the tentative many.
Sometimes she would stroll about the hall with a girl on either
side, or one only. She had a curious little trick of catching the
girl she spoke with by the elbow, and pushing her gently along
as she talked, bending over (she was very tall) and enveloping.
Everybody knew the ' Gendarme Stunt ' as Cynthia Griffiths
irreverently termed it, and no one would have dreamed of
approaching or interrupting such a *tête-à-tête*.

Nevertheless, Miss Hartill had not exchanged three sentences
with Louise Denny on the morning of Olivia Pring's arrival,
before every girl in Big Hall knew of it, and twice the number
of eyes were following them, with an elaborately accidental gaze,
in their progress.

Possibly Clare was a little touched by Louise's delight at the invitation. At any rate she managed, in spite of her headache, to be a very charming companion. She confessed to the headache, and asked Louise for advice. And Louise, deeply concerned, could think of nothing but a recipe she had found in Clare's own Culpeper, in which rhubarb and powdered dormice figured largely. She suggested it in a doubtful little voice. The school would have given a good deal to know what made Miss Hartill laugh so.

Miss Hartill told Louise all about her visitor, whom, she declared, she depended on Louise to entertain, and added a couple of comical tales of their mutual school-days. Unfortunately Clare's *novelli* owed their charm more to her inventive touches and graphic manner than to the actual underlying fact. Louise was left with the impression of an Olivia Pring who had been Friar Tuck to Clare's Robin Hood. She appreciated the honour of being asked to meet her to a degree that would have tickled Clare, had she guessed it.

' Miss Olivia Pring ! ' Louise meditated all day over Miss Olivia Pring. Evidently Miss Hartill's best friend. . . . She hoped Miss Olivia Pring would like her. . . . How dreadful it would be if she didn't . . . for what might she not say of her to Miss Hartill ? Louise must be careful, oh, so careful, of her manners and her speech. . . . It was rather hard luck that she would not have Miss Hartill to herself. . . . It would be dreadfully uncomfortable—talking before a stranger. . . . Except for the delightfulness of being asked by Miss Hartill, she could have wished that Miss Hartill had not asked her. Rather an ordeal for a thirteen-year-old—supper with Miss Hartill and Miss Olivia Pring.

Now shyness, like any other painful sensation, is inexplicable to such as have not experienced it, is at once forgotten by such as outgrow it, but to those at its mercy is sheer suffering, paralysing, stultifying, a spiritual Torture of the Pear.

Clare Hartill should have understood; she had her own furtive childhood for reference; but Clare Hartill had a headache, and she was very tired of Olivia Pring. Olivia was so placid, so shapeless, so ridiculous, in her pink flannel blouse, and the reckless glasses, that were ever on the point of toppling over the precipice of her abbreviated nose into the abyss of her half-open mouth. It certainly did not occur to Clare that Louise could feel the slightest discomfort on account of Olivia Pring.

K

But Louise was blind to the flannel blouse, and the foolish face, and the unmanageable glasses. She was wearing glasses of her own, rose-coloured affairs, through which Miss Pring appeared, not only as a ' grown-up ' and a stranger, but as the intimate of Deity in Undress. Miss Pring did nothing to dispel the illusion—she had conscientiously flattened the high spirits out of too many little girls to be interested in a new specimen. She addressed herself chiefly to Clare—recalling incessantly, and enlarging upon, trifling incidents of their mutual past, which every fresh sentence of the badgered hostess contrived to recall to her elastic memory. Louise, always sensitive, her shyness growing with every word, could but take each unexplained allusion as a personal snub, and feeling herself entirely superfluous, began to imagine that Miss Hartill was already regretting the invitation. Panic-struck she tried to remedy matters by effacing herself as completely as possible. It was wonderful what a small and insignificant person Louise could sometimes look, and did look that evening in one of Clare's big arm-chairs. Her prim little whisper and deprecatory smile might have struck Clare as pathetic if Clare had not been so very tired of the affectionate reminiscences of Olivia Pring. As it was, she was annoyed. She had asked Louise of the bright eyes and quick stammer and extravagant imagery, to supper with her—the panther-cub, not the leveret. She had talked of Louise too— had looked forward to putting the child through its paces, if only for the benefit of Olivia Pring. She had even surmised that Louise would take Olivia's measure, and at a nod from Clare would be delicately, deliciously impertinent. Indeed, she had thought her capable of it. But it was only a schoolgirl after all—a silly, tongue-tied schoolgirl—that she had for an instant compared with Alwynne : Alwynne, monstrously absent, a match for ten Olivias.

She yawned, shrugged her shoulders, and suggested, in fine ironic fit, a game of ' Old Maid.' Olivia was extremely pleased. She so much preferred Old Maid—or Beggar-my-Neighbour, perhaps ?—to Bridge. She did not approve of Bridge. In her position it did not do. Clare would remember that she had always said. . . .

Clare fetched the cards.

Louise ! Louise ! You have done yourself no good to-night. Shy ? Nonsense ! What is there to be shy about ? A few words from Miss Hartill—a prompting or two—a leading question

—could have broken the ice of your shyness for you, eh? And Miss Hartill knows it, as well as you, if not better. That shall not avail you. Who are you, to set Miss Hartill's conscience itching? Miss Hartill has a headache. Pull up your chair, and deal your cards, and stop Miss Hartill yawning, if you can. Believe me, it's your only chance of escape.

Louise was a clumsy dealer. Her careful setting out of cards irritated Clare to snatching point. Olivia triumphed in every game. On principle, Clare disliked losing, even at Beggar-my-Neighbour. And they played Beggar-my-Neighbour till ten o'clock.

Louise grew more cheerful as the evening progressed, ventured a few sentences now and then. Clare was dangerously suave with both her guests; but Louise, taking all in good faith, hoped after all, that she had not appeared as stupid as she felt. It had been dreadful at first, she reflected, as she put on coat and hat. But it had gone better afterwards. . . . She didn't believe Miss Hartill was cross with her. . . . That had been a silly idea of her own. . . . Miss Hartill was just as usual.

She made her farewells. Clare came out into the hall and ushered her forth.

"Good-bye!" Louise smiled up at her. "It was so kind of you to have me. I have so much enjoyed myself." Then, the formula off her tongue: "Miss Hartill, I do hope your head's better?"

"Thank you!" said Clare inscrutably. "Good-night!" Then, as the maid went down the stairs: "Louise!"

"Yes, Miss Hartill?"

Clare was smiling brilliantly.

"Don't come again, Louise, until you can be more amusing. At any rate, natural. Good-night!"

She shut the door.

CHAPTER XVII

LOUISE spent her Easter holidays among her lesson books. Miss Hartill and Miss Durand were in Italy, all responsibilities put aside for four blessed weeks, but for Louise there could be no relaxation. The examinations were to take place a few days before the summer term began, and their imminence overshadowed her. Useless for Miss Durand to extract a promise to rest, to be lazy, to forget all about lessons. Louise promised readily and broke her promise half-an-hour after she had waved the train out of the station. Impossible to keep away from one's History and Latin and Mathematics with examinations three weeks ahead. Miss Durand might preach; her overtaxed brain cry pax; her cramped body ache for exercise; but Louise knew herself forced to ignore all protests. She would rest when the examinations were over. Till then—revision, repetition—repetition, revision—with as little time as might be grudged to eating and sleeping and duty walks with Mrs. Denny.

There was no time to lose. The nights swallowed up the days all too swiftly.

Yet, waking one morning with a start to realize that the day of days had dawned at last, she found it incredible. The morning was exactly like other mornings, with the sun streaming blindingly in upon her, because she had forgotten, as usual, to draw her blind at night, her head already aching a little, hot and heavy from uneasy sleep. All night long her brain had been alert, restless, beyond control. All night long it had tugged and fretted, like a leashed dog, at the surface slumber that tethered it. She felt confused, burdened with a half-consciousness of vivid, forgotten dreams.

She dressed abstractedly, lesson books propped against her looking-glass, and wedged between soap-dish and pitcher. For the hundredth time she conned the technicalities of her work, and making no slips, grew more cheerful, for it had been the letter, not the spirit, that had troubled her—little

matters of rules and exceptions, of dates and derivations, that
would surely trip her up. But she was feeling sure of herself
at last, and thrilling as she was with nervous excitement, could
yet be glad that the great day had dawned, and ready to laugh
at all her previous despondencies. Things were turning out
better than she had expected. There was bracing comfort in
beginning with her own subject—Miss Hartill's own subject.
She could have no fears for herself in the Literature examination.
French in the afternoon, that was less pleasant. But she would
manage—must, literally. ' Miss Hartill expects——' She
laughed. She supposed the sailors felt just the same about
Nelson as she did about Miss Hartill. She wondered if Lady
Hamilton had minded his only having one eye and one arm?
Suppose Miss Hartill had only one eye and one arm? Oh! If
anything happened to Miss Hartill. . . .! She shivered at the
idea and instantly witnessed, with all imaginable detail, the
wreck of the train as it entered Utterbridge station, and she
herself rescuing Miss Hartill, armless and blind, from the blazing
carriage. She had her on the sofa, five years later, in the prettiest of invalid gowns, contentedly reliant on her former pupil.
And Louise, blissfully happy, was her hands and feet and eyes,
her nurse, her servant, her—(hastily Louise deprived her alike
of income and friends) her bread-winner and companion. Here
her French Grammar, slithering over the soap to the floor, woke
her from that delicious reverie.

She picked it up, and applied herself for a while to its dazing
infinitives. But teeth-brushing is a rhythmic process : her
thoughts wandered again perforce. She had got to be first.
. . . Miss Hartill would be so pleased. . . . It would be heavenly
to please Miss Hartill again as she used to do. . . . Nothing
had been the same since Cynthia came. . . . She flushed to the
eyes at the recollection of her last unlucky visit—— ' You
needn't come again unless you can be more amusing. You
might at least be natural. . . .' Yet Miss Hartill had been
so kind at the last . . . had waved to her from the train. . . .

The postman's knock startled her, disturbed her meditations
anew. Letters ! Was it possible ? Would Miss Hartill have
remembered ? Have sent her, perhaps, a postcard ? Stranger
things had been. She had for weeks envisaged the possibility.
She finished her dressing and tore downstairs.

The maid was hovering over the breakfast-table.

" Are there any letters, Baxter ? Are there any letters ? "

But she had already caught sight of a foreign postcard on her plate, a postcard with an unfamiliar stamp. She scurried round the table, her heart thumping.

But the big, adventurous handwriting was hatefully familiar. The postcard was from Miss Durand.

She waited a moment, her lips parted vacantly, as was her fashion when controlling emotion; waited till the maid had gone.

Then she crumpled and tore the thin cardboard in her hand and flung it at last on the floor, in a passion of disappointment. "She might have written!" cried Louise. "Oh, she might have written! It wouldn't have hurt her—a postcard."

Presently a thought struck her. She groped under the table for the torn scraps of paper and spread them in her lap, piecing them eagerly, laboriously. Miss Hartill might have written on Miss Durand's postcard.

She had the oblong fitted together at last and read the scrawl with impatient eagerness. Miss Durand was just sending her a line to wish her all imaginable luck. She and Miss Hartill were having a glorious time. They were sitting at that moment where she had made a cross on the picture postcard. She wished Louise could be with them to see the wonderful view over the valley and with good wishes from them both, was her Alwynne Durand. . . .

Louise's eyes softened—' from them both.' That was something! Miss Hartill had sent her a message. She sighed as she wrapped the scraps carefully in her handkerchief. Life was queer. . . . Here was Miss Durand, so kind, so friendly always —yet her kindness brought no pleasure. . . . And Miss Hartill, who could open heaven with a word—was not half so kind as Miss Durand. Louise marvelled that Miss Hartill could be so miserly. She was sure that if she, Louise, could make people utterly happy by kind looks and kind words, stray messages and occasional postcards, that she would be only too glad to be allowed to do it. To possess the power of giving happiness. . . . And with no more trouble to yourself than the writing of a postcard! Queer that Miss Hartill did not realize what her mere existence meant to people. . . . She couldn't realize it, of course . . . that was it. . . . She thought so little about herself. . . . It was her own beautiful selflessness that made her seem, occasionally, hard—unkind even. . . . She didn't realize what she meant to people. . . . If she had, she would have written. . . . Of course she would have written . . . just a word . . . on Daffy's postcard. . . .

Louise sighed again. One didn't ask much. . . . But it seemed the more humble one grew—the less one asked—the more unlikely people were to throw one even that little. . . . At any rate there was the examination to tackle. . . . If she did well—! She lost herself again in speculations as to the form Miss Hartill's approval might take.

The family trooped in to breakfast as the brisk maid dumped a steaming dishful of liver and bacon upon the table.

Louise occupied her place and began to spread her bread-and-butter, avoiding her father's eye. But, as she foresaw, she was not permitted to escape.

Mr. Denny pounced upon the butter-dish.

"Not with bacon," he remarked, with reproachful satisfaction, and removed it.

Louise said nothing. She was careful not to look at her parent, for she knew that her expression was not permissible. His harmless tyrannies irritated her as invariably as her tricks of personality grated upon him. She thought him smug and petty, and despised him for his submissive attitude to her stepmother. His noisy interferences with her personal habits she thought intolerable, though she had learned to endure them stolidly. But most of all, she hated to see his fat, pudgy hands touching her food. She was accustomed to cut bread for the family. No one guessed why she had arrogated to herself that duty.

And he, good man, would look at his daughter occasionally, and wonder why she was so unlike his satisfactory sons and their capable mother : would be vaguely annoyed by her silences, and by a certain expression that reminded him uncomfortably of his first 'fine-lady' wife; would have an emotion of disquieted responsibility; would hesitate : would end by presenting his daughter with a five-shilling-piece, or be delivered from a dawning sense of responsibility by crumbs on the carpet, the muddy boots of a son and heir, or, as in the present instance, an unjustifiable predilection for butter.

"Bread with your meat," he said firmly and handed her a full plate.

Then he watched her with interest. His conception of the duties of fatherhood was realized in seeing that his children slightly over-ate themselves at every meal. He did as he would be done by.

Louise picked up knife and fork unwillingly. She was dry-mouthed with excitement and the beginnings of a headache, and the liberal portion of hot, rich food sickened her. But any-thing was better than a fuss. She sliced idly at the slab of liver.

Opportunity beckoned Mr. Denny.

" Don't play with your food," said the father sharply.

She ate a few mouthfuls, conscious of his supervision. Satis-fied, he turned at last to his own breakfast.

There was a peaceful interval.

The children talked among themselves. Mrs. Denny, hidden behind her tea-cosy, was exclusively concerned with the table manners of the youngest boy. The moment was propitious.

Softly Louise rose and slipped to the sideboard. Her plate once hidden behind the biscuit-tin. . . .

Mr. Denny looked up. He was ever miraculously alert at breakfast.

" More bacon, Louise ? "

" No, thank you, Father," said Louise fervently.

" Have you finished your plate ? "

" Yes, Father."

Her brothers gave tongue joyously.

" Oh-h ! You whopper ! "

" Oh, Father, she hasn't ! "

" Mother, did you hear ? Louise says she's finished her bacon. She hasn't."

" Not near ! "

" Not half ! "

" Not a quarter ! "

" Well—of all the whopping lies ! "

Mr. Denny sprang up, his eyes glistening. He, too, enjoyed a scene. The plate was retrieved from its hiding-place and its guilty burden laid bare.

" Emma, do you see this ? Emma ! Leave that child alone and attend to me ! Flagrant ! Flagrant disobedience ! Louise, I told you to eat it. Turning up your nose at good food ! There's many a child would be thankful—Emma ! Am I to be disobeyed by my own children ? And a lie into the bargain ! If that is the way you are taught at your fine school, I'll take you away. Disgraceful ! Eat it up now. Emma ! Are you or are you not going to back me up? Is all that food to be wasted?"

Mrs. Denny's calm eyes surveyed the excited table.

"Don't fuss, Edwin. Louise, eat up your bacon."

"I can't," said Louise sullenly.

"Then you shouldn't have taken so much."

"I didn't. It was Father——"

"Eat it up at once," said Mrs. Denny peremptorily, as the baby cast his spoon upon the carpet. The tone of her voice ended the discussion.

Mr. Denny watched his daughter triumphantly, as she toiled over her task, called her attention to a piece of bacon she had left on the edge of her plate, and when she had finished told her she was a good girl and that it would do her good. After which he gave her a shilling.

"I don't want it," muttered Louise.

"You don't want it?" repeated Mr. Denny incredulously.

Louise looked at him. There was a world of uncomprehending contempt in the eyes of father and child alike, though the father's were amused, where the child's were bitter.

Mr. Denny laughed jollily.

"I say, kids! Hear that? Your sister here hasn't any use for a shilling. Bet you haven't either! Eh? I don't think!"

Ensued clamour, with jostling and laughter and clutching of coins, from which the head of the house retired to his chair by the fire, chuckling and content. He enjoyed distributing largesse, especially where there was no great need for it, though he was liberal enough to famous charities. He never gave to beggars, on principle.

Louise slipped out of the room under cover of the noise, and was dressed and departing when her step-mother called her back.

"Louise! You stay to lunch to-day, don't you?"

"At school? Oh no, Mamma. Holidays, you know! They only open a class-room for the exam."

"The fifty-pound job, eh?" Her father eyed her over the top of his paper approvingly. For once his daughter was showing a proper spirit. "Go in and win, my girl! I've given you the best education money could buy. If you don't get it, you jolly well ought to. Fifty quid, eh? I wasn't given the chance of earning fifty quid when I was thirteen. Shop-boy, I was. Started as shop-boy like me father before me."

His wife cut in sharply.

" Isn't there an afternoon examination ? I understood——"

" Yes, Mamma. But no dinners. It's all shut."

Mrs. Denny frowned.

" It's annoying. I wanted you out of the way. Nurse is taking the children for an outing. I've enough to do without providing lunches—you must take some sandwiches—spring cleaning—maids all busy——"

" I'd rather take sandwiches ! " Louise's face brightened.

" I thought the cleaning was over—not a comfortable room in the house for the last fortnight." ·Mr. Denny was testy.

His wife answered them thickly, her mouth full of pins as she adjusted her dusting apron.

" Very well ! Ask cook to—no, she's upstairs. Cut them yourself. There's plenty of liver. Perfectly absurd ! Do you want the house a foot deep in dust ? You leave the household arrangements to me ! The top-floor hasn't been done for years —not thoroughly."

" The top floor ? Not the attics ? " said Louise.

" Yes ! I'm re-arranging the rooms. John's getting too big for the nursery. He needs a room to himself. I'm putting him in cook's old room."

Louise paused, the slice of bread half cut.

" Where's cook going ? " said her father.

She awaited the answer, a fear catching at her breath.

" Oh, in the lumber-room," said Mrs. Denny easily.   " It only wants papering. A nice, big room ! A sloping roof, of course. But with her wages, if she can't put up with a sloping roof— ! But it'll take some clearing ! You wouldn't believe what an amount of rubbish has collected."

" It's not rubbish," said Louise. Her voice was low with passion. " It's not rubbish ! You shan't touch it."

Mrs. Denny spun round amazedly. Her step-daughter, the loaf clutched to her breast with an unconscious gesture, the big knife gleaming, was a tragi-comic figure.

" What on earth—— ? " she began.

Louise leaned forward, hot-eyed.

"Mamma ! You won't ! You can't ! You mustn't ! Father, don't let her ! That's Mother's room ! If you put cook in Mother's room——" She choked. A priestess defending her altars could have used her accents.

Mr. Denny put down his paper.

"What's the matter with the girl?" he demanded.

Mrs. Denny shrugged her shoulders.

"I've no idea! I don't know what she means. Put down that knife, Louise—you'll cut yourself. And mind your own business, please."

"You don't understand!" Louise fought for calmness, for words that should enlighten and persuade. "I didn't mean to interfere. But the big attic! Mamma! Father! That's my room. I always go there—do my lessons there—I love it! You don't know how I love it. You see——" She paused helplessly.

"But you've got the nursery to sit in," said Mrs. Denny, equally helpless. "I'm sorry, Louise, if you've taken a fancy to the room—but I want it for cook."

Louise made her way to the hearth and stood between the pair.

"Mamma—please! Please! Please! There's the other attic for cook—not this one!"

"Now, be quiet, Louise!" Mrs. Denny was getting impatient.

Suddenly Louise lost grip of herself.

"It's not right! It's not right! You've got all the house! Every room is yours and you grudge me that one! Nobody's ever wanted it but me! It's mine! You've got your lovely rooms—drawing-room, and dining-room, and morning-room, and bedroom, and summerhouse, and the boys have got the nursery and the maids have got the kitchen, and yet you won't let me have the attic! It's not fair! It's mean! Why can't cook have the other attic? Not this one! Not this one!"

"But why? Why?" Mrs. Denny was more bewildered than angry. She looked down at her step-daughter as a St. Bernard looks at an aggressive kitten. Desperately Louise tore off her veils.

"Because of Mother. Can't you understand? All her things are there. She's there! So I've always played up there. Oh, won't you understand?"

Mrs. Denny flushed.

"You talk a lot of nonsense, Louise. Finish your sandwiches. You'll be late."

"Then you will leave it, as it is?"

"Certainly not. I told you—I need it for cook."

Louise turned to her father with a frenzied gesture.

"Father! Don't let her! Don't let her touch it! Oh, how can you let her touch it?"

Mr. Denny put down his paper, staring from one to the other.

" Emma ? What's she driving at ? "

" To control the household, apparently. She's a very impertinent child," said Mrs. Denny impatiently.

" Father ! I'm not ! I don't ! Father ! I only want her to leave my attic alone ! Father——"

" Don't worry your father now," began Mrs. Denny.

" He's my father ! I can speak to him if I choose," cried Louise shrilly.

" Now then, now then ! " reasoned Mr. Denny heavily. " Can't have you rude to your mother, you know."

Louise gave herself up to her passion.

" She's not my mother ! I call her Mamma ! She's not my mother ! Mother wouldn't be so cruel ! To take away all I've got like that. Her books are there ! Her things ! It's always been our room—hers and mine ! And to take it away ! To put cook—it's horrible ! It's wicked ! It's stealing ! I hate her ! I hate you—all of you ! I'll never forget—never— never—never ! "

She stopped abruptly on a high note, stared blindly at the outraged countenances that opposed her, and fled from the room.

They listened to the clatter of umbrellas in the hall stand, to the furious hands fumbling for mackintosh and satchel, to the bang of the hall door.

Mr. Denny whistled.

" Hot stuff ! What ? I never knew she had it in her." There was a curious element of approval in his tone. He respected volubility.

His wife frowned; then, she, too, began to laugh. She was as incapable as he of imagining the state of nerves that could lead, in Louise, to such an outburst. To speak one's mind, noisily and emphatically, was a daily occurrence for her. Silence was stupidity, and meekness irritating. This ' row ' was unusual because Louise had taken part in it, but she certainly thought no worse of her step-daughter on that account. The child should be sent to bed early as a punishment, she decided, but goodhumouredly enough. She was too thick-skinned to be pricked by Louise's repudiation. She dismissed it as ' temper.' Its underlying criticism of her character escaped her utterly.

By the time the attic was cleared and the paperhanger at work, she had forgotten the matter.

CHAPTER XVIII

It is not impossible to sympathize with Ahab.

It must have been difficult for him, with his varied possessions, to realize the value to Naboth of his vineyard. He had offered compensation. Naboth would undoubtedly have gained by the exchange. Ahab, owning half Palestine, must have been genuinely puzzled by this blind attachment to one miserable half-acre. One wonders what would have happened if they had met to talk over the matter. Ahab, convinced of the generosity of his offer, courteously argumentative, carefully repressing his not unnatural impatience, would have contrasted favourably with the peasant, black, fierce, dumb, incapable of explaining himself, conscious only of his own bitter helplessness in the face of oppression and loss.

The Naboth mood is a dangerous one. Fierce emotions, unable to disperse themselves in speech, can turn in again upon the mind that bred them, to work strange havoc. The affair of the attic, outwardly so trivial, shook the child's nature to its foundation. Though one's house be built of cards, it is none the less bedazing to have it knocked about one's ears. To Louise, the loss of her holy place, but yet more the manner of its loss, was catastrophic. Her nerves, frayed and strained by weeks of overwork and excitement, snapped under the shock. Her sense of proportion failed her. Miss Hartill, the examination, all that made up her life, faded before this monstrous desecration of an ideal. She suffered as Naboth, forgetting also his greater goods of life and kith and kin, suffered before her.

Before she reached the school the violence of her emotion had faded, and she was in the first stage of the inevitable physical reaction. She felt weak and shaken. She was going, she knew, to her examination. She wondered idly why she did not feel nervous. She tried to impress the importance of the occasion upon herself, but her thoughts eluded her—sequence had become impossible. She gave up the attempt, and her mind, released,

141

returned to the scene of the morning in incessant, miserable
rehearsal.

Mechanically she made her way into the school by the unfamiliar mistresses' entrance, greeted the little knot of competi-
tors assembled in the hall. But if she were introspective and
distraught, so were they : her silence was unnoticed.

The nervous minutes passed jerkily. Louise thought that the
clock must be enjoying himself. He was playing overseer; he
wheezed and grunted as her father did at breakfast; had just
such a bland, fat face. Her father would be a fat, horrible old
man in another ten years. She was glad. Every one would
hate him, then, as she hated him, show it as she dared not do.

Miss Vigers interrupted her meditations; Miss Vigers, utterly
unreal in holiday smiles and the first hobble-skirt in which her
decent limbs had permitted themselves to be outlined. She
marshalled the procession.

The Lower Fifth class-room, newly scrubbed and reeking of
naphthaline, with naked shelves and treble range of isolated
desks, was unfamiliar, curiously disconcerting. Louise, ever
perilously susceptible to outward conditions, was dismayed by
the lack of atmosphere. She wriggled uneasily in her desk. It
was uncomfortable, far too big for her : Agatha's initials, of an
inkiness that had defied the charwoman, stared at her from the
lid. She was at the back of the room. Between Marion's neat
head and the coiffure of the little Jewess, the bored face of the
examiner peered and shifted. He was speaking—

" You will find the questions on your desks. Write your names
in the top right-hand corner of each page. Full name. Kindly
number the sheets. You are allowed two and a half hours."

A pause. Some rustling of papers and the snap and rattle
of pencil-boxes. Then the voice of the examiner again —

" You may begin."

Instantly a furious pen-scratching broke the hush. Louise
glanced in the direction of the sound, and smiled broadly.
Agatha had begun. Miss Hartill would have seen the joke,
but the examiner was already absorbed in the book he had taken
from his pocket. Louise gazed idly about her. So this was what
the ordeal was like ! There were her clean, blank papers on
the desk before her, and the printed list of questions. She
supposed she had better begin. . . . But there was plenty of
time. She had a curious sense of detachment. Her body surrounded her, rigid, quiescent, dreading exertion. Her mind,

on the contrary, was bewilderingly active, consciously alive with thoughts, as she had once, under a microscope, seen a drop of water alive with animalculi : thoughts, however, that had no connection with real life as it at the moment presented itself : thoughts that admitted the fact of the examination with a dreamy impersonality that precluded any idea of participation. Her mind felt comfortable in its warm bed of motionless flesh, would not disturb its repose for all the ultimate gods might offer : but was interested nevertheless in its surroundings, gazing out into them with the detached curiosity of an attic-dweller, peering out and down at a dwarfed and distant street. Yet each trivial object on which her eyes alighted gave birth to a train of thought that led separately, yet quite inevitably, to the memories that would shatter her quietude, as conscious and sub-conscious self struggled for possession of her mind

She stared at the intent backs of her neighbours. One by one they hunched forward, as each in turn settled to work. Louise considered them critically. What ugly things backs were ! It was funny, but girls with dark skirts always pinned them to their blouses with white safety-pins, and *vice versa*. It made them look skewered. . . . Yet Miss Durand had said that backs were the most expressive part of the whole body. . . . That was the day they had seen the Watts pictures. But then the draperies of the great white figure in ' Love and Death ' were not fastened up in the middle with safety-pins. . . . That had been a wonderful picture. . . . She knew how the boy felt, how he fought. . . . How long had he been able to hold the door ? she wondered. Characteristically, she never questioned the ultimate defeat. It was terrible to be so weak. . . . But the Death was beautiful. . . . pitying . . . One wouldn't hate it while one resisted it, as one hated Mamma. . . . Mamma, forcing her way into an attic. . . . Louise writhed as she thought of it.

The girl in front of her coughed, a hasty, grudging cough, recovered herself, and bent again to her work. Louise was amused. What a hurry she was in ! What a hurry every one was in ! How hot Marion's cheeks were ! And Agatha . . . Agatha was up to her wrists in ink. . . . Like the women in the French Revolution. . . . Though that was blood, of course. . . . They were steeped in gore. . . . It would be fascinating to write a story about the knitting women . . . click—click—clicking—like a lot of pens scraping. . . . What were they all

scribbling like that for ?   Of course, it was the examination. . . .
There was a paper on her own desk too. . . . How funny !
   ' Distinguish between Shelley the poet, and Shelley the
politician. Illustrate your meaning by quotations.'
   Shelley ?   The name was familiar. . . . She sells sea-shells. . . .
   ' Give a short account of the life of Shakespeare.'
   He had a wife, hadn't he ?   A narrow, grudging woman, who
couldn't understand him. . . . A woman like Mamma. . . .
Mamma, who was turning out the attic and laughing at Louise. . . .
Not that that mattered—but to clear the attic—to take away
Mother's things. . . . What would Mother do—little, darling
Mother. . . ? It was holidays. . . . Mother would know. . . .
Mother would be there, waiting for Louise. A hideous picture
rose up in Louise's mind. With photographic clearness she saw
the attic and the faint shadow of her mother wavering from
visibility to nothingness as the sunlight caught and lost her
impalpable outlines : there was a sound of footsteps—Louise
heard it : the faint thing held out sweet arms and Louise strained
towards them; but the door opened, and Mrs. Denny and the
maids came in. Mamma pointed, while the maids laughed and
took their brooms and chased the forlorn appearance, and it
fled before them about the room, cowering, afraid, calling in its
whisper to Louise. But the maids closed in, and swept that
shrinking nothingness into the dark corner behind the old trunk :
but when they had moved the trunk, there was nothing to be
seen but a delicate cobweb or two. So they swept it into the
dustpan and settled down to the scrubbing of the floor.
   The picture faded. Louise crouched over her desk, her head
in her hands. About her the pens scratched rhythmically.
   For a space she existed merely. She could not have told how
long it was before thoughts began once more to drift across the
blankness of her mind like the first imperceptible flakes that
herald a fall of snow.
   She moved stiffly in her seat. The thoughts came thicker—
thoughts of her mother still, of the dream presence that she
would not feel again. . . . Never again ?   There was the Last
Judgment, of course. . . . She would see her then. . . . And
who knew when the Judgment would come. . . . In a thousand
years ?   In the next five seconds ?   She counted slowly, holding
her breath : " One—two—three—four—five——" and stared
out expectantly into space through the lashes of her dropped
lids.

All about her sat forms, bowed like her own, scarcely moving. Of course, of course—she nodded to herself—satisfied with her own acuteness. Obviously, the Last Judgment. . . . They were all waiting for God. . . . He hadn't arrived yet, it seemed. . . . Well, one might look about a little first. . . . How queer Heaven smelt! The heart of Louise leapt within her. . . . Now was the opportunity to find Mother. . . . Mother would be somewhere among the dead. . . . But they all had ugly backs. . . . But Mother . . . Of course Mother would be standing on that high platform place like a throne. . . . It was her place. . . . She always stood there. . . . Or did she? Was there not some one else? very like her . . . with eyes . . . and a smile . . . whom Louise knew so well? Wasn't it Mother? With patient deliberation she strove to disentangle the two personalities, that combined and divided and blurred again into one. There was Mother—and the Other—one was shape and one was shadow—but which was real? There was Mother—and the Other—who was Mother? No, who was—who was—The Other was not Mother—but if not, who?—who?—who?—

A chorus of angels took up the chant: Who? who? who? They had flat, faint voices, that gritted and whispered, like pens passing over paper.

Who? who? who?

The answer came thundering back out of infinite space in the awaited voice of God. . . .

" You have ten minutes more."

Louise gave a faint gasp. Reality enveloped her once more, licking up her illusion as instantly and fiercely as an unnoticed candle will shrivel up a woman's muslins. She stood naked amid the ashes of her dreams.

She glanced wildly about her. The girls at her elbows were furiously at work. The little examiner had put away his book and was staring at her. Her eyes fell. Before her lay foolscap, fair and blank, save for her name in the corner, and a close-printed paper that she did not recognize, clamouring for information anent Shelley, and Carlyle, and the Mermaid Tavern. Because, of course, she was at the Literature examination, and there were ten minutes more.

And she had written nothing.

An instant she sat appalled. Then she snatched up her pen and wrote. . . .

Her pen fled across the paper at Tam o' Shanter speed, leaving its trail of shapeless, delirious sentences. She never paused to consider—she wrote. She knew only that she had ten—twelve— fifteen questions to answer, and ten minutes in which to do it. Ten minutes for a two and a half hours' paper! No matter—if one stopped to think. . . . Hurry! hurry! Shelley was born in 1792—he was the son of Sir Timothy Shelley, of Field Place, near Horsham——

When the examiner collected the papers, she had written exactly two pages.

CHAPTER XIX

THE examination had taken place early in May, but the summer term was nearly over before news of the results arrived. When it came, it made but a small sensation. The school had tired of waiting. Not only was its own more intimate examination drawing near, but its many heads were filled, to the exclusion of all else, with the excitements and rivalries of the summer theatricals.

The school play was an institution. Of late years—ever since she had joined the staff indeed—it had grown into an annual personal triumph for Miss Hartill.

Clare was blessed—cursed—with that sixth sense, the *sens du théâtre*. Her own nature was, in essence, theatrical; her frigid and fastidious reserve warring incessantly with her irrepressible love of the scene for its own sake. She was aware of the trait and humiliated by its presence in her character. Usually she would curb her inclination with a severity that was in itself histrionic : at times she indulged it with voluptuous recklessness.

As a girl, the stage had appealed to her strongly; but her excessive squeamishness, with her acute sense of personal, bodily dignity, closed it to her as a career. Also her love of power. Though she knew little of stage life she had sufficient intuition to gauge correctly what she might become. Successful necessarily—dominant never. And she required a dais. But the compelling woman, she knew, is successful through her combination of intellectual strength with sexual charm. She must not scruple to use all the weapons at her service. Clare had told herself that there were some weapons to which she would never condescend. If sting had lain in the fact that, though she would, they were not hers to use, she did not acknowledge it, even to herself. Resolutely she put from her the idea of fostering a useless talent; and the desire to exploit it, save surreptitiously in social intercourse, dulled as she grew older.

Nevertheless, the yearly plays were to Clare a source of

excitement and gratification. She alone was responsible for the production. In five successful years they had become an event, a festival—not only to the school, but to the entire neighbourhood. Two, and then three public performances were given each summer, and the proceeds benefited the school charities. *As You Like It*, *Twelfth Night*, *Verona*, and *The Merchant of Venice*, followed upon the *Midsummer Night's Dream*, and exhausted the list of entirely suitable plays; but after some hesitation, Clare had devised for her next venture scenes from *King John*. Several forms were studying the period, the Sixths and Fifths were reading the play, politically also it was apropos. (Clare had ever sound reasons to gild her decisions.) Privately she had been slightly embarrassed by the fact that the classes she supervised had that year proved themselves unusually poor in dramatic ability. She could depend, indeed, on a score of keen and capable children, but in Louise Denny alone had she glimpsed an actress who could do her credit. The child's physique precluded her from rôles that, otherwise, she could easily have filled, but as Prince Arthur, she could be made the central, unforgettable figure of an otherwise trite performance. " *King John*," quoth Clare; " decidedly, the very play." And *King John* was chosen.

Since the beginning of the term, with Clare as generalissimo and Alwynne most ingenious of adjutants, staff and school had worked enthusiastically. Costumes were finished, staging painted and planned, and the various scenes were, at length, receiving their final polish. Alwynne was responsible for the interpretation of the minor parts, while Clare, in her spare time, devoted herself to the principals, attacking alternately the exaggerations of Agatha's 'Constance,' Marion's stolid ' Hubert,' a certain near-sighted amiability in the spectacled ' King John.'

Clare was a born stage-manager, patient, resourceful, compelling. The children trusted her; she had the habit of success. Her air of authority cushioned them, denied the possibility of failure. Clare, wholly in earnest, Clare at unusual hours, intimate and relaxed, Clare appealing, exhorting, inspiring, was irresistible. She got what she wanted from them and was not ill content. She knew to the last ounce their capabilities.

With Louise alone she had difficulties. The child was almost too easily trained. Responsive, quickly fired or chilled, she was, in fact, too delicately and completely attuned to Clare herself.

Clare could be crude : she had her gusty moods : the little æolian harp quivered to snapping point before them. Originally this extreme sensitiveness had fascinated Clare ; she felt like a musician exploring the possibilities of an unknown instrument ; but she tired of it in time. As Louise became saturated with the stronger personality, she had, in her passionate desire to satisfy Clare, grown into her mere replica ; reproducing her phraseology, voicing her opinions, reflecting her moods, stifling, in the exquisite delight of abnegation, all in her that had originally attracted the older woman. That the effect had been, first to amuse, then to irritate, finally to bore Clare's fickle humour, was natural enough. Clare, had she cared, could have guided the child, despite the great disparity of age, into a pleasant path of affection and friendship, but that she did not choose. She was disappointed, and showed it : and there, for her, the matter ended. That she was in any way responsible, she would not admit.

She did not, indeed, fully realize the extent of the change in Louise until the rehearsals began. For all her growing indifference, in spite of the marked deterioration that automatically it had caused in the girl's work, she had still a high and just opinion of her capabilities. She was positive that as Prince Arthur, Louise would give a fine and original performance, and anticipated with amused interest her initial rendering of the character.

At the first rehearsal Louise did not disappoint her. She was neither stiff nor self-conscious, and her acting, which proved to be entirely instinctive, carried conviction. Though Clare worked from the head, she could appreciate the more primitive method, but even then, the character as portrayed by Louise amazed her. The deliberate pathos, the cloying charm, did not seem to exist for Louise. She played as in an ecstasy of terror. The text, Clare knew, could permit the reading, and the conception interested her ; but the temptation to criticize, alter and improve, was natural. Here and there, as rehearsals progressed, she pulled and patched and patted—quite genuinely in the interest of the play as a whole. But the result was discouraging. The Louise of former days would have defended her own version, delighting Clare with shy impudences and flashes of insight, naïve parries and counter-attacks, till between them they had attained notable results. But the sparkle had been drilled out of Louise. She was humble, anxiously acquiescent, agreeing with every alteration, accepting every suggestion, however foreign to her own instinctive convictions, while the vividness faded slowly from her reading, leaving it lifeless and forced.

" It's patchwork," said Clare disgustedly to Alwynne, at the end of the third week, " pure patchwork. She does everything I tell her—and the result is dire. What it will be like on the night, heaven knows ! And there's nobody else. Yet she *can* act. That first performance was quite excellent."

" And she tries."

" She slaves ! She would be less irritating if she didn't. You know, Alwynne, I let myself go yesterday. I told her how impossible she was. And all she did was to look at me like a mournful monkey ! "

" Inarticulate. Exactly."

Clare lifted her eyebrows. Alwynne looked at her quaintly.

" You know perfectly well what's wrong. Why on earth don't you leave her alone ? "

" Uncoached ? "

" That as well, of course. You said yourself she was excellent at first. Why don't you leave her to herself ? It's safe. She's not like the others. She's a nectarine, not a potato. Give her a free hand till the dress-rehearsal. It won't be your reading— I prefer yours, too ; at least I think I do——"

" I'm glad you say ' think.' But think again. There's no question of which you ought to prefer. But I, my good child, must consider my public ! It wants to enjoy itself ! It wants to weep salt tears ! Louise's reading would cheat it of its emotions ! "

" At least it will be a reading, not a repetition. I don't mean that, though, when I say—leave her alone. Clare—you won't realize what you mean to people ! "

" I don't follow——" but Clare laughed a little.

" You do. You know you've made Louise crazy about you." Clare shrugged impatiently.

" I dislike these enthusiasms."

" But you cause them. I think it is rather mean to shirk the consequences."

" Really, Alwynne ! " But Clare was still smiling.

" You do. You begin by being heavenly to people—and then you tantalize them."

" Does it hurt, Alwynne ? Are you going to run away ? " Alwynne smiled.

" Oh, you won't get rid of me so easily. I'm a limpet. Do

you know, I couldn't imagine existence without you now. I've never been so gloriously happy in my life. You wouldn't ever get really tired of me, would you ? "

" I wonder."

" I know."

" I've warned you that I'm changeable. Instance your Louise."

" Oh, Clare, do be nicer to Louise."

" Oh, Alwynne, do mind your own business. I'm as nice as is good for her. But I believe you're right about this acting. I'll wash my hands of her till the dress-rehearsal, if you like. You can tell her I said so."

But Alwynne, whispering to Louise that perhaps the old way was better after all, that Miss Hartill had said she didn't mind, achieved little.

" Oh, Miss Durand—don't let her think I'm hopeless. I shall get it right in time. I'd rather stick to the way she showed me. Miss Durand—do you think she's angry ? Honestly, I will get it right. Miss Durand—I suppose there's no news ? "

The child's face was very drawn; her eyes seemed larger than ever; she looked like a little old woman; Alwynne was concerned; she felt vaguely responsible. She, too, wished that the news, good or bad, would come, and put an end at least to the tension.

And one morning, all unexpectedly, the news did come.

The performances were but two days away. The decorous Big Hall was in confusion. The school sat, picnic-fashion, for its prayers; and the head mistress, entering between half-hung cloths, mounted a battlemented rostrum to address it. She carried a sheaf of papers. Louise, sitting with her class at the further end of the hall, outwardly decorous enough, was in reality paying little attention. Her vague, unhappy thoughts were concerned with the coming rehearsal; she could not remember what Miss Hartill's last directions had been; she was sure she should stumble. Sometimes the mere words seemed to evade her. Yet the play was on her shoulders—Miss Durand had said so. She supposed Prince Arthur was really fond of Hubert ? Not pretending, because he was afraid ? But of course it was easy to love a person and yet be terrified of them. She stole a look at Clare, prominent in the grave group of mistresses. They were all very intent. It dawned on her that the head mistress had been speaking for several minutes.

Suddenly there was an outburst of clapping. The spectacled girl at the end of the row grew pink and stared at her hands.

" What is it ? " breathed Louise. " Oh, what is it ? What is it ? "

A neighbour caught the murmur and looked down at her curiously.

" Are you asleep ? It's the lists. Your exam. You'll be second, I expect."

But Marion was second.

The clapping crackled up anew.

So the news was come !

It was cruel to let it spring upon you thus. . . . You would have asked so little . . . ten minutes . . . a bare five . . . in which to brace yourself. . . . Surprise was horrible. . . . it caught you with your soul half-naked . . . it shocked like sudden noise. . . .

There came a fresh outburst.

It was wicked to make such sounds. . . . like all the policeman's-rattles in the world. . . .

The reading proceeded; it calmed her; it barely stirred the beautiful silence. But presently the neat voice altered. Old Edith Marsham was a kindly soul. She had not quite forgotten her own school-days. She realized, perfunctorily, as the successful do, the blankness of defeat. Louise heard her name pronounced, a trifle hurriedly. Louise Denny—failed.

She made no sign. She sat erect, listening to the conclusion of that matter, clapped in due course, stood, kneeled, rose again, as applause, hymns and prayers buzzed about her, filed with her class from the hall and added her shy word to the clamour of congratulation in the long corridors. Inwardly, she was stunned by the evil that was upon her.

The irregular morning classes (the imminent entertainment had disorganized the entire system of work) gave her time to rouse, to review her position.

She turned helplessly within herself, wondering how she should begin to think—and where. She wondered idly if this was how soldiers felt, when a shell had blown them to pieces ? She wondered how they collected themselves afterwards ? Where did they begin ? Did an arm pick up the legs and head, or how ?

The picture thus conjured up struck her as excessively funny She began to giggle. The mistress's astonished voice roused her to the necessity for self-control. She picked up her pen. The thoughts flowed more clearly—yes, like ink in a pen. So it had come.

All along she had known that she must have failed : known it from the day of the examination itself. The burden of that knowledge had been upon her for weeks like a secret guilt. Daily she had gone to prayers in cold fear, thinking : " Now—now—now —they will read it out." Daily she had studied Clare's face, to each change of expression, each abstraction or transient sternness, her heart beating out its one thought, " She has heard ! she knows ! " And yet behind her academic certainty of failure had lain a little illogical hope. There was just a chance—an examiner more kind than just. . . . a spilled ink-bottle . . . an opportune fire. The child in her could still pray for miracles, for help from fairyland, and half believe it on the way.

And now the daily terrors, the daily reliefs, were alike over. Louise, who had learned, as she thought, to do without hope these many weeks, realized pitifully her self-deception. This hopelessness, this dead weight of certainty, was a new burden— a Sisyphus rock which would never roll for her. She was at the end.

Her mind, for all its forced and hot-house development, had, in matters of raw fact, the narrow outlook of the schoolgirl, superimposed upon the passions, the more intense for their utter innocence, of the child. Her sense of proportion, that latest developed and most infallible sign of maturity, was embryonic. The examination, so intrinsically unimportant, appeared to her a Waterloo. She could not see beyond it.

Clare, inexplicably altering, daily sterner and more indifferent, save for stray gleams of whimsical kindness, that stung and maddened the child by their sweetness and rarity, would, Louise considered, be effectually alienated. But Louise could not conceive life possible without Clare. The future was a night of black misery without a hint of dawn.

CHAPTER XX

THE morning wore to an end. Clare had come in at the mid-morning break to announce that the dress rehearsal would take place on the afternoon of the following day. All costumes were to be ready. The day-girls were to lunch at the school. She was brief and businesslike, inaccessible to questions. She did not look at Louise.

Alwynne, later in the morning, supplementing her instructions, paused a moment at the child's desk. But Louise gave no sign. Alwynne hesitated. She herself was averse from verbal sympathy. Also she was pressed for time, and Clare, she knew, wanted her. The one o'clock bell shattered her indecision. She gave her directions and hurried away.

Louise packed her books together and went home.

She endured the cheerful noisy lunch; carried out some small commissions for her stepmother; shepherded the troop of small boys into the paddock behind the garden and saw them established at their games. She stayed a moment with the round two-year-old, sprawling by the pile of coats, but he, too, had his amusements. Every pocket tempted his enquiring fingers. He ignored her.

She went back to the house. Habit brought her for the fiftieth time to the attic, and she had opened the door before she remembered. She looked about her. An iron bedstead, covered by a crude quilt, stood where the trunk of books had lain. A square of unswept carpet lay before it. There was a deal night-table and a candlestick of blue tin, with matches and a guttered candle. Across a chair lay a paper-back, face downwards, and a pair of soiled red corsets. The ivy had been cut away from the window, and the sunlight cast no fantastic frieze, but a squared, black shadow on the floor. The air was close, and a little rank. Louise shrank from it.

"Mother?" she said; and then: "You've gone away, haven't you? It's no use calling?"

She waited. The uneven water-jug rattled in its basin.

She spoke again—

" Mother, I know it's all spoiled here, but couldn't you come ? Just for a little while, Mother ? I'm most miserable. Please, Mother ? "

There was no answer.

" What shall I do ? " cried Louise wildly. " What shall I do ? Oh, what shall I do ? "

She turned from that empty place, stumbled to her room, and flung herself across her bed. She was shaken by her misery, as a dog shakes a rat. She cried, her head on her arms, till she was sick and blinded. Loneliness and longing seared her as with irons.

The clock ticked, and the sunshine poured into the room. The shouts of the children, the crack of ball on bat sounded faintly. The house slept. Two hours passed.

Somewhere a clock chimed and boomed. Four o'clock.

Slowly and stiffly Louise roused herself and got off her bed. She was cramped and shivering. She stood in the middle of the room and held out her hands to the brassy sunlight, but it did not warm her. She felt dazed and giddy; her head burned as if there were live coals in it. Her thoughts flowed sluggishly; she found it impossible to hurry them; they split apart into fragments that were words and meaningless phrases, or stuck like cogged wheels. Her mind moved across immense spaces to adjust these difficulties, but she policed them in vain. There was one sentence, in particular, that she could not deal with. It would not move along and make room for other thoughts. It danced before her; its grin spanned the horizon; it inhabited her mind; it was reversible like a Liberty satin; it ticked like a clock : " What next ? What next ? What next ? Next what ? Next what ? Next what ? "

What next ? . . . Dully she reckoned it up. The tea-bell— homework—bedtime. Night—and the false dreams. Morning —and the anger of Miss Hartill. Day and week and month— and the anger of Miss Hartill. The years stretched out before her in infinite repetition of the afternoon's agony, till her raw nerves shrank appalled. Kneeling down, she told God that it was impossible for her to endure this desolation. She implored Him, if He should in truth exist, not to reckon her doubt against her, but to be merciful and let her die. It was not the first time that she had prayed thus, but never before with such fierce insistence. If He existed He could impossibly refuse. . . .

Speaking her thoughts, even to so indefinite a Listener, steadied her. A ghost of hope had drifted through her mind. A ghost indeed; a messenger that whispered not of waking but of sleep, not of arduous renewing but of an end. Death was life upon his lips and life, death; yet he was none the less a hope.

The familiar text upon the wall above her bed caught her eye. The message seemed no more miraculous than the pansies and mistletoe that wreathed about its gilt and crimson capitals. ' God is our Refuge and Strength, a very present Help in Trouble.' ' Ask and it shall be given unto you ' confirmed her from the other wall.

She sat between those tremendous statements and considered them.

God had never yet answered any prayer of hers. . . . Not, she supposed, that He could not, but because He did not choose. . . . He was rather like Miss Hartill. . . . But Miss Hartill would never understand. . . . At least one could explain things to God—if God were. . . . And she asked so little of Him—just to let her die and be at peace. . . . She thought He might—if He had even time for sparrows. . . . She wondered how He would manage it ? If He would only be quick—because red-hot wires ran through her head when she tried to think, and she was afraid—afraid—afraid—of to-morrow and Miss Hartill. . . .

The tea-bell pealed across the garden.

She tidied her hair, and fetching the sponge and towel stood before the glass, trying to trim her marred face into some semblance of composure. The boys would be clamouring—and one never knew. . . . There might be tainted food—a loose baluster —a tag of carpet. . . . He had His ways. . . . She must not baulk Him. . . .

She went downstairs.

The children were tired and cross and quarrelsome—the heat had soured even cheerful Mrs. Denny. It was not a pleasant meal. But it could not oppress Louise. Outwardly docile and attentive, her mind had withdrawn into itself and sat aloof, inviolate, surveying its surroundings much as it would have watched the actors in a moving picture. She was impervious to bickerings and querulous comment. What did it matter ? She would never have tea with them again. . . . She was going away from it all. . . . If only God did not forget. . . .

All through the breathless evening she awaited His pleasure.

Long after the house was quiet, and Mrs. Denny, tucking up her children, had come and gone, Louise lay wakeful—still waiting.

It was an airless night. Every other moment the little unaccountable noises of a sleeping building broke the warm silence. Shadows scurried across the counterpane and over her face like ghostly mice, as the trees outside her window bent and nodded to a radiant moon.

She was weary to the point of exhaustion. Momently her body seemed to shrink away from her into the depths of the bed —warm, fathomless depths—leaving her essential self to float free and uncontained. She would resign herself luxuriously to the sensation of disintegration, but with maddening regularity her next breath clicked body and soul together anew. Yet, as she drowsed, the space between breath and breath lengthened slowly, till they lay divided by incredible æons in which her thoughts wandered and lost themselves, grew hoar and died and were born again; while the dead-weight of her body sank ever deeper into sleep, was recalled to consciousness with ever increasing effort.

She speculated languidly upon her sensations. They recalled a day at the dentist's, years before. A tube had been placed over her mouth and she had struggled, remembering a hideous story of a woman—a French marquise—that she had read in a magazine. The name began with a ' B' or a ' V.' ' Brin—' something. The Funnel—*The Leather Funnel*—that was the name of the story. . . . But there came no choking water— only sweet, buzzing air. . . . And then her body had dropped away from her, as it was doing now. . . . She recalled the sensation of rest and freedom; she had passed, like a bird planing down warm breezes, into exquisite oblivion. . . . She had returned, centuries later, to a dull aching pain, harsh noises, and lights that were like blows. . . . But if she had not returned ? She would have been dead. . . . They would have buried her. . . . Such things had happened. . . . So that was death—that cradling, beautiful sleep. And God was sending it to her now; flooding her, drowning her in its warm comfort. . . . God was very good. . . . She was sorry—sorry that she had often not believed in Him. . . . But Miss Hartill didn't. . . . But she would never see Miss Hartill any more. . . . Perhaps, years after, when she was tired of sleeping, she would go back and see her again. . . . There was All Souls' Night, when you woke up.

But she would not frighten Miss Hartill. . . . She laughed a
little, to think that she could ever frighten Miss Hartill. . . .
She would just kiss her, a little ghost's kiss that would feel like
a puff of air . . . and then she would go back and sleep and
sleep and sleep . . . with only the yew-berries pattering on to
her gravestone to tell her when another year had drifted past. . . .
It was funny that people could be afraid to die. . . . She wondered if ghosts snored, and if you heard them, if your grave were
very close ? It was her last thought as she slid into slumber.

Instantly the breakfast gong came crashing across her peace.
She fought against waking. Her eyelids lifted the weight upon
them as violets press upwards against a clod of rotten leaves.
She lay dazedly, her mind cobwebbed with dreams, her thoughts
trickling back into the channels of the previous night. Slowly
she took in her situation. There was the window, and a shining
day without : she could hear the starlings quarrelling on the
lawn, and the squeak of an angry robin. . . . There was her
room, and the tidy pile of clothes by the bed . . . the bed, and
she herself lying in it. . . . So she was not dead ! There was
to-day to be faced, and Miss Hartill's anger, and all the other
hundreds and thousands of days. . . .

And she must get up at once.

Her sick mind shrank from that, as from a culminating terror.
She was desperately tired; her body ached as if it had been
beaten. Dressing was a monstrous and impossible feat. . . .
It could not be. . . . Yet her stepmother would come—she was
between God and Mrs. Denny—and God had left her in the lurch.

She lay shielding her eyes from the strong light.

The pressure on her eyeballs was causing the usual kaleido-
scopic ring of light to form within her closed lids. The phenomenon
had always been a childish amusement to her; she was adept
at the shifting pressure that could vary colour and pattern. She
watched idly. Red changed to green, purple followed yellow,
and the ring narrowed to a pin-point of light on its background
of watered silk; then it broke up as usual into starry fragments.
But they danced no dazzling fire-dance for her ere they merged
again into the yellow ring : to her distracted fancy they were
letters—fiery letters, that formed and broke and formed again.
G—O—D—then an H and a P and an L. She puzzled over
them. " God hopes ? "   " God helps ? "   But He hadn't. . . .
" God helps ? "   A Voice in her ears exactly like her own took it
up—" Those that help themselves."   It spoke so loudly that

she shrank. The universe echoed to Its boom : yet she knew so well that the Voice was only in her own head.

No wonder her head ached, when it was all full of Lights and Voices. . . . And Miss Hartill would be angry if she took Them to school. . . . If only she need not go to school. . . . Why—why had God cheated her ? " He helped those——" Was that what They meant ?

She looked about her, brightening yet uncertain; then her long plait of hair caught her eye. Lazily she lifted it, disentangled a strand no thicker than coarse string, and doubling it about her throat, began to tighten it, using her fingers as a lever, till the blood sang in her ears. She had sat upright in bed for the greater ease. Suddenly she caught sight of her face in the wardrobe mirror. It was growing pink and puffy : the eyes goggled a little. The sensation of choking grew unendurable. Instinctively her fingers freed themselves and the noose fell apart. She swung forward, panting, and watched her features grow normal again.

" It's no good. Oh, I am a coward," cried Louise, wearily.

Her mother's old-fashioned travelling-clock, chiming the quarter, answered her, and for a moment forced her thoughts back from those borderlands where sanity ends. Habit asserted itself; she was filled with everyday anxieties. She was late, certainly for breakfast, probably for school. She jumped out of bed, washed and dressed in panic speed, collected her belongings and hurried from the house.

Her father, hearing the gate clack, glanced up from his newspaper.

" Has that child had any breakfast ? " he demanded, uneasily.

There was no answer. He was late himself, and his wife had poured his coffee and left the room. He could hear her heavy footfall in their bedroom overhead.

He returned to his reading.

CHAPTER XXI

LOUISE ran up the steep hill, her satchel padding at her back, the soft wind disordering her hair and whipping a colour into her white cheeks. She gained the deserted cloakroom, flung off her hat, and fled upstairs. But she was later than she guessed. Racing, against all rules, through the upper hall and down the long corridor, the drone of voices as she passed the glass-panelled doors warned her that no hurrying could avail her. She was definitely late. Her speed slackened.

The passage ended at right-angles to a small landing, into which her class-room opened. She paused, sheltering in the curve of the wall, listening. The class was still. The single voice of a mistress rang muffled through the walls. She could not distinguish the accents.

It was Miss Durand's class; but when everything was so upset. . . . one never knew . . . it might be Miss Hartill herself. . . . That would be just Louise's luck. . . . She hated you to be late. . . . But there was no point in hesitating. . . .

Yet she hesitated, shifting her weight uneasily from foot to foot, till a far-off step in the corridor without, ended her uncertainty. Some one was coming. . . . That again might be Miss Hartill. . . . Louise must be in her place. . . . Yet surely it was Miss Hartill's voice in the form-room ?

She crept to the door and peered through the glass.

Miss Durand was standing at the blackboard.

Louise entered, brazen with relief, and began her apologies. But Alwynne was no Rhadamanthus, and her official reprobation was marred by a twinkle. She would have been late herself that morning, but for Elsbeth—poor dear Elsbeth, who conceded, without remotely comprehending, the joys of that extra twenty minutes. And when had Louise been late before ? Little, good, frightened Louise ! She entered the name in the defaulters' book, but her manner sent the child to her desk quieted.

Alwynne, at sentry-go between blackboard and rostrum, dictating, supervising, expounding, yet found time to watch her. Louise was always a little on her motherly young mind. The child's shrinking manner worried her—and her pain-haunted eyes. Pain was Alwynne's devil. She was selfish, as youth must be, but at least, unconsciously. Hint trouble, and all of her was eager to serve and save. She was the instinctive Samaritan. But her perception was blurred by her profound belief in Clare. Louise, she knew, was in good hands, in wise hands; where she had known ten children, Clare had trained a hundred; if Clare's ways were not hers—so much the worse for hers.

Yet this disciplining of Louise was a long business; she wished it need not make the child so wretched. Surely Clare forgot how young she was. . . . There would be new trouble over the affair of the papers. . . . If Clare would but be commonplace for once, laugh, and say it didn't matter, and perhaps ask Louise to tea. . . . The child would be radiant for another six months—and work better too. . . . But, of course, it was absurd for her to dictate to Clare. . . . Louise had had such a pretty colour when she came in; it was all gone now. . . . She looked dreadfully thin. . . . Alwynne wondered if it would do any good to speak to Clare again. . . . Dear Clare—she was so proud of her girls, so eager to see them successful. . . . Louise was a bitter disappointment to her. . . . Yet, if she could have been gentler —but, of course, Clare knew best. . . . Alwynne only hoped the rehearsal would be a success. If Louise did well, it might adjust the tension. . . .

She watched the child, sitting apparently attentive, noted the moving lips, the little red volume half hidden in her lap. Shakespeare had no business in a physiology lesson, but Alwynne let her alone.

The hour was over all too quickly for Louise. Earlier in the year, when she had been at her most brilliant, and Miss Hartill's classes the absorbing joy of her day, she had yet welcomed the hours with Miss Durand. They alone had not seemed, in comparison, a waste of priceless time. They were jolly hours, quick-stepping, cheerful, laughter-flecked; void of excitements, yet never savourless; above all restful. Unconsciously she had counted on them for their recuperative value. Even now, exhausted, overwrought, beyond all influence, the kindly atmosphere could at least soothe her. Wistfully

M

her eyes followed Alwynne, as the young mistress left the room.

Clamour arose; slamming of desk-lids, thud of satchels and rattle of pencil-cases mingling with the babble of tongues. The next lesson was French Grammar. The little Frenchwoman was invariably late. She dreaded the lesson as much as her audience enjoyed it. They welcomed it as a pleasant interlude—the hour for conversation. Agatha did not even trouble to keep an eye on the door, as she turned to Louise, immobile beside her.

" I say, were you late ? "

" Didn't you see ? "

" Why were you late ? Weren't you called ? Didn't you wake up ? "

" No."

" Why ? "

" Oh, the housemaid died in the night. Smallpox." Louise stooped over her book, her shoulders hunched against questions.

" No, but tell me. Did you get in a row ? "

" You heard what Daffy said. I want to learn, Agatha."

" Oh, not that. Did you get in a row about the rehearsal ? "

" What rehearsal ? "

" The rehearsal yesterday."

Louise sat up, her eyes widening.

" There was no rehearsal yesterday ? " she said anxiously.

" Wasn't there just ! "

" But I never heard; nobody told me."

" Why, Daffy came in herself, yesterday morning. Every-one was there. I suppose you were moonstruck as usual. Do you mean to say you didn't hear ? I don't envy you."

" Was she angry ? " said Louise, in her smallest voice.

Agatha began to enjoy herself.

" Angry ? She was raving ! "

" What did she say ? "

" Well, she didn't say much," admitted Agatha. " Just asked where you were, and if not, why not—you know her way. Then we got started and went all through it, and had a gorgeous afternoon. She read your part. I say, she can act, can't she ? But she was pretty mad, of course."

" Was she——" said Louise. But it was not a question.

" Oh, and you're to go to her at break, this morning. Don't go and forget, and then say I didn't tell you." And she turned to greet the entering mistress with a flood of Anglo-French.

Louise had three parts of an hour in which to assimilate the message. How unlucky she was! She remembered the previous morning as one remembers a nightmare. . . . Miss Durand had certainly drifted through its dreadfulness—but of what she had said or done, Louise remembered nothing. But it was certain that she had managed to annoy Miss Hartill more than ever. To miss a special rehearsal! Now she was to go to her, and Miss Hartill would be so angry already, that when the question of the papers arose, the last chance of her leniency was gone. . . . For, of course, she would speak of the examination. . . . What would she say? Her imagination stubbed; it could not pierce the terror of what Miss Hartill would say.

The break was half over before she had wrenched herself out of her desk, along the length of the school, and up the staircase to Clare's little sanctum.

She knocked timidly. Clare's answering bell, that invariably startled her, rang sharply. She hesitated—the bell rang again, a prolonged, shrill peal. She pulled herself together, opened the door, and went in.

The floor was littered with gay costumes. Miss Durand, in a big apron, laughter-flushed, with her pretty hair tumbling down her back, was sorting them into neat heaps.

Clare, at ease in a big arm-chair, directing operations, while her quick fingers cut and pasted at a tinsel crown, was laughing also.

" How happy they look," thought Louise.

Clare glanced up.

" Well, Louise," she said, not unkindly.

Louise stammered a little.

" Miss Hartill—I'm very sorry—I'm most awfully sorry. They said—the girls said—there was rehearsal yesterday, and you wanted me. I honestly didn't know. I've only just heard there was one."

Clare kept her waiting while she clipped at the indentations of the crown. The scissors clicked and flashed. It seemed an interminable process.

Finally she spoke to Alwynne, her eyes on her work.

" Miss Durand! You gave my message to the Fifths? "

Yes, Alwynne had told the girls.

" Wasn't Louise in the room at the time? "

Alwynne's unwilling eyes took in every detail of the forlorn figure between them. She lied swiftly, amazing herself—

" As a matter of fact—I believe Louise was not in the room at the time. It was my fault : I should have seen that she was told. I'm so sorry."

Louise gave a little gasp of relief—more audible than she realized.

Clare roused at it. She disliked a check. She disliked also the obvious sympathy between the child and the girl.

" No, it was my fault. I should have gone myself. It's always wiser. It saves trouble in the long run. Never mind, Louise. You couldn't help it. Are you sure of your words ? "

Louise, infinitely relieved, was quite sure of her words.

" Very well. Shut the door after you—oh, Louise ! "

Louise turned in the doorway.

" Yes, Miss Hartill."

" I may as well explain to you now. I am re-arranging the classes."

Louise questioned her mutely.

" You will be in the Upper Fourth next term."

Louise stood petrified. She had never thought of this.

" You are moving me down ? I am third still."

" We think—Miss Marsham agrees with me—that the work in the Fifth is too much for you. It is not your fault."

" Miss Hartill, I have tried—I am trying."

Clare smiled quite pleasantly.

" I am quite sure of it. I tell you that I'm not blaming you. I blame myself. If I expected more of you than you could manage—no one but myself is to blame. I am sure you will do well in the Fourth."

Louise broke out passionately—

" It is because of the examination."

Clare held out her crown at arm's length, and eyed it between criticism and approval as she answered Louise.

" I think," said Clare smoothly, " we had better not discuss the examination."

Louise stood in the doorway, her mouth quivering.

Alwynne could stand the scene no longer. She jerked herself upright, and, going to the child, slipped her arm about her and pushed her gently from the room.

Clare was still admiring her crown, as Alwynne shut the door again. Alwynne must try it on. It would suit Alwynne.

Alwynne peeped at herself in the little mirror, but her thoughts were with Louise on the other side of the door.

"Clare," said Alwynne uneasily, "you hurt that child."

Clare looked at her oddly.

"Do her good," she said. "Do you think no one has ever hurt me?"

Alwynne was silent. At times her goddess puzzled her.

CHAPTER XXII

To the schoolgirls the dress rehearsal was, if possible, more of an ordeal than the performances themselves. The head mistress attended in state with the entire staff and such of the girls as were not themselves acting. Stray relatives, unable to be present at the play proper, dotted the more distant benches, or were bestowed in the overhanging galleries, while the servants, from portly matron to jobbing gardener, clustered at the back of the hall.

The platform at the upper end had been built out to form a stage, and when, late in the afternoon, the final signal had been given and the improvised curtains drew audibly apart, Clare had fair reason to plume herself on her stage-management.

The long blinds of the windows had been let down and shut out the sceptical sunshine; and the candle footlights, flickering unprofessionally, mellowed the paintwork and patterned the home-made scenery with re-echoing lights, pools of unaccountable shadow, and shaftlike, wavering, prismatic gleams, flinging over the crude stage-setting a veil of fantastic charm.

The play opened, however, dully enough. The scenes chosen had had inevitably to be compressed, run together, mangled, and Clare had not found it easy work. Faulconbridge, bowdlerized out of all but existence, could not tickle his hearers, and King John, not yet broken in to crown and mantle, gave him feeble support. But with the entrance of Constance, Arthur and the French court, actors and audience alike bestirred themselves.

Agatha, her dark eyes flashing, her lank figure softened and rounded by the generous sweep of her geranium-coloured robes, looked an authentic stage queen. Her exuberant movements and theatrical intonation had been skilfully utilized by Clare, who, playing on her eager vanity, had alternately checked and goaded her into a plausible rendering of the part. She was the reverse of nervous; her voice rolled her opening speech without a tremor; her impatient, impetuous delivery (she hardly let her fellow-actors finish their lines) fitted the character and was effective enough.

Yet to Clare, note-book in hand, prepared to pounce, cat-like, on deficiencies, neither she nor her foil dominated the stage, nor the row of schoolgirl princes. Her critical appreciation was for the little figure, wavering uncertainly between the shrieking queens, with scared anxious eyes, that swept the listening circle in faint appeal, quivering like a sensitive plant at each verbal assault, shrinking beneath the hail of blandishments and reproaches. The one speech of the scene, the reproof to Constance, was spoken with un-childlike, weary dignity—

> "'Good my mother, peace!
> I would that I were low laid in my grave;
> I am not worth this coil that's made for me.'"

Yet it was not Arthur that spoke, nor Louise—no frightened boy or overwrought, precocious girl. It was the voice of childhood itself, sexless, aloof; childhood the eternal pilgrim, wandering passive and perplexed, an elf among the giants; childhood, jostled by the uncaring crowd, swayed by gross energies and seared by alien passions.

" She's got it," muttered Clare to Alwynne, reporting progress in the interval; " oh, how she's got it ! " She laughed shortly. " So that's her reading. Impudent monkey ! But she's got her atmosphere. Uncanny, isn't it ? It reminds me—do you remember that performance of hers last autumn with *Childe Roland*? I told you about it. Well, this brings it back, rather. Clever imp. I wonder how much of my coaching in this act she'll condescend to leave in ? "

" You gave her a free hand, you know," deprecated Alwynne.

" I did. But it's impudence——"

" Inspiration——"

" Impudence all the same. When the rehearsal is over I must have a little conversation with Miss Denny." She showed her white teeth in a smile.

Alwynne caught her up uneasily—

" Clare—you're not going to scold ? It wouldn't be fair. You know you're as pleased as Punch, really."

Clare shot a look at her, but Alwynne's face was innocent and anxious. She shrugged her shoulders.

" Am I ? I suppose I am. I don't know. On my word,

Alwynne, I don't know!   But run along, my deputy.   There's
an agitated orb rolling in your direction from the join of the
curtains."

Alwynne fled.

The opening scene of the second division of the play—as Clare
had planned it—showed Arthur a prisoner to John and the old
queen.   The child's face was changed, his manner strained; his
startled eyes darted restlessly from Hubert to the king and back
again to Hubert; the pair seemed to fascinate him.   Yet he
shrank from their touch and from Elinor's embrace, only to
check the instinctive movement with pitiful, propitiatory haste,
and to submit, his small fists clenched, to their caresses.   His
eyes never left their faces : you saw the tide of fear rising in his
soul.   Not till the interview with Hubert, however, was the
morbid drift of the conception fully apparent.   He hung upon
the man, smiling with white lips; he fawned; he babbled;   he
cajoled;   marshalled his poor defences of tears and smiles, frail
defiance and wooing surrender, with an awful, childish cunning.
He watched the man as a frightened bird watches a cat;   turned
as he turned, confronting him with every muscle tense.   His
high whisper premised a voice too weak with terror to shriek.
Yet at the entrance of the attendants there came a cry that made
Clare shiver where she sat.   It was fear incarnate.

Clare fidgeted.   It was too bad of Louise. . . . And what
had Alwynne been thinking of ?   A free hand, indeed !   Too
much of a free hand altogether !   The fact that she was listening to a piece of acting, that, in a theatre, would have overwhelmed her with admiration, added to her annoyance.   A
school performance was not the place for brilliant improprieties.
Certainly impropriety—this laborious exposure of a naked emotion was, in such a milieu, essentially improper—Louise must be
crazy !   And in what unholy school had she learned it all—this
baby of thirteen ?   And what on earth would staff and school
say ?

She stole a look at her colleagues.   Some were interested, she
could see, but obviously puzzled.   A couple were whispering
together.   A third had chosen the moment to yawn.

Her contradictory mind instantly despised them for fools
that could not appreciate what manner of work they were privileged to watch.   She saw her path clear—her attitude outlined
for her.   She would glorify a glorious effort (it was pleasant that
for once justice might walk with expediency) and her sure, instant

tribute would, she knew, suffice to quiet the carpers. But, for all that, the performances themselves should be, she promised herself, on less dangerous lines than the dress-rehearsal. She would have a word with Louise : the imp needed a cold douche. . . But what an actress it would make later on ! Clare sighed enviously.

The scene was nearly over. With the glad cry— "'Ah! now you look like Hubert,'" the enchantment of terror broke. A few more sentences and Arthur was left alone on the stage.

As the door clanged (Alwynne was juggling with hardware in the wings) the child's strained attitude relaxed and the audience unconsciously relaxed with it. He swayed a moment, then collapsed brokenly into a chair. The long pause was an exquisite relief.

But before long the small face puckered into frowns; a backwash of subsiding fear swept across it. The hands twitched and drummed. You felt that a plan was maturing.

At last, after furtive glances at the door, he rose with an air of decision, and crossed quickly to the alcove of the window. For an instant the curtains hid him, and the audience stared expectantly at an empty stage. When he turned to them again, holding the great draperies apart with little, resolute fists, his face was alight with hope, and, for the first time, wholly youthful. In the soft voice ringing out the last courageous sentences, detailing the plan of the escape, there was a little quiver of excitement, of childish delight in an adventure. He ended; stood a moment smiling; then the heavy folds hid him again as they swept into position.

There was a tense pause.

Suddenly as from a great distance, came a faint wailing cry. Thereon, silence.

The curtains wheezed and rattled into place.

Alwynne, hurrying on to the stage to shift scenery for the following act, nearly tripped, as she dismantled the alcove, over a huddle of clothes crouched between backing and wall. She stooped and shook it. A small arm flung up in instant guard.

"Louise? Get up! The act's over. Run out of the way. Stop—help me with this, as you're here."

Obediently the child scrambled to her feet. She gripped an armful of curtain, and trailed across the stage in Alwynne's wake. Till the curtains rose on the final act, she trotted after her meekly, helping where she could.

With King John embarked on his opening speech, Alwynne
drew breath again. She ran her eye over the actors, palpitant
at their several entrances, saw the prompter still established
with book and lantern, and decided that all could go on without
her for a moment. She put her hand on Louise's shoulder and
drew her into the passage.

" What is it, Louise ? "

" Nothing."

" What were you doing just now ? Were you scared ? Was
it stage fright ? "

" Oh no." Louise smiled faintly.

" Then what were you doing ? "

Louise considered.

" I was dead. I had jumped, you know. I was finding out
how it would feel."

" Louise ! You gruesome child ! "

" I liked it—it was so quiet. I'd forgotten about shifting the
scenery. I'm sorry. Does it—did it hurt him, do you think,
the falling ? "

Alwynne put both her hands on the thin shoulders and shook
her gently.

" Louise ! Wake up ! You're not Prince Arthur now !
Gracious me, child—it's only a play. You mustn't take it so
seriously."

Louise made no answer; she did not seem to understand.

Alwynne was struck by a new idea. She took the child's
face in her hand and turned it to the gaslight.

" Did I see you at lunch, Louise ? I don't believe I did. Do
you know you're a very naughty child to take advantage of the
confusion ? "

" Miss Durand, I had to learn. I was forgetting it all. I
slipped the last two lines as it was—you know, the ' My uncle's
spirit is in these stones ' bit. I wasn't hungry."

" And you were very late, too. What did you have for
breakfast ? "

An agitated face peered round the corner.

" Miss Durand, which side do I come on from ? Hubert's
nearly off."

" The left." Alwynne hurried to the rescue, dragging Louise
after her. She hustled the anxious courtier to his entrance,
twitched his mantle into position, and saw him safely on the stage.
Then she turned to Louise.

" Louise, will you please go to the kitchen and ask Mrs. Random
for two cups of tea and some buns—at once. There is some tea
made, I know. I'm tired and thirsty—two cups, please. Bring
it to me here, and don't run into any one with your hands full.
Be quick—I'm dying for some."

Louise darted away on her errand. Poor Daffy did look
hot and flustered. . . . Daffy was such a dear . . . every one
worried her . . . it was a shame. . . . Wouldn't Daffy have been
a pleasant mother ? Better than shouting Constance. . . . What
was it she had asked for ? A plum, a cherry and a fig ? No,
that wasn't it. Oh, of course, tea—tea and buns.

Alwynne looked after her, smiling and frowning; she was not
in the least thirsty. What a baby it was. . . . But nothing to
eat all day ! Mrs. Denny ought to be ashamed of herself. . . .
She, Alwynne, would keep a vigilant eye on her to-morrow,
poor little soul. . . . Had she really lost herself so entirely in the
part—or was there a touch of pose ? No, that was more Agatha's
line. . . . Agatha was enjoying herself. . . . She listened amus-
edly, watching through a crack in the screen, till a far-away
chink caught her ear. She went out again into the passage,
and met Louise with a laden tray.

Alwynne drank with expressive pantomime and motioned to
the other cup.

" Drink it up," she commanded.

" It's a second cup—for you——" began Louise.

" Be a good child and do as you're told ! I must fly in a minute."

The child looked doubtful; but the steaming liquid was
tempting and the new-baked, shining cakes. She obeyed.
Alwynne watched the faint colour flush her cheeks with a satisfaction that surprised herself.

" Finish it all up—d'you hear ? I must go." She hesitated :
" Louise—you were very good to-day. I am sure Miss Hartill
must have been awfully pleased."

She went back to the stage. She had had the pleasure of
bringing a look of relief to Louise's face. Alwynne could never
remember that the kindest lie is a lie none the less.

In the part of Arthur the child, unconsciously, had seen
embodied her own psychological situation. She had enacted
the spirit, if not the letter, of her own state of mind, and in the
mock death had experienced something of the sensations, the
sense of release, of a real one. Left to to herself, she might gradually have dreamed and imagined and acted herself out of her

troubles, have drifted back to real life again, cured and sane.   But
Alwynne, with her suggestion of good cheer, had destroyed the
skin of make-believe that was forming healingly upon the child's
sore heart.   Louise awoke, with a pang of hope, to her real
situation.

' I am sure Miss Hartill must have been awfully pleased.' . . .
So pleased that, who knew, she might yet forgive the crime
of the examination ?   If it might be. . . . " What might be must
be," cried the child within her.

There came a crash of clapping;   the rehearsal was over at
last, and in a few moments flocks of girls, chattering and excited,
came trooping past Louise on their way to tea.

She did not follow them.   She was suddenly aware of her
boy's clothes.   She must change them. . . . She could not find
Miss Hartill till she was tidy, and she had determined to speak
with her.

Miss Durand had said. . . . She would do as Arthur did to
Hubert—she would besiege Miss Hartill, force her to be kind,
till she could say, " Oh, now you look Miss Hartill ! all this while
you were disguised."   She shivered at the idea of undergoing
once more the emotional experience of the scene—but the vision
of Miss Hartill transfigured drew her as a magnet pulls a needle.

She went towards the stairs.

The big music-room at the top of the house had been temporarily converted into a dressing-room, and she thought she
would go quickly and change, while it was still quiet and spacious.
But as she pushed open the swinging doors that divided staircase
from passage, she saw Clare coming down the long corridor.
There was no one else in sight.   Again wild, unreasoning hopes
flooded her.   She would seize the opportunity. . . . She would
speak to Miss Hartill there and then. . . . She would ask her
why she was always angry. . . . Perhaps she would be kind ?
' I am sure Miss Hartill must have been awfully pleased. . . .'
She must have speech with her at once—at once. . . .

She waited, holding open the door, her heart beating violently,
her face steeled to composure.

Clare, passing with a nod, found her way barred by a white-
faced scrap of humanity, whose courage, obviously and pitifully,
was desperation.   But Clare could be very blind when she did
not choose to see.

" Miss Hartill, may I speak to you ? "

" I can't wait, Louise.   I'm busy."

"Miss Hartill, was it all right? Were you pleased? I tried furiously. Was it as you wanted it?"

"Oh, you played your own version." Clare caught her up sharply.

"But Miss Durand said—you said I was to."

"I expect it was all right," said Clare lightly. "I'm afraid I was too busy to attend much, even to your efforts, Louise." She smiled crookedly. "And now run along and change."

She pushed against the door, but Louise, beyond all control, caught back the handles.

"Miss Hartill—you shall listen. Are you always going to be angry? What have I done? Will you never be good to me again as you used to be?"

Clare's face grew stern.

"Louise, you are being very silly. Let me pass."

"Because I can't bear it. It's killing me. Couldn't you stop being angry?"

Clare, ignoring her, wrenched open the door. Louise, flung sideways, slipped on the polished floor. She crouched where she fell, and caught at Clare's skirts. She was completely demoralized.

"Miss Hartill! Oh, please—please—if you would only understand. You hurt me so. You hurt me so."

Clare stood looking down at her.

"Once and for all, Louise, I dislike scenes. Let me go, please."

For a moment their eyes strove. And suddenly Louise, relaxing all effort, let her go. Without another look, Clare retraced her steps and entered the Common-room. Louise, still crouching against the wall, watched her till she disappeared. The doors swung and clicked into rigidity.

There was a sudden uproar of voices and laughter and scraping chairs. A distant door had opened.

Louise started to her feet, and sped swiftly up the stairs, flight on flight, of the tall old house, till she reached the top floor and the music-room. It was empty. She flung-to the door, and fumbled with the stiff key. It turned at last, and she leaned back against the lock, shaking and breathless, but with a sense of relief.

She was safe. . . . Not for long—they would be coming up soon—but long enough for her purpose.

But first she must recover breath. It was foolish to tremble so. It only hindered one . . . when there was so little time to lose.

Hurriedly she sorted out her little pile of everyday clothes— some irrelevant instinct insisting on the paramount necessity of changing into them. Mrs. Denny would be annoyed if she spoiled the new costume. She re-dressed hastily and, clasping her belt, crossed to the window.

It was tall and divided into three casements. The centre door was open. A low seat ran round the bay. She climbed upon it and stood upright, peering out.

How high up she was ! There was a blue haze on the horizon, above the line of faint hills, that melted in turn into a weald, chequered like the chessboard counties in *Alice.* So there was a world beyond the school ! Nearer still, the suburb spread map-like. She craned forward. Directly under her lay the front garden, and a row of white steps that grinned like teeth. It was on them that she would fall—not on the grass. . . .

She imagined the sensation of the impact, and shuddered. But at least they would kill one outright. . . . One would not die groaning in rhymed couplets, like Arthur. . . .

Clasping the shafts, she hoisted herself upwards, till she stood upon the inner sill. Instantly the fear of falling caught her by the throat. She swayed backwards, gasping and dizzy, steadying herself against the stout curtains.

" I can't do it," whispered Louise hoarsely. " I can't do it."

Slowly the vertigo passed. She fought with her rampant fear, wrenching away her thoughts from the terror of the death she had chosen, to the terror of the life she was leaving. She stood a space, balanced between time and eternity, weighing them.

With an effort she straightened herself, and put a foot on the outer ledge. Again, inevitably, she sickened. Huddled in the safety of the window-seat, stray phrases thrummed in her head : *My bones turn to water—There is no strength in me.* He knew—that Psalmist man. . . .

She slipped back on to the floor, and walked unsteadily to the littered table. Her hands were so weak that she could hardly lift them to pour out a glass of water.

She leaned against the table and drank thirstily. What a fool she was. . . . What a weak fool. . . . An instant's courage —one little second—and peace for ever after. . . . Wasn't it worth while ? Wasn't it ? Wasn't it ? She turned again to her deliverance.

As she pulled herself on to the seat, she heard a noise of footsteps in the passage without, and the handle of the door was rattled impatiently. In an instant she was on the sill. This was pursuit—Miss Hartill, and all the terrors! There must be no more hesitation. Once more she crouched for the leap, only, with a supreme effort, to swing herself back to safety again. Her hands were so slippery with sweat that they could barely grip the window-shafts. There was a banging at the door and a sound of voices calling. She swayed in a double agony, as fear strove against fear.

She heard the voice of a prefect—

"Who is it in there? Open the door at once."

They would break open the door. . . . They would find her. . . . They would stop her. . . . Coward that she was—fool and coward. . . . One instant's courage—one little movement!

She stiffened herself anew. Poised on the extreme edge of the outer sill, she pushed her two hands through the belt of her dress, lest they should save her in her own despite. She stood an instant, her eyes closed.

Then she sprang. . . . .

CHAPTER XXIII

CLARE was enjoying tea and triumph. She had worked hard for both, and was virtuously fatigued. The rocking-chair was comfortable, and the little gym mistress had brought her her favourite cakes. The Common-room, tinkling its tea-cups, buzzed criticism and approval. The rehearsal had been a success.

The talk centred, while opinion divided, on the Constance and the Prince Arthur. The general standpoint seemed to be that Agatha had reached the heights. Her royal robes had been effective; she reminded nearly every one of a favourite actress. Louise was less popular. A curious performance— very clever, of course—only one had not thought of Arthur quite like that! Now the Constance——

Clare, watching and listening, purred like a sleepy cat. She wondered why Alwynne was absent . . . she was missing a lot. . . . Louise was annoying—she had been excessively irritated with her ten minutes before—and there was the debacle of the scholarship papers—but to class her with Agatha! What fools these women were!

The discussion had become argument, and was growing faintly acrimonious, when a deep voice cut across it.

Miss Hamilton, a visiting music mistress, always had a hearing when she chose to speak. She was a big woman, with a fine massive head and shrewd eyes. She dressed tweedily and carried her hands in her pockets, slouching a little. It was her harmless vanity to have none. Teaching music was her business; her recreations, hockey, and the more law-abiding forms of suffrage agitation. She was a level-headed and convincing speaker, with a triumphant sense of humour that could, and had, carried her successfully through many a fantastic situation. Rumours of her adventures had spread among the staff, if not through the school, and beglamoured her; she could have had a following if she had chosen. But her healthy twelve stone crashed through pedestals, and she established comradeship, as she helped you, laughter-shaken, to pick up the pieces.

A postponed lesson had given her time to attend the rehearsal, and she had afterwards joined the flock of mistresses at tea. Clare, who thought more of her opinion than she·chose to own, had eyed her once or twice already, and at the sound of her voice she stopped her lazy rocking.

"But they are not in the same category! Any schoolgirl could have played Constance as What's-her-name played it, given the training she has had." Miss Hamilton nodded pleasantly to the rocking-chair. She appreciated Clare's capacities. "But Arthur——"

"Well, I thought Agatha was splendid," repeated a junior mistress stubbornly.

"She was. An excellent piece of work! 'But the hands were the hands of Esau.'"

"They always are," said the little gym mistress fervently.

Clare gave her a quick, brilliant smile. She blushed scarlet.

The music mistress laughed; she enjoyed her weekly glimpse of school interdependencies.

"Why did you single out *King John*, Miss Hartill?" she inquired politely.

Clare was demure, but her eyes twinkled.

"The decision lay with Miss Marsham," she murmured.

"Of course. But having a Cinderella on the premises—eh?"

"If you know of a glass slipper——"

"You fit it on! Exactly! Where did you discover her?"

"Starving—literally starving, in the Lower Third." Clare thawed to the congenial listener. "It was an amazing performance, wasn't it? Of course, there was nothing of the actual Arthur in it——"

Miss Hamilton nodded.

"That struck me. It was a child in trouble—not a boy. Not a girl either—but, of course, only a girl would be precocious enough to conceive and carry out the idea. If she did, that is?"

"Oh, it was original," Clare disclaimed prettily. "It had little to do with me. I had to let her go her own way."

Miss Hamilton liked her generosity.

"You're wise. It's all very well to trim the household lamps, but a burning bush is best left alone. I don't altogether envy you. Genius must be a disturbing factor in a school."

" You think she has genius ? "

" It was more than precocity to-day—or talent. The Constance
had talent."

" And was third in the scholarship papers. Louise failed
completely. Isn't it inexplicable ? What is one to do ? Of
course, it was disgraceful : she should have been first. I expected
it. I coached her myself. I know her possibilities. Frankly,
I am deeply disappointed."

Miss Hamilton pulled her chair nearer. She was interested ;
Clare was not usually so communicative. But their further
conversation was interrupted by the opening of the door, and
old Miss Marsham appeared on a visit of congratulation, accepting
tea and dispensing compliments with equal stateliness.

" An excellent performance ! We must felicitate each other—
and Miss Hartill. But we are accustomed to great things from
Miss Hartill. There can be no uneasiness to-morrow. The
child in the green coat, in that scene—ah, you remember ? I
thought her a trifle indistinct. Perhaps a hint——? Altogether it was excellent. Especially the Constance—most
dramatic. If I may criticize—acting is not my department—
but the Prince Arthur ? Now, were you satisfied ? Louise is
a dear child, but hardly suitable, eh ? "

Clare stiffened.

" I thought her acting remarkable."

" Did you ? Now I can't help feeling that Shakespeare never
intended it like that. He makes him such a dear little boy.
It's so pathetic, you know, where he begs the man not to put
out his eyes. So childlike and touching. Like little Lord
Fauntleroy. I know I cried when I saw it, years ago. Now
this child was not at all appealing."

Clare shrugged her shoulders.

" It is not a pretty scene, Miss Marsham, though the managers
conspire to make us think so. A child at the mercy of brutes,
knowing its own danger, terrorised into the extreme of cunning,
parading its poor little graces with the skill of a mondaine—
it's not pretty ! And Louise spared us nothing."

Miss Marsham fidgeted.

" If that is your view of the scene, Miss Hartill, I wonder
that you consider it fit for a school performance."

Clare hedged.

" My private view doesn't matter, after all. Traditionally
it is inadmissible, of course. But if you would like the treat-

ment altered a little, I will speak to Louise. It is only the dress rehearsal, of course."

Miss Marsham looked relieved.

"Perhaps it would be better. A little more childlike, you know. But don't let her think me annoyed, Miss Hartill; I am sure she has worked so hard. Just a hint, you know. I should not like her feelings to be hurt. Poor child, the results were a sad disappointment to her, I'm afraid. You spoke to her about the change of class?"

"Yes."

"I hope she was not distressed?"

Clare remembered the look on Louise's face. She hesitated.

"She will get over it," she said.

The kind old woman looked worried.

"You must not let her feel that she has failed over this, Miss Hartill—on the top of the other trouble. You will be judicious?"

A door slammed in the distance; there was a blurr of voices, a sound of hurrying footsteps.

Clare rose impatiently; she was tired of the subject.

"It will be all right, Miss Marsham. I understand Louise. What in the world is that disgraceful noise?"

But the door was flung open before she could reach it. Alwynne stood in the aperture, panting a little. In her arms lay Louise, her head falling limply, like a dead bird's. Behind them, peering faces showed for a moment, white against the dusk of the passage. Then Alwynne, staggering beneath the dead weight, stumbled forward, and the door swung to with a crash.

The roomful of women stared in horrified silence.

"She's dead," said Alwynne. "I found her on the steps. She fell from a window. . One of the children saw it. She's dead."

She swayed forward to the empty rocking-chair, and sat down, the child's body clasped to her breast. She looked like a young mother.

Clare, watching half stupefied, saw a thin trickle of blood run out across her bare arm.

It woke her.

"Send for a doctor!" screamed Clare. "Send for a doctor! Will nobody send for a doctor?"

CHAPTER XXIV

THE sudden death of Louise Denny had shocked, each in her degree, every member of the staff. The general view was that such a deplorable accident could and should have been impossible. Every one remembered having long ago thought that the old-fashioned windows were unsafe, and having wondered why precautions had never been taken. Every one, the first horror over, canvassed the result of the unavoidable inquest, and speculated whether any one would be censured for carelessness. The younger mistresses were so sure that it was nobody's business to be on duty in the dressing-room at that particular hour that they spent the rest of the hushed, horror-stricken day in telling each other so, proclaiming, a trifle too insistently, their relief that they at least had nothing, however remote, to do with the affair: while inwardly they ransacked their memories to recall if perchance some half-heard order, some forgotten promise of standing substitute or relieving guard could, at the last moment, implicate them.

But the task of quieting and occupying the frightened children, and of clearing away, as far as might be, all traces of the dress rehearsal, was at least distraction. On the heads of the school, real and nominal, the strain was immeasurably greater. It was first truly felt, indeed, many hours later. Old Miss Marsham, in whom the shock had awakened something of her old-time decision of character, had conducted the interview with the decorously grieving parents with sufficient dignity; had overseen the temporary resting-place of the dead child; had communicated with doctors, lawyers and officials. But the spurt of energy had subsided with the necessity for it. She had retired late at night to her own apartments and the ministrations of her efficient maid, a broken old commander, facing tremulously the calamity that had befallen her life-work: foreseeing and exaggerating its effect on the future of the school, planning feverishly her defence from the gossip that must ensue. An accident . . . of course, an accident . . . a terrible yet unfore-

seeable accident. . . . That was the point. . . . At all costs
it must be shown that it was an accident pure and simple, with
never a whisper of negligence against authority or underling.
. . . But she was an old woman. . . . She needed, she supposed
bitterly, a shock of this kind to humble her into realizing that
her day was over. . . . She had been driving with slack reins
this many a long year. . . . She had known it and had hoped
that no one shared her knowledge. And none had known. . . .
So there came this pitiful occurrence to advertise her weakness
to the world. . . . The poor child! Ah, the poor little child!
There had been a lack of supervision, no doubt . . . some such
gross carelessness as she, in her heyday, would never have
tolerated. . . . And she was grown too old, too feeble to hold
enquiry—to dispense strict justice. . . . She must depend on
the lieutenants who had failed her, to hush the matter up—to
make the administration of the school appear blameless. . . .
They could do that, she did not doubt, and so she must be
content. . . . But in the day of her strength she would not
have been content. . . . But she was old. . . . It was time for
her to abdicate. . . . She must put her affairs in order, name
her successor—Clare Hartill or the secretary, she supposed. . . .
They knew her ways. . . . There was that bright girl who had
faced her to-day with the little child in her arms . . . what
was her name? Daughter or niece of some old pupil of her
own. . . . She could more easily have seen her in her seat than
either of her vice-regents. . . . So young and strong and eager.
. . . She had been like that once. . . . Now she was a weak
old woman, and because of her weakness a little child lay dead
in her house. . . . Yes, Martha might put her to bed. . . .
Why not? She was very tired.

Henrietta Vigers had also her anxieties. She had so long
claimed the position of virtual head that there was no doubt
in her own mind that other people would consider her as responsible as if she had been the actual one. She worried incessantly.
Should she have had bars put up to those old-fashioned windows?
She, who was responsible for all the household arrangements?
Ought she not to have foreseen the danger and guarded against
it? And there was the matter of the dressing-room mistress.
. . . For the school machinery she had made herself even
more pointedly responsible. . . . She should have arranged
for some one to oversee the children. . . . But the dressing-
room had been a temporary one and she had overlooked the

necessity. . . . Yet if some one had been in the room the
accident could impossibly have happened. . . . She felt that
she would be lucky to escape public censure, that loss of prestige
in the eyes at least of the head mistress was inevitable.

But the more or less selfish perturbation, as distinct from
the emotion of sheer humanity, that was aroused by the death
of the little schoolgirl in the two older women, was as nothing
to the sensation of sick dismay that it awoke in Clare Hartill.
She, too, through the night that followed on the accident, lay
awake till sunrise, considering her position. She was stunned
by the unexpectedness of the catastrophe; a little grieved for
the loss of Louise, but, above all, intensely and quite selfishly
frightened. She felt guilty. She remembered, remorselessly
enlightened, the afternoon, the expression in Louise's eyes, and
not for one instant did she share the general belief in the accidental nature of her death. Her conscience would not allow
her the comfort of such self-deception. Later she might lull it to
sleep again, but for the moment it was awake, and her master.
This same keen-witted conscience of hers, this quintessence of
her secret admirations and considered opinions, her epicurean
appreciation of what was guileless and beautiful and worthy,
co-existing, as it did, with the intellectualized sensuality of her
imperious and carnal personality, was no small trial to Clare.
Though it could not sway her decisions nor influence her actions
by one hair's-breadth, it was at least cynically active, as now,
to prick and fret at her peace. It was, indeed, at the root of
the whimsical irritability that, for all her charm, made her an
impossible housemate.

Essentially, her attitude to life was simple. It was an orange,
to be squeezed for her pleasure. It must serve her; but she
owed it, therefore, no duty. She found that she achieved a
maximum of pleasurable sensations by following the dictates
of that mind which is the mouthpiece of body, while indulging,
as Lucullus ate turnips, in austere flirtations with that other
mind, which is the mouthpiece of spirit. So she served Mammon,
or rather, she allowed Mammon to serve her, but she was, on
occasions, critically interested in God. And this was her undoing.
Could she have been content to be frankly selfish, she might
have been happy enough, but her very interest in the kingdom
of Heaven had created her conscience, and had laid her open
to its attacks. She ignored it, and it made her wretched : she
compromised with it, and became a hypocrite.

She resented the death of Louise because it challenged her whole scheme of life. She was furiously angry with the dead child for what she felt to be an indictment of her legitimate amusements. Louise, so meek and ineffectual, had yet been able to steal a march on her, had stabbed in the back and run away, beyond reach of Clare's retaliation. . . . Louise had fooled her. . . . She, Clare, proud of her insight, her complete knowledge of character, her alert intuition, had yet had no inkling of what was passing in that childish mind. . . . If she had guessed, however vaguely, she could have taken measures, have scourged the mere suggestion of such monstrous rebellion out of that subject soul. . . . But Louise, secure in her insignificance, had tricked her, planned her sure escape. . . . But how unhappy she must have been ! . . . .

In a sudden revulsion of feeling Clare grew faint with pity, as she tried to realize the child's state of mind during the past months. Her thoughts went back to the Christmas Day they had spent together. She had been happy enough then. . . . Half sincerely she tried to puzzle out the change in Louise, the gradual deterioration that had led to the tragedy. Had she been to blame ? Louise had grown tiresome, and she had snubbed her. . . . There was the thing in a nutshell. . . . If she was to be so tender of the feelings of all the silly girls who sentimentalized over her, where would it end, at all ?

Poor little Louise. . . . She had been really fond of her at the beginning. . . . She had thought for a time that she might even supplant Alwynne. . . . But Louise had disappointed her. . . . She had let her work go to the dogs. . . . All her originality and charm fizzled out. . . . She had ceased to be interesting. . . . And she, Clare, had naturally been bored and had shown it. . . . Why couldn't the child take it quietly ? If Louise had only known—and had conducted herself with tact—Clare had been preparing to be nicer to her again. . . . She had been deeply interested in her performance of the morning, had recognized its uncanny sincerity—had thought, with a distinct quickening of interest, that Louise was recovering herself at last, and that it might be as well to take her in hand again. . . . Oh, she had been full of benevolent impulses ! But then Louise had been tiresome again . . . had stopped her and made a scene. . . . She hated scenes . . . at least (with a laugh) scenes that were not of her own devising. . . .

She supposed she should have recognized that the child was

overwrought—terribly overwrought by the emotions aroused
by such an interpretation as she had insisted upon giving. . . .
She ought never to have been allowed to play it like that. . . .
That was Alwynne's doing. . . . Alwynne had persuaded Clare
to leave Louise to her own devices. . . . Alwynne was so
headstrong. . . . She hoped that Alwynne would never need
to realize how much she was to blame. . . .

Here she became aware that her conscience was convulsed
with cynical laughter. She flushed in the darkness, her opportune
sense of injury increasing.

Alwynne might well be distressed. . . . If any awkward
questions should be asked, Alwynne might find herself uncomfortably placed. . . . People would wonder that she had not
noticed how unbalanced Louise was growing. . . . Every one
knew how intimate, how ridiculously intimate, she and Louise
had become. . . . Alwynne had fussed over her like an old
hen . . . had even on occasion questioned her, Clare's, method
with her. . . . She must have known what was in Louise's
mind. . . . Yet Clare had no doubt that people would be only
too ready to accuse her, rather than Alwynne, of criminal obtuseness. . . . Henrietta Vigers, for instance. . . . Henrietta would
be less prejudiced than many others, though. . . . She was no
friend to Alwynne. . . . It might do no harm to talk over the
matter with Henrietta Vigers. . . . A word or two would be
enough. . . .

Of course it would be considered an accident. . . . But if
by any chance, vague suspicions were rife, a judicious talk
with Henrietta would have served, at least, to prevent Clare
from being made their object. . . . She had her enemies, she
knew. . . . Alwynne, with her easy popularity, had none save
Henrietta. . . . A few waspish remarks from Henrietta would
not hurt Alwynne. . . . Clare would protect Alwynne from
serious annoyance, of course. . . . If the mistresses—the
school—oh, if the whole world turned against Alwynne, Clare
would make it up to her. . . . What did Alwynne want, after
all, with any one but Clare ? The less the world gave Alwynne,
the more she would be content with Clare, the more entirely
she would be Clare's own property. . . . It was a good idea. . . .
She would certainly speak to Miss Vigers. . . .

She was outlining that conversation till she fell asleep.

CHAPTER XXV

On the following afternoon Clare and Henrietta were sitting together in the mistresses' room. The afternoon classes were over and the day pupils and mistresses had gone home. The boarders were at supper and the staff with them.

But Henrietta had taken no notice of the supper-hour. She had more work in hand than she could well compass—letters to write and answer, of explanation, and enquiry, and condolence. She could have found time for her supper, nevertheless, but when she was overworked she liked her world to be aware of it. Clare, contrary to her custom, had stayed late. She was waiting for Alwynne. She had offered, perfunctorily enough, her assistance, but Henrietta had refused all help from her. Yet Henrietta had turned over the bulk of her formal correspondence to Alwynne, who sat, hard at work, in the adjacent office. She disliked Alwynne, but accepted the very necessary help from her more easily than from Clare Hartill. Yet she was softened by Clare's offer, which she had refused, and not at all grateful for Alwynne's help, though she accepted it.

She wrote busily for more than an hour, and Clare, silent, scarcely moving, sat watching her. Henrietta had, for once, no feeling of impatience at her idle supervision. She did not experience her usual sensation of intimidated antagonism. It was as if the stress of the last twenty-four hours had temporarily atoned the two incongruous characters. Neither by look or gesture had Clare flouted any suggestion or arrangement of Henrietta's—indeed, her presence had been quite distinctly a support. Henrietta had appealed more than once, and even confidently, to her. Henrietta had thought, with a touch of compunction, how strangely trouble brought out the best in people. Miss Hartill had been very proud of Louise Denny; evidently felt her death. The shock was causing her to unbend. Not, as one would have expected, to Alwynne Durand—she hoped, by the way, that Miss Durand was addressing those

envelopes legibly : she did so dislike an explosive handwriting—
no, Miss Hartill was turning, very properly, to herself in the
emergency. . . . She was pleased. . . . There should be free-
masonry between the heads of the school. . . . And Clare
Hartill, for all her lazy indifference, was influential and enormously capable. . . . Henrietta wondered if it would be safe
to consult her. . . . She might, without acknowledging a definite
uneasiness, find out cautiously whether it had occurred to Miss
Hartill that she, Henrietta, might be considered to have been
negligent.

She glanced across at her inscrutable colleague. Clare was
staring thoughtfully at her. Her lips were puffed a little,
as if in doubt.

Their eyes met for a moment in a glance that was almost
one of understanding.

Henrietta hesitated, for the first time not at all disconcerted
by Clare's direct gaze. But the sparkle of gay malice that
attracted half her world, and disconcerted the other half, was
gone from Clare's eyes. Their expression, for the time being,
was calm, possibly friendly ; at any rate, irreproachably matter-
of-fact.

Henrietta flung down her pen with a sigh of fatigue, and
bent and unbent her cramped fingers. But it was not fatigue
that made her stop work. She wanted to talk to Clare Hartill,
and had a queer conviction that Clare Hartill wanted to talk
to her.

" Finished ? " Clare spoke from the shadow of her deep
chair. Her back was to the light, but Henrietta faced the
west window. The evening sun laid bare her face for Clare's
inspection. Not a flicker of expression could escape her, if
she chose to look.

" More or less. I want half-an-hour's rest."

" I don't wonder. You've had everything to see to." Clare's
voice was delicately sympathetic.

Henrietta unbent.

" A secretary's work isn't showy, Miss Hartill, but it's necessary : and any happening that's out of the common doubles it.
The correspondence over this unhappy affair alone——"

" I know. Of course, at Miss Marsham's age——"

" It all falls on me ! People don't realize that. The extra
work is enormous. Miss Marsham depends on me so entirely,
of course."

" Yes, yes," murmured Clare appreciatively.

Henrietta played with her papers.

" I feel the responsibility very strongly," she said abruptly; but her tone was confidential.

Clare nodded.

" Yet, of course—as far as nominal responsibility goes—I am not the head of the school. I cannot be held responsible—any oversight——"

Clare nodded.

" Oh, Miss Vigers—you merely carry out instructions, like the rest of us "—she hesitated imperceptibly—" officially," she added slowly.

Henrietta looked relieved.

" I am so glad you see what I mean."

" Oh, I do, entirely," Clare assured her grimly.

" I'm not heartless," said Henrietta suddenly, flushing. Her tone justified herself against unuttered criticism. " And the poor child's death was as much a shock to me as to any one. But I was not fond of her—as you were, for instance——"

Clare's pose never altered.

" I was very proud of her," she said gently. " I thought her an exceptional child. But, as Miss Durand said to me only a few days ago—I didn't really know her : not, at least, as she did. Alwynne, I know, thinks we. have lost a genius. But you're right—it was a shock to me—a terrible shock."

" It was that to everybody, naturally. But in a way it's curious," said Henrietta meditatively, " how much we all feel it—how oppressively, at least : for I don't think any one was very fond of Louise."

" Oh, Miss Durand was deeply attached to her," Clare protested, her beautiful voice low with emotion.

" Yes, of course ! Oh, I've noticed that." Clare's unusual accessibility made Henrietta anxious to agree. Also, though she had noticed nothing unusual, she did not wish to appear lacking in penetration. She recalled Alwynne's haggard face; recollected how much she had had to do with the child; and decided that Clare was probably right.

" But except for her," she went on, " and your interest in her——"

" I've never had such a pupil," said Clare calmly. " Industrious—original—oh, I shall miss her, I know. But you're right—she was not popular——"

" Yet everybody feels her death—among ourselves, I mean—
to an extraordinary degree. After all—an accident is only an
accident, however dreadful! But there's a sort of oppression
on us—a kind of fear. Do you know what I mean? I think
we all feel it. It draws us together in a curious way."

" *The Tie of Common Funk*," rapped out Clare, forgetting
her rôle.

Henrietta stiffened.

" I don't think it is an occasion for slang," she said. " The
child's not buried yet."

Clare bit back a flippancy.

" I thought you would realize," continued Henrietta severely,
" that the situation is trying for us all——"

" Of course I do." Clare hastened to soothe her. " But
seriously, Miss Vigers, I do not think you need be anxious.
The inquest—oh, a painful ordeal, if you like. But you, at
least, can have no reason to reproach yourself."

Henrietta relaxed again.

" No! As I say, I'm not the head of the school. I'm not
responsible for regulations—only for carrying them out. And
accidents will happen."

" I only hope," said Clare, as if to herself, " that it will be
considered an accident——"

Henrietta stared.

" But Miss Hartill! Of course it was an accident! "

Clare looked at her wistfully.

" Yes! It was, wasn't it? Yes, of course! It must have
been an accident." Her tone dismissed the matter.

But Henrietta was on the alert. Her own anxieties had been
skilfully allayed. Her mind was recovering poise. She nosed
a mystery and her reviving sense of importance insisted on
sharing the knowledge of it.

" Miss Hartill—you are not suggesting——? " Her tone
invited confidence.

Clare gave a little natural laugh.

" Oh, my dear woman—I'm all nerves just at present. Of
course I'm not suggesting anything. One gets absurd ideas
into one's head. I'm only too relieved to hear you laugh at
me. Your common sense is always a real support to me, you
know. I've grown to depend on it all these years. I'm afraid
I've got into the way of taking it too much for granted."

She gave a charming little deprecatory shrug.

Henrietta flushed: she felt herself warming unaccountably to Clare Hartill. She wondered why she had never before taken the trouble to draw her out. . . . She was evidently a woman of heart as well as brain. She felt vaguely that she must constantly have been unjust to her. But these sensations only whetted her eager curiosity. She pulled in her chair to the hearth.

"But what ideas, Miss Hartill? If you will tell me—I should be the last person to laugh. I have far too much respect for—I wish you would tell me what is worrying you. Does anything make you think it was not an accident?"

Clare was the picture of reluctance.

"Impressions—vague ideas—is it fair to formulate them? Even if Louise were unbalanced—but, of course, I did not see much of her out of class. I confess I thought her manner strained at times. But I teach. I have nothing to do with the supervision of the younger children."

"That is Miss Durand's business," remarked Henrietta crisply.

"Oh, but if she had noticed anything——" began Clare. Then, lamely, "Obviously she didn't——"

"It was her business to. She should have reported to me. Why, she coached Louise, didn't she?"

"Of course, if Louise had really overworked—badly——" reflected Clare, with the distressed air of one on whom unwelcome ideas are dawning. "One hears of cases—in Germany—but it's impossible!"

Henrietta looked genuinely shocked, but none the less she was excited.

"She failed in that exam.——" she adduced.

"Yes! Miss Durand coached her for that, you know. Poor Miss Durand! How she slaved over her! She was dreadfully disappointed," said Clare indulgently.

"Of course, she let her overdo herself!" cried Henrietta triumphantly. "But you coached her too—didn't you notice either?"

"I coach the whole class. You know how busy I am. I'm afraid I left Louise a good deal to Alwynne," said Clare regretfully.

"But she's supposed to be grown up—an asset to the school, according to Miss Marsham," said Henrietta tartly. "But, I must say, if she couldn't see that the child was doing too much, she's not fit to teach——"

" Oh, my dear ! " cried Clare, distressed. " You mustn't say such things. You've no idea how conscientious Alwynne is. She may have worked Louise too hard—but with the best intentions. She would be heartbroken if you suggested it."

" Oh, you are always very lenient to Miss Durand," began Henrietta, with a touch of jealousy.

" Ah ! She's so young ! So full of the zeal of youth. Besides, I'm very fond of her." Clare's smile took Henrietta into her confidence—confessed to an amiable weakness.

Henrietta brooded.

" Oh, Miss Hartill, you talk of my common sense. I wish— I wish you could see Miss Durand from my point of view for a moment." She eyed Clare, attentive and plastic in her shadows, and took courage. " This—appalling—probability——"

" Possibility——" Clare deprecated.

" Oh, but it seems terribly probable to me—only carries on my idea of Miss Durand. She is so ignorant—so inexperienced— so undisciplined—she cannot possibly have a good influence on young children——"

" She is my friend ! " Clare reminded her, with gentle dignity.

" And if your suspicions are correct—if Louise's death were not accidental—if it had anything to do with her state of mind— if it were the effect of overwork—I consider—I must consider Miss Durand in some measure reponsible. I feel that Miss Marsham should be told."

Clare shook her head. Her solemn, candid eyes abashed Henrietta.

" Miss Vigers—we are speaking in confidence. I should never forgive myself if anything I've said to you were repeated."

" Of course, of course ! " Henrietta appeased her hastily. " But I've had my own suspicions—oh, for a long time, I assure you. I've not been blind. And I might feel it my duty—on my account, you understand—after all Miss Marsham depends on me implicitly—to speak to her—for the sake of the school——"

Clare considered.

" That, of course—I can't prevent. But Miss Vigers—forgive me—but—don't let your sense of responsibility make you unfair. And for heaven's sake, don't let my vague uneasiness— it's really nothing more—affect your judgment. We may both be utterly mistaken. I am sure the result of the inquest will prove us mistaken after all—it will be found to have been an accident."

Henrietta closed her lips obstinately.

Clare rose in her place.

"It was an accident!" she cried passionately. "In my heart I am sure. I wish I'd never said anything to you. I'd no right to be suspicious. Think of what Miss Durand's feelings would be if she realized——" She flung out her hands appealingly. "Oh, we're two overwrought women, aren't we? Sitting in the dusk and scaring ourselves with bogies. It was an accident, Miss Vigers—a tragic accident! Make yourself think so! Make me think so too!" Her beautiful eyes implored comfort.

Henrietta, quite touched, patted her awkwardly on the arm. She enjoyed her transient superiority.

"Of course, of course, we'll try to think so. Now you must go home. You are quite overwrought. It will be a trying day for us all to-morrow. I shall go to bed early too. Won't you go home now?"

Clare nodded, mute, grateful. She went to her peg, and took down her hat and jacket.

"Have you finished with Miss Durand? She was going home with me."

"Oh! Miss Durand!" Henrietta's tone grew crisper. "Yes, of course. I'll see if she has done. I'll send her to you. And you mustn't let yourself worry, Miss Hartill. Leave it all to me. These things are more my province. Good-night!" said Henrietta cordially.

She left the room.

Clare, pinning on her hat, stared critically at herself in the inadequate mirror.

"I think," she said confidentially, "we did that rather well." She smiled. The cynical lips smiled back at her.

"You beast!" cried Clare, with sudden passion. "You beast! You beast!"

She was still staring at herself when Alwynne came for her.

CHAPTER XXVI

CLARE HARTILL'S precautions proved to be unnecessary as the alarms of her colleagues. The inquest was a formal and quickly concluded affair, and the only corollary to the verdict of accidental death was an expression of sympathy with all concerned.

Whereon, there being no further cause for the detaining of Louise Denny above ground, she was elegantly and expeditiously buried.

The whole school attended the funeral. The flowers required a second carriage, and for the first time in his life, Mr. Denny was genuinely proud of his daughter. He did not believe that his own death could have extracted more lavish tributes from the purses of his acquaintances.

Clare Hartill, writing a card for her wreath of incredible orchids, did not regret her extravagance. After all—one must keep up one's position. . . . There would certainly not be such another wreath in the churchyard. . . . How Louise would have exclaimed over it ! Poor child. . . . It was all one could do for her now. Clare hesitated, pen arrested—' With deepest sympathy.' It was not necessary to write anything more. . . . Her name was printed already. . . . But Louise would have liked a message. . . . After all, she had been very proud of Louise. . . .

She reversed the card, and wrote, almost illegibly, in a corner, ' Louise—with love. C. H.' She paused, lips pursed. Sentimental, perhaps ? Possibly. . . . But let it go. . . .

Hastily she impaled her card on its attendant pin, and thrust it, print upward, among the flowers. The message was for Louise; no one else need see it.

Alwynne, too, sent flowers. But as usual she had spent all but a fraction of her salary. Seven and sixpence does not make a show, even if the garland be home-made. The shabby wreath was forgotten among the crowd of hot-house blooms. It lay in a corner till the day after the funeral. Then the housemaid threw it away.

So Louise had no message from Alwynne.

By the end of a fortnight Louise was barely a memory in the school. A month had obliterated her entirely.

Yet her short career and sudden death had its influence on school and individual alike. Miss Marsham had had her lesson; she began to make her preliminary preparations for giving up her head mistress-ship, and selling her interest in the school; though it was the following spring before she began to negotiate definitely with Clare, on whom her choice had finally fallen. She would not be hurried; she would not appear anxious to settle her affairs; but she had determined, between regret and relief, that the next summer should be the last of her reign.

Henrietta, though her anxieties were abated by the turn affairs had taken, was still doubtful whether Miss Marsham were as blindly reliant upon her as usual. But, though feeling her position still somewhat insecure, her spirits had risen, and her natural love of interference had risen with them. She could not forget her conversation with Miss Hartill : an amazing conversation—a conversation teeming with suggestions and possibilities. . . . Of course, Miss Hartill had had no idea, poor distracted woman, of how skilfully Henrietta had drawn her out. . . . Henrietta felt pleased with herself. Without once referring to Miss Hartill, she could follow out her own plans as far as Miss Durand was concerned. . . . Later, Miss Hartill might remember that apparently innocent conversation and realize that Henrietta had stolen a march on her. . . . Yet, though she might be loyally angry, for her friend's sake, she could not do anything to cross Henrietta's arrangements . . . could not wish to do anything, because essentially, if reluctantly, she had approved them, had recognized that it was time to curtail Miss Durand's activities. . . .

Henrietta felt virtuous. Miss Durand had brought it on herself. . . . She wished her no harm. . . . But it was right that Miss Marsham should realize how far she was from an ideal school-mistress. . . . She had been engaged as scholastic maid-of-all-work. . . . Yet in a few terms she had become second only to Miss Hartill herself. . . . It was not fit. . . . Let her go back to her beginnings. . . . She, Henrietta, had only to open Miss Marsham's eyes. . . . But to that end there must be evidence. . . .

For the rest of the term, patient and peering as a rag-picker,
she went about collecting her evidence.

Clare did not give another thought to her conversation with
the gimlet-eyed secretary. It had served its purpose—had
been a barrier between herself and the possibility of attack—
had given her a feeling of security. She perceived, nevertheless,
that her transient affability had made Henrietta violently her
adherent. Clare was resigned to knowing that the change of
face would be temporary—she could not allow a parading of
herself as an intimate, and thither, she shrewdly suspected,
would Henrietta's amenities lead. But she found it amusing
to be gracious, as long as no more was expected of her. She
did not like Henrietta one whit the better; felt herself, indeed,
degraded by the expedient to which she had resorted, and
fiercely despised her tool. Henrietta should be given rope,
might attack Alwynne unhindered, nevertheless she should hang
herself at the last. . . . Clare would ensure that. . . . Once—
Henrietta had called her a cat. . . . Oh, she had heard of it!
Well—for the present, she would purr to Henrietta, blank-eyed,
claws sheathed. . . . Let her serve her turn.

But Clare, beneath her schemes and jealousies, was, nevertheless, deeply and sincerely unhappy. The removal of the
entirely selfish and cold-blooded panic that had been upon
her since Louise's death, left her free to entertain deeper and
sincerer feelings. She thought of Louise incessantly, with a
growing feeling of regret and responsibility. She hated responsibility, though she loved authority—she had always shut her
eyes to the effects of her caprices. But the more she thought
of Louise, the more insistent grew her qualms. That the child
was dead of its own will, she never doubted; but she fought
desperately against the suggestion that her own conduct could
have affected its state of mind, was ready to accept the most
preposterous premise, whose ensuing chain of reasoning could
acquit her. But nobody having accused her, no ingenuity of
herself or another, could, for the time being, acquit her. She
was merely a prey to her own intangible uneasinesses. Yet it
needed but a key to set the whole machinery of her conscience
in motion against her. The key was to be found.

The term was drawing to an end, and Alwynne, rounding
off her special classes and generally making up arrears, was
proportionately busy. She still spent her week-ends with
Clare, but she brought her work along with her. She had

her corner of the table, and Clare her desk, and the two would work till the small hours.

But by the last Sunday evening, Clare's piles of reports and examination papers had disappeared, and she was free to lie at ease on her sofa, and to laugh at Alwynne, still immersed in exercise books, and tantalize her with airy plans for the long, delicious holidays. It had been, in spite of the season, a day of rain and cold winds. The skies had cleared at the sunset, with its red promise of fine weather once more, but the remnant of a fire still smouldered on the hearth. Alwynne was flushed with the interest of her work, but ever and again Clare shivered, and pulled the quilted sofa-wrap more closely about her. She wished that Alwynne would be quick. . . . Surely Alwynne could finish off her work some other time. . . . It wouldn't hurt her to get up early for once, for that matter. . . . She was bored . . . She was dull. . . . She wanted amusement. . . . She wanted Alwynne, and attention, and affection, and a little butterfly kiss or two. . . . Alwynne ought to be awake to the fact that she was wanted. . . .

She watched her, between fretfulness and affection, æsthetically appreciative of the big young body in the lavender frock, and the crown of shining hair, pleased with her property, intensely impatient of its interest in anything but herself.

" Alwynne——? " There was a hint of neglect in her voice. Alwynne beamed, but her eyes were abstracted.

" Only another half-hour, Clare. I must just finish these. You don't mind, do you ? "

" I ? Mind ? " Clare laughed elaborately. She picked up a book, and there was silence once more.

Leaves fluttered and a pen scraped. The light began to fade. Suddenly Alwynne gave a smothered exclamation. Clare looked up and pulled herself upright, angry enough.

" Alwynne ! Your carelessness—you've dropped your wet pen on my carpet. It's too bad."

Alwynne groped hastily beneath the table. But even the prolonged stooping had not brought back the colour to her cheek, as she replaced her pen on the stand.

" I'm sorry. I was startled. It hasn't marked it. Clare— just listen to this."

" What have you got hold of ? " demanded Clare irritably. She disliked spots and spillings and mess, as Alwynne might know.

"It's Louise's composition book. I always wondered where it had got to, when I cleared out her desk. It must have lain about and got collected in with the rest, yesterday."

"Well?" said Clare, with a show of indifference.

"Here's that essay on King John and his times. Do you remember? You gave it to them to do just before the play. It's not corrected. Not finished." She hesitated. "Clare! It's rather queer."

"Is it any good?" said Clare meditatively.

"What for?"

"The School Magazine. We're short of copy. The child wrote well. But I suppose it wouldn't do to use it—though I don't see why not."

Suddenly Alwynne began to read aloud.

"*Another way by which King John got money from the Jews was by threatening them with torture. He was all-powerful. He could draw their teeth, tooth by tooth, twist their thumbs, or leave them to rot in dark, silent prisons. They could not do anything against him. If he could not force them to yield up their treasure he would have them burned, or cause them to be pressed to death. This is a horrible torture. I read about a woman who was killed in this way in the 'Hundred Best Books'; and there was a man in Good King Charles's days whom they killed like this. It is the worst death of any. They tie you down, so that you cannot move at all, and there is a slab of stone that hangs a little above you. This sinks very slowly, so that all the first day you just lie and stare at it and wonder if it really moves. People come and give you food and laugh at you. You are scarcely afraid, because it moves so little and you think nobody could be really so cruel and hurt you so horribly, and that you will be saved somehow. But all the time the stone is sinking — sinking — and the day goes by and the night comes and they leave you alone. And perhaps you go to sleep at last. You are horribly tired, because of the weeks of fear that are behind you. Perhaps you dream. You dream you are free and people love you, and you have done nothing wrong and you are frightfully happy, and the one you love most kisses your forehead. But then the kiss grows so cold that you shrink away, only you cannot, and it presses you harder and harder, and you wake up and it is the stone. It is the sinking stone that is pressing you, pressing you, pressing you to death — and you cannot move. And you shriek and*

*shriek for help within your gagged mouth, and no one comes,
and always the stone is pressing you, pressing you, pressing
you——*"

Clare caught the exercise-book from Alwynne's hand and
thrust it into the heart of the half-dead fire. It lay unlighted,
charring and smouldering. The unformed handwriting stood
out very clearly. Clare caught at a matchbox, and tore it
open; the matches showered out over her hand on to the rug
and grate. She struck one after another, breaking them before
they could light. Silently Alwynne took the box from her
shaking fingers, lit a match and held it to the twisting papers.
A thin little flame flickered up, overran them eagerly, wavered a
second, and died with a faint whistling sigh.

"Do you hear that? Did you see that?" Clare knelt
upright on the hearth. She held up her forefinger. "Listen!
Like a voice! Like a child's voice! A child sighing! Light
the candles—light all the candles! I want light everywhere.
No room for any shadow."

But as Alwynne moved obediently, she caught at her hand.

"Alwynne! Stay with me! Don't go into another room.
Alwynne, I'm frightened of my thoughts."

Alwynne put her hand shyly on her shoulders, talking at
random.

"Clare, dear, do get up. Come on to the sofa. You mustn't
kneel there. You'll strain yourself. I always get tired kneeling
in church. It makes one's heart ache."

Clare would not move.

"Don't you think my heart aches?" she said. "Don't you
think it aches all day? You're young—you're cold—you can
sit there reading, reading—with a ghost at your shoulder——"

An undecipherable expression flashed across Alwynne's face.
It came but to go—and Clare, absorbed in her own passion,
saw nothing.

"It's Louise!" she cried, between sincerity and histrionics.
"Calling to some one. Calling from her grave. They call it
an accident, like fools. Oh, can't you hear? She died because
she was forced. She's complaining—plaining—plaining—— I
tell you it's nothing to do with me. It wasn't my fault!"

She flung her arms about Alwynne's waist and clutched her
convulsively. She was sincere enough at last.

"Alwynne! Alwynne! Say it was not my fault."

Alwynne sank to her knees beside her and held her close.

They clung to each other like scared children. But Clare's abandonment awoke all Alwynne's protective instincts. She crushed down whatever emotions had hollowed her eyes and whitened her cheeks in the last long weeks, and addressed herself to quieting Clare. Clare, stepped off her pedestal, unpoised, clinging helplessly, was a new experience. In the face of it she felt herself childish, inadequate. But Clare was in trouble and needed her. The very marvel of it steadied. All her love for Clare rose within her, overflowed her, like a warm tide.

By sheer strength she pulled Clare into a chair and dropped on to the floor beside her, face upturned, talking fast and eagerly.

"You're not to talk like that. Of course it's not your fault. As if anything could be your fault. Clare, darling, don't look like that. You must lean back and rest. You're just tired, you know. We've talked of it so often. You know it was an accident. Why can't you believe it, if every one else does?"

"Do you?" said Clare intently.

Alwynne's eyes met hers defiantly.

"I do. Of course I do. It's wicked to torment yourself. But if I didn't—if the poor baby was overtired and overworked —is it your fault? You only saw her in class at the last. You couldn't help it if the exams. and the play were suddenly too much—if something snapped——"

"You see, you do think so," said Clare bitterly. "I've always known you did. Well—think what you like—what do I care?" She put up her clenched hands and rubbed and kneaded at her dry aching eyes.

Alwynne watched her, desperately. Here was her lady wanting comfort, and she had found none. She wracked her brains as the sluggish minutes passed.

Clare's hands dropped at last. She met Alwynne's anxious gaze and laughed harshly.

"Well? The verdict? That I was a brute to Louise, I suppose?"

Alwynne looked at her wistfully.

"Clare, I do love you so."

Clare stiffened.

"Then I warn you—stop! I'm not good for you. I hurt people who love me. You always pestered me about hurting Louise. You needn't protest. You always did. And now you lay her death at my door. I see it in your face. Can't I read you like a book? Can't I? Can't I?" Her face was distorted by the conflict within her.

Alwynne's simplicity was convinced. Here, she felt, was tragedy. Awe and pity tore at her sense of reality. Love loosened her tongue. Her words rushed forth in a torrent of incoherent argument. She was so eager that her fallacies had power to convince herself, much more Clare.

"Clare, I won't have it. You don't know what you say. What is this mad idea you've got? What would poor Louise think if she heard? Why, she adored you. And you were kind—always kind—only when you thought it better for her, you were strict. It's folly to torment yourself. If you do—what about me?"

"You?" Clare's eyes glinted suddenly.

"Me! If you are to blame, how much more I? Oh, don't you see?" Alwynne's face grew rapt. Here was inspiration; her path grew suddenly clear. "Clare, don't you see? If she did—" she paused imperceptibly—"I ought to have seen what was coming. I knew her so much better than you."

Clare repressed a denial.

"Oh, darling—you mustn't worry. It's my responsibility. Try and think—at the play, for instance. Did you think her manner strained? No, of course you didn't. But I did. I thought at the time it had all been too much for her. I did notice—I did! I thought—that child will get brain-fever if we're not careful—— I meant to speak to Elsbeth. I meant to speak to you. Oh, I'd noticed before. Only I was busy, and lazy, and put it off. She was unhappy at failing—I knew. I wanted to tell you that I knew how much it meant to her—and I didn't. I was afraid——" She broke off abruptly; her eloquence ended as suddenly as it had begun.

But she had succeeded in her desire. Clare was recovering poise; would soon have herself all the more rigidly in control for her recent collapse. She stiffened as she spoke.

"Afraid of whom?"

"I mean I was afraid all along of what might happen," Alwynne concluded lamely. "You see, it was my fault?" There was an odd half-query in her voice.

"If you noticed so much and never tried to warn me, you are certainly to blame." Clare's voice was full of reluctant conviction. "I can't remember that you tried very hard."

" Oh, Clare ! " began Alwynne. Their eyes met. Clare's face was hard and impassive—all trace of emotion gone. Her eyes challenged. Alwynne's lids dropped as she finished her sentence. " That is—no, I didn't try very hard."

" And why not ? "

Inconceivably an answer suggested itself to Alwynne, an unutterable iconoclasm. Her mind edged away from it horrified and in an instant it was not. But it had been.

" I don't know," she stammered.

" You realized the responsibility you incurred ? " Clare went on.

" I didn't. No, never ! " Alwynne supplicated her.

" You do now ? "

" Oh, yes," she said despairingly. She rejoiced that Clare could believe and be comforted, but it hurt her that she believed so easily. It alarmed her, too, made her, knowing her own motives, yet doubt herself. She felt trapped.

" I'm sorry you told me," said Clare abruptly.

They sat a moment in silence. A ray from the dying sun illuminated their faces. In Alwynne an innocent air of triumph fought with distress, and a growing uneasiness. Clare was expressionless.

Clare put up her hand to shelter herself, and her face was scarcely visible as she went on. She spoke softly.

" My dear, I can't say I'm not relieved. I feel exonerated—completely. Yet I wish you hadn't told me. I'd have rather thought it my fault than known it——"

" Mine," said Alwynne huskily.

Clare bent towards her, tender, gracious, yet subtly aloof : confessor, not friend.

" Oh, Alwynne ! Why will you always be so sure of yourself ? Why not have come to me for advice as you used to ? What are we elder folk for ? I love your impetuosity—your self-reliance—and I believe, I shall always believe, that you wanted to spare me trouble and worry. I know you. But you're not old enough, Alwynne, to decide everything for yourself. You wouldn't believe it, I suppose—oh, I was just the same. But doesn't all this dreadful business show you ? A few words—and Louise might have been with us now. Of course you acted for the best, but—— There, my dear, there, there——" for her beautiful, pitiful voice had played too exquisitely on Alwynne's nerves, and the girl was sobbing helplessly.

And Clare was very kind to Alwynne, and let her cry in peace. And when she was tired of watching her, she braced her with deft praises of courage and self-control. Self-control appealed very strongly to Clare, Alwynne knew. While she dried her eyes, Clare whispered to her that the past was past and that one couldn't repair one's mistakes by dwelling on them. Let devotion to the living blot out a debt to the dead. She must try and forget. Clare would help her. Clare would try to forget too. They would never speak of it again. Never by word or look would Clare refer to it. It should be blotted out and forgotten.

And after a discreet interval, when there was no chance of big, irrepressible tears dropping into the gravy, or salting the butter, Clare thought she would like her supper.

She made quite a hearty meal, and Alwynne crumbled bread and drank thirstily, and watched her with humble, adoring eyes.

Clare, in soft undertones, was delicately amusing, full of dainty quips that coaxed Alwynne gently back to smiles and naturalness. She spared no pains, and sent Alwynne home at last, with, metaphorically speaking, her blessing.

But Alwynne stooped as she walked, as though she carried a burden.

CHAPTER XXVII

THE summer holidays came and went, eight cloudless weeks of them. Clare loved the sun; was well content to be out, day after day, cushioned and replete, on the sunniest strip of sand in the sunniest corner of a parched and gasping England. She found it wonderfully soothing to listen with shut eyes to the purr of the sea and the distant cries of gulls and children, with Alwynne to fan her and shade her, and clamber up and down two hundred feet of red cliff for her when the corkscrew was forgotten, or the salt, or Clare's bathing-dress, or a half-read magazine. Clare grew brown and plump as the drowsy days went by. Alwynne grew brown, too, but she certainly did not grow plumper. But then the heat never suited Alwynne. She had often said so, as she reminded Elsbeth. For, when Alwynne came back to her for the three weeks at home that she had persuaded Clare were due to Elsbeth, Elsbeth was difficult to satisfy. Elsbeth was inclined to be indignant. What sort of a holiday had it been, if Alwynne could come back so thin, and tired, and colourless under her tan ? What had Miss Hartill been about to allow it ?

But Alwynne's account of their pleasant lazy days was certainly appeasing. . . . It must have been the heat. . . . Not even the most suspicious of aunts could conscientiously suspect Clare of having anything to do with it. . . . Wait till September came, with its cooling skies. . . . Alwynne would be better then.

In the meantime Elsbeth tried what care and cookery and coddling could do, and Alwynne submitted more patiently than usual.

Alwynne, indeed, was unusually gentle with Elsbeth in the three weeks they spent together before the autumn term began. She was always good to Elsbeth, considerate of her bodily comforts, lovingly demonstrative. But Clare had taught Alwynne very carefully that she was growing up at last, becoming financially and morally independent, free to lead her own life, that if she stayed with Elsbeth it was by favour, not by duty. And Alwynne, immensely flattered by the picture of herself as a woman of the world, had lived up to it with her usual drastic enthusiasm. Elsbeth, not unused to disillusionment and hopes deferred, could sigh and smile and acquiesce, knowing it for the phase that it was and forgiving Alwynne in advance. But Clare, who owed her neither gratitude nor duty, she never forgave. She was a very human woman, for all her saintliness.

She got her reward that summer, when Alwynne came back, quieted, grave, very tender with Elsbeth, clinging to her sometimes as if she were nearer nine than nineteen. But Elsbeth was fated never to have her happiness untainted. She was haunted by the conviction that Alwynne's subduement was not natural. Her pleasure in being with her aunt was so obvious that Elsbeth was worried, and knowing how infallibly Alwynne turned to her in any trouble, she expected revelations. But none came—only the manner was there that always accompanied them. Yet something was wrong. . . . A quarrel with Clare Hartill?

But Alwynne, delicately questioned, chattered happily enough of their holiday, and there were frequent letters—— She was over-anxious, too, to protest that she was perfectly well, and, in proof, exhausted herself in unnecessary housework. But she continued restless and abstracted, jumped absurdly at any sudden noise, and followed Elsbeth about like a homeless dog.

And she had contracted an odd habit of coming late at night into Elsbeth's room, trailing blankets and a pillow under her arm, to beg to sleep on Elsbeth's sofa—just this once! She would laugh at herself and pull Elsbeth's face down to her for a kiss, but she never gave any good reason for her whim. But she came so often that Elsbeth had a bed made up for her at last, and she slept there all the holidays, or lay awake. Elsbeth suspected that she lay awake two nights out of three.

With the autumn term Alwynne seemed to rouse herself, and flung herself into her work with her usual energy. Elsbeth saw less of her. The school claimed all her days, and Clare the bulk of her evenings. She had moved back into her own room again, and Elsbeth, her door ajar, would lie and watch the crack of light across the passage, and grieve over her darling's sleeplessness, and the shocking waste of electric light.

She wondered if the girl were working too hard. . . . Could that be at the root of the matter? She grew so anxious that she could even consult Clare on one of the latter's rare and formal calls.

"I am so glad to see you. Alwynne is changing; she'll be down in a minute. I made her lie down. Miss Hartill, I'm very distressed about the child. Do you think she looks well?"

Clare, less staccato than usual, certainly didn't think so.

"So thin—she's growing so dreadfully thin. Her neck! You should see her neck—salt-cellars, literally! And she had such a beautiful neck! But you've seen her in evening dress."

Yes, Clare had seen her.

"And so white and listless! I don't know what to make of her. I don't know what to do."

Clare, with unusual gentleness, would not advise Elsbeth to worry herself. Possibly Alwynne was doing a little too much. Clare would make enquiries. But she was sure that Elsbeth was over-anxious.

But Elsbeth was not to be comforted. She nodded to the open door.

"Look at her now—dragging across the hall."

But Alwynne, in her gay frock, cheeks, at sight of Clare, suddenly aflame, did not look as if there were much amiss. She was thinner, of course . . . .

Elsbeth, however, had made Clare uneasy. She attacked Alwynne on the following day.

"Your aunt says you're dying, Alwynne. What's the matter?"

"Dear old Elsbeth!" Alwynne laughed lightly.

"*Is* anything wrong?" Clare did not appear to look at her; nevertheless she did not miss the slight change in Alwynne's face, as she answered with careful cheeriness—

"What should be wrong in this best of all possible——"

Clare caught her up.

"I'm not a fool, Alwynne. What's the matter?"

"I wish you wouldn't discuss me with Elsbeth," said Alwynne uneasily. "I don't like it. I won't have you bothered."

"I'm not," said Clare coolly. "At the same time——"

Alwynne braced herself. She knew the tone.

"—I don't like any one about me with a secret grief and a pale, courageous smile. I can't stand a martyr."

"I'm not!" Alwynne was wincing. Then, suddenly:

"What has Elsbeth been saying? Honestly, I didn't know she'd noticed anything."

"What is the matter?" said Clare again, gently enough. "Tell me, silly child!"

Alwynne shrugged her shoulders.

"Nothing! Just life!"

Clare waited.

"I'm sorry if I've been horrid—" she paused—"to Elsbeth."

Clare opened her eyes.

"What about me?"

"I'm never horrid to you," said Alwynne with compunction. "That's what's so beastly of me."

"Well, upon my word!" cried Clare blankly.

"Oh, you know what I mean." Alwynne jumbled her words. "I always want to be nice to you. It's perfectly easy. And then I go home to Elsbeth, the darling, and am grumpy and snappy, and show her all the hateful side of me. Heaven knows why! Only yesterday she said, 'You wouldn't speak to Clare Hartill like that,' in her dear, hurt voice. I felt such a brute."

A little smile hovered at the corners of Clare's mouth.

"I was always so sorry," said Clare smoothly, "that you couldn't spend Christmas Day with me last year."

Alwynne wrinkled her forehead.

"What's that got to do——?"

Clare caught her up.

"With your secret griefs? Nothing whatever! You're quite right. But what are they, Alwynne? Who's been worrying you? Have you got too much to do?"

"It's not that," said Alwynne unwillingly.

"Then what?"

"Oh, things!"

"What things?"

"Miss Vigers, for one," Alwynne began. Then she burst out: "Clare, I don't know what I've done to her! She never leaves me alone."

Clare stiffened.

"Miss Vigers? What has she to say to you? You're responsible to me—after Miss Marsham."

"She doesn't seem to think so. It's nag, nag, nag—fuss, fuss, fuss. Are the girls working properly? Am I not neglecting this? Or overdoing that? Do I remember that Dolly Brown had measles three terms ago? Why is Winifred Hawkins allowed to sit with the light in her eyes? Do I make a habit of keeping So-and-so in? and if so, why so? And Miss Marsham doesn't approve of this, and Miss Marsham evidently doesn't know of that—and my manner is excessively independent—and will I kindly remember. . . ? Oh, Clare, it's simply awful. I get no peace. And you know how driven I am, with Miss Hutchins away. You'd think I'd done something awful from the way she treats me. Everlastingly spying and hinting——"

"Hinting what?" Clare's voice was icy.

"That's what I can't make out. That's the maddening part of it. Do you think I'm such a failure? Do you think I'm not to be trusted? I get on with the children—they work well! Truly, Clare, I don't know why she dislikes me so. You'd think she was trying to worry me into leaving."

"You should have told me before," said Clare curtly, and changed the subject so abruptly that Alwynne feared she was angry, and wished that she had held her tongue.

She was right. Clare was angry. Clare had conveniently forgotten her little conversation with Henrietta on that panic-stricken summer day : was naturally surprised and indignant to find it bearing the fruit she had intended it to bear. This was what came of confiding in people! And Henrietta, she had no doubt, would be prepared to give chapter and verse for her surveillance, if Clare should, directly or indirectly, call it in question. . . . Henrietta would appear to have Clare in a cleft stick : and Alwynne was to suffer in consequence. Clare (a great deal fonder of Alwynne than she, or Alwynne, or any one save Elsbeth, guessed) laughed to herself, once, softly, and her eyes snapped. Wait a while, Henrietta . . . wait a wee while !

Thoughtfully she approached the question of the counter-attack. That was inevitable, a sop to her own conscience. Besides, it would be amusing. . . . It was necessary, however, to decide upon the weapon.

It was a small matter—the refusal of a boarder for lack of space—that provided it. Quietly, she went to work.

For the first time, for her own departments had allowed her energy its outlet, she set herself to disentangle the lines on which the school was run. She found many knots. Half day, half boarding school, grown from a timid beginning into one of the most flourishing of its kind, it was, indeed, like the five hundred-year-old town in which it stood, a marvellous com-

pound of ancient custom and modern usage. The ' Seminary
for Young Ladies ' of the 'seventies was three parts obliterated
by the 'nineties' High School regimen, on which, in its turn,
was superimposed the cricket and hockey of the twentieth
century's effemination of the public-school system; the whole
swollen, patch-work concern held together by the personality
of its creator, and its own reputation.

Clare nodded. It was obvious to her, that with the retirement
of Miss Marsham, accomplished already in all save name, the
school would fall to pieces. A pity . . . it had a fine past . . .
was a valuable property still. . . . With a vigorous woman at
its head, judiciously iconoclastic, no stickler for tradition, it
should revive its youth. . . . She herself, for instance. . . . She
toyed with the idea.

Miss Marsham was looking out for a successor. . . . She herself had been sounded. . . . Should she ? She shook her head.
Life was very pleasant as it was. . . . She knew that she hated
responsibility as much as she liked power. . . . She sat on the
school's shoulders, at present. . . . As head mistress the school
would sit on hers. . . . No, thank you ! She had better uses
for her spare time. . . . There were books . . . idleness. . . .
Alwynne. . . . Imagine never having time to play with
Alwynne !

Nevertheless it would be fascinating to plan out the reorganiza-
tion of the school . . . . and carry it out, for that matter. She
could do it, she knew. She would get all pat and then have some
talks—some suggestive talks—with Miss Marsham. . . . She,
Clare, had some little influence. . . . And there was life in
the old warhorse yet. . . . Anything that she could be persuaded to believe would benefit her school would have her instant
sanction. . . . She would be nominally responsible, of course,
and would give Clare, nevertheless, a free hand. . . . And
Clare, sweeping clean, would sweep away whatever withstood
her. . . . Henrietta would have little energy left for Alwynne
when Clare had finished her spring-cleaning. . . .

For the next few weeks, Clare spent nearly all her spare time
at the school. She would stay to supper, and even, on occasion,
superintend ' lights out.' She would ask artless questions, and
the matron and the younger mistresses found her " so sympathetic when you really got her to yourself. So sensible, you
know—always sees what you mean."

Finally, Clare shut herself up for a Saturday and a Sunday

with a neat little notebook, and drew up plans and made some calculations. Then she went to see Miss Marsham. She went to see Miss Marsham several times.

The plan was certainly an excellent one. . . . Miss Marsham could not follow the details very well . . . but that, of course, would be dear Clare's affair. . . . A great saving . . . an immense improvement. . . . There would be changes, of course. . . . This idea of separate houses, for instance. . . . It would mean taking extra premises—but Clare was quite right, they were overcrowded—had had to turn away girls. . . . She quite agreed with Clare. . . . she had always preferred boarders herself; one had a freer hand. . . . With a mistress responsible for each house, though, what would there be left for Miss Vigers to do? . . . Yes—she might take over a house, of course. . . . But Miss Marsham paused uneasily. She anticipated trouble with Henrietta.

She was justified. Henrietta refused utterly to discuss the suggested alterations. Miss Marsham must excuse her; she had her position. . . . One house? after controlling the entire school's economy? She did not suggest that Miss Marsham could be serious—that was impossible . . . Miss Marsham was serious? Then there was no more to be said. . . .

She said a good deal, however, and at considerable length; ended, breathless, waspish, leaving her resignation in her principal's hands. Neither she nor Miss Marsham dreamed that it would be accepted.

But Clare Hartill, consulted by Miss Marsham, was puzzlingly relieved. Very delicately she congratulated her chief on being extricated from a difficult position; praised Miss Vigers's tact —or her sense of fitness. Unusual good sense. . . . People so seldom realized their limitations, unprompted. . . . poor Miss Vigers was certainly no longer young. . . . hardly the woman for a modern house-mistress-ship. . . . Old fashioned. . . . in these days of degrees and college-training so much more was expected. . . . and after that affair in the summer no doubt she had lost confidence in herself. . . . Clare was sure that Miss Vigers had appreciated Miss Marsham's forbearance, but of course, she must know, in her own heart, that if she had taken proper precautions—it was her business to arrange for a mistress to be on duty, wasn't it?—the accident could not have happened. Poor little Louise! Oh, and of course, poor Miss Vigers too! . . . Well, it was for the best, she supposed. . . . and Miss Vigers

seemed to feel that it was time for her to go. . . . Perhaps it
was. . . . But they would all be sorry to lose her. . . . Clare
really thought that she would like to get up a presentation
from the school. . . . Now what did Miss Marsham consider
appropriate ?

So Henrietta found herself taken at her word. She left,
passionately resentful, at the half-term; hoping, at least, to
embarrass her employer thereby. (But Clare Hartill knew of
such a nice suitable woman—Newnham.)

Henrietta Vigers was forty-seven when she left. She had
spent youth and prime at the school, and had nothing more to
sell. She had neither certificates nor recommendations behind
her. She was hampered by her aggressive gentility. Out of a
£50 salary she had scraped together £500. Invested daringly
it yielded her £25 a year. She had no friends outside the school.
She left none within it.

Miss Marsham presented her with a gold watch, decorously
inscribed; the school with a handsomely bound edition of
Shakespeare.

Heaven knows what became of her.

CHAPTER XXVIII

SAID Clare to Elsbeth at their next meeting—

"I found out what the trouble was. Henrietta Vigers has been slave-driving her. I should have guessed before, but you know how that sort of thing can go on in a school unnoticed."

"Oh, yes," said Elsbeth.

Clare shot a suspicious glance at her, but Elsbeth's face was impassive.

"But she'll be all right now. Miss Vigers is leaving us at half-term."

"So I hear."

Their eyes met. Clare flushed faintly.

"I couldn't have Alwynne bullied."

"I know exactly how you feel," said Elsbeth quietly. Then, with a direct glance, "Has Miss Vigers got another post?"

"I haven't enquired."

"You're a bad enemy," Elsbeth's tone was quaintly reflective, almost admiring.

"But a good friend, I hope?" Clare laughed.

"I hope so," said Elsbeth doubtfully, and Clare laughed again. It amused her to cross swords with Elsbeth. At times she felt, that had it not been for Alwynne—that bone of contention— she could have liked her.

"You can't be one without the other," she instructed her. "I don't pretend to be a saint. And you'll see how much better Alwynne will be next term."

But the spring term came, and Alwynne was no better. She flagged like a transplanted tree. She went about her business as usual, but even Clare, not too willing to acknowledge what interfered with her scheme of things, realized that her efficiency was laborious, that her high spirits were forced, her comicalities not spontaneous, that she was in fact, not herself, but merely an elaborate imitation.

But where Elsbeth grew anxious Clare grew irritated. She

spied a mystery. Some obscure, yet powerful instinct prevented her from probing it, but she was none the less piqued at being left in the dark. It annoyed her too, that Alwynne should be obviously and daily losing her health and good looks. Clare required above all vitality in her associates. It had been, in her eyes, one of Alwynne's most attractive characteristics. This changing Alwynne, whitened, quieted, submissive, the sparkle gone from her eyes and the snap from her tongue, was less to her taste. Alwynne, very conscious of her shortcomings and of Clare's irritation at them, grew daily more nervously propitiatory —ever a fatal attitude to Clare. It roused the petty tyrant in her. There were jarrings, misunderstandings, exhausting scenes and more exhausting reconciliations. Yet the two were always together. Clare, viciously adroit as she grew in those days in piercing the armour of Alwynne's peace, exacted nevertheless her incessant service. And never had Alwynne so strained every nerve to please her.

Elsbeth, guessing at the situation, could give thanks when influenza, sweeping over the school, claimed Alwynne as its earliest victim. Her turn had come. She nursed Alwynne through the attack, prolonged her convalescence, excluded all enquirers, censored messages and letters. When Alwynne grew better, and talked, restless yet unwilling, of fixing the date of her return, Elsbeth, lips firmly set, went out one afternoon to pay a call upon Miss Marsham, and returning, sat down to write a letter. She busied herself for the rest of that day and all the next over Alwynne's wardrobe, mending and pressing and freshening.

Alwynne protested.

" Elsbeth dear, do leave my things alone. I'll mend them some time—honestly. They're all right. I wish you wouldn't fuss."

But Elsbeth fussed placidly on.

In the evening came letters for them both. Alwynne read hers hurriedly.

" Elsbeth, it's from Clare ! She wants to know why I'm not coming back. What does she mean ? Of course I'm coming back. Mademoiselle Charette is already, and she was ill after I was ! "

Elsbeth sniffed.

" She was only in bed two days—Miss Marsham said so. You're not going back this term, Alwynne. I've seen Miss

Marsham myself. I told her what the doctor said. I've arranged things. She agrees with me—you're not fit to. It's only a month to end of term. They can manage. You've simply got to have a change. So I wrote to Dene—to the Lumsdens, and Alicia's answer has just come. They're delighted to have you. I knew they would be, of course. They have asked us so often. Such a nice letter. Such a lovely place. Now, my dear, be a sensible child and don't argue, because I've made up my mind. It'll do you good to get away."

For in Alwynne's face astonishment had been succeeded by indignation. Elsbeth prepared herself resignedly to face a storm of protest, if not a blank refusal. To be arranged for as if she were a child—unconsulted—Clare—the school—the coaching—leaving Elsbeth alone—Dene—utter strangers—perfectly well—simply ridiculous ! Elsbeth saw it all coming.

"My dear Elsbeth ! What a preposterous——" began Alwynne. Then the weakness of convalescence swamped her. She sank back in her chair.

"Perhaps it will," said Alwynne wearily. "All right, Elsbeth ! I'll go if you want me to. Anyway, I don't much care."

CHAPTER XXIX

A WEEK later Alwynne was sitting in a diminutive go-cart, drawn by a large pony, and driven by a large lady with a wide smile and bulgy knees, with which, as the little cart jolted over the stony road, she unconsciously nudged Alwynne, imparting an air of sly familiarity to her pleasant, formal talk. This, Alwynne supposed, was Alicia. She liked her, liked her fat kind face, her comfortable rotundity, and her sweet voice. She liked her cool disregard of her own comical appearance, wedged in among portmanteaux and Alwynne and a basket of market produce, with an old sun-hat tied bonnet-fashion to shade her eyes, and her scarf ends fluttering madly, as she thwacked and tugged at the iron-mouthed pony.

She was more than middle-aged, a woman of flopping draperies and haphazard hookings, and scatter-brained grey locks, that had been a fringe in the days of fringes. She moved, as Alwynne noticed later, like a hurried cow, and tripped continually over her long skirts. Yet, in spite of her ramshackle exterior, she was not ridiculous. The goodmen and stray children they encountered greeted her with obvious respect. Alwynne, comparing the keen eyes and their cheerful crowsfeet, with the chin, firm enough in its cushion of fat, guessed her the ruling spirit of the Dene household, and wondered why she had not married a vicar.

But Alicia, though Alwynne listened politely to her flow of talk, and answered prettily when she must, did not long occupy her attention.

She was in her own country again. She loved the country— woods, fields, hedges and lanes—as she loved no city or sea-town of them all. London, Paris, Rome—Swiss mountains or Italian lakes—she would have given them all for Kent and Hampshire and the Sussex Weald. But Clare would never hear of a country holiday. Alwynne took deep breaths of the clean, kindly air, and wondered to herself that she had taken the proposal of her

213

holiday so dully. She had not realized that she was going into
the country—she had not realized anything, except that she
was tired, and that Elsbeth would not leave her alone. She had
shrunk painfully from the idea of meeting strangers, from the
exertion of accommodating herself to them. But this good air
made one feel alive again. . . .

She stared over the pony's ears at the gay spring landscape.

" Those are the Dene fields," said Alicia, following her glance.
" There are two Denes, you know—Dene Village and Dene
Fields. There's a couple of miles between them. We are in the
hollow, where the road dips, at the foot of Witch Hill."

" Witch Hill ? "

Alicia flourished her whip at the sky-line. The fields were spread
over the hillside in sections of chocolate and magenta and silver-
green, with here and again a parti-coloured patch, where oats
and dandelions, pimpernel and sky-blue flax choked and strangled
on an ash-heap. From the slopes Witch Hill lifted a brow of
blank white chalk, crowned and draped in woodland, lying
against pillows of cloud, for all the world like a hag abed, knees
hunched, and patch-work quilt drawn up to ragged eyebrows.
Round her neck the road wound like a silver riband; looped,
dipped, disappeared, for two unfenced miles—to flash into view
but a parrot's flight away, and swerve, with a steep little rush,
round a house with French windows thatched in yellow jessamine.

Alwynne's eyes lit up.

" What a good name ! Who was she before she was turned
into that ? " She stopped, flushing. Alicia would think her
stupid.

Alicia laughed pleasantly.

" Do you like fairy tales ? You've come to the right place—
the country-side's full of them. There's a fairy fort—Roman
I suppose, really, and a haunted barn out beyond Dene Compton,
besides Witch Hill and the Witch Wood just behind our house.
There's a story, of course. I don't know it—you must ask
Roger. He's always picking up stories."

" Roger ? "

" My nephew, Roger Lumsden. Hasn't Elsbeth——? "

" Oh yes, of course."

" He's away just now. Look, now you can see the house
properly."

" Behind the hill ? " Alwynne had caught sight of a group
of buildings crowning a secondary slope.

" No, no—that's the school, Dene Compton."

" A school ? " Alwynne screwed up her eyes to look at it.
" What a big place ! Girls or boys ? "

" Both."

" Oh ! A board school ! " Alwynne's interest flagged.

" Scarcely ! " Alicia laughed. " Haven't you hear of Dene
Compton ? And you a schoolmistress ! "

Alwynne was politely blank.

" The thin end of the co-educational wedge. It's unique—
or was, till a few years ago. There are several now, dotted about
England. You ladies' seminaries should be trembling in your
shoes."

" Boys and girls ! What a mad idea ! Yes, I believe Clare—
I believe I did hear something about it. It's all cranks and
simple lifers and socialists though, isn't it ? "

" You'd better come up one day and see. I'll take you."

" Why, do you know them ? "

" I teach there."

" You ? Oh—I beg your pardon," cried Alwynne strickenly.
Alicia laughed.

" I'm accustomed to it. Jean will be delighted with an ally.
She pretends to disapprove. But Roger and I are generally
too much for her."

" Is he a master, then ? "

" Good gracious, no ! But he has a lot of friends at the school.
He ought to be interested—it's his land, you know. His people
lived there for generations—the Lumsdens of Dene Compton.
The head master has the old house, but the school itself is new—
all those buildings you see. No, not those— " Alwynne's eyes
were caught by a glitter of glass roofs— " those are Roger's
houses. He's a gardener, you know. He lives for his bulbs and
his manures."

The tiny cart rocked as the pony bucketed down the dip of
the road and whirled it through the gates and up the short drive.
Alwynne clutched the inadequate rail.

" He will do it," said Alicia resignedly. " He wants his tea.
There's Jean. Mind the door."

She pulled up the rocketing pony as the ridiculous little door
burst open and Alwynne and her baggage were precipitated on
to the gravel.

A little woman ran out from the porch.

" Are you hurt ? It always does that. I'm always asking

Alicia to tell Bryce to take it to be seen to. Alicia—I shall speak to Roger if you don't. My dear, I hope you haven't hurt yourself. That pretty frock—but it will all brush off. And how is Elsbeth, and why didn't you bring her with you? Come in at once and have some tea. Alicia has driven round to the stables. It's Bryce's afternoon off."

Jean was a prim little red-haired woman, some years younger than Alicia, with brisk ways, and a clacking tongue. She had Alwynne in a chair, had given her tea, deplored her white looks, suggested three infallible remedies, recounted their effect on her own constitution and Alicia's and her nephew's, and, digressing easily, was beginning a detailed history of Roger's health since, at the age of five or thereabouts, he had come under her care, before Alwynne had had time to realize more than that the room was very cheerful, Jean very talkative, and she herself very, very tired. She could not help being relieved when Alicia returned. Jean, with her neat dress and knowledgeable ways and little air of apologizing for her slap-dash elder, should, by all the rules, have been the more reliable of the cousins. Yet Alwynne turned instinctively to Alicia; and Alicia, spread upon a chair, fanning herself cyclonically with her enormous hat, did not fail her.

"Jean! The child's as white as a sheet. You can ask about Elsbeth to-morrow, and Roger will keep. Take her up to her room, leave her to unpack and lie down in peace and quiet, and come back and give me my tea. Supper's at seven, Alwynne. Take my advice and have a good rest. There are plenty of books—oh, yes, I know all about your likes and dislikes. Elsbeth's a talker too—on paper! Jean—if you're not down in five minutes, I'll come and fetch you."

Alwynne, half an hour later, curled comfortably upon a sofa, in front of a blazing fire, with a lazy hour before her and a Copperfield upon her knee, thought that Alicia was a perfect dear. And Jean? Jean, pulling out the sofa, poking the fire, pattering about her like a too intelligent terrier—Jean was a dear too. . . . They were a couple of comical dears.

And 'The Dears' was Alwynne's name for them from that day on.

CHAPTER XXX

ALWYNNE settled down with an ease that surprised herself. Much as she loved the country, a country life would have bored her to death, Clare had often assured her, as a permanent state; but for a few weeks it was certainly delightful. She enjoyed pottering about the garden with Jean, and jogging into the village on her own account behind the obstinate pony, who, approving her taste in apples, allowed her to believe that she more or less regulated his direction and pace. She enjoyed the complicated smells of the village store, half post office, half emporium, and the taste of its gargantuan bulls'-eyes. She sent, in the first enthusiasm of discovery, a tinful heaped about with early primroses to Clare; but Clare was not impressed.

Clare disapproved strongly of Alwynne's holiday, needed her too much to allow it necessary. Her first letters were a curious mixture—half fretfulness over Alwynne's absence, half assurance of how perfectly well she, Clare, got on without her. Alwynne would have been exquisitely amazed could she have known how eagerly Clare awaited her bi-weekly budget. Alwynne was afraid her letters were dull enough. She apologized constantly—

Of course, Clare, this will seem very small beer to you—but little things are important down here. It's all so quiet, you see. I've been perfectly happy this morning because I found a patch of white violets in a clearing, and Jean and Alicia were just as excited when I told them at lunch: and we went off with a tea-basket afterwards, and dug violet roots for an hour, or more, and then spread our mackintoshes over a felled trunk and made tea. The ground was sopping, but it was fun. You'd love my cousins. They're as old as Elsbeth but full of beans, and they've travelled and are interesting—only they will talk incessantly about this nephew they've got. It's ' Roger ' this and ' Roger ' that—he seems to rule them with a rod of iron—can't do wrong! He comes back next week. I rather wonder what

*he'll be like. The Dears make him out a paragon ; but I'm
expecting a prig, myself ! There are photographs of him all
over the place. He's quite good-looking.*

But before Alwynne could tire of the lanes and village, of
gardening with Jean, and hints of how Roger stubbed up roots
and handled bulbs, Alicia had provided her with a new interest.
She remembered her promise one morning and took her up to
Dene Compton.

Alicia gave Italian lessons twice a week, and from her Alwynne
had gleaned many quaint details of the school and its workings.
What she heard interested her, though she was prepared to be
merely, if indulgently, amused. She looked forward to the visit
if only to get copy for a letter to Clare. Clare, too, liked to be
amused.

The gong was clanging for the mid-morning break when Alicia,
Alwynne in her wake, led the way into the main building, and
waving her airily towards a mound of biscuits, bade her help
herself and look about her for a while, because she, Alicia, had
got to speak to—— She dived into the crowd.

Alwynne, thus deserted, stood shyly enough in a roofed corner
of the great brick quadrangle, munching a fair imitation of a dog-
biscuit, and watching the boys and girls who swarmed past her
as undisturbed by her presence as if she were invisible. At the
boys she smiled indulgently as she would have smiled at a string
of lively terriers, but of the girls she was sharply critical. They
wore curious, and as she thought hideous, serge tunics : she
jibbed at their utilitarian plaits : but she conceded a good carriage
to most of them and was impressed by a certain pleasant fearless-
ness of manner. A couple of men, Alicia, and a bright, emphatic
woman in a nurse's uniform, wandered through the crowd, which
made way courteously enough, but seemed otherwise in no degree
embarrassed by their propinquity. Alwynne had a sudden
memory of Clare's triumphal progressions ; compared them uneasily with the fashion of these quiet people.

She watched a small girl dash panting to the loggia at the
opposite side of the quadrangle, where a slight man in disreput-
able tennis-shoes, leaned against a shaft and observed the pleasant
tumult. There was a moment's earnest consultation, and the
small girl darted away again and disappeared down a corridor.
The man resumed his former pose—head on one side, smiling a
little.

Alwynne ventured out of her corner and caught at Alicia as she passed.

" Cousin Alice ! I like all this. I'm glad you brought me. Who's that ? " She nodded towards the man in tennis-shoes.

" The Head."

" The head master ? "

" Why not ? "

" But—but—when Miss Marsham comes in—you can hear a pin drop—— Is he nice ? "

Alicia laughed.

" I'll introduce you."

She did.

" Well," said Alicia with a twinkle as they walked home together later, " what did you think of him ? "

Alwynne flushed, but she laughed too.

" Cousin Alice—it was too bad of you. He just said ' How do you do ? ' and smiled politely. Then he said nothing at all for five minutes, and then he clutched at one of the girls and handed me over to her with another smile—an immensely relieved one—and drifted away. I've never been so snubbed in my life."

" You're not the first. So you didn't like him ? "

" Oh—I liked him," conceded Alwynne grudgingly.

They walked on in silence for a while.

" What's that ? " Alwynne pointed to a large grey building half way down the avenue.

" The girls' house, Hill Dene. They sleep there ; and have the needlework classes, and housewifery, I believe."

" Do they have everything else with the boys ? "

" Practically."

" Does it answer ? "

" Why not ? Girls with brothers and boys with sisters have an advantage over the solitary specimens, everybody knows. This is only extending the principle."

Alwynne giggled suddenly.

" You know that girl he dumped me on to—she was showing me round, and we ran into some boys in the gym. I couldn't make out why, but she jolly well sent them flying."

" Out of hours, I expect."

" But the coolness of it, Cousin Alice ! She was a bit of a thing—the boys were half as high again ! "

" But not prefects."

"Oh, I see." Alwynne meditated. "Oh, Cousin Alicia, that girl asked me to go with them next Saturday for a tramp. Over Witch Hill. She and another girl and some boys. Imagine! they're going by themselves—without a master or a mistress or anything!"

"Why not?"

"We don't. We crocodile. Two and two, and two and two, and two and two. And I trot along at the side and see that they don't take arms. But of course, you can't control the day-girls. One of them asked two of the boarders out for the day one Sunday, at least her mother did, and we met them after church on the promenade, arm in arm—all three! I tell you, there was a row. They were locked up in their bedrooms for three days, and nobody might speak to them for the rest of the term. Miss Marsham said it was defiance and that they might remember they were ladies."

"I don't think they want 'ladies' here," said Alicia. "They're quite content if they produce gentlewomen. Your school must be peculiar."

"Oh, no," said Alwynne, opening her eyes. "There are dozens of schools like Utterbridge. I was at two myself when I was young. It's this place that's peculiar. It's like nothing I've heard of. I want to explore. He said I could. Yes, I forgot—he did say that—that I was to come up whenever I liked."

And for the next week Alwynne spent a good half of her days at Dene Compton. She clung to Alicia's skirts at the first, afraid of appearing to intrude. But she soon found that she might go where she would without arousing curiosity or even notice, though boys and girls alike were friendly enough when she spoke to them. Accustomed to her mistress-ship, she was half-piqued, half-amused to find herself so entirely unimportant.

But the great school fascinated her. It was scarce a third larger than her own in point of numbers, but the perfection of its proportions made it impressive. The arrangements for the children's physical well-being reflected the methods employed for their spiritual development. There was an insistence on sunlight and fresh air and space—above all, space. There was no calculation of the legal minimum of cubic feet: body and mind alike were given room in which to turn, to stretch themselves, to grow.

Gradually she realized that she had been living for years in a rabbit warren.

With her discoveries she filled many sheets of notepaper. But Clare's letters were nicely calculated to divert enthusiasm. Their tone was changing; they allowed Alwynne to guess herself missed. There was in them a hint of appeal : a suggestion of lonely evenings—— Never a word of Alwynne's doings. Yet, by implication, description of her new friends and their outlook was dismissed as unnecessary. Clare, Alwynne was to realize, would smile pleasantly as she read, and think it all rather silly.

Elsbeth—*so pleased that they are so kind to you at Alicia's school*—was more genuinely uninterested. Dene Compton had been the home of a certain John Lumsden for Elsbeth. She did not care for descriptions of its metamorphosis. She wanted to hear about Dene, and her cousins, and how Alwynne was eating and sleeping, and if Roger Lumsden had come back yet. She asked twice if Roger Lumsden had come back yet. But Alwynne had an annoying habit of leaving her questions unanswered through eight closely written sheets. It was not only Clare who was very tired of co-education and Dene Compton.

But Elsbeth got her news at last, and was satisfied with it as Macchiavellis usually are, whose plots are being developed by unconscious and self-willed instruments. Alwynne, who in her spare time had discovered what spring in the country could mean, tucked in the news at the end of an epistle that was purely botanical—

. . . and cuckoo-pint and primroses and violets ! Have you ever seen larches in bud ? Oh, Elsbeth, why can't we live in the country ? Every collection of buildings bigger than Dene Village ought to be razed by Act of Parliament. I expect the earth hates cities as I hated warts on my hands when I was little. Well, I must stop. Oh—the Lumsden man turned up a day or two ago. The Dears were in ecstasies, and he let himself be fussed over in the calmest way, as if he had a perfect right to it. I think he's conceited. I don't think you'd like him. He's back for good, apparently, but he won't worry me much. I'm only in at meals. The Dears are always busy and let me do as I like, and I either go up to Compton, or prowl, or take a rug and book into the garden. It's quite hot, although it's barely April— so you needn't worry. The garden is jolly, big and half wild : only ' Roger ' is beginning to trim it—the vandal !

He's by way of being a gardener, you know. Great on bulbs and roses, I believe.

By the way is he a relation? Even The Dears are only very distant cousins, aren't they? Because he will call me 'Alwynne' as if he were. I call it cheek. I was very stiff, but he's got a hide like a rhinoceros. When I said 'Mr. Lumsden,' he just grinned. So now I say 'Roger' very markedly whenever he says 'Alwynne.' I can't see what Jean and Alicia see in him; but of course I have to be polite. They are dears, if you like—are giving me a lovely time.

I hope you're not very dull, Elsbeth dear. You must try and get out this lovely weather. Why not have Clare to tea one day? You'd both enjoy it. I heard from her yesterday—such a jolly letter!

Heaps of love from Jean and Alicia—and you know what a lot from me!

ALWYNNE.

P.S.—I found these violets to-day on a bank behind the church. They'll be squashed when you get 'em, but they'll smell still.

P.S.—The Lumsden man saw me writing, and said, would I send you his love, and do you remember him? I told him I'd scarcely heard you mention his name, so it wasn't probable—but he just smiled his superior smile. He reminds me of Mr. Darcy in P. and P. I can't say I like him.

CHAPTER XXXI

Roger Lumsden had been home a week. Alwynne, save at meals, had seen little of him, and that little she did not intend to like. There was a memory of a passage of arms at their first meeting which rankled.

Roger had been enquiring when the Compton holidays began. Alicia hesitated—

" Let me see—the play's Tuesday week——"

" Wednesday week," put in Alwynne.

" Tuesday——"

" No, Wednesday," Alwynne persisted. " Because, you know, Mr. Bryant is so afraid that Gertrude Clarke won't be out of the ' San.' He says he can never coach up another Alkestis in the time. Besides, there isn't any one. He's been tearing his hair."

Alicia laughed.

" She knows more about it than I do, Roger! She's been half living there, haven't you, Alwynne ? "

Roger turned to her with a smile and the first touch of personal interest that he had shown.

" Jolly place, isn't it ? You teach, don't you ? I wonder how it strikes you ! "

But he was a stranger and Alwynne was nervous. She answered flippantly, as she always did when she was not at her ease—

" Oh, I can't get over their dresses! Appalling garments! Imagine that poor girl trying to rehearse Alkestis in a pea-green potato sack! It must be delicious. And their hair! Doesn't anybody ever teach them to do their hair ? "

He eyed her thoughtfully, from her carefully dressed head to her shining shoe-buckles, and shrugged his shoulders.

" Is that all you see ? " said Roger dispassionately, and withdrew interest.

Alwynne grew hot with annoyance. Idiot! All she saw. . . . As if she had meant anything of the kind. . . . One said things

like that. . . . One just said them. . . . Especially when one was
nervous. . . . Taking a remark like that seriously. . . . Oh
well, if he liked to think her a fool—let him ! Silly prig !

She endeavoured to put him out of her mind. But his mere
existence disturbed her. She was not accustomed to tobacco,
for instance. . . . and it was disconcerting to find him in her
favourite corner of the library or occupying the writing-table
that no one had seemed to use but herself. He appeared to
have forgotten that he had snubbed her and was unquenchably
friendly. She found herself being pleasanter than she intended,
but she made it a point of honour never to agree with him. That,
at least, she owed herself.

She watched him furtively, alert for justification of her ill-
humour. She told herself that it would be easier to be nice to
him if everybody else did not fuss over him so. . . . It was
ridiculous to see how Jean, especially, brightened at the sight of
him. . . . He was good to her, certainly : she was argumentative,
without being shrewd, but he never lost patience, as Alwynne,
in secret was inclined to do. Even Alicia, so stoutly the head
of her household, submitted every difficulty, from an unexpected
legacy to a dearth of eggs. And he would sit down solidly and
think the matter out. And his advice, from a flutter in rubber
to pepper in the chicken pail, would be followed literally, and
generally, Alwynne admitted, with success.

But she jibbed furiously when the sisters began to consult him
about her personal affairs.

" Roger, don't you think that Alwynne—— ? "

But here Roger was invariably offhand and non-committal.
Curiously, however, this attitude, correct as it was, did not
appease Alwynne. But she was forced, at least, to admit that
he could, on occasion, be tactful.

The last week of the term had begun. Alicia, at breakfast
behind the coffee urn, was making her plans.

" It's a busy week. The Swains want us to go to lunch, Jean,
only we haven't a day before Sunday, have we ? At least—
there's Tuesday ; it's only the dress-rehearsal. I can get out of
that. Alwynne can represent me." She nodded benevolently.

There was a slight pause. Roger, glancing up, stared openly.
Alwynne had turned as white as paper. Her words came
stickily.

" Cousin Alice, I can't. I mean—I'd rather—I don't want to
go much, if you don't mind."

Alicia blessed herself.

" But, my dear ! Why not ? I thought you'd be looking forward—— Oh, I suppose you've watched it so often, already."

" No—I haven't seen it; I'm afraid rehearsals bore me——" Alwynne broke off with an attempt at a light laugh.

" But you've been up to Compton so much," Alicia's tone was reproachful. " I should have thought you would have been sufficiently interested——"

" Oh, I am ! Only—you see I've got letters to write—to Elsbeth——"

" Well, you've got all the week to write in ! Are you so afraid of being bored ? Compton wouldn't be flattered. We rather pride ourselves on our acting, you know ! My dear, we're expected to go—must give the performers some sort of an audience to get them into training for the night. You ought to understand, of all people ! Don't you ever give plays at your school ? "

Alwynne was silent, but prompted by an instinct she could not have explained, she turned to Roger, stolid behind his eggs and bacon. She said nothing, but she looked at him desperately. He gave an imperceptible nod. He had been watching her intently.

" But, dear Alwynne——" Jean was chirruping her version of Alicia's remarks when Roger's calm voice interrupted—

" I say, Alicia ! I thought you and Jean were coming with me ! I can't go on the night itself. Of course you must come. Go to your lunch on Sunday—I'll look after Alwynne. But I'm not going up to Compton without you. Spoil all the fun."

" Of course, if Roger wants us——" began Jean quickly.

" Oh, I didn't want to miss it," retreated Alicia hastily. " I only thought the Swains—— But of course Sunday would do."

" I met old Swain yesterday," said Roger, " travelled up to town with him. He was very full of his daughter's engagement."

" Engagement ! " Alicia and Jean swooped to the news, like gulls to a falling crust. It kept them busy till breakfast was over.

And Roger returned to his eggs and bacon with never a glance at Alwynne.

Alwynne, half an hour later in her own room, fighting certain memories, arguing herself fiercely out of her weakness, had yet time to puzzle her head over Roger Lumsden. How quick he had been—and how kind. . . . Or had he noticed nothing ? Had that adroit change of subject been accidental ? That was much more likely.

She dismissed him from her mind. She wished she could dismiss all the thoughts that filled her mind as easily.

Alwynne was grateful enough to Roger, however, when Tuesday came and he set out for Compton, an aunt on either arm : but on Sunday she had to pay for her non-attendance. Hurrying down, a little late, to lunch, she was half-way through her usual apologies before she realized that neither Jean nor Alicia were in their places. Of course—they were going to the Swain's . . . Their nephew, however, waiting gravely behind his chair, admitted her excuses with a little air of acknowledging them to be necessary that ruffled her at once, though she had promised herself to be pleasant. After all, she was staying, as she had told herself several times already, with Jean and Alicia. Once more she applied herself, quite unsuccessfully, to snubbing his air of host. Roger listened to her in some amusement ; her ungracious ways disturbed him no more than the rufflings and peckings of an angry bird, and her charming manner to his aunts and occasional whim of friendliness to himself, had prevented him from pigeonholing her definitely as a pretty young shrew. He was inclined to like her, for Jean and Alicia had confessed themselves absurdly taken with the girl, and he was accustomed to be influenced by their judgment ; but the touch of hostility that usually showed itself in her manner to him puzzled as much as it amused him.

He enjoyed baiting her, yet he thought, carelessly, that it was a pity she should have inaugurated guerilla warfare. She looked as if she could have been pleasant company for his spare time if she had chosen. However, he would have little enough spare time, for the next few weeks, anyhow. . . . he had promised Jean to set to work seriously at the renovation of her garden. . . . He should be thankful for a visitor requiring neither escort nor attention .

Yet, naturally, her independence piqued him. He eyed her swiftly, as she sat at his right hand. She was a curious girl, he thought, to be so pretty and well-dressed, and yet so self-sufficing. Girls, apparently of her type, (he thought of his American cousins) usually needed a good deal of admiration to keep them contented.

She did not look altogether contented, though. . . . there were lines and puckers at the corners of her large eyes, that were surely out of place. . . . nineteen, wasn't she ? She had had a breakdown, of course. . . . rather absurd, for such a child. . . . Jean had hinted a guess at some trouble. . .

A love affair, he supposed. That would account for her thorniness, her occasional air of absence and depression, that contrasted with her usual cheerfulness. . . . Yet that curious whim the other day—what had it meant ? More than a whim, he imagined —her very lips had grown white. . . . He was quite sure that he had helped her out of a hole. . . . She might at least show a certain decent gratitude. . . . He wondered what she was thinking about, sitting there so silently. . . . she was generally talkative enough. . . . pretty quarrelsome, too. He supposed she was having a fit of the blues. . . . He had better talk to her, perhaps. . . .

Alwynne, eating her wing of chicken, was merely and sheerly shy. She was garrulous enough with women, but she did not in the least know how to talk to men. Therefore and naturally she was full of theories. She had vague ideas that they had to be amused as babies have to be amused, but confronted with the prospect of a prolonged *tête-à-tête*, without Alicia or Jean to retire upon, she had nothing whatever to say. Yet she had been taught by Elsbeth to consider a lack of table-talk as a lack of manners, and was irritated with herself for her silence, and still more irritated with Roger for his.

She met his belated attempts at conversation none too graciously—was bored by the boat-race, and would have nothing to say to the weather; though she thawed to his catalogue of copses and plantations in the neighbourhood, where certain wild flowers she had not yet discovered might be found.

But it was impossible for Alwynne to be silent long, and by the time they had adjourned to the drawing-room, the pair were talking easily enough. Roger did not find himself bored. He had, from the beginning, recognized that she was no fool, that her remarks owed their comicality to her phrasing of them, and that essentially they were shrewd, her acrobatic intellect swinging easily across the gaps in her education. The gaps were certainly there. He would marvel at her amazing ignorance, only to be tripped up by her unexpected display of authoritative knowledge. Gradually he began to analyse and discriminate, to see that she was naturally observant. Her remarks on life as she knew it, were as illuminating as original. She had humour and a nice sense of caricature. But when she, as it were, hoisted herself on the shoulders of the women about her, and from that level peered curiously at an outer, alien world, her insight failed her, her views grew distorted and merely grotesque. He thought he guessed the reason. She was no longer gazing, critical and clear-eyed, at known surroundings, but, still supported by the opinions of the women of her circle, was seeing what she had expected to see, what she had been told by them that she would see.

For all her air of modern girl, her independence, her store of book experience, she was comically conventual in her curiosities and intolerances, in her prim company manners and uncontrollable lapses into unconventionality. She had an air of not being at her ease; yet he guessed that it was merely the unaccustomed environment that disturbed her poise. He could see her handling surely enough a crowd of schoolgirls. He was equally certain that she ruled through sheer, easy popularity. She had dignity in spite of her whimsies, but he could not imagine her intimidating even a schoolgirl.

But most of all her attitude to himself amused him. She had a certain veiled antagonism of manner, that was allied to the antagonism of the small child to any innovation. She talked to him readily enough (and he, for that matter, to her) yet she was always on the defensive, inquisitive yet wary. He felt that if she had been ten years younger, she would have circled about him and poked.

A stray phrase explained her to him.

They had discussed the latest raid. At Alwynne's age and period all conversational roads led to the suffrage question, and he had found her re-hash of Mona Hamilton's arguments sufficiently entertaining. He guessed a plagiarism of the matter, but the manner was obviously her own. She was full of second-hand indignation over the conduct of a certain Cabinet Minister.

" He won't even see them ! " she explained grievously. " Not even a deputation from the constitutional section ! Just because some women are fools—and burn things——" The pause was eloquent. " It's so utterly unreasonable," declaimed Alwynne. " But of course men are unreasonable," said Alwynne, pensively reflective.

" Are they ? "

" All I know are, anyhow."

He considered her ingenuous countenance—

" If it's not a delicate question—how many do you know ? " said Roger softly.

She looked at him, mildly surprised.

" Hundreds ! In books, that is."

" Oh—books ! I meant real life."

" Surely a page of Shakespeare is more real than dozens of real people's lives."

" Side issue ! I'm not to be deflected. How many men do you know, in real life, well enough to discuss the suffrage with ? "

" I'm always kept at school the day the vicar comes to tea," she said suggestively.

" Who else ? "

She saw his drift, but defended herself, smiling.

" The assistants are most intelligent at the circulating library."

" Who else ? "

" There were music masters at school. I didn't mean *you* were unreasonable," she deprecated.

He began to laugh, openly, mischievously, delighting in her discomfiture.

" Anyhow, I know a lot about women," said Alwynne heatedly.

He eyed her respectfully.

" I'm sure you do. But we were talking of men. And on the whole—you make me a polite exception—as a result of your wide knowledge, your complicated experience of Us—as a class—you consider that we are unreasonable ? "

But he spoke into space. Alwynne had retired, pinkly, to a sofa and a novel. But he thought, as he settled to his own reading, that he heard a strangled chuckle. Alwynne, caught napping, always tickled Alwynne.

Over the top of his book, he considered her bent head approvingly. He liked her sense of fun. It was not every girl who could appreciate the smut on her own nose. . . . quite a pretty nose too. . . . indeed the whole profile was unexceptionable. . .

He noticed how well the patch of sky and the slopes of Witch Hill framed it. . . . and her hair. . . . it regularly mopped up the sunlight ! He felt that he wanted to take the great heavy rope and twist it like a wet cloth till the gold dropped out on to the floor in shining pools.

He supposed she would be called a beautiful woman. . . . He had always looked upon a beautiful woman as an improbable possibility, like a millionaire or an archbishop—whom you might meet any day, but somehow never did. . . . Yet he was in the same house with one—and she his semi-demi cousin. . . . Yes—she was certainly beautiful. . . .

Here Alwynne, who had not been entirely absorbed, looked

up and caught his eye. Neither quite knew how to meet the other's unexpected scrutiny. Roger, less agile than Alwynne, stared solemnly until she looked away.

Alwynne gave a little inaudible sigh. She was boring him, of course. . . . It was pretty obvious. . . . Yet he had been quite nice all through lunch. . . . It was a pity. . . . She wondered if he wanted to read, or if she ought to go on talking ? She racked her brains for something to say to him. It was not so easy to talk if he would not do his share. . . . She supposed she had talked too much about the suffrage. . . . Men never liked to be contradicted. . . . She glanced at him swiftly, and met his look once more, and once more he stared, till her dropping lids released him. Then he lit his pipe.

She shrugged her shoulders.

She thought it very rude of him to leave off talking. . . . Silence was oppressive unless you knew people well. . . . It snubbed you. . . . Especially when you had been, as Alwynne feared she had, holding forth a trifle. . . . She supposed he had put her down as a talkative bore. . . . Elsbeth always said that strangers thought her enthusiasms were pose. . . . as if it mattered what strangers thought ! She hated strangers. . . . She was always fantastic with new acquaintances. . . . It was the form her shyness took. If Roger chose to think she was posing. . . . It didn't affect her anyway. . . . She was only too glad to be able to read in peace. . . . Hang Roger !

She settled herself to her reading.

For five long minutes they both read steadily. But Alwynne's book was not interesting; she began to flutter the pages, her thoughts once more astray.

It was rather a shame of The Dears to desert her . . . . to leave her to entertain a strange man who didn't like her. . . . It made her look a fool. . . . She hated boring people. . . . If she bored their precious nephew as much as the book on her lap bored her ! . . . She wondered why, with all the library to choose from, she had pitched on it. Of course, it was Roger's suggestion. . . . Well, she didn't think much of his taste. . . . Or perhaps he imagined it was the sort of stuff to appeal to her ? She flung up her chin indignantly, to find his serious and critical eyes once more concerned with her. She met them with a raising of eyebrows—a hint of cool defiance. It was Roger's turn to retire into his book.

He was an odd sort of a man. . . . She wondered what Clare would think of him? As if Clare would bother her head. . . . But then he wasn't Clare's cousin. But Clare would be out in the woods after the wild hyacinths. . . . Somebody had said it was blue with them in the little wood behind the house. . . . She must send Clare a boxful to-morrow. . . . or to-day? She supposed there was an evening post. . . . It was a pity to waste such a heavenly afternoon. . . .

She stole yet another glance at Roger; he was evidently engrossed at last. It would not be rude? After all, what did it matter? He wasn't too polite himself! She drove her book viciously down the yielding side of the Chesterfield, swished to the open French window, and so out. The gravel crunched moistly beneath her thin shoes; she could feel every pebble. She glanced back into the drawing-room. All quiet. But by the time she had changed, the man might have come out. . . . She would change afterwards. . . . The smooth lawn sloped invitingly—beyond lay the rose walk and the wood, little Witch Wood that she had never yet explored, just because it was always at hand.

She picked up her silken skirts and took to her heels.

It was exactly half an hour later that Roger's book also grew dull to the point of imbecility. He shut it with a bang, stirred the sun-drowned fire, and knocked out his pipe against the shining dogs. Then he too walked out on to the terrace.

He wondered where the girl had got to. Then he frowned. Little half-moons dinted the wet yellow path and the stretch of grass beyond it. It was very careless, cutting up the turf like that. . . . If there was one thing he hated. . . . Of course she was town-bred. . . . could not be expected to realize the sacredness of a lawn. . . . But he must certainly tell her. . . . He might as well find her and tell her at once. . . . Then he laughed. Alwynne's high heels had betrayed her. The tracks led straight to the wood. So that was the lure. . . . He remembered saying that the hyacinths would probably be out. . . .

He wondered if she knew her way. . . . It wasn't a large wood. . . . Perhaps he had better go and see. . . . and warn her off the lawn coming back? He hesitated. His eyes fell on Jean's forgotten bodge, lying by the border. If the hyacinths were out, she would need a basket. . . . She had not taken one. . . . Trust her to forget such a detail. . . . She would be glad of it though. . . . He tipped out the weeds into a neat pile and jumping the narrow bed, ran down, in his turn, towards the wood.

Alicia and Jean, home to tea, were annoyed to find the fire out.

The gardener, rolling the lawn next day, thought as ill of hob-nailed boots as of high French heels.

CHAPTER XXXII

ALWYNNE left the garden behind her and crossed the stretch of grass, half lawn, half paddock, that lay between kitchen-garden and wood. It was fenced with riotous hedges, demure for the moment in dove-grey honeysuckle and star of Bethlehem, with no hint in their puritan apparel of the brionies and eglantines that were to follow. About the hedge borders the grass grew tall and rank, and, as she watched, the wind would stir it into a sea of emerald and the parsley-blossoms sway above it like snatches of drifting foam. Beyond the hedge shadow, 'Nicholas Nye,' the one-eyed donkey, reposed Celestially among the buttercups, which, making common cause with the afternoon sun, had turned his grazing ground into a Field of the Cloth of Gold.

For a moment she was minded to content herself with all the buttercups on earth to gather, and to go no further that day; but staring down the dazzling slope, her eyes rested once more upon the pleasant darkness of the goal for which she had been bound. Among the nearer tree trunks were stripes and chequerings of blue—the blue that is lovelier than the sea, the one blue in the world to the flower-lover. At once, indifferently, she left the buttercups to Nicholas Nye and hurried on and into the wood.

There were hyacinths everywhere, hyacinths by the million. It was as if the winds had torn her robes from the faint, spring sky, and had flung them to earth, and she now bent above them naked and shivering.

Alwynne wandered from patch to patch in an ecstasy of delight. As usual, her pleasure shaped itself into exclamations, phrases, whole sentences of the letters she would write to Clare Hartill of her experiences. If only she could have Clare with her, she thought, to see and hear and touch and smell—to share the loveliness she was enjoying. Her thoughts flew to Italy, to their crowded month of beautiful sights together. She

233

laughed—she would discard all those memories for love of this present vision. . . . If only Clare could see it. . . . She could never describe it properly. . . . adjectives welled up in her mind and dispersed again, like bubbles in a glass of water. The stalks and the hoarse ring of the hyacinth bells fascinated her. Clare was forgotten. She began to pick for the sake of picking.

The hot silence of early afternoon lay upon tree and bird and air. Alwynne, moving from blue clump to blue clump, grew ashamed of the rustle of her dress and the scrunch of twigs and soaked leaves beneath her feet, and trod softly; even her own calm breathing sounded too loudly for the perfect peace of the place and the hour.

She picked steadily, greedily—she had never before had as many flowers as she wanted, and there was inexpressible pleasure in filling her arms till she could hold no more; yet, some twenty minutes later, as she straightened herself at last, a little giddily, and looked about her over the pile of azure bells, there was no sign of bareness, for all she had gathered; she still stood to her knees in a lake of blue and green and gold.

She stretched herself lazily as she considered the flowers about her and wondered at their luxuriance. They were thicker and longer-stemmed than the mass of those she carried : the leaves were juicy and shining like dark swords : the last dozen of her armful had flecked her hands and dress with milky syrup. The ground, too, was black and boggy, and sucked at her feet as she moved. Suddenly she realized that the trees grew thick and close together—that the patches of sunlight were far apart —and that she had wandered farther into the wood than she had intended. She thought that she had picked enough, more than enough for Elsbeth as well as Clare; that it was time to be getting home. She had no idea of the hour. . . . It would not do to risk being late. . . .

She moved forward uncertainly.

She had had a blessed afternoon : she had surrendered herself to the sounds and sights and smells of the spring, to the warmth of the sun and the touch of the wind, till every sense was drunken with pleasure. But her ecstasy had been impersonal and thoughtless : she had enjoyed too completely to have had knowledge of her enjoyment. With the return to realization of place and time, her mood was changing. She was no longer of the wood, but in it merely; wandering in the dark heart of it, no dryad returned and welcome, but a stranger, one Alwynne

Durand, in thin shoes and an unsuitable dress, with the wood's flowers, not her own, in her hands. Stolen flowers—their weight was suddenly a burden to her. She felt guilty, and had an odd, sudden wish to put them down tenderly at the foot of a tree, hide them with grasses and run for her life. She laughed at the idea as she looked for the path—what were flowers for, but picking? Yet she could not get rid of the feeling that she had been doing wrong, and that even now she was being watched, and would, in due time, be caught and punished, her stolen treasures still in her hands.

But wild flowers are free to all—and the wood was Roger Lumsden's wood! He had told her that he rented it.

She moved backwards and forwards, turning hurriedly hither and thither, trampling the hyacinths and stumbling on the uneven ground, unreasonably flurried that she could not find any path. She could not even track her own footsteps.

It was very strange, she thought, when she had penetrated so easily the depths of the wood, that the return should be so difficult. She had thought it a mere copse. She put her free hand to her eyes, scanning the wall of greenery in all directions. She fancied that at one point the trees grew less densely, and set out, scrambling over rough ground towards the faint light.

But in spite of her hurry she advanced slowly. The thin switches of the undergrowth whipped her as she pushed them aside, and the huge briars twisted themselves about her like live things. Twice the slippery moss brought her to her knees, and the faint light grew no stronger as she pressed forward. She began to feel frightened, though she knew the sensation to be absurd. It was impossible to be lost in a little wood, half a mile across. . . . It was merely a question of walking straight on till one emerged on open fields. . . .

She told herself so, and tried to be amused at her adventure, and hummed a confident little tune as she plodded on, very careful not to look behind her. Her shoes, thudding and squelching in the wet mess of mould and green stuff, made more noise than one would have thought possible for one pair of feet, and woke the oddest echoes.

Of course, it was impossible that any one could be following her. . . . But the wood was so horribly silent that her own breathing and clumsy footfalls (there could be nothing else) counterfeited the noises of pursuit. . . . She could have sworn there was a presence at her elbow, in her rear, moving as she moved, stumbling as she stumbled. Twice she faced round abruptly, standing still—but she saw nothing but the wall of vegetation, motionless, silent, yet insistently alive. She felt that every tree, every leaf, every blade of grass, was watching her with green, unwinking eyes. There was nothing more in the wood than there had been a pleasant hour ago—less indeed, for she realized suddenly that the sun had gone in and that it was cold; yet she owned to herself at last that she was nervous, vaguely uneasy. Instantly, by that mere act of recognition, fright was born in her—unreasonable and unreasoning fright, that, in the length of a thought, pervaded her entire personality, crisping her hair, catching at her throat, paralysing her mind. The wood-panic had her in its grip—the age-old terror that still lies in wait where trees are gathered together, though the god that begot it be dead these nineteen hundred years.

She began to run.

It was impossible to pass quickly through the tangled undergrowth; but sheer fright gave her skill to avoid real obstacles, strength to crash over and through the mere wreckage of the wood. She turned and doubled like a hare, yet desperately, with the hare's terror of the sudden turn that might confront her with the presence at her heels. She could endure its pursuit, but she knew that its revelation would be more than she could bear. She was so far merely and indefinitely frightened, but to face the unknown would be to confront fear itself. And she was more frightened of fear than of any evil she knew. She could, she thought, meet pain or sickness or any mere misery, with sufficient calmness, but the fear of fear was an obsession. She tore through the wood, shaken and gasping with terror of the greater terror she every moment expected to be forced to undergo; for almost the only clear thought remaining to her, in that onrush of panic, was the realization that there was, at her elbow, in her heart, physical or metaphysical, she knew not which, some as yet veiled fact waiting to be revealed, in view of which her present agitation was trivial and meaningless.

She ran on, blind and blundering; yet her feet were so clogged by the weight of earth and wet, her thoughts by the sweat of the fear that was on them, that neither seemed to move for all her willing. And all the while, another part of her consciousness sat aloof, critical and detached, laughing at her for an excitable fool, analysing, in Clare's crispest accents, the illusions which were bewildering her, and wondering coolly that any girl of her age could so let her imagination run away with her.

She pulled herself together with an immense effort of will.

That was the truth. . . . It was her own imagination that was literally and physically running away with her, whipping her tired body into unnecessary exertion, flogging her into mad flight from this pleasant, harmless place, with its hideous and horrible suggestion of evil at hand. . . . But the evil was in her own mind. . . . There was nothing pursuing her, no vague ghost at her elbow. . . . The horror was in herself, to be faced, and fought, and trampled. . . . . Running would not help her . . . she would only carry her terror with her. . . . For an instant she had a lightning glimpse of the reasons of the Sadducean attitude to personality, and its desperate denials of future existence. She was suddenly appalled at the hideous possibility of existing eternally with her own undying thoughts for company. She wondered if there were really such a thing as soul suicide, and thought that, if so, many must have chosen to commit it.

Here her shifting, crowding thoughts blotted out the glimmer of understanding, as flies clustering on a window-pane can blot out light; yet the word *suicide* remained in her mind, disturbing, vaguely suggestive. It was connected with something terrible—she could not remember what—that in its turn was one with the vague horror at her elbow, that walked with the echo of her footsteps and panted with the echoes of her breaths, and yet was not real at all, but only in her mind.

She did not believe she should ever find her way out of the wood. . . . The hyacinths in her arms were so heavy—a queerly familiar weight : and the sun had gone in, which had, somehow, something to do with the trouble. . . . She felt the black depression of the winter months that she had left Utterbridge to escape settling down on her once more. She turned hopelessly to elude it, but it surrounded her like a fog, as indeed she half believed it to be. She supposed they had sudden fogs in the country, when the sun went in. . . . And the sun had gone in because she had picked all the hyacinths. . . . She remembered the story clearly enough now. . . . The sun had played at quoits with a child, and had thrown amiss, and killed it, and the purple blood had trickled down from the child's forehead. . . . So the sun had turned it into purple hyacinths. . . . But she, Alwynne, had been gathering all the hyacinths, and they were a heavy bunch, heavy as a dead child's body . . . and in another minute they would be disenchanted, and she would be carrying a dead child's body in her arms. . . .

She stood still, gazing down at the flowers, white and glassy-eyed with terror, wondering that she was still alive and not yet mad. For she knew that the fear she had feared was upon her at last. She dared not blink lest in that second the change should take place, and she should find Louise, long buried, in her arms. Because, of course, it was Louise who had been following her all the while. . . . Louise—who had committed suicide. . . . She was following Alwynne, because it was Alwynne's fault. . . . Clare had said so. . . . Well—at least she could tell Louise that she had meant no harm. . . .

She waited, swayed back against a tree trunk, the flowers a dead weight over her arm. She held them gently, lest a rough movement should wake the horror they hid. With what was left of sanity she prayed.

The trees encircled her, watching. From far away there came once more a sound of footsteps.

CHAPTER XXXIII

Roger set out at a quick pace for the wood, the basket rattling lightly on his arm; but the track of Alwynne's shoes was lost in the deep grass of the paddock, and he hesitated, wondering where he should look for her. Followed a cupboard-love scene with Nicholas Nye, who accompanied him to the boundary of his kingdom, snuffling windily in the empty bodge. He brayed disgustedly when Roger left him, his ancient lips curling backward over yellow stumps, in a smile that was an insult. He had the air of knowing exactly where Roger was going, and of being leeringly amused.

For ten minutes Roger wandered about, starting aside from the pathway half a dozen times, deceived by a swaying branch, or the deceptive pink and white of distant birch bark. He tramped on into the thickness of the wood, till at last, through a thinning of trees, a hundred yards to his left, he caught a glimpse of gold, that could only, he told himself, be Alwynne's hair. He frowned. It was just like the girl to go floundering into the only boggy bit of the wood, when two thirds were drained and dry, and thick with flowers. . . . It was sheer spirit of contradiction! She would catch cold of course; and he would, not to mince matters, be stunk out with eucalyptus for the next ten days . . . and The Dears would fuss . . . he knew them! His fastidiousness was always revolted by a parade of handkerchiefs and bleared eyes. He was accustomed to insist that disease was as disgraceful as dirt : and that there was not a pin to choose between Dartmoor and the London Hospital as harbourage for criminals. But he could always dismount from his hobby-horse for any case of suffering that came his way. He could give his time, his money, or his tenderness, with a matter-of-course promptitude that relieved all but a tender-skinned few of any belief that they had reason to be grateful to him.

Roger, his eye on the distant halo, crashed through the undergrowth at a great rate, emerging into a little natural clearing, to find Alwynne facing him, a bare half-dozen yards away.

The full sight of her pulled him up short.

She was standing—lying upright, rather, for she seemed incapable of self-support—flattened against a big grey oak. One arm, flung backwards, clutched and scrabbled at the bark; the other, crooked shelteringly, supported a mass of bluebells. Her face was grey, her mouth half open, her eyes wide and pale. Very obviously she did not see him.

" Alwynne ! " he exclaimed.

She cowered. He exclaimed again, astonished and not a little alarmed—

" Alwynne ! Are you ill ? What on earth has happened ? "

She flung up her head, staring.

" Roger ? " she said incredulously.

Then her face began to work. He never forgot the expression of relief that flowed across it. It was like the breaking up of a frozen pool.

" Why, it's you ! " cried Alwynne. " It's you ! It's only you ! " The flowers dropped lingeringly from her slack hands, and she swayed where she stood. He crossed hastily to her and she clung helplessly to his arm. She looked dazed and stupid.

" Of course it is," he said. " Who did you think it was ? " Alwynne looked at him.

" Louise," she said, " I thought it was Louise. She's come before, but never in the daytime. A ghost can't walk in the daytime. But this place is so dark, she might think it was night here, don't you think ? "

He gave her arm a gentle shake.

" Let's get out of this, Alwynne," he began persuasively. " I think you're rather done for. There's been a hot sun to-day, and you've been stooping till you're dizzy. Come on. What a lot of flowers you've picked ! Come, let's get out of this place."

" Yes," she said; " let's get out of this place."

" What about your bunch ? " he questioned, glancing down at the hyacinths' heaped disorder. " Don't you want it ? "

He felt her shiver.

" No," she said, " no." She hesitated. " Could we hide it ? Cover it up ? It ought to be buried. I can't leave it—just lying there——" There was a catch in her voice.

He concealed his astonishment and looked about him.

" Of course not," he said cheerfully. " Here—what about this ? "

A huge tussock of bleached grass, its sodden leaves as long as a woman's hair, caught his eye. He parted the heavy mass and showed her the little cave of dry soil below.

" What about this ? They'll be all right here," he suggested gravely.

Alwynne nodded.

" Yes—put it in quickly," she said.

Without a word, as if it were the most natural thing in the world, he did as she asked. Then, rising and slipping her arm through his own, he pushed on quite silently, holding back the strong pollard shoots, clearing aside the brambles, till they reached the uneven footpath once more, that led them in less than five minutes to the further edge of the wood. As they emerged into the open fields, he felt the weight on his arm lessening. He glanced at his companion, and saw that there was once more a tinge of colour in her cheek.

She drew a deep breath and looked at him.

" I thought I should never get out again," she said dispassionately, as one stating a bald fact.

" Get where ? "

" Out of that wood. You were just in time. I thought I was caught. I should have been, if you hadn't come."

Then she grew conscious of his expression, and answered it—

" I suppose you think I'm mad."

" I do rather."

" I don't wonder. It doesn't much matter——" Her voice flagged and strained.

They walked on in silence.

She began again abruptly.

" Of course you thought I was mad. I knew you would. I do myself, sometimes. Any one would. Even Clare. That's why I never told any one. But it never happened when I was awake before."

" I wonder if you would tell me exactly what happened ? "

" I was frightened," she began irresolutely.

" For a moment I wondered if a tramp——"

She laughed shakily.

" I'm a match for the average tramp, I think. I'm head of the games."

He was amused.

" You'd tell him what you thought of him, I'm sure."

But already her smile had grown absent; she was relapsing into her abstraction.

They had crossed the field as they talked, and struck into the little gravelled path that led to the monster glass-houses on the the other side of the hedge. A wide gate barred their progress. Roger manipulated the rusty chain in silence for a moment, then, as the gate yawned open, turned to her pleasantly——

" Won't you have a look round, as we've come so far ? You're in my territory now, and I've a houseful of daffodils just bursting."

His calm matter-of-fact manner had its effect. Alwynne absorbed in her sick thoughts, found herself listening to his account of his houses and his experiments, as one listens subconsciously to the slur of a distant water-course. She did not take in the meaning of his words, but his even voice soothed her fretted nerves.

Roger was perfectly aware of her inattention. He was not brilliant, but he was equipped with experience and common-sense and kindness of heart; and above all he was observant. The Alwynne of his acquaintance, pretty, amusing, clever, had attracted him sufficiently, had even, as he admitted to himself as he went in search of her, been able to entice him from his Sunday comfort to wander quarrelling in wet fields. But the Alwynne he had come upon half-an-hour later was a revelation ; at a glance every preconceived notion of her character was swept away.

His first idea was that she had been frightened by roughs, but her manner and expression speedily contradicted it. She was, he perceived, struggling, and not for the first time, with some overwhelming trouble of the mind. He had been ap-palled by the fear in her eyes. He remembered Jean's account. Elsbeth had been worried about her for a long time : ill-health and depression : she believed there had been some sort of a shock—a child had died suddenly at the school. . . .

Alwynne's gay and piquant presence had made him forget, till that moment, such rudiments of her history as he had heard. But seeing her distress, he was angry that he had been obtuse, and amazed at her skill in concealing whatever trouble it might be that was oppressing her. All the kindliness of his nature awoke at sight of her haunted, hunted air; he bestirred himself to allay her agitation; he resolved then and there to help her if he could.

He had recognized at once that she was in no state for argument or explanation, and had devoted himself to calming her, falling in with her humour, and showing no surprise at the extravagance of her remarks. He had her quieted, almost herself, by the time they had reached his nursery and descended brick steps into a bath of sweet-smelling warmth.

Alwynne exclaimed.

The glass-house was very peaceful. Above a huge Lent lily the spring's first butterfly hovered and was still awhile, then quivered again and fluttered away, till his pale wings grew invisible against the aisles of yellow bloom. The short, impatient barks of Roger's terrier outside the door came to them, dulled and faint. The sun poured down upon the already heated air.

Alwynne walked down the long narrow middle way, hesitating, enjoying, and moving on again, much, Roger thought, as the butterfly had done. She said little, but her delight was evident. Roger was pleased; he liked his flowers to be appreciated. But he, too, said little; he was considering his course of action.

At the end of the conservatory was a square of brick flooring on which stood a table with a tobacco jar, and a litter of magazines; beside it an ancient basket-chair. Roger pulled it forward.

"This is my sanctum," he said. "Won't you sit down? I do a lot of work here in the winter."

Alwynne sank into the creaking wicker-work with a sigh of relief.

"I shall never get up again," she said. "It's too comfortable. I'm tired."

"Of course." He smiled at her. "Don't you worry. You needn't budge till you want to. I'll get some tea."

"You mustn't bother. It'll be cold. It's miles to the house," said Alwynne wearily.

He made no answer, but began to clear away the rubbish on the table. He moved deftly, light-footed, without clumsy or unnecessary noise; in spite of his size, his movements were always silent and assured.

She closed her eyes indifferently. She had said that she was tired; the word was as good as another where none were adequate to express her utter exhaustion. She felt that, in a sense, she was in luck to be so tired that she could not think. . . . She knew that later she must brace herself to an examination of the nightmare experience of the afternoon, to renew her struggle against the devils of her imagination; but for the moment her weakness was her safeguard, and she could lie relaxed and thoughtless, mesmerized by the flooding sunshine and the pulsing scents and the quiet movements of the man beside her. She wondered what he was doing, but she was too tired to open her eyes, or to interpret to herself the faint sounds she heard. She thought dreamily that he was as kind as Elsbeth. She was grateful to him for not talking to her. He was a wonderfully understanding person. . . . He might have known her for years. . . . He made her feel safe . . . that was a great gift. . . . If she, Alwynne, had been like that, kind and reassuring, to poor little Louise— if only she had understood—Louise would have come to her, then, instead of brooding herself to death. . . . Poor Louise. . . . Poor unhappy Louise. . . . And after all she had not been able to kill herself. . . . She was still alive, lying in wait for her, though she knew that Alwynne could not help her. . . . She would never go away, though they had left her outside in the cold—in the cold of the wood—and were safe in this warm summerland . . . she would be waiting when they came out again. . . . She shuddered as she thought of retracing her steps. She would ask Roger to take her home another way. . . . She would not have to explain. . . . He had not wanted explanation. . . . She was passionately grateful to him because he had not overwhelmed her with questions at their meeting. She could never explain, of course, because people would think her mad. . . . They might even send her to an asylum, if she told them. . . . She longed for the relief of confession, yet who would believe that she was merely a sane woman rendered desperate by evil dreams? Not Clare, certainly—not Elsbeth, though they loved her. . . . She would just have to go on fighting her terrors as best she could, till she or they were crushed. . . .

She sighed hopelessly and opened her eyes.

"Had a doze? Good! Tea's ready! I expect you want it," said Roger cheerfully.

She was surprised into normality, and began to smile as she looked about her.

The rickety table had been covered by a gay, chequered cloth. There was crockery, and a little green tea-pot, and a pile of short-bread at her elbow. A spirit-lamp and kettle were shelved incongruously between trays of daffodils.

Roger sat upon an upturned flower-pot, and beamed at her.

"Oh, how jolly!" cried Alwynne, the Alwynne once more of his former acquaintance. "Where did it come from?"

He showed her a cupboard against the wall, half hidden by a canopy of smilax.

"I always keep stores here," he confessed boyishly. "I used to when I was a kid. This is the old glass-house, you know, on Great House land. I've built all the others. I used to be Robinson Crusoe then, and now it's useful, when I'm busy, not to have to go up to the house always. Won't you pour out?"

Alwynne flashed a look at him.

"I don't believe it's that. You enjoy the—the marooning still. I should. I think it's perfectly delightful here."

"Well, Harris—my head-gardener—doesn't approve. Think's it's *infra dig*. He told me once that he knew ladies enjoyed making parlours of their conservatories, and letting in draughts and killing the plants; but he was a nurseryman himself. How ever, I've broken him in to it. Oh, I say, there's no milk!"

"I don't take it. Clare—a friend of mine—never does, so I've got accustomed to it." She drank thirstily. "Oh, it's good! I didn't know I wanted my tea so."

"I did," he said significantly.

She coloured painfully : she would not look at him.

"I was very tired," she said lamely.

"Were you?" he asked her. "You weren't gone half an hour. Do you know it's only half-past three?"

He was very gentle; but she felt herself accused. She played uneasily with her rope of beads as she chose her words. Roger, for all his intentness, could not help noticing how white and slender her hands showed, stained though they were with hya-cinth-milk, as they fingered the blue, glancing chain. They were thin though; and following the outline of her wrist and arm and bare neck, he thought her cheek, for all its smooth youth-fulness, was thin also, too thin—altogether too austere, for her age and way of life.. She had always been flushed in his presence, delightfully flushed with laughter, or anger, or embarrassment, and he had noticed nothing beyond her pretty colour. But now, he saw uneasily that there were hollows round her eyes, as if she slept little, and that there were hollows as well as dimples in her cheeks. He was astonished to find himself not a little perturbed at his discovery, so perturbed that he did not, for a moment, realize that she was speaking to him.

"I am very sorry," she was saying. "I'm afraid you thought —I'm afraid I was rather silly—in the wood. I was disturbed when you found me." Her words came jerkily. "I had not expected—that is—I did not expect——" She broke off. Her eyes implored him to leave her alone.

He would not understand their appeal.

" Yes, you expected——" he prompted her.

She controlled her voice with difficulty.

" Heavens knows ! " She laughed, with a pitiful little air of throwing him off the scent. " One gets frightened for no reason sometimes."

" Does one ? "

" In the country—I'm town-bred." She smiled at him.

He made up his mind, though he felt brutal.

" You were expecting—Louise ? "

There was a silence. Slowly she lifted shaking hands, warding him off.

" No, no ! " she said. " For pity's sake. You are calling her back." Then, struck with a new idea, she grew, if possible, whiter still. " Unless," she said, whispering, " you saw her— you too ? Then there is no hope. I thought it was in my mind— only in my mind—but if you saw her too——" Her voice failed.

He thrust in hastily, ready enough to comfort her, but knowing well that the time had not come. Yet he felt like a surgeon at his first operation.

" No, you are mistaken. There was no one. I don't even know who Louise is. Only you mentioned her—once or twice, you see."

" Did I ? " she said. Then, with an effort at a commonplace tone : " I was stupidly upset. You must excuse——"

He broke in.

" Who is Louise ? " he asked her bluntly.

" A ghost," said Alwynne, white to the lips.

Again they were blankly silent.

Then she spoke, with extraordinary passion—

" If you laugh—it will be wicked if you laugh at me."

" I'm not thinking of laughing," he said, with the petulance of extreme anxiety.

She met his look and shrugged her shoulders.

" Then you think I'm crazy," she began defiantly. " I can't help it, what you think." She changed the subject transparently. " Roger, it's nice here. What are the names of all these flowers ? Are those big ones daffodils, or jonquils, or narcissi ? I never know the difference. I never remember——" Her voice trailed into silence.

" But look here," he began, and stopped again abruptly, deep in thought.

The flame of the spirit-lamp on the shelf between them flickered and failed, and sputtered up again noisily. Mechanically he rose to extinguish it, and, still absently, cleared the little table of its china and eatables.

Then he sat down once more, and leant forward, his arms on the table, his expression determined, yet very friendly.

" Alwynne," he said, in his most matter-of-fact voice, " hadn't you better tell me all about it ? "

" You ? "

" Why not ? " he said comfortably. " You'll feel ever so much better if you get it off your chest."

For an instant she hesitated : then she shook her head wearily.

" I would like to tell some one. But I can't. I sound mad, even to myself. I couldn't tell any one. I couldn't tell Elsbeth even."

" Of course not," he agreed. " You can't worry your own people."

" No, you can't, can you ? " she said, grateful for his comprehension.

" Of course not. But you see—I'm different. Whatever your trouble is, it won't worry me—because I don't care for you like Elsbeth and your friends. So you can just ease off on me—d'you see ? If I do think you mad, it just doesn't matter, does it ? What does it matter telling some one a secret when you'll never see them again ? Don't you see ? " he argued reassuringly.

She nodded dumbly. The cheerful, impersonal kindness of his voice and air made her want to cry. She realized how she had been aching for sympathy.

" Don't you see ? " he repeated.

" You wouldn't make fun ? " she asked him. " You wouldn't tell any one ? You wouldn't talk me over ? "

" No, Alwynne," he said gravely.

For a moment her eyes searched his face wistfully ; then with sudden decision, she began to speak.

CHAPTER XXXIV

ALWYNNE'S words, after the months of silence, came rushing out, breaking down all barriers, sweeping on in unnatural fluency. Yet she was simple and direct, entirely sincere ; accepting him at his own valuation, impersonally, as confessor and comforter, without a side glance at the impression she might make, or its effect on their after relations.

She told him the story of Louise ; and he felt sick as he listened. Unintentionally, for she was obviously absorbed in her school and uncritical in her attitude to it, she gave him a vivid enough impression of the system in force, of the deliberate encouragement of much that he considered unhealthy, if not unnatural. He detected an hysterical tendency in the emulations and enthusiasms to which she referred. The gardener in him revolted at the thought of such congestion of minds and bodies. He felt as indignant as if he had discovered a tray of unthinned seedlings. Alwynne conveyed to him, more clearly than she knew, an idea of the forcing-house atmosphere that she, and those still younger than she, had been breathing. The friend she so constantly mentioned, repelled him ; he thought of her with distaste, as of an unscrupulous and unskilful hireling ; he was amazed at the affection of Alwynne's references to her. Only in connection with the dead child was there a hint of uncertainty in her attitude. There perhaps, she admitted, had ' Clare ' been, not unkind—never and impossibly unkind—but perhaps, with the best of motives, mistaken. She had not understood Louise. Roger agreed silently and grimly enough. She had not understood Louise, whom she had killed, nor this loyal and affectionate child, whom she was driving into melancholia, nor any one it appeared, nor anything, but the needs of her own barrenly emotional nature. . . . He was horrified at the idea of such a woman, such a type of woman, in undisputed authority, moulding the mothers of the next generation. . . . He had never considered the matter seriously, but he supposed she

was but one of many. . . . There must be something poisonous
in a system that could render possible the placing of such women
in such positions. . . .

"Then what happened, after that poor child's death ? " he
asked. "She left, of course ? "

"Who ? "

"Your friend—' Clare '—Miss—— ? "

"Hartill. Oh, no ! Why should she ? "

"I should have thought—suicide—bad for the school's
reputation ? "

"Then you think it was—that—too ? It was supposed to
be an accident."

"How do you mean, ' supposed ' ? "

"There was an inquest, you see. I had to go. I was so
frightened all the time, of what I might slip into saying. But
they all agreed that it was an accident. She was fond of curling
up in the window-seats with her books. Oh, she was a queer
little thing ! When you came on her suddenly, she used to
look up like a startled baby colt. She always looked as if
she wanted some one to run to. Well, there was no guard,
you see, only an inch of ledge—she had not been well—she
must have felt faint—and fallen. They all said it was that.
I was so thankful—for Clare's sake. She could not reproach
herself—after such a verdict. It was ' Accidental Death.'
Only—I—of course—I knew. Some of them guessed—Clare—
and I believe Elsbeth, though we never discussed it—and I
knew. But nobody said anything—nobody has, ever since,
except once Clare told me—what she feared. I never managed
to persuade her that it was an accident, but at least she doesn't
know for certain, and at least she knows she couldn't help it.
And now we never speak of it. But *I* know——"

"What do you know ? " he said. "You found out something ? "

"She did—she did kill herself," said Alwynne. "Oh, Roger,
she did. I've known it all along—I should have guessed anyway, I think, because I knew how unhappy she was. I knew
how awfully she cared about Clare. Clare was very good to
her sometimes. Clare was fond of her, you know. Clare takes
violent fancies like that, to clever people. And Louise was
brilliant, of course. Clare was charmed with her. Only Louise
—this is how I've thought it out ; oh, I've had time to think it
out—she just got drunk on it, the happiness, I mean, of being

cared for. She hadn't much of a home. She was rather an ugly duckling to her people, I think. Then Clare made a fuss of her, and you see, she was so little, she couldn't see that—it didn't mean much to Clare. And I don't think grown-up people understand how girls are—they have to worship some one, at that age. Clare doesn't quite understand, I think. She is too sensible herself to realize how girls can be silly. She is awfully good to them, but, of course, she never dreams how miserable they get when she gets bored with them. She can't help it."

Roger's face was expressive—but Alwynne was staring at the uneasy butterfly.

"It doesn't matter, as a rule. Only Louise had no one else—and it just broke her heart. If she had been grown-up it would have been like being in love."

Roger made an inarticulate remark.

"Don't you see?" said Alwynne innocently.

"I see." He was carefully expressionless.

"And then she was run down and did her work badly. And Clare hates illness—besides—she thought Louise was slacking. I tried to make her see—— Oh," she cried passionately, "why didn't I try harder? It's haunting me, Roger, that I didn't try enough. I ought to have known how she felt—I was near her age. Clare couldn't be expected to—but Louise talked to me sometimes—I ought to have seen. I did see. All that summer she went about so white and miserable—and Clare was angry with her—and I hadn't the pluck to tackle either of them. I was afraid of being a busybody—I was afraid of upsetting Clare. You see—I'm awfully fond of Clare. She makes you forget everything but herself. And, of course, she never realized what was wrong with Louise. I didn't altogether, either—you do believe that?" She broke off, questioning pitifully, as if he were her judge.

He nodded.

"Right till the day of the play, I never really saw how crazily miserable she was growing. She was crazy—don't you think?"

"You want to think so?" He considered her curiously.

"It mitigates it."

"That she killed herself?"

"It's deadly sin. Or don't you believe——?"

"No," he said. 'There's such a thing as the right of exit—but go on."

" What do you mean ? "

" I'll tell you what I think presently. I want all your thoughts now—— There were signs——? "

" Of insanity ? No. But she was—exaggerated—too intelligent—too babyish—too brilliant—too everything. She felt things too much. She failed in an exam.—sheer overwork—just before."

" I see. Was she ambitious ? "

" Only to please Clare. Clare didn't like her failing."

" Did she tell the child so ? " His tone was stern.

" Oh, no ! "

" You're sure ? "

" Clare would have told me if they had had a row. She tells me everything."

He smiled a little.

" How old is your friend ? "

She looked surprised.

" Oh—thirty-three—thirty-four—thirty-five. I don't really know. She never talks about ages and looks and that sort of thing. She rather despises all that. She laughs at me for—for liking clothes . . ." Her little blush made her look natural again. " But why ? "

" I wondered. Then there was nothing to upset the child ? "

" Only the failing. And then the play. I told you. She was awfully strange afterwards. That's where I blame myself. I ought to have seen that she was overwrought. But she drank the tea, and cheered up so when I told her Clare was pleased with her acting—— "

" Was she ? " He was frowning interestedly.

" I'm sure she must have been—it was brilliant, you know."

" She said so ? "

" Oh, not actually—but I could tell. And it cheered the child up. I was quite easy about her—and then ten minutes later—— " She shuddered.

" Then it might have been an accident," he suggested soothingly.

" It wasn't," she said, with despairing conviction.

" My dear girl ! Either you're indulging in morbid imaginings—or you've something to go on ? "

She shook her head with a frightened look at him.

" No ! " she said hurriedly. " No ! "

" Then why," he said quietly, meeting her eyes, " were you frightened at the inquest ? "

She averted her eyes.

" I wasn't—I mean—I was nervous, of course."

" You were frightened of what you might slip into saying. You told me so ten minutes ago."

" Oh, if you're trying to trap me ? " she flashed out wrathfully.

He rejoiced at the tone. It was the impetuous Alwynne of his daily intercourse again. The mere relief of discussion was, as he had guessed, having a tonic effect on her nerves.

He smiled at her pleasantly.

" Don't tell me anything more, if you'd rather not."

She subsided at this.

" I didn't mean to be angry," she faltered. " Only I've guarded myself so from telling. You see, I lied at the inquest. It was perjury, I suppose." There was a little touch of importance in her tone. " But I'll tell you."

She hesitated, her older self once more supervening.

" Afterwards—when the doctor had come, and they took Louise away—after that ghastly afternoon was over——" She whitened. " It was ghastly, you know—so many people—crowding and gaping—I dream of all those crowded faces——"

" Well ? " he urged her forward.

" I went up to the room where she had changed, to see that the children had gone——"

" She fell from that room ? "

" She must have. After she had changed. She'd locked the door—to change. I broke it open. I thought she had fainted—a baby told me something about Louise falling—lisping so, I couldn't make out what she meant—and I'd run up to see. It turned out afterwards that little Joan had been in a lower room, and had seen her body as it fell past the window."

" How beastly ! " he said, with an involuntary shudder.

" And when I got the door open—an empty room. Something made me look out of the window. She was down below—right under me—on the steps."

She was silent.

" But afterwards ? " he urged her. " You went up again ? "

" I had to. I was afraid already—recollecting little things. I looked about, in case she'd—left a message. And on the window-ledge—there were great scratches. Then I knew."

She was forgetting him, staring into space, peopled as it was with her memories.

" I don't understand," he said.

She did not answer.

" Alwynne ! " he said urgently.

She looked at him absently.

" Scratches ? What are you driving at ? "

" Oh," she said dully, " there was a nail in her shoe. She had tried to hammer it in at morning school. It had made scratches all over the rostrum. I was rather cross about it."

" But I don't see," he began, and stopped, realizing suddenly her meaning.

" You mean—she must have stood on the ledge—to make those marks ? "

" Yes," said Alwynne. Then, fiercely, " Well ? "

" Yes, that's conclusive," he admitted. He looked at her pityingly. " You poor child ! And you never told ? "

" I got a paint-box," she said defiantly, " and painted them brown—like the paintwork. It would have broken up Clare to know—and all the questions and comments. What would you have done ? "

He ignored the challenge, answered only the misery in the tone.

" It can't have been easy for you—that week," he said gently.

" Easy ? " She began to laugh harshly. " And yet I don't know," she reflected. " I don't think I felt anything much at the time. It was like being in a play. Almost interesting. Entirely unreal. At the inquest—I lied as easily as saying grace. I wasn't a bit worried. What did worry me was a bit of sticking-plaster on the coroner's chin. One end was un-curled, and I was longing for him to stick it down again. It seemed more important than anything else that he should stick it down. It would have been a real relief to me. I'm not trying to be funny."

" I know," he said.

" And when it was over—I was quite cheerful. And at the funeral—I know they thought I was callous. But I didn't feel sad. Only cold—icy cold—in my hands and my feet and my heart. And I felt desperately irritated with them all for crying. People look appalling when they cry." She paused. " So they banked up Louise with wreaths and we left her." She paused again.

" Well ? " he prompted.

" I went home at the end of that week. Elsbeth sent me to bed early. I was log-tired all of a sudden. Oh, I was tired! I had hardly slept at all since she died. I'd stayed at Clare's, you know. She's a bad sleeper, too, and it always infects me— and we used to sit up till daylight, forgetting the time, talking. We've always heaps to talk about. Clare's a night-bird. She's always most brilliant about midnight." She smiled reminis- cently. " We picnic, you know, in our dressing-gowns. She has a great white bearskin on the hearth. Her fires are piled up, and never go out all night. And I brew coffee—and we talk. It's jolly. I wish you knew Clare. She's an absorbing person."

" You're giving me quite a good idea of her," he said. Then, carelessly : " But she must have realized that after such a shock —and the strain——"

" Oh, it was much worse for Clare," she broke in quickly. " Think—her special pupil ! She had had such hopes of Louise. And Clare's so terribly sensitive—she was getting it on her mind. Do you know, she almost began to think it was her fault, not to have seen what was going on ? Once, she was absolutely frantic with depression, poor darling, until I made her understand that, if it was any one's, it must be mine. Of course, when I told her everything, how I'd guessed Louise was pretty miserable, and tried to tell her again and then funked it—well, then she saw. As she said, if I'd only spoken out. . . . She was very kind—but, of course, I soon felt that she thought I was responsible—indirectly—for the whole thing——" Her voice quavered.

Roger, watching her simple face, wanted to do something vigorous. At that moment it would have given him great satisfaction to have interviewed Miss Hartill. Failing that, he wanted to take Alwynne by the shoulders and shake the nonsense out of her. He repressed himself, however. He was in his way, as simple as Alwynne, but where she was merely direct, he was shrewd. He knew that she must show him all the weeds that were choking her before he could set about uprooting them and planting good seed in their stead.

She went on.

" But even then, though I had been neglectful—oh, Roger, what made Louise do it ? Just then ? She looked happier ! It couldn't have been anything I'd said ? I know I cheered her up. It's inconceivable! She was smiling, contented—and she went straight upstairs and killed herself!"

He shook his head.

"Inconceivable, as you say. You're sure—of your facts?"

"How?"

"I mean—you were the last person to see her?"

"Oh, yes, Roger! every one was at tea."

"Miss Hartill?"

"Clare would have said——"

"Of course," he said, "she tells you everything."

She nodded, in all good faith—

"Besides, Clare was in the mistresses' room."

"Impossible for her to have spoken with Louise?"

"Quite. Clare would have told me——"

"Yet there remains the fact that Louise was, as you say, happier after seeing you. Within fifteen minutes she is dead. Either she went mad—which I don't believe, do you?"

"I want to——"

"But you don't—knowing the child. Neither do I, from what you tell me. She seems to have been horribly sane. Sane enough, anyhow, to throw off a burden. So if, as we agree, she didn't suddenly go mad—something occurred to change her mood of comparative happiness to actual despair. I think, if you ask me, that she did see Miss Hartill after she left you."

"But Clare would have told me," repeated Alwynne stubbornly.

"I'm not so sure."

"But she said nothing at the inquest, either."

"Did you?" he retorted. "If she had had a row with the child it would have sounded pretty bad."

"But Clare's incapable of deceit."

"She might say the same of you."

"But—if your guess were true, it would be Clare's fault—all Clare's fault—not mine at all!" she deduced slowly.

"It's not your fault, anyway," he assured her.

"But it would have been too utterly cruel of Clare not to have told me. She knew what I felt at the time—why not have told me?"

"She might have been afraid—you might have shrunk——"

"From Clare?" She smiled securely. Then, with a change of tone: "No, Roger. All this is guessing, far-fetched guessing."

"Anyhow, Alwynne," he said sharply, "there was gross

cruelty in her treatment of that child. You can't excuse it. Directly or indirectly, she is responsible for her death."

She flushed.

" You have not the shadow of right to say that."

" I do say it."

She put out her hand to him with a touch of appeal.

" Please—won't you leave Clare out of it ? You are utterly wrong. You see, you don't know her. If you did you would understand. I am so grateful to you for being kind. I don't want to be angry. But I must, if you talk like that. Please— if you can, make me sure it wasn't my fault. But if it involves Clare—I'd rather go on being—not quite happy. Yet I hoped, perhaps, you would help me."

" Of course I'm helping you," he said, quick to catch and adopt her tone. He had no wish to intimidate. He liked her pathetic little dignities and loyalties. He was, so far, content ; he had, he knew, in spite of her protestations, sown a seed of distrust in her mind. Time would ripen it. He felt no compunction in enlightening her blind devotion. He had quick antipathies, and he had conceived an idea of Clare Hartill that would have appalled Alwynne, and which justified to himself any measure that he might see fit to take. In his own mind he referred to her as ' that poisonous female.' There were no half-measures with Roger.

CHAPTER XXXV

ALWYNNE leant back in her chair and regarded Roger with some intentness.

" Well ? " he said politely.

" I was thinking—— " she said lamely.

" Obviously."

" That it was rather queer—that I should tell you all this, when I couldn't even tell Elsbeth."

" Don't you think it's often easier to talk to strangers ?   One's personality can make its own impression—it has no preconception to fight against."

" Yes. But I hate strangers, till they've stopped being strange. And, you know "—she hesitated—" I haven't really liked you. Have you noticed it ? "

" In streaks," he admitted. " But why ? "

" You patronize so ! " she flared. " You make me feel a fool. This afternoon—— Of course, it's quite true that I don't know much about men. I suppose you knew I was—inexperienced : but you needn't have rubbed it in. And you've always talked down to me."

" I don't think I did," he considered the matter unsmiling. " I think it's rather the other way—the tilt of your nose disturbs my complacence. You listen to me at meals like Disapproval incarnate. You make me nervous."

" Do I ? " she asked delightedly.

" Yes." He laughed. " I hide it under a superior air, of course."

" Yes, of course," she sympathized. " That's what I do always."

" It is useful," he agreed.

" People may think you disagreeable, but at least you're dignified. *You have chosen your fault well, I really cannot laugh at it.* Do you remember ? I told Elsbeth that you were like Mr. Darcy."

" And that you don't like me ? "

" Well—I didn't. That's why it's so queer—that I can talk to you so easily. I am grateful. It has helped, just talking."

" I knew it would."

" I feel better." She stirred in her seat. " Is it late ? Ought we to be going home ? "

He chose his words, his eyes on her, though he spoke casually enough.

" No hurry. We can always take a cut through the wood, you know."

She flinched at that, as he expected; spoke uneasily, furtive-eyed.

" I think I'd rather go at once—round by the road. Isn't there a road ? " She rose and looked about her, taking farewell of the daffodils.

" Yes, there's a road. Wouldn't you like a bunch ? " He took a pair of scissors from the wall, and began to select his blooms. Alwynne followed him delightedly. She thought she would have a surprise for Clare, after all. And Elsbeth ! Elsbeth was an after-thought. But she hoped there would be enough for Elsbeth.

" Why won't you go back through the wood ? " he said quietly, as, hands full, he at last replaced the scissors on their particular nail, and twitched a strand from the horse-tail of bass that hung beside them. " Tell me." Then, calmly, " Here—put your finger here, will you ? "

Mechanically she obeyed and he tied the knot that secured the great yellow sheaf and gave it to her.

" Now tell me. What frightened you in the wood ? What was wrong ? " He spoke quietly, but his tone compelled her.

" If you dreamed a dream——" she began unwillingly, " night after night—month after month—something ghastly——"

" Yes—" he encouraged her.

" Ah, well—at least you've the comfort of knowing it's a dream. But suppose, one day—you dreamt it while you were awake—— ? "

" Dreamt what ? " He guessed her meaning, but he was deliberately forcing her to reduce her terrors into words—the more they crystallized, the easier she would find it to face and destroy them.

" Do you believe in hell ? " she flung at him.

" I should jolly well think so."

"For children?" Her tone implored comfort.

"I'm afraid so."

"But how can it be fair? They're so little. They don't know right from wrong."

"I knew a kid," he said meditatively, an eye on her tormented face, "only eight—used to act, if you please. Hung about London stage-doors, and bearded managers in their dens for a living. Quick little chap! Father drunk or ill; incapable, anyhow. The child supported them both. I've seen that child kept hanging about three or four hours on end. And what he knew! It made you sick and sorry. He must be twelve by now—getting on, I believe, poor kid! And a cheerful monkey! He's certainly had his hell, though."

She had hardly listened, she was absorbed in her thoughts; but she caught at his last words—

"In this life? Oh, yes! That's cruel enough. But not afterwards? Not eternal damnation? I don't mind it for myself so much—but for a baby that can't understand why—— It isn't possible, is it?"

He began to laugh jollily.

"Alwynne—you utter fool! Don't you believe in God?"

"I suppose so," she admitted.

"Of course, if you didn't——"

"Yes," she thrust in. "Then it would be all right. I could be sure she was asleep—dead—like last year's leaves——"

"But why should God complicate matters?"

"Well—heaven follows—and hell—don't they? *Their worm dieth not*—and all the rest."

"Oh, I follow."

"Miss Marsham—the head mistress, you know—of course she's very old—but she believes—terribly. It's an awfully religious school. It scares some of the children. I used to laugh, but now, since Louise died, it scares me, though I am grown up. I've no convictions—and she is certain—and then I get these nightmares. I hear her calling—for water."

The flat matter-of-fact tone alarmed him more than emotion would have done.

"Water?"

"*For I am tormented in this flame*. I hear her every night—wailing." Her eyes strained after something that he could not see.

He found no words.

She returned with an effort.

"Of course, when it's over—I know it's imagination. My sense tells me so—in the daytime. Only I can't be sure. If only. I could be sure! If some one would tell me to be sure. It's the reasoning it out for myself—all day—and going back to the dreams all night."

"How long has this been going on?" he asked curtly.

"Ever since—when I came home from Clare's—that night. I'd slept like a log. Then I woke up suddenly. I thought I heard Louise calling. I'd forgotten she was dead. Every night it happens—as soon as I go to sleep, she comes. Always trying to speak to me. I hear her screaming with pain—wanting help. Never any words. Do you think I'm mad? I know it's only a dream—but every night, you know——"

"You're not going to dream any more," he said, with a determination that belied his inward sense of dismay. "But go on—let's have the rest of it."

"There isn't much. Just dreams. It's been a miserable year. I couldn't be cheerful always, you know—and I used to dread going to bed so. It made me stupid all day. And Clare—Clare didn't quite understand. Oh—I did want to tell her so. But you can't worry people. I'm afraid Elsbeth got worried—she hates it if you don't eat and have a colour. She packed me off here at last."

She drew a long breath.

"This blessed place! You don't know how I love it. I feel a different girl. All this space and air and freedom What is it that the country does to one's mind? I've slept. No dreaming. Sleep that's like a hot bath. Can you imagine what that is after those months? Oh, Roger! I thought I'd stopped dreaming for good—I was forgetting——"

"Go on forgetting," he said. "You can. I'll help you. You had a shock. It made you ill. You're getting well again. That's all."

"I'm not," she said. "I'm going mad. To-day, in that wood. . . . Louise came running after me—and I was awake. . . ."

Suddenly she gave a little ripple of high-pitched laughter.

"Oh, Mr. Lumsden! Isn't this a ridiculous conversation? And your face—you're so absurd when you frown. . . . You make me laugh. . . . You make me laugh. . . ."

She broke off. Roger, with a swift movement, had turned and was standing over her.

"Now shut up!" he said sharply. "Shut up! D'you hear? Shut up this instant, and sit down." He put his hand on her shoulder and jerked her back into her chair.

The shock of his roughness checked her hysteria, as he had intended it should. She sat limply, her head in her hand, trying not to cry. He watched her.

"Pull yourself together, Alwynne!" he said more gently.

Her lips quivered, but she nodded valiantly.

"I will. Just wait a minute. I don't want to make a fool of myself." Then, with a quavering laugh, "Oh, Roger, this is pleasant for you!"

He laughed.

"You needn't mind me," he said calmly. "Any more than I mind you. Except when you threaten hysterics. I bar hysterics. I wouldn't mind if they did any good. But we've got lots to do. No time at all for them. We've got to work this thing out. Ready?"

Alwynne waited, her attention caught.

"Now listen," he said. "First of all, get it into your head that I know all about it, and that I'm going to see you through. Next—whenever you get scared—though you won't again, I hope—that you are just to come and talk it over. You won't even have to tell me—I shall see by your face, you know. Do you understand? You're not alone any more. I'm here. Always ready to lay your ghosts for you. Will you remember?"

He spoke clearly and patiently—very cheerful and reassuring.

"You've got to go home well, Alwynne. Because, you know, though you're as sane as I am, you've been ill. This last year has been one long illness. You had a shock—a ghastly shock—and, of course, it skinned your nerves raw. My dear, I wonder it didn't send you really mad, instead of merely making you afraid of going mad. If you hadn't put up such a fight—— Honestly, Alwynne! I think you've been jolly plucky."

The sincere admiration in his voice was wonderfully pleasant to hear.

Alwynne opened her eyes widely.

"I don't know what you mean," she began shyly.

"I'm not imaginative," he said, "but if I'd been hag-ridden as you have——" He broke off abruptly. "But, at least, you've fought yourself free," he continued cheerfully. "Yes, in spite of to-day." And his complete assurance of voice and manner had its effect on Alwynne, though she did not realize it.

"You're better already. You say yourself you're a different girl since you got away from—since you came here. And when you're quite well, it'll be your own work, not mine. I'm just tugging you up the bank, so to speak. But you've done the real fighting with the elements. I think you can be jolly proud of yourself."

Alwynne looked at him, half smiling, half bewildered.

"What do you mean? You talk as if it were all over. Shall I never be frightened again? Think of to-day."

"Of course it's all over," he assured her truculently. "To-day? To-day was the last revolt of your imagination. You've let it run riot too long. Of course it hasn't been easy to call it to heel."

"You think it's all silly imaginings, then?"

"Alwynne," he said. "You've got to listen to this, just this. You say I'm not to talk about your friend, that I don't know her—that I'm unjust. But listen, at least, to this. I won't be unfair. I'll grant you that she was fond of the little girl, and meant no harm, no more than you did. But you say yourself that she was miserable till you relieved her mind by taking all the blame on yourself. Can't you conceive that in so doing you did assume a burden, a very real one? Don't you think that her fears, her terrors, may have haunted you as well as your own? I believe in the powers of thought. I believe that fear—remorse—regret—may materialize into a very ghost at your elbow. Do you remember Macbeth and Banquo? Do you believe that a something really physical sat that night in the king's seat? Do you think it was the man from his grave? I think it was Macbeth's thoughts incarnate. He thought too much, that man. But let's leave all that. Let's argue it out from a common-sense point of view. You said you believed in God?"

"Yes," she said.

"And the devil?"

"I suppose so."

"Well—I'm not so sure that I do," he remarked meditatively. "But if I do—I must say I cannot see the point of a God who wouldn't be more than a match for him : and a God who'd leave a baby in his clutches to expiate in fire and brimstone and all the rest of the beastliness—— Well, is it common sense?" he appealed to her.

"If you put it like that——" she admitted.

" My dear, would you let Louise frizzle if it were in your hands ? Why, you've driven yourself half crazy with fear for her, as it is. Can't you give God credit for a little common humanity ? I'm not much of a Bible reader, but I seem to remember something about a sparrow falling to the ground—— Now follow it up," he went on urgently. " If Louise's life was so little worth living that she threw it away—doesn't it prove she had her hell down here ? If you insist on a hell. And when she was dead, poor baby, can't you trust God to have taken charge of her ? And if He has—as He must have—do you think that child—that happy child, Alwynne, for if God exists at all, He must exist as the very source and essence of peace and love—that that child would or could wrench itself apart from God, from its happiness, in order to return to torment you ? Is it possible ? Is it probable ? In any way feasible ? "

Alwynne caught her breath.

" How you believe in God ! I wish I could ! "

Roger flushed suddenly like an embarrassed boy.

" You know, it's queer," he confided, subsiding naïvely, " till I began to talk to you, I didn't know I did. I never bother about church and things. You know——"

But Alwynne was not attending.

" Of course—I see what you mean," she murmured. " It applies to Louise too. Why, Roger, she was really fond of me—not as she was of Clare, of course—but quite fond of me. She never would have hurt me. Hurt ? Poor mite ! She never hurt any one in all her life."

" I wonder you didn't think of that before," remarked Roger severely. " I hope you see what an idiot you've been ? "

" Yes," said Alwynne meekly. She did not flash out at him as he had hoped she would : but her manner had grown calm, and her eyes were peaceful.

" Poor little Louise ! " said Alwynne slowly. " So we needn't think about her any more ? She's to be dead, and buried, and forgotten. It sounds harsh, doesn't it ? But she is dead—and I've only been keeping her alive in my mind all this year. Is that what you mean ? "

" Yes," he said. " And if it were not as I think it is, sheer imagination—if your grieving and fear really kept a fraction of her personality with you, to torment you both—let her go now, Alwynne. Say good-bye to her kindly, and let her go home."

She looked at him gravely for a moment. Then she turned from him to the empty house of flowers.

" Good-bye, Louise ! " said Alwynne, simply as a child.

About them was the evening silence. The sun, sinking over the edge of the world, was a blinding glory.

Out of the flowers rose the butterfly, found an open pane and fluttered out on the evening air, straight into the heart of the sunlight.

They watched it with dazzled eyes.

CHAPTER XXXVI

ALWYNNE had gone to bed early. She confessed to being tired, as she bade her cousins good-night, and, indeed, she had dark rings about her eyes; but her colour was brilliant as she waited at the foot of the stairs for her candle. Roger had followed her into the hall and was lighting it. The thin flame flickered between them, kindling odd lights in their eyes.

"Good-night," said Alwynne, and went up a shallow step or two.

"Good-night," said Roger, without moving.

She turned suddenly and bent down to him over the poppy-head of the balustrade.

"Good-night," said Alwynne once more, and put out her hand.

"You're to sleep well, you know," he said authoritatively.

She nodded. Then, with a rush—

"Roger, I do thank you. I do thank you very much."

"That's all right," said Roger awkwardly.

Alwynne went upstairs.

He watched her disappear in the shadows of the landing, and took a meditative turn up and down the long hall before he returned to the drawing-room.

He felt oddly responsible for the girl; wished that he had some one to consult about her. . . . His aunts? Dears, of course, but . . . Alicia, possibly. . . . Certainly not Jean. . . . Nothing against them . . . dearest women alive . . . but hardly capable of understanding Alwynne, were they? Without at all realizing it he had already arrived at the conviction that no one understood Alwynne but himself.

He caught her name as he re-entered the room.

"Ever so much better! A different creature! Don't you think so, Roger?"

"Think what?"

"That Alwynne's a new girl? It's the air. Nothing like

Dene air. But, of course, you didn't see her when she first
came. A poor white thing! She'd worked herself to a shadow.
How Elsbeth allowed it——"

Jean caught her up.

"Overwork! Fiddlesticks! It wasn't that. I'm convinced
in my own mind that there's something behind it. A girl
doesn't go to pieces like that from a little extra work. Look
at your Compton women at the end of a term. Bursting with
energy still, I will say that for them. No—I'm inclined to
agree with Parker. I told you what she said to me? 'She
must have been crossed in love, poor young lady, the way she
fiddle-faddles with her food!'"

Alicia laughed.

"When you and Parker get together there's not a reputation
safe in the three Denes. If there had been anything of the
kind, Elsbeth would have given me a hint."

"I should have thought Elsbeth would be the last person——"
Jean broke off significantly.

Roger glanced at her, eyebrows lifted.

"What's she driving at, Aunt Alice?"

"Lord knows!" said Alicia shortly.

Jean grew huffed.

"It's all very well, Alicia, to take that tone. You know
what I mean perfectly well. Considering how reticent Elsbeth
was over her own affairs to us—she wouldn't be likely to confide
anything about Alwynne. But Elsbeth always imagined no
one had any eyes."

Alicia moved uneasily in her chair.

"Jean, will you never let that foolish gossip be? It wasn't
your business thirty years ago—at least let it alone now."

Jean flushed.

"It's all very well to be superior, Alice, but you know you
agreed with me at the time."

Roger chuckled.

"What are you two driving at? Let's have it."

Alicia answered him.

"My dear boy, you know what Jean is. Elsbeth stayed with
us a good deal when we were all girls together—and because
she and your dear father were very good friends——"

"Inseparable!" snapped Jean. She was annoyed that the
telling of the story was taken from her.

"Oh, they had tastes in common. But we all liked him.

I'm quite certain Elsbeth was perfectly heart-whole. Only Jean has the servant-girl habit of pairing off all her friends and acquaintances. I don't say, of course, that if John had never met your dear mother—but she came home from her French school—she'd been away two years, you know—and turned everybody's head. Ravishing she was. I remember her coming-out dance. She wore the first short dress we'd seen —every one wore trains in those days—white gauze and forget-me-nots. She looked like a fairy. All the gentlemen wanted to dance with her, she was so light-footed. Your father fell head over ears ! They were engaged in a fortnight. And nobody, in her quiet way, was more pleased than Elsbeth, I'm sure. Why, she was one of the bridesmaids ! "

"She never came to stay with them afterwards," said Jean obstinately, " always had an excuse."

"Considering she had to nurse her father, with her mother an invalid already——" Alicia was indignant. "Ten years of sick-nursing that poor girl had ! "

"Anyhow, she never came to Dene again till after John died. Then she came, once. When she heard we were all going out to Italy. Stayed a week."

"I remember," said Roger unexpectedly.

"You ! You were only five," cried Jean. The clock struck as she spoke. She jumped up. "Alicia ! It's ten o'clock ! Where's Parker ? Why hasn't Parker brought the biscuits ? You really might speak to her ! She's always late ! "

She flurried out of the room.

Roger drew in his chair.

"Aunt Alice, I say—how much of that is just—Aunt Jean ? "

Alicia sighed.

"My dear boy ! How should I know ? It's all such a long while ago. Jean's no respecter of privacy. I never noticed anything—hate prying—always did."

"She never married ? "

"She was over thirty before her mother died. She aged quickly—faded somehow. At that visit Jean spoke of—I shall never forget the change in her. She was only twenty-six, two years older than your mother, but Rosemary was a girl beside her, in spite of you and her widow's weeds. And then Alwynne was left on her hands and she absorbed herself in her. She's one of those self-effacing women—— But there—she's quite contented, I think. She adores Alwynne. Her letters are cheerful enough. I always kept up with her. I'd like to see her again."

" Why didn't you ask her with Alwynne ? "

" I did. She wouldn't come. Spring-cleaning, and one of her whimsies. Wanted the child to have a change from her. That's Elsbeth all over. She was always painfully humble. I imagine she'd sell her immortal soul for Alwynne."

" Well—and so would you for me," said Roger, with a twinkle.

" Don't you flatter yourself," retorted Alicia with spirit. Then she laughed and kissed him, and lumbered off to scold Jean up to bed.

Roger sat late, staring into the fire, and reviewing the day's happenings.

There was Alwynne to be considered. . . . Alwynne in the wood. . . . Alwynne in the daffodil house. . . . Alwynne hanging over the bannisters, a candle in her hand. . . . And Elsbeth. . . . . Elsbeth had become something more than a name. . . . Elsbeth had known his mother—had been 'pals' with his father. . . . He chuckled at the recollection of Jean's speculations. . . . Poor old Jean ! She hadn't altered much. . . . He remembered her first horror at Compton and its boys and girls. . . . But Elsbeth was evidently a good sort . . . appreciated Alwynne. . . . He would like to have a talk with Elsbeth. . . . He would like to have her version of that disastrous summer; have her views on Alwynne and this school of hers . . . and that woman . . . what was her name ? . . . Hartill ! Clare Hartill ! Yes, he must certainly get to know Alwynne's Elsbeth. . . . In the meantime . . .

He hesitated, fidgeting at his desk; spoiled a sheet or two; shrugged his shoulders; began again; and finally, with a laugh at his own uncertainty, settled down to the writing of a long letter to his second cousin Elsbeth.

Elsbeth, opening a boot-boxful of daffodils on the following evening, had no leisure for any other letter till Alwynne's was read.

. . . I hope they'll arrive fresh. Roger packed them for me himself. He's frightfully clever with flowers, you know ; you should just see his greenhouses ! But he goes in chiefly for roses ; he's going to teach me pruning and all that, he says, later on. The Dears were out all day, but he looked after me. He's really

awfully nice when you get to know him. One of those sensible people. I'm sure you would like him. Etcetera, etcetera, etcetera.

Elsbeth smiled over her daffodils. She had to put them in water, and arrange them, and re-arrange them, and admire them for a full half-hour before she had time for the rest of her post, for her two circulars and the letter in the unfamiliar handwriting.

But when, at last, it was opened, she had no more eyes for daffodils; and though she spent her evening letter-writing, Alwynne got no thanks for them next day.

" Not even a note ! " declaimed Alwynne indignantly. " She might at least have sent me a note ! It isn't as if she had any one else to write to ! "

Roger was most sympathetic.

CHAPTER XXXVII

Alwynne's visit had been prolonged in turn by Alicia, Jean and Roger; and Elsbeth had acquiesced—her sedate letters never betrayed how eagerly—in each delay.

Alicia was flatteringly in need of her help for the Easter church decorations, and how could Alwynne refuse? Jean was in the thick of preparations for the bazaar: Alwynne's quick wits and clever fingers were not to be dispensed with. Alwynne wondered what Clare would say to her interest in a bazaar and a mothers' meeting, and was a little nervous that it would be considered anything but a reasonable excuse for yet another delay. Clare's letters were getting impatient—Clare was wanting her back. Clare was finding her holidays dull. Yet Alwynne, longing to return to her, was persuaded to linger—for a bazaar— a village bazaar! That a bazaar of all things should tempt Alwynne from Clare! She felt the absurdity of it as fully as ever Clare could do. Yet she stayed. After all, The Dears had been very good to her. . . . She should be glad to make some small return by being useful when she could. . . .

And Alwynne was pleasantly conscious that she was uncommonly useful. A fair is a many-sided gaiety. There are tableaux—Alwynne's suggestions were invaluable. Side-shows —Alwynne, in a witch's hat, told the entire village its fortunes with precision and point. Alwynne's well-drilled school-babies were pretty enough in their country dances and nursery rhymes; and the stall draperies were a credit to Alwynne's taste. Alwynne's posters lined the walls; and her lightning portraits— fourpence each, married couples sixpence—were the success of the evening. The village notabilities were congratulatory: The Dears beamed: it was all very pleasant.

Her pleasure in her own popularity was innocent enough. Nevertheless she glanced uneasily in the direction of Roger Lumsden more than once during the evening. He was very big and busy in his corner helping his aunts, but she felt herself under observation. She had an odd idea that he was amused at her. She thought he might have enquired if she needed help during the long evening, when the little Parish Hall was grown crowded. Once, indeed, she signed to him across the room to come and talk to her, but he laughed and shook his head, and turned again to an old mother, absorbed in a pile of flannel petticoats. Alwynne was not pleased.

But when the sale had come to its triumphant end, and the stall-holders stood about in little groups, counting coppers and comparing gains—it was Roger who discovered Alwynne, laughing a trifle mechanically at the jokes of the ancient rector, and came to her rescue.

She found herself in the cool outer air, hat and scarf miraculously in place.

"Jean and Alicia are driving, they won't be long after us. I thought you'd rather walk. That room was a furnace," said Roger, with solicitude.

She drew a deep breath.

"It was worth it to get this. Isn't it cool and quiet? I like this black and white road. Doesn't the night smell delicious?"

"It's the cottage gardens," he said.

"Wallflowers and briar and old man. Better than all your acres of glass, after all," she insinuated mischievously. Then, with a change of tone, "Oh, dear, I am tired."

"You'd better hang on to my arm," said Roger promptly. "That's better. Of course you're tired. If you insist on running the entire show——"

"Then you did think that?" Alwynne gave instant battle. "I knew you did. I saw you laugh. I can walk by myself, thank you."

But her dignity edged her into a cart-rut, for Roger did not deviate from the middle of the lane.

He laughed.

"You're a consistent young woman—I'm as sure of a rise—— You'd better take my arm. Alwynne! You're not to say 'Damn.'" A puddle shone blackly, and Alwynne, nose in air, had stepped squarely into it.

She ignored his comments.

"I wasn't interfering. I had to help where I could. They asked me to. Besides—I liked it."

"Of course you did."

She looked up quickly.

" Did I really do anything wrong? Did I push myself forward? "

" You made the whole thing go," he said seriously. " A triumph, Alwynne. The rector's your friend for life."

" Then why do you grudge it? " She was hurt.

" Do I? "

" You laugh at me."

" Because I was pleased."

" With me? "

" With my thoughts. You've enjoyed yourself, haven't you? "

She nodded.

" I never dreamed it would be such fun." She laughed shyly. " I like people to like me."

" Now, come," he said. " Wasn't it quite as amusing as a prize-giving? "

She looked up at him, puzzled. He was switching with his stick at the parsley-blooms, white against the shadows of the hedge.

" I suppose your goal is a head mistress-ship? " he suggested off-handedly.

" Why? " began Alwynne, wondering. Then, taking the bait : " Not for myself—I couldn't. I haven't been to college, you know. But if Clare got one—I could be her secretary, and run things for her, like Miss Vigers did for Miss Marsham. We've often planned it."

" Ah, that's a prospect indeed," he remarked. " I suppose it would be more attractive, for instance, than to be Lady Bountiful to a village? "

" Oh, yes," said Alwynne, with conviction. " More scope, you know. And, besides, Clare hates the country."

" Ah ! " said Roger.

They walked awhile in silence.

But before they reached home, Roger had grown talkative again. He had heard from his aunts that she was planning to go back to Utterbridge on the following Saturday—a bare three days ahead. Roger thought that a pity. The bazaar was barely over—had Alwynne any idea of the clearing up there would be to do? Accounts—calls—congratulations. Surely Alwynne would not desert his aunts till peace reigned once more. And the first of his roses would be out in another week; Alwynne ought to see them; they were a sight. Surely Alwynne could spare another week.

Alwynne had a lot to say about Elsbeth. And Clare. Especially Clare. Alwynne did not think it would be kind to either of them to stay away any longer. It would look at last as if she didn't want to go home. Elsbeth would be hurt. And Clare. Especially Clare.

But the lane had been dark and the hedges had been high, high enough to shut out all the world save Roger and his plausibilities. By the time they reached the garden gate Alwynne's hand was on Roger's arm—Alwynne was tired—and Alwynne had promised to stay yet another week at Dene. On the following day, labouring over her letters of explanation, she wondered what had possessed her. Wondered, between a chuckle of mischief and a genuine shiver, what on earth Clare would say.

But if Roger had gained his point, he gained little beside it. The week passed pleasantly, but some obscure instinct tied Alwynne to his aunts' apron-strings. He saw less of her in those last days than in all the weeks of her visit. He had assured her that The Dears would need help, and she took him at his word. She absorbed herself in their concerns, and in seven long days found time but twice to visit Roger's roses.

Yet who so pleasant as Alwynne when she was with him? Roger should have appreciated her whim of civility. It is on record that she agreed with him one dinner-time, on five consecutive subjects. On record, too, that in that last week there arose between them no quarrel worthy of the name. Yet Roger was not in the easiest of moods, as his gardeners knew, and his coachman, and his aunts. The gardeners grumbled. The coachman went so far as to think of talking of giving notice. Alicia said it was the spring. Jean thought he needed a tonic— or a change. Roger, cautiously consulted, surprised her by agreeing. He said it was a good idea. He might very well take a few days off, say in a fortnight, or three weeks. . . .

Only Alwynne, very busy over the finishing touches of Clare's birthday present, paid no attention to the state of Roger's temper. She was entirely content. The anticipation of her reunion with Clare accentuated the delights of her protracted absence. Indeed, it was not until the last morning of her visit that she noticed any change in him. That last morning, she thought resentfully, as later she considered matters in the train, he had certainly managed to spoil. Roger, her even-minded, tranquil Roger—Roger, prime sympathizer and confederate—Roger, the entirely dependable—had failed her. She did not know what had come over him.

For Roger had been in a bad temper, a rotten bad temper, and heaven knew why. . . . Alwynne didn't. . . . She had been in such a jolly frame of mind herself. . . . She had got her packing done early, and had dashed down to breakfast, beautifully punctual—and then it all began. . . . She re-lived it indignantly, as the telegraph poles shot by.

The bacon had sizzled pleasantly in the chafing-dish. She was standing at the window, crumbling bread to the birds.

" Hulloa ! You're early ! " remarked Roger, entering.

" Done all my packing already ! Isn't that virtue ? " Alwynne was intent on her pensioners. " Oh, Roger—look ! There's a cuckoo. I'm sure it's a cuckoo. Jean says they come right on to the lawn sometimes. I've always wanted to see one. Look ! The big dark blue one."

" Starling," said Roger shortly, and sat himself down. " First day I've known you punctual," he continued sourly.

" I'm going home," cried Alwynne. " I'm going home ! Do you know I've been away seven weeks ? It's queer that I haven't been homesick, isn't it ? "

" Is it ? " said Roger blankly.

" So, of course, I'm awfully excited," she continued, coming to the table. " Oh, Roger ! In six hours I shall see Clare ! "

" Congratulations ! " He gulped down some coffee.

Alwynne looked at him, mildly surprised at his taciturnity.

" I've had a lovely time," she remarked wistfully. " You've all been so good to me."

Roger brightened.

" The Dears are such dears," continued Alwynne with enthusiasm. " I've never had such a glorious time. It only wanted Clare to make it quite perfect. And Elsbeth, of course."

" Of course," said Roger.

" So often I've thought," she went on : " " Now if only Clare and Elsbeth could be coming down the road to meet us—— ' " she paused effectively. " I do so like my friends to know each other, don't you ? "

Roger was cutting bread—stale bread, to judge by his efforts. His face was growing red.

" Because then I can talk about them to them," concluded Alwynne lucidly.

" Jolly for them ! " he commented indistinctly.

Alwynne looked up.

" What, Roger ? "

" I said, ' Jolly for them ! ' "

" Oh ! " Alwynne glanced at him in some uncertainty. Then, with a frown—

" Have you finished—already ? "

" Yes, thank you."

" I haven't," remarked Alwynne, with sufficient point. Roger rose.

" You'll excuse me, won't you ? I've a busy morning ahead of me."

He got up. But in spite of his protestations of haste he still stood at the table, fidgeting over his pile of circulars and seed catalogues, while he coughed the preliminary cough of a man who has something to say, and no idea of how to say it.

Alwynne, meanwhile, had discovered the two letters that her napkin had hidden, and had neither ears nor eyes for him and his hesitations.

Roger watched her gloomily as she opened the envelopes. The first enclosure was read and tossed aside quickly enough, but the other was evidently absorbing. He shrugged his shoulders at last, and, crossing the room, took his warmed boots from the hearth. The supporting tongs fell with a crash.

Alwynne jumped.

" Oh, Roger, you are noisy ! "

" Sorry," said Roger, but without conviction.

She looked across at him with a hint of perturbation in her manner. She distrusted laconics.

" I say—is anything the matter ? "

" Nothing whatever ! " he assured her. " Why ? " He bent over his boots.

" I don't know. You're rather glum to-day, aren't you ? "

" Not at all," said Roger, with a dignity that was marred by the sudden bursting of his over-tugged bootlace. His ensuing exclamation was vigorous and not inaudible. Alwynne giggled. It is not easy to tie a knot in four-sided leather laces. She watched his struggles without excessive sympathy. Presently a neat twist of twine flicked through space and fell beside him.

" ' Just a little bit of string,' " murmured Alwynne flippantly. But getting no thanks, she returned to her letter. Roger fumbled in silence.

" The Dears are late," remarked Alwynne at last, as she folded her sheets.

" No—it's we who are early. I got down early on purpose. I thought you might be, too. I wanted——" he broke off abruptly.

" Yes, I always wake up at daybreak when I'm excited," she said joyously. " Oh, Roger! How I'm looking forward to getting home! Clare says she may meet me—if she feels like it," she beamed.

" Oh! " said Roger.

Alwynne tapped her foot angrily.

" What's the matter with you? " she demanded. " Why on earth do you sit there and grunt at me like that? Why won't you talk? You're an absolute wet blanket—on my last morning. I wish The Dears would come down."

" I think I hear them moving," he said, and stared at the ceiling.

" I hope you do." Alwynne flounced from the table and picked up a paper.

He stood looking at her—between vexation and amusement, and another sensation less easily defined.

" Well, I must be off," he said at last.

He got no answer.

" Good-bye, Alwynne. Pleasant journey."

Alwynne turned in a flash.

" Good-bye? Aren't you coming to see me off? " she demanded blankly.

He hesitated, looking back at her from the open window, one foot already on the terrace.

" I'm awfully busy. It's market-day, you know—and the new stuff's coming in. The Dears will see you off."

" Oh, all right." Alwynne was suddenly subdued. She held out a limp hand.

He disregarded it.

" Do you want me to come? " He spoke more cheerfully.

" One always likes one's friends to see one off," she remarked sedately.

" And meet one? " He glanced at the letter in her hand.

" And meet one. Certainly." Her chin went up. " I hadn't to ask Clare. But you needn't come. Good-bye! "

" Oh, I'm coming—now," he assured her, smiling.

Alwynne's eyebrows went up.

" But it's market-day, you know——"

" Yes."

" You're awfully busy."

" Yes."

" The new stuff's coming in."

" Yes."

" Are you coming, Roger ? "

" Yes, Alwynne."

" Then, Roger dear—if you are coming, and it's no bother, and you can spare them, would you bring me a tiny bunch of your roses ? Not for me—for Clare. She does love them so. Do, Roger ! "

" I'm hanged if I do," cried Roger, and went his wrathful way.

But he did. A big bunch. More than enough for Clare.

CHAPTER XXXVIII

ALWYNNE was out of the train a dangerous quarter minute before it came to a standstill, and making for the bunch of violets that bloomed perennially in Elsbeth's bonnet. There followed a sufficiency of kissing. It was like a holiday home-coming, thought Alwynne, of not so very long ago. But not so long ago she would have been exclusively occupied with Elsbeth, and her luggage, and her forgotten compartment; would not have turned impatiently from her aunt to scan the length of the platform. Not a sign of Clare? And Clare had promised to meet her. . . .

She prolonged as long as she might her business with porters and ticket collectors and outside-men, but Clare did not appear; and she left the station at last, at her aunt's side, sedately enough, with the edge off the pleasure of her home-coming.

A telegram on the hall stand, however, contented her. Clare was sorry; Clare was delayed; would be away another four days; was writing. Alwynne shook off her black dog, and the meeting with Clare still delightfully ahead of her, was able to devote herself altogether to Elsbeth. Elsbeth spent a gay four days with an Alwynne grown rosy and cheerful, affectionate and satisfyingly garrulous again; found it very pleasant to have Alwynne to herself, her own property, even for four days. Elsbeth might know that she was second fiddle still, but though it cost her something to realize that she could never be first fiddle again, she could be content to give place to Roger Lumsden. She shook her head over her inconsistency. She could school herself, rather than lose the girl's confidence, to accept Clare Hartill as the main theme of Alwynne's conversation, till she was weary of the name, but she could not hear enough of Roger. All that Alwynne let fall of incident, description, or approval— Roger, Elsbeth discovered, had, in common with Clare, no faults whatever—she stored up to compare, when Alwynne had gone to bed, with letters, half-a-dozen by this time, that she

278

kept locked up, with certain other, older letters, in the absurd little secret drawer of her desk. And she would patter across into Alwynne's room at last, to tuck in a sheet or twitch back a coverlet or merely to pretend to herself that Alwynne was a baby still, and so, with a smile and a sigh, to her own room, to make her plain toilet and to say her selfless prayers to God and her counterpane. Happy days and nights—four happy days and nights for Elsbeth.

Then Clare came back.

It was natural that Alwynne should meet her and go home with her, portmanteau in hand, to spend a night or two. . . . Elsbeth agreed that it was natural. . . . Three nights or even four. . . . But when a week passed, with no sign from Alwynne but a meagre, apologetic post-card, Elsbeth thought that she had good cause for anger. Not, of course, with Alwynne . . . never, be it understood, with Alwynne . . . but most certainly with Clare Hartill. Alwynne was so fatally good-natured. . . . Clare, she supposed, had kept the child by a great show of needing her help. . . . Of course, school was beginning, had begun already. . . . Clare would find Alwynne useful enough. . . . No doubt it was pleasant to have some one at her beck and call again in these busy first days of term. . . . Possibly—probably—oh, she conceded the ' probably '—Clare had missed Alwynne badly. . . . Had not Elsbeth, too, missed Alwynne ?

But she answered Alwynne's post-card affectionately as usual. If Alwynne were happier with Clare, Elsbeth would give no hint of loneliness. A hint, she knew, would suffice. Alwynne had a sense of duty. But she wanted free-will offering from Alwynne, not tribute.

In spite of herself, however, something of bitterness crept into her next note to Roger Lumsden, who had inveigled her, she hardly knew how, into regular correspondence. Her remark that *Alwynne has been away ten days now*, was set down baldly, with no veiling sub-sentences of explanation or excuse.

Had she but known it, however, she was not altogether just to Alwynne. The first hours of re-union did certainly drive her aunt out of Alwynne's mind, but after a couple of days she was ready to remind herself and Clare that Elsbeth, too, had some claim on her time. It is possible, however, that had she been happier, she would have been less readily scrupulous. Clare had certainly been glad to see her, had, for an hour or two, been entirely delightful. But with the resumption of their mutual life Clare was not long in falling back into her old bad ways, and in revenge for her two months' boredom, in sheer teasing high spirits at Alwynne's return, as well as in unreasoning, petulant jealousy, led Alwynne a pretty enough dance. For Clare was jealous, jealous of these eight weeks of Alwynne's youth that did not belong to her, and between her jealousy and her own contempt for her jealousy, was in one of the moods that she and Alwynne alike dreaded.

The mornings at the school came as a relief to them both, but no sooner were they together again than Clare's pricking devil must out. Scenes were incessant—wanton, childish scenes. Yet Alwynne, sore and bewildered as she was by Clare's waxing unreasonableness, was yet not proof against the sudden surrenders that always contrived to put her in the wrong. She would repeat to herself that it must be she who was unreasonable, that she should be flattered rather than distressed, for instance, that Clare would not let her go home. . . . She would rather be with Clare than Elsbeth, wouldn't she? Of course! well, then! . . . Nevertheless she could not help wondering if any letters had come for her; if Elsbeth, expecting her daily would bother to send them on. . . . Roger had promised to write. . . . She thought that really she ought to go home.

But Clare would not hear of her leaving. Elsbeth wanted Alwynne? So did she. Didn't Elsbeth always have Alwynne? Surely Alwynne was old enough to be away from Elsbeth for a fortnight, without leave granted! Really, with all due respect to her, Alwynne's aunt was a regular Old Man of the Sea.

" Clare ! " Alwynne's tone had a hint of remonstrance.

" Oh, I said 'with all respect.' But if she were not your aunt I should really be tempted to get rid of her—have you here altogether. You would like that, Alwynne, eh ? "

Alwynne refused to nod, but she laughed.

" ' Get rid ' ? Clare, don't be absurd."

Clare looked at her, smiling, eyes narrowed in the old way.

" Do you think I couldn't get rid of her if I wanted to ? I always do what I set out to do. Look at Henrietta Vigers."

Alwynne sat bolt upright.

" Miss Vigers ? But she resigned ! She had been meaning to leave ! She told us so ! Do you mean that she didn't want to leave ? Do you mean that she had to ? "

" Have you ever seen a liner launched ? You press an electric button, you know—just a touch—it's awfully simple——"
She paused, eyes dancing.

But Alwynne had no answering twinkle.

" I wouldn't have believed it," she said slowly. Then, distractedly, " But why, Clare, why ? What possessed you ? "

" She got in my way," said Clare indolently.

Alwynne turned on her, eyes blazing.

" You mean to say—you deliberately did that poor old thing out of her job ? If you did—— But I don't believe it. If you did—— Clare, excuse me—but I think it was beastly."

" *Demon ! With the highest respect to you*——" quoted Clare, tongue in cheek.

But Alwynne was not to be pacified.

" Clare—you didn't, did you ? "

" My dear, she was in the way. She worried you and you worried me. I don't like being worried."

Alwynne shivered.

" Don't, Clare ! I hate you to talk like that—even in fun. It's—it's so cold-blooded."

" In fun ! " Clare laughed lightly. Alwynne's youthful severity amused her. But she had gone, she perceived, a trifle too far. " Well, then, in earnest—joking apart——"

Alwynne's face relaxed. Of course, she had known all along that Clare was in fun. . . .

" Joking apart—it was time for Miss Vigers to go. I admit saying what I thought to Miss Marsham. I am quite ready to take responsibility. She was too old—too fussy—too intolerant —I can't stand intolerance. She had to go."

Alwynne looked wicked.

" Clare, you remind me of a man I met, down at Compton. You ought to get on together. He's great on tolerance too. So tolerant that five hundred years ago he'd have burned every one who wasn't as tolerant as he. As it is, he shrugs them out of existence, *à la* Podsnap. Just as you did Miss Vigers just now."

" Who was he ? "

" Don't know—only met him once. But he tickled me awfully. He hadn't the faintest idea how funny he was."

" Did he shrug you out of existence ? "

" My dear Clare—could any one snub me ? You might as well snub a rubber ball."

" Yes, you're pretty thick-skinned." Clare paid her back reflectively.

Alwynne winced.

" Am I? I'm sorry. I didn't mean to be. How, just now? " Clare yawned.

" Well, for one thing, you needn't flavour your conversation exclusively with Denes. They bore me worse than if they had an ' a ' in them."

" I'm sorry." Alwynne paused. Then she plucked up courage. " Clare, I stayed there two months. The Dene people are my friends, my great friends. I don't think you need sneer at them."

Clare yawned again.

" I wonder you ever came back, if they're so absorbing. What is the particular attraction there, by the way? The old women or the young men? "

Alwynne's lips quivered.

" Clare, what has happened? What is the matter with you nowadays? Why are you grown so different? Why are you always saying unkind things? "

Clare shrugged her shoulders.

" Really, Alwynne, I am not accustomed to be cross-examined. Such a bore, giving reasons. Besides, I haven't got any. Oh, don't look such a martyr."

" I think I'll go home," said Alwynne in a low voice. " I don't think you want me."

" But Elsbeth does, doesn't she? "

Clare settled herself more comfortably in the comfortable Chesterfield as she watched Alwynne out of the room. She lay like a sleepy cat, listening to the muffled sounds of Alwynne's packing; let her get ready to her hat and her gloves and the lacing of her boots, before she called her back, and played with her, and forgave her at the last. Yet she found Alwynne less pliable than usual : convicted of sin, she was yet resolved on departure, if not to-day—no, of course she would not go to-day, after behaving so ill to her Clare—then, the day following. That would be Friday—a completed fortnight—and Saturday was Clare's birthday—had Clare forgotten? Alwynne hadn't, anyhow. Oh, she must come for Saturday, and what would Elsbeth say to that? There must be one evening, at least, given to Elsbeth in between. After all, it was jolly dull for Elsbeth all by herself.

Clare, good-tempered for the first time that afternoon, supposed it was, rather.

But on that particular day, Alwynne's qualms of conscience were unnecessary. Elsbeth was not at all dull. Elsbeth, on the contrary, was tremendously excited. And Elsbeth had forgotten all about Alwynne, was not missing her in the least. Elsbeth had received a letter from Dene that morning, and was expecting Roger Lumsden to supper.

CHAPTER XXXIX

ELSBETH spent her day in that meticulous and unnecessary arrangement and re-arrangement of her house and person, with which woman, since time was, has delighted to honour man, and which he, the unaccountable, has as inevitably failed to notice. The clean cretonnes had arrived in time and were tied and smoothed into place; the vases new-filled; and the fire, though spring-cleaning had been, sprawled opulently in a brickless grate. The matches, with the fifty cigarettes Elsbeth had bought that forenoon, hesitating and all too reliant upon the bored tobacconist, lay, aliens unmistakable, near Roger's probable seat, and the knowledge of the supper laid out in the next room fortified Elsbeth as, years ago, a new frock might have done. Alwynne, in every age and stage, dotted the piano and occasional tables, and a photograph that even Alwynne had never seen was placed on the mantelshelf, that Roger, greeting Elsbeth, might see it and forget to be shy.

But it was Elsbeth that was shy, when Roger, very punctual, arrived amid the chimes of the evening service. Yet Elsbeth had been ready since five. They greeted each other in dumb show and sat a moment, smiling and taking stock, while the clamour swelled, insisted, ebbed and died away.

Roger, still silent, began to fumble at a case he carried, while Elsbeth found herself apologetically and for the thousandth time wondering to her guest why she had taken root so near a church, while within herself a hard voice cried exultantly, "He's his father, his father over again! Nothing of Rosemary there!" and she tasted a little strange flash of triumph over the dead woman she had been too gentle to hate.

But suddenly her lap was filled with roses, bunch upon tight masculine bunch, and the formal sentences broke up into incoherence as Roger stooped and kissed his second cousin Elsbeth.

They soon made friends. Roger, who had never quite forgotten her, found the pleasant-faced spinster as attractive as

284

the pretty lady of his childhood. He examined her as he ate his supper. A spare figure, soft grey hair, and square, capable hands; a kind mouth, not a strong one, set in lines firmer than were natural to it; gentle eyes, no longer beautiful, and a cheerful, tired smile; a sweet face, thought Roger, not a happy one. Yet she had Alwynne! She fluttered a little over the meal, and was anxious about his coffee, and full of little enquiries and attentions that were never irritating. There was a faint scent of verbena as she moved about him, and her silk gown did not crackle like younger women's dresses. She listened well, but he guessed her no talker, and later in the evening, gauged her affection for Alwynne by her breathless fluency. He thought her charming and a little pathetic, and wondered why nobody had ever insisted on marrying her.

Elsbeth's shyness soon dwindled; she slipped quickly into the informal ' aunt and nephew ' attitude that he evidently expected, and found his friendliness and obvious pleasure in her as delightful as it was astonishing. She supposed, with a wistful little shrug, that she was near the rose! Nevertheless she enjoyed herself.

They talked in narrowing circles : of his father a little; more of his mother; of Dene, and Elsbeth's former visits. He described Compton and The Dears, and his gardens and his roses. Then, with a chuckle, an unauthorized attempt of Alwynne at pruning that had ended in disaster; and so plunged into confidences.

" I expect you've guessed that I intend—that I want to marry Alwynne—with your permission," he added hastily, smiling down at her.

Elsbeth envied him his inches. For Alwynne's sake she did not intend to be dominated; but she found his mere masculinity a little overpowering, and did not guess that her frail dignity had made its own impression.

She smiled back at him.

" I'm glad you put that in. You should respect grey hairs."

" But I do."

" No. You imply that I'm a very blind and foolish guardian ! My dear boy," her pretty voice shook a little, " I've hoped and prayed for this. You, John's boy, and—and dear Rosemary's, of course—and Alwynne, who's dearer to me than a daughter ! Why, that's why I sent her down to Dene ! " She blushed the rare blush of later middle age. " Oh, my dear—it was shameless! I was matchmaking! I was! And I've always considered it so indelicate. But I wished so strongly that you two might come together. When Alwynne wrote of you so often, I hoped: and then your letters made me sure. You had got on so well without me these twenty-five years—and then to feel the ties of kinship so very strongly all of a sudden—it was transparent, Roger."

He laughed.

"I hadn't forgotten really—though it's the vaguest memory. You gave me a rabbit in a green cabbage that opened. And one Sunday we shared Prayer Books. You had a blue dress—a pale blue that one never sees nowadays, and very pink cheeks."

"Ah! the *crêpe de Chine*," said Elsbeth absently.

"I always remembered—though I'd forgotten I did. Alwynne brought it back. She's like you in some ways, you know. She made me awfully curious to see you again. From the way she talked I knew you'd be decent to me." He smiled. "Elsbeth—I'm tremendously in love."

"Have you told her so?"

"Alwynne's rather difficult to get hold of. She doesn't understand anything but black and white."

"Clare Hartill—I suppose you've heard of Clare Hartill?"

"Have I not!"

"Clare Hartill says she has an uncanny ear for nuances."

"Also that she's thick-skinned! The woman's a fool."

"Oh, she's quite right, Roger, though I expect she was in a temper when she said it. But it only means that Alwynne has been trained to listen to women. She can't follow men yet. She has been advised that they are grown-up children and that her rôle is to be superior but tactful."

He chuckled.

"Yes. When Alwynne's tactful—she's tactful! You can't mistake it, can you? Have you ever seen her sidling out of a room when she thought she wasn't wanted? Still, she can hold her own, on occasion. She simply walked through my hints. But—how does she talk of me, Elsbeth, if she does at all, that is?"

"She likes you, in the 'good old Roger' fashion."

"But you do think I have a chance?"

"That's why I wanted to see you. Frankly, at present I don't think you have."

He looked at her coolly, not at all depressed.

" Why not ? "

" Clare Hartill."

" Ah ! " He sat down at the table again, his chin in his fist. " You think her the obstacle ? "

" I taught her once. Alwynne has been absorbed in her for two years. Alwynne talks——" they both smiled. " I could compare. I ought to know her pretty well."

" Yes. But how can she affect Alwynne and me ? Of course I know what a lot Alwynne thinks of her. She's rather delightful on the subject. Thinks her perfection, and so on. Alwynne is naïve ; conveys more than she knows or intends, sometimes. And she never looks at her god's feet, does she ? ' Clare ' and ' Clare ' and ' Clare.' Personally, I imagine her a bit of a brute."

" I try to be fair. She is fond of Alwynne."

" Why not ? But what's that got to do with Alwynne's caring for me, if I am lucky enough to make her ? And I'm— conceitedly sure—that it's only a question of waking Alwynne up."

" You don't know Clare. If once she knows, she'll never let the child go."

" But if Alwynne were engaged to me ? "

" She'll never allow it. She'll play on Alwynne's affection for her."

" But why ? I shouldn't interfere with their friendship."

" My dear Roger—marriage ends friendship automatically. Clare would be shrewd enough to see that. And even—other- wise—she would never share. You don't guess how jealous women are."

Roger leant back in his chair with a gesture of bewilderment.

" My dearest cousin ! The age of sorcery is over. You talk as if Alwynne were under a spell."

" Practically she is. Of course Clare would put it on the highest grounds—unsuitability—a waste of talents. She pre- tends to despise domesticity. Alwynne would be hypnotized into repeating her arguments as her own opinion."

" Hypnotism ? "

" Oh, not literally. But she really does influence some women, and young girls especially, in the most uncanny way. I've watched it so often."

" She's not married ? "

" She hardly ever speaks to a man. I've seen her at gaieties, when she was younger. She was always rather stranded. Men

left her alone. Something in her seems to repel them. I think
she fully realized it. And she's a proud woman. There's
tragedy in it."

" Does she repel you ? "

" Not in that way. I dislike her. I think her dangerous.
I'm intensely sorry for her. And I do understand something
of the attraction she exercises, better than you can, though
it has never affected me. You see—eccentricity—abnormality
—does not affect women as it does men. And she's brilliantly
clever."

" So is Alwynne—you wouldn't call her abnormal ? "

" Alwynne ? Never ! She's as sound and sweet as an apple.
But—and it means a good deal at her age—she's in abnormal
hands. Clare Hartill *is* abnormal, spiritually perverse—and
she's fastened on the child. They adore each other. It's
terribly bad for Alwynne. As it is, it will take her months
to shake off Clare's influence, even with you to help her. That
is, if you succeed in detaching her. I'm useless, of course.
Loving—just loving—is no good. You can only influence if
you are strong enough to wound. I merely irritate. I'm weak.
But you could do as you like, I believe. Take her away from
that selfish woman, Roger ! It's blighting her."

" You think," he said, " that she would be content with
me—with marriage as a career ? Of course, Miss Hartill's right
about her talents."

" Alwynne ? I don't think—I know. All her gifts are so
much surface show; she's a very simple child underneath.
Content ? Can't you see her, Roger—with children ? Her own
babies ? "

Roger beamed.

" It's rather a jolly prospect. Well, I must take my chance."

" Of course, you must wait; it's too soon yet. Even later,
if Clare really wants her—wants her enough to suppress her
own perverse impulses—I'm afraid you've little chance. But
it's possible that she will not want her as much as that."

" I don't follow."

" I mean that Clare, with that impish nature of hers, may
hurt Alwynne."

" I should think she has already, often enough."

" Yes—but Alwynne has never realized it, never realized that
it was deliberate. She is always so sure that it was her fault
somehow. If once she found out that Clare was hurting her

for—for the fun of it, you know—for the pleasure of watching her suffer—as I'm sure she does—it might end everything. Alwynne hates cruelty. That poor child's death shook her. A little more, and she will be disillusioned."

" But loyal still ? "

" Probably. But the glamour would be gone. She would be extremely unhappy. There your chance would come. Though I don't think Clare will give it you—for I believe Alwynne does mean more to her than most things. But she's an unaccountable person : there is the chance."

" I see," Roger rose and straightened himself. " Practically I'm not to depend on my own—attractions—at all." He laughed a little. " I am to watch the whims of this—this unpleasant school-marm, and be grateful to her for forcing Alwynne to prefer my deep sea to her devil. The situation is hardly dignified."

Elsbeth laughed too.

" Love is always undignified, Roger. What does it matter if you want her ? " But she watched him anxiously as he walked to the window, and stood staring out.

There was a silence. At last he turned—

" Elsbeth, dear, it's a beautiful scheme, and a woman could carry it through, I daresay—but it's no good to me. It's too— too tortuous, too feminine. I don't mean anything rude. It's merely that I'm not—subtle enough, or patient. At least, I haven't got that cat-and-mouse kind of patience. I can wait, you know. That's different. I can wait all right. But I can't intrigue."

Elsbeth flushed.

" There is no intrigue. It's a question of understanding Alwynne and of using the opportunity when it comes."

" To trick and surprise and over-persuade her into caring for me ! It's no good, Elsbeth. It isn't possession I want— it's Alwynne. Can't you see ? We should neither of us be happy. She would always distrust me and remember that I'd taken an advantage. I should end by hating her, I believe. Can't you see ? "

Elsbeth was shaken by her own thoughts.

" I see," she said finally. " And I see that you don't love her—or you'd take her on any terms."

" Would you ? "

" Yes."

U

" Well, I wouldn't. And I do love her. But I want Alwynne on my terms. Do I sound an awful prig ? Cousin Elsbeth, hear my way ! I'm going to have it out with Alwynne."

" At once ? "

" At once. As soon as I see her—no beating about the bush."

" Roger—she may be utterly out of the mood."

" Hang moods ! I beg your pardon, Elsbeth. But I'm going to tell her—certain things. If she doesn't like it I'm going back to Dene. She'll know where to find me when she changes her mind. Elsbeth, don't look so hopeless."

" You don't understand Alwynne."

" I don't want to understand her—I want to marry her. I must stick to my own way. Can't you conceive that all this consideration, all this deference to moods and dissection of motives, this horribly feminine atmosphere that she seems to have lived in, of subtleties, and reservations, and simulations— may be bad for her ? It seems to me that she's always being thought about. You, with your anxious affection—that unholy woman with her lancet and probe—you neither of you leave her alone for a second. She's always being touched. Well, I'm going to leave her alone. It gives her a chance."

" I've never spoiled her." Elsbeth was off at a tangent.

" I'm sure of it. I can remember Father holding you up to Mother once. He said you were the most judicious woman with children that he knew."

" Did he ? " said Elsbeth.

" Mother was awfully annoyed." Roger chuckled. " I'd been bawling for my fourth doughnut—and got it."

" I've never spoiled Alwynne," repeated Elsbeth tonelessly.

" No one could," remarked Roger with conviction.

Elsbeth looked up and laughed at him.

" So you are human ! " she said. " I was beginning to doubt it."

" When I get on the subject of Alwynne's adorableness——" he laughed back at her, " we're obviously cousins, aren't we ? But, really, I've been trying to be detached, and critical, and analytical, and all the things you feel are important. I wanted to see what you meant, Cousin Elsbeth ; and I do see that we both want the same thing. But as to the means—I believe I must go my own way."

She eyed him doubtfully. But he looked very big and solid in the little room, comfortingly sure of himself.

" You think me a frantic old clucking hen, don't you ? And are just a little sorry for the duckling."

" I think you're a perfect dear," said Roger.

" You'll come to-morrow ? Alwynne will be back, I hope."

" What time is she likely to turn up ? "

" About four, if she comes. She would lunch with Clare, I expect."

He nodded whimsically.

" Very well. To-morrow, at four precisely, there will be a row royal. To-morrow I am calling on Miss Hartill to fetch Alwynne home. Good-bye, Cousin Elsbeth."

He turned again in the doorway.

" Elsbeth, there's a house at Dene I've got my eye on. There's a turret room. My best roses will clamber right into it. That's to be yours. And Elsbeth ! Nobody but you shall run the nursery."

He had shut the door before she could answer, and she heard him laugh as he ran, two at a time, down the shallow steps.

She went to the window and watched till his strong figure had disappeared in the dusk.

" He is very like his father," said Elsbeth wistfully, glancing across at the faded likeness.

The dusk deepened and the stars began to twinkle.

" He will never be the man his father was," cried Elsbeth, suddenly and defiantly.

Her hands shook as she cleared away the remnants of the meal. She swept up the hearth, picked the coals carefully apart, and tidied the tidy room. Roger's roses still lay in a heap in the basket chair. She gathered them up and carried them into the tiny bathroom, that they might drink their fill all night. Their scent was strong and sweet. Then she lit her candle and prepared for bed.

The sheets were very cold. She tried not to think of Roger's father, lying in the grave she had never seen. The old, cruel longing was upon her for the sound of his voice and the sight of his face and the sweetness of his smile. She broke into painful weeping.

The hours wore past.

Of course he would marry Alwynne. . . . Alwynne would be happy. . . . there was comfort in that . . . Roger would be kind to her. . . . A good boy . . . a dear boy. . . .

" And he might have been my son," cried out Elsbeth to the uncaring night.

CHAPTER XL

ROGER never fought his battle-royal with Clare, for at the turn of Friar's Lane he met Alwynne herself, dragging wearily along the cobblestones, weighed down by paper parcels and the heavy folds of the waterproof hanging on her arm. Her hair was roughened by the wind that tugged and strained at her loosened hat; her face was drawn and shadowy; she had an air of exhaustion, of indefinable demoralization that Roger recognized angrily. He had seen it in the first weeks of her visit to Dene. Her thoughts were evidently far away, and she would have passed him without a look if he had not stopped her. She started violently as he spoke—it was like rousing a nightmare-ridden sleeper—then her face grew radiant.

"Roger!" she cried, and beamed at him like a delighted child.

He possessed himself of her parcels and they walked on, Alwynne's questions and exclamations tumbling over each other. Roger at Utterbridge! Why had he come? How long was he staying? How were The Dears and how did Dene spare him? When had he arrived?

Roger dropped his bomb.

"Yesterday. I went to supper with Elsbeth. We had a long talk."

His tone conveyed much. The brightness died out of Alwynne's face. She looked surprised and excessively annoyed.

"She knew you were coming?"

"She did."

"Why on earth didn't she let me know? Why, she doesn't know you! She hasn't seen you since you were a kid! It's extraordinary of Elsbeth."

"I wouldn't let her."

"Wouldn't let her?" Alwynne looked at him blankly. "Roger—I think you're cracked."

"Terse and to the point! Don't you worry. Elsbeth and I understand each other. Besides, we've been corresponding."

" You and Elsbeth ? "

" Yes. That's partly why I came. I wanted to get to know her. You see, your description and her letters didn't tally. So I came. We got on jolly well. I burst in on her again at breakfast this morning. She didn't fuss—took it like a lamb. I fancy you underrate our cousin—in more ways than one. She knows it too; she's no fool ! I found that out when we talked about you."

" Elsbeth discussed me ?—with you ? " Alwynne's tone foreboded a bad half-hour to Elsbeth.

" Why not ? You're not sacred, are you ? " Roger chuckled.

Alwynne felt inclined to box his ears. Here was a new Roger. Roger—her own property—to take such an attitude—to ally himself with Elsbeth—to leave her in the dark ! Roger ! It was unthinkable. . . . And she had been so awfully glad to see him . . . absurdly glad to see him . . . he had made her forget even Clare. . . . Clare. . . . She began to occupy her mind once more with the scene of the previous day, recalling what she had said ; contrasting it with what she had intended to say ; stabbed afresh by Clare's manner ; writhing at her own helplessness ; when Roger's slow voice brought her thoughts back to the present.

" You've been away from Elsbeth a fortnight," he said accusingly, as they entered the Town Gardens.

She flared anew at his tone.

" Certainly. I've been staying with friends. Have you any objection ? "

" A friend," he corrected.

She flushed.

" Clare Hartill is my best friend——"

" Your worst, you mean."

She turned on him.

" How dare you say that ? How dare you speak of my friends like that ? How dare you speak to me at all ? "

He continued, quite unmoved—

" Don't be silly, Alwynne. Your best friend is your Aunt Elsbeth—you ought to know that. You don't treat her well, I think. You've been away a fortnight with that—friend of yours ; you stayed on without consulting her——"

" I telephoned," cried Alwynne, in spite of herself.

" Since then you've sent her one post-card. She isn't even sure that you're coming back to-day ; she's just had to sit tight and wait until it's your—no, I'll give you your due—until it's your friend's pleasure to send you back to her, fagged out, miserable—just like my dog after a thrashing. And Elsbeth's to comfort you, and cosset you, and put you to rights—and then you'll go back to that woman again, to have the strength and the spirit drained out of you afresh—and you walk along talking of your best friend. I call it hard luck on Elsbeth."

Alwynne's careful dignity was forgotten in her anger. She turned on him like a furious schoolgirl.

"Will you stop, please? How dare you speak of Clare? If Elsbeth chooses to complain—— What affair is it of yours, anyhow? I'll never speak to you again—never—or Elsbeth either." Her voice broke—she was on the verge of tears.

Roger took her by the arm, and drew her to a seat.

"You'd better sit down," he said. "We've heaps to talk over yet, more than you've a notion of. And if we're to have a row, let's get it over in the open—far less dangerous. Never get to cover in a thunderstorm. I know what you want." He had watched her fumbling unavailingly in bag and pocket and had chuckled. He knew his Alwynne. He produced a clean silk handkerchief and dangled it before her. She clutched at it with undignified haste.

"'Thank you,' first," he said, holding it firmly. A moment victory hung in the balance. Then—

"Oh! Oh, thank you," said Alwynne, with fine unconcern, and secured it. Their eyes met. It was impossible not to smile.

"At the same time," remarked Alwynne, a little later, "you've no right to talk to me like that, Roger, whatever you choose to think. You're not my cousin."

"I'm Elsbeth's. It strikes me she needs defending."

Alwynne laughed.

"You know I'm awfully fond of Elsbeth. You know I am. I am a beast sometimes to her, you're quite right—but she doesn't really need defending. Honestly."

"Not from you, I know. But frankly, without wanting to be rude to your friend—I think she makes you careless of Elsbeth's feelings. Elsbeth was awfully hurt this week, and she's the sort of dear one hates to see hurt."

Alwynne looked at him wistfully.

"Roger," she said hesitatingly, "suppose some one were unkind to me—hurt me—hurt me badly, very often, almost on purpose—would you defend me? Would you care at all?"

" I shouldn't let 'em," he grunted.

" If you couldn't help it?"

" I shouldn't let 'em," he repeated doggedly.

" But should you care?"

" Of course I should. What rot you talk. Of course I should. But I shouldn't let them."

" Oh, Roger," she cried, suddenly and pitifully, " they do hurt me sometimes—they do, they do."

Roger looked around him with unusual caution. The Gardens were empty. There was not even a loafer in sight. He put his arm round her, and drew her clumsily to him. She yielded like a tired child, and lay quietly, staring with brimming eyes at the gaudy tulip-bed on the further side of the walk.

" I believe you're about fed up with that school of yours," he said, after a time, as if he had not followed the allusion to Clare.

She nodded.

" I'm not lazy, Roger; you know it's not that. It's just the atmosphere, and the awful crowding. Such a lot of women at close quarters, all enthusiasm and fussing and importance. They're all hard-working, and all unselfish and keen—more than a crowd of men would be, I believe. But that's just it— they're dears when you get them alone, but somehow, all together, they stifle you. And they all have high voices, that squeak when they're keenest. D'you know, that was what first made me like you, Roger—your voice? It's slow, and deep, and restful—such a reasonable voice. You mustn't think me disloyal to the school. The girls are all frightfully interesting, and the women are dears, and there's always Clare—only we do get on each other's nerves."

" A boys' school is just the same."

" Is it? I've only seen Compton. I don't know how co-education affects the boys, but I'm sure it's good for the girls, and the mistresses too. Of course, they're not really different to my lot, but they seemed so. They had room to move. They weren't always rubbing up against each other like apples in a basket. It all seemed so natural and jolly. Fresh air everywhere. And since I've been back, I've felt I couldn't breathe. I believe it's altered me, just seeing it all; and I can't make Clare understand. She thinks I liked Dene because I wanted to flirt."

"That type would."

"Yes, I know you think that," she answered uneasily, "but she isn't—that horrid type. That's why it hurts so that she can't understand. As if I ever thought of such a thing until she talked of it! Only I like talking to men, you know, Roger; because they've often got quite interesting minds, and it's easier to find out what they really think than with women. But they bore Clare."

"Do they?" Roger had his own opinion on the question. But he found that it was difficult to refrain from kissing Alwynne when she looked at him with innocent eyes and made preposterous statements; so he stared at the tulips.

"You see, she thinks—we both think, that if you've got a— a really real woman friend, it's just as good as falling in love and getting married and all that—and far less commonplace. Besides the trouble—smoking, you know—and children. Clare hates children."

"Do you?" Roger looked at her gravely.

"Me? I love them. That's the worst of it. When I grew old, I'd meant to adopt some—only Clare wouldn't let me, I'm sure. Of course, as long as Clare wanted me, I shouldn't mind. To live with Clare all my life—oh, you know how I'd love it. I just—I love her dearly, Roger, you know I do—in spite of things I've told you. Only—oh, Roger, suppose she got tired of me. And, since I've been back, sometimes I believe she is."

"Poor old girl!"

"It's a shame to grizzle to you; it can't be interesting; and, of course, I don't mean for one moment to attack Clare; only everything I do seems wrong. When she sneers, I get nervous; and the more nervous I get, the more I do things wrong—you know, silly things, like spilling tea and knocking into furniture. And she gets furious and then we have a scene. It's simply miserable. We had one yesterday, and again this morning. It's my fault, of course—I get on her nerves."

"You never get on my nerves," said Roger suggestively.

"Not when I chop up your best pink roses?" She looked at him sideways, dimpling a little.

"As long as you don't chop up your own pink fingers—you've got pretty fingers, Alwynne——"

"Roger, you're a comforting person. I wish—I wish Clare

would treat me as you do, sometimes. You pull me up too, but you never make me nervous. I'm sure I shouldn't disappoint her so often, if she did."

"Alwynne," he returned with a twinkle, "stop talking. I've made a discovery!"

"Well?"

"You're ten times fonder of me than you are of that good lady. Now, own up."

"Roger!" Alwynne was outraged. She made efforts to sit upright, but Roger's arm did not move. It was a strong arm and it held her, if anything, a trifle more firmly. "You're talking rot. Please let me sit up."

"You're all right. It's quite true, my child, and you know it. Ah, yes—they're a lovely colour, aren't they?"

For Alwynne was gazing at the tulips with elaborate indifference. Secretly she was a little excited. Here was a new Roger. . . . He was quite mad, of course, but rather a dear. . . . She wondered what he would say next. . . .

"To examine our evidence. You were very glad to see me—now weren't you?"

"I'm always pleased," remarked Alwynne sedately to the tulips, "to see old friends."

"Yes—but we're not old friends exactly, if you refer to length of acquaintanceship. If to age—I was thirty last March. I'm not doddering yet."

"I wasn't speaking of ages. Thirty is perfectly young. Clare's thirty-five. You do fish, Roger."

"Yes. I'm going to have a haul some day soon, I hope. But to resume. Firstly, you were jolly glad to see me. Secondly, you took your lecture very fairly meekly—for you! and you've already had one talking-to to-day during which, I gather, you were anything but meek."

"I never told you——"

"But there was a glint in your eye—— You've no idea how invariably your face gives you away, Alwynne. Thirdly, you've hinted quite half-a-dozen times that Miss Hartill would be all the better for a few of my virtues. Tenth, and finally, you've made my coat collar thoroughly damp—you needn't try to move—and I don't exactly see you spoiling your Clare's Sunday blouse that way, often, eh?"

Alwynne was obliged to agree with the tulips.

"I thought so. Therefore I say, after considering all the evidence—in your heart of hearts you are ten times fonder of me than of Miss Clare Hartill."

The trap was attractively baited. Impossible for an Alwynne to resist analysis of her own emotions. She walked into it.

"I don't know—I wonder if you're right? Perhaps I am *fonder* of you. I love Clare—that's quite a different thing. One couldn't be fond of Clare. That would be commonplace. She's the sort of wonderful person you just worship. She's like a cathedral—a sort of mystery. Now you're like a country cottage, Roger. Of course, one couldn't be fond of a cathedral."

"A cottage," remarked Roger to the tulips in his turn, "can be a very comfortable place. Especially if it's a good-sized one —Holt Meadows, for instance. My tenants leave in June, did you know? There's a south wall and a croquet ground."

"Tennis?"

Roger was afraid the tulips would find it too small for tennis.

"But a court could be made in Nicholas Nye's paddock," Alwynne reminded them.

Roger thought it would be rather fun to live there, tennis or no tennis—didn't the tulips think so?

The tulips did, rather.

"One could buy Witch Wood for a song, I believe; you know it runs along the paddock. Think of it, all Witch Wood for a wild garden."

"And no trespassers! No trampled hyacinths any more! Or ginger-beer bottles! Oh, Roger!" A delighted, delightful Alwynne was forgetting all about the tulips; but they nodded very pleasantly for all that.

"A footpath through to The Dears' garden, and my glass-houses. And chickens in a corner of the paddock. You'd have to undertake those."

"All white ones!"

"Better have Buff Orpingtons. Lay better. Remember Jean's troubles: 'Really, the Amount of Eggs——'"

"Dear Jean. And besides, I shall want some for clutches. I adore them when they're all fluff and squeak; and ducklings too, Roger. We won't have incubators, will we?"

"Rather not. Lord, it will be sport. You're to wear print dresses at breakfast, Alwynne—lilac, with spots."

"You're very particular——"

"Like that one you wore at the Fair—you know."

" Oh, that one ! Do you mean to say—— All right. But I shall wear tea-gowns every afternoon—with lace and frillies. Elsbeth says they're theatrical."

" All right ! We'll eat muffins——"

" And read acres of books——"

" May I smoke ? "

" It'll get into the curtains——"

" I'll get you a new lot once a week——"

" And we won't ever be at home to callers——"

" Just us two."

Alwynne sighed contentedly.

" Oh, Roger, it would be rather nice. You can invent beautifully."

He laughed.

" Then we'll consider that settled."

He bent his head and kissed her.

A very light kiss—a very airy and fugitive attempt at a kiss—a kiss that suited the moment better than his mood; but Roger could be Fabian in his methods. Alwynne rather thought that it was a curl brushing her forehead : the tulips rather thought it wasn't. Roger could have settled the matter, but they did not like to appeal to him. They were all a little disturbed—more than a little uncertain how to act. The tulips' attitude was frankly alarming to Alwynne, who (if the kiss had really happened) was prepared to be dignified and indignant. The tulips, however, appeared to think a kiss a pleasant enough indiscretion. " To someone, at any rate, we are worth the kissing," quoth the tulips defiantly, with irreverent eyes on a vision of Clare's horrified face. Then, veering smartly, they reminded Alwynne, that from a patient, protective Roger it was the most brotherly and natural of sequels to their make-believe. Alwynne was not so sure; Roger was developing characteristics of which the kiss (had it taken place) was not the least exciting and alarming symptom. He was no longer the Roger of Dene days, not a month dead; or rather, the Dene Roger was proving himself but a facet of a many-sided personality—big, too—that was more than a match for a many-sided Alwynne, with moods that met and enveloped hers, as a woman's hands will catch and cover a baby's aimless fist. More than his strength, his gentleness disturbed her. So long a prisoner to Clare, ever bruising herself against the narrow walls of that labyrinthine mind—she would have been indifferent to any

harshness from him; but his kindliness, his simplicity, unnerved
her. He had been right—she had her pride. Clare did not
often guess when her self-control was undermined. But with
Roger—what was the use of pretending to Roger? It had
been comforting to have a good cry. His kiss had been comforting too. She remembered the first of Clare's rare kisses—
the thin fingers that gripped her shoulders; the long, fierce
pressure, mouth to mouth; the rough gesture that released her,
flung her aside.

But Roger—if, indeed, she had not dreamed—had been comforting. Here the tulips broke in whimsically with the brazen
suggestion that it would be delightful to put one's arms round
Roger's neck and return that supposititious kiss. A remark,
of course, of which no flower but a flaunting scarlet tulip could
be capable. Alwynne was horrified at the tulips. Horrified by
the tulips, worried by her own uncertainties, puzzled by the
imperturbable face smiling down at her. Certainly not a
conscience-stricken face. Probably the entire incident was a
wild imagining of the tulips. She had watched those nodding
spring devils long enough. Time to go home: at any rate it
was time to go home.

It puzzled her anew that Roger's arm was no longer about
her, that he should make no effort to detain her, or to reopen
the conversation; that he should walk at her side in his usual
fashion, originating nothing. Once or twice, glancing up at
him, she surprised a smile of inscrutable satisfaction, but he did
not speak; he merely met her eyes steadily, still smiling, till
she dropped her own once more. A month ago she would have
challenged that smile, cavilled and cross-examined. To-day
she was quaintly intimidated by it. Indeed a new Roger!
She never dreamed of a new Alwynne.

Yet for all her perplexity and very real physical fatigue,
Alwynne walked with a light step and a light heart. As
usual she was absurdly touched by his unconscious protective
movements—the touch on her arm at crossings—the juggle of
places on the fresh pathway—the little courtesies which the
woman-bred girl had practised, without receiving, appealed to
her enormously. She felt like a tall schoolchild, 'gentleman'
perforce at all her dancing lessons, who, at her first ball, comes
delightedly into her own.

She gave Roger little friendly glances as they walked home,
but no words; though she could have talked had he invited.

But Roger was resolutely silent, and for some obscure reason this embarrassed her more than his previous loquacity. Gradually she grew conscious of her crumpled dress and loosened hair; that a button was missing on her glove; trifles not often wont to trouble her. She wondered if Roger had noticed the button's absence; she hoped fervently that he had not. She glanced obscurely at shop-windows, whose blurred reflections could not help her to the conviction that her hat was straight. Also it dawned upon her that Roger was weighed down by preposterous parcels; that the parcels were her own. She was sure the string was cutting his fingers. She was penitent, knowing that she would not be allowed to relieve him, and hugely annoyed with herself. She had been scolded often enough for her parcel habit, and had laughed at Elsbeth; and here was Elsbeth proved entirely right. Weighing down Roger like this! What would he think of her? He had not spoken for ten minutes. . . . Of course—he was annoyed. . . . They had better get home as quickly as might be. . . .

CHAPTER XLI

ELSBETH, sitting at the window, had seen them come down the street, and was at the door to welcome them. Alwynne was kissed, rather gravely, but Elsbeth and Roger greeted each other like the oldest of trusted friends. Alwynne's eyebrows lifted, but Elsbeth ignored her. She scolded Roger for being late, showed him his roses, revived and fragrant in their blue bowls; and when Alwynne turned to go and dress, declared that he looked starved, that supper was long overdue, and must be eaten at once. Roger seconded her, and to supper they went.

Alwynne raged silently. What was the matter with Elsbeth? She had barely greeted her. . . . And now to be so inconsiderate. . . . To insist on sitting down to supper then and there, without giving her time to make herself decent ! Couldn't she see how tired Alwynne was, how badly in need of soap and water and a brush and comb, let alone a prettier frock ? It wasn't fair ! Elsbeth might know she would want to look nice—with Roger there. . . . She did not choose to look a frump, however Elsbeth dressed herself. . . .

It dawned on her, however, as Elsbeth, resigning the joint to Roger, began to mix a salad under his eye, after some particular recipe of his imparting, that Elsbeth, on this occasion, was looking anything but a frump. She wore her best dress of soft, dark purple stuff, and the scarf of fine old lace, that, as Alwynne very well knew, saw the light on high and holy days only; and a bunch of Roger's roses were tucked in her belt. Her hair was piled high in a fashion new to Alwynne : a tiny black velvet bow set off its silvery grey : it was waved, too, and clustered becomingly at the temples. Alwynne, gasping, realized that Elsbeth must have paid a visit to the local coiffeur. She realized also, for the first time, how pretty, in delicate, pink-may fashion, her aunt must once have been.

At any other time Alwynne would have been delighted at the

improvement, for she was proud of Elsbeth, in daughterly fashion, and had wrestled untiringly with her indifference to dress. She knew she should have hailed the change, but, to her own annoyance, she found it irritating. It displeased her that she herself should be dishevelled and day-worn, while Elsbeth faced her, cool and dainty and dignified. Roger was so obviously impressed. . . . Roger, to whom Elsbeth had been so carefully, so deprecatingly explained. . . . It made Alwynne look such a fool. . . . How was she to know that Elsbeth would have this whim? She had never guessed that Elsbeth could make herself look so charming. . . . And she to be in her street clothes . . . with her hair like a mouse's nest! It was too bad! However, it didn't seem to matter. . . . Roger, it was clear enough, had no eyes for her. . . .

Her resentment grew. She attempted to join in the conversation, but though Roger listened gravely, and answered politely—she never caught the twinkle in his eye—he invariably flung back the ball to Elsbeth as quickly as might be. She mentioned Dene; made intimate allusions to their walks and adventures; and he turned to explain them, to include Elsbeth, with a pointedness that made Alwynne pink with vexation. She began to long to get him to herself . . . to quarrel or make peace, as he pleased . . . but anyhow to get him to herself. . . . Couldn't one have a moment's conversation without dragging Elsbeth into it? So absurd of Roger. . . .

Slowly she realized that neither Roger nor Elsbeth were finding her indispensable, and her surprise was only rivalled by her indignation. Elsbeth particularly—it was simply beastly of Elsbeth—was being, in her impalpable way, unapproachable. . . . She was angry about something. . . . Alwynne knew the signs. . . . She, Alwynne, supposed that she ought to have written. . . . But she did write a post-card. . . . One couldn't be everlastingly writing letters. . . . Any one but Elsbeth would have waived the matter, with a visitor present, but Elsbeth was so vindictive. . . . Here Alwynne's rebellious conscience allied itself with her sense of humour, to protest against the picture of a vindictive Elsbeth. They bubbled with tender laughter at the idea. Alwynne must needs laugh with them, a trifle remorsefully, and admit that the idea was fantastic; that Elsbeth, in all the years she had known her, had been the most meek and forgiving of guardians; and that she, Alwynne, had been undeniably negligent. Nevertheless,

why must Elsbeth show Roger the kitchen? What was he
saying to her out there? And why were they both laughing
like that?

" Cackle, cackle, cackle," muttered Alwynne viciously; " awfully funny, isn't it? "

She continued her reflections.

Fussing over clearing the supper still! One of Elsbeth's
absurd ideas, just because it was the maid's evening out. . . .
Let her do it when she came back! Such a fuss and excitement
always! What would Roger think of them? What a long
time they were! She might take the opportunity of going to
change her frock. . . . She hesitated. What was that? What
was Roger saying? She caught the murmur of his deep voice
and her aunt's staccato in answer, but the words were blurred.

After all—why should she bother to change? Elsbeth would
be sure to make unnecessary remarks. . . . And Roger wouldn·t
care—he was too occupied with Elsbeth. . . . Nobody cared—
nobody wanted her. . . . She would go back to Clare to-morrow.
. . . . But if Clare were in to-day's humour still?

What a wretched week it had been. . . . Even if Clare had
not been so moody, Alwynne would have felt ill at ease . . .
she had known perfectly well that she owed the first weeks of
her return to her aunt . . . but at a hint from Clare she had
stifled her conscience and stayed. . . . And now Elsbeth, she
could tell, was deeply hurt. . . . Once away from Clare, Alwynne
could reflect and be sorry. . . . She wouldn't have believed
that she could be so careless of Elsbeth's feelings. . . . She was
suddenly and generously furious with herself. How selfish,
how abominably selfish she had been. . . . No wonder Roger
had been shocked! Of course neither he nor Elsbeth could
ever understand how difficult it was to withstand Clare. . . . It
had been possible once. . . . Her thoughts strayed to that early
Christmas when she had resisted all Clare's arguments. . . .
But now she had no choice. . . . However determined one
might be beforehand—and she had intended to return that
first day—one's will was beaten aside, blown about like a straw
in a strong wind. . . . If only Roger would understand that.
. . . She hated him to think her so selfish. . . . Elsbeth needn't
have told him, she thought resentfully . . . . it was not like
Elsbeth to give her away. . . . She supposed she had hurt
Elsbeth's feelings pretty badly. . . . Why, oh why, hadn't she
been firmer with Clare? She had only to say, quite quietly,

that she must do what she felt to be right. . . . Clare couldn't
have eaten her. . . .

She began to rehearse the conversation; it soothed her to
compose the telling phrases she might have uttered. They
sounded all right . . . but, of course, face to face with Clare
she could never have said them. . . . Clare, in indifference,
displeasure or appeal, would have conquered without battle
given . . . in her heart she knew that.

She moved uneasily about the room, deep in thought. For
the first time her attitude to Clare struck her as contemptible.
. . What had Roger said ? ' Like a dog after a thrashing.'
Intolerable ! She flung up her head, her pride writhing under
the phrase. So that was how it struck outsiders ! Outsiders ?
She didn't care a dead leaf for outsiders. . . . Let them think
what they chose ! But Roger ? And Elsbeth ? Did they
really think her weak and enslaved ? It stung her that Roger
should think so meanly of her. She told herself that the loss
of his opinion in no way affected her—and instantly began to
revolve within herself phrases, explanations, actions, wherewith
to regain it. And there was Elsbeth. . . . He had thought
her unkind to Elsbeth. . . . He was right there ! She saw,
remorsefully, with her usual thoroughness, that she had been,
for many a long year, as the plagues of Egypt to her Elsbeth.

She flung herself on the prim little sofa, and stared at the
closed door uncertainly. She was too proud to do what she
wanted to do—invade the kitchen, and regardless of Roger's
eyes and presence, confess to Elsbeth, and receive absolution.
A word, she knew, would be enough. . . . If Elsbeth felt as
miserable as she did—a word would be more than enough. . .

Elsbeth and Roger, returning to the sitting-room, ended her
indecision. Their manner had changed—Roger was quieter—
less talkative—but Elsbeth was so radiant that Alwynne decided
that contrition could wait. More than ever she realized that
two were company. . . .

Her anger grew again as she watched and listened.

Elsbeth had produced cards, and suggested three-handed
bridge. Alwynne excused herself, and Roger, who had been
her partner on occasion at Dene, was obviously relieved. His
Alwynne was the One Woman—but she could not play bridge !

He settled down to double-dummy with Elsbeth. The conversation became a rapt and technical duet, punctuated with
interminable pauses.

Alwynne fumed.

So this was Elsbeth's idea of a really pleasant evening! Cards! Beastly, idiotic cards! Roger, her Roger, had come up all the way from Dene to play cards with Elsbeth! Had he just? All right then! He should have all the cards he wanted—and more! As for Elsbeth—catch Alwynne telling her she was sorry now!

The striking of the clock gave her her opportunity. She rose, yawning elaborately.

" I'm going to bed," she remarked to the card-table.

" Are you, dear? " said Elsbeth.

" Oh! Oh, good-night," said Roger casually, rising and sitting down again. " Your shout, Elsbeth."

Elsbeth went " no trumps."

Alwynne lingered.

" Of course the kitchen fire's out? " she said, with sour suggestiveness.

" Do you want a bath? Yes, of course. Do you know, my dear, you're looking rather grubby?" Elsbeth paid her sweetly. " I expect the water will still be hot, if you're quick. Don't forget to turn the light off, will you, when you've finished? "

Alwynne made no answer, but she still lingered. Elsbeth, finishing her hand, spoke over her shoulder—

" Alwynne, dear, either go out, or come in and sit down. There's such a draught."

There was a swish of skirts, and all the innumerable ornaments rattled on their shelves. Alwynne had permitted herself the luxury of banging the door.

Roger laughed like a schoolboy.

" ' All is not well! ' " he quoted.

Elsbeth laughed too, yet half against her will.

" My poor Alwynne! She hates me to be annoyed with her. It infuriates her. She'll be awfully penitent to-morrow. It's really rather comical, you know. She'll take criticism from any one else—but I must approve implicitly! And you being here didn't improve matters. She was longing to be nice, and I didn't help her. She was quite aware that she was showing you her worst side, and quite unable to get out of the mood. I knew, bless her heart! "

She looked at him with a quick little gesture of appeal.

" Roger—you do understand? That—tantrum—meant—nothing. She's such an impulsive child."

He smiled.

" I know. Don't you worry. Besides, it was my fault. I was teasing her all the evening. It was not what she expected. Oh, I'm growing subtle enough to please even you, Elsbeth. You know, she's had rather a full day. Evidently a scorching afternoon with that delightful friend of hers, to start with——"

" Ah ? " said Elsbeth, her eyes brightening.

" Oh yes; she was distinctly chastened. I improved the occasion, and you've about finished her off, the poor old girl ! I was expecting that little exhibition."

" I believe—I believe you enjoy upsetting her," began Elsbeth, rather indignantly.

" Of course I do. It's as good as a play ! "

Elsbeth sighed.

" Well—I suppose it's all right. You'll have to manage her for the future, not I."

" Oh, she'll do all the managing," said Roger ruefully. " I foresee that this is my last stand. She's just a trifle in awe of me, at present, you know, though she doesn't know it. But it won't last. And then—heaven help me ! But, you know, Cousin Elsbeth—to be henpecked by Alwynne—don't you think it will be quite pleasant ? "

" It is. She's bullied me since she was three. Oh, Roger, I shall miss her." She blinked rapidly.

Roger stared away from her in awkward sympathy.

" You shan't, not very much," he said. " We'll fix things. You'll have to come and settle near us."

Elsbeth fidgeted.

" You know, you took my breath away in the kitchen just now," she said. " Are you quite sure it's all right ? Does Alwynne *know* she's engaged to you ? "

He perpended.

" Well, frankly—I don't think she did quite take it in."

" Roger ! "

" But I'm buying the engagement ring to-morrow," he added hastily. " That'll clear things up."

Elsbeth looked at him helplessly.

" Roger, either you're a genius or a lunatic. I'm not sure which—but, I think, a lunatic."

" Oh, well ! We shall know to-morrow," he observed consolingly. " I shall turn up about eleven. Keep Alwynne for me, won't you ? "

Elsbeth struck her hands together.

" It's Clare Hartill's birthday ! I'd almost forgotten her ! Alwynne will be engrossed. Oh, Roger ! You've been telling me fairy tales. We've forgotten Clare Hartill."

Roger picked up the scattered cards. With immense caution he poised a couple, tent fashion, and builded about them, till a house was complete. He added storey after storey, frowning and absorbed. At the sixth, the structure collapsed. He looked up and met Elsbeth's eyes.

" People in card-houses shouldn't raise Cain. It's an expensive habit," he remarked sententiously. " Elsbeth, don't worry ! But keep Alwynne till I come to-morrow, won't you ? "

" I'll try."

" Of course, if she's still in a temper—— Hulloa ! "

The door had been softly opened. Alwynne, in her gay dressing-gown stood on the threshold. Her hair was knotted on the top of her head, and small damp curls strayed about her forehead. The folds of her wrapper, humped across her arm, with elaborate care, hinted at the towels and sponges concealed beneath. She looked, in spite of her bigness, like an extremely small child masquerading as a grown-up person.

Her eyes sought her aunt's appealingly. Roger, she ignored.

" Elsbeth," she said meekly, " please won't you come and tuck me up ? "

She disappeared again.

Elsbeth laughed as she rose.

" I knew she wouldn't be content. Isn't she a dear, Roger, for all her little ways ? "

" She's all right," said Roger, with immense conviction.

CHAPTER XLII

ALWYNNE was spending a contented morning. She had made her peace with Elsbeth over-night, and at the ensuing breakfast had been something of a feasted prodigal. Elsbeth had made no objection to her plans for the afternoon, but had suggested that, as Roger was coming to lunch, Alwynne might take him for a walk in the morning. He was sure to arrive by twelve. Alwynne, her head full of Clare's birthday and Clare's birthday present, acquiesced graciously. Indeed, she was herself anxious to talk to him again, to show him how completely she and Elsbeth were in accord, to prove to him, once and for all, though with kindly firmness, how uncalled for his comments had been. She believed that they had not parted the best of friends last night. . . . A pity—Roger could be such a dear when he chose. . . . Yesterday afternoon, for instance. . . . She found herself blushing hotly, as she recalled the details of yesterday afternoon.

Her thoughts were divided evenly between Roger and Clare as she sat at her work-table, running the last ribbon through the foamy laces and embroideries. She was proud of her work, and thrilled with pleasurable anticipations of Clare's comments. Clare would be pleased, wouldn't she?

Elsbeth, helping her to fold the dainty garment, and wondering wistfully if Alwynne would ever be found spending a tenth of the time and trouble on her own trousseau that she lavished on presents for people who did not appreciate them, was quite sure that Clare would be more than pleased. She could not cloud Alwynne's happy face; but she hoped to goodness that Roger would come soon. . . . She was sick of the word Clare.

Alwynne despatched her parcel by messenger-boy. She would not trust it to the post—yet it must arrive before she did. Clare hated to be confronted with you and your gift together. She hoped that Clare would not be in a mood when gifts were anathema. You never knew with Clare.

She paid the boy with a bright shilling and a slice of inviolate

309

company cake, and was guiltily endeavouring so to squeeze and compress its girth, that Elsbeth would not notice the enlarged gap at tea-time, when Roger arrived.

She slid the tin hastily back into the cupboard.

"I won't shake hands," she said. "But it's stickiness, not ill-feeling."

Roger frowned aside the remark. He was looking excited, extremely pleased with himself, yet a trifle worried. He had the air of a man who had been priding himself on doing the right thing, and is suddenly stricken with doubt as to whether, after all, he had not made a mess of the business. He confronted her.

"I expect I've got it wrong," he remarked, with gloomy triumph. "I hate coloured stones myself."

"What are you talking about?" demanded Alwynne.

"Which is it, anyhow?"

"Which is what?"

"Which is your favourite stone?"

Alwynne gazed at him blankly.

"What on earth——?" she began.

Roger frowned anew.

"Don't argue with me. Which is your favourite stone?"

"I don't know—emeralds, I think."

He gave a sigh of relief, not entirely make-believe.

"Of course! I knew I was right. Elsbeth swore to pearls."

"Oh, I've always coveted her string. She's going to give it me when I'm forty. I'd like to know what you're talking about, Roger, if you don't mind?"

"Why forty?"

"Years of discretion! You are tidy and never lose anything once you're forty. But why? Were you having a bet?"

"Not exactly." Roger searched his pockets. "Here, catch hold!"

He had produced a small package, gay with sealing-wax and coloured string. He handed it to her awkwardly, with immense detachment.

She opened it curiously.

In a little white kid case lay an emerald, round and shining like a safety signal. It was set in silver, quaintly carven.

Alwynne exclaimed.

"Oh, Roger! How gorgeous! How perfectly ripping! Where did you pick it up? Was it awfully expensive?"

Roger had been beaming in a gratified fashion, but at her question his jaw dropped.

"Well," he began. "Well—I——"

His expression struck her.

"Do you mind my asking? It's only because it is so exactly what I've always longed to give Clare. I'm saving. I'm going to, some day. Clare loves emeralds."

"Perhaps," said Roger, with elaborate irony, "you'd like to give her this? Don't mind me."

She glanced up at him, startled, puzzled.

"This?"

"It happens to be your engagement ring," he remarked offendedly.

Alwynne began to laugh, but a trifle uncertainly. To laugh without accompaniment or encouragement is uneasy work, and Roger's face was entirely expressionless. She felt that her laughter was sounding affected, and ceased abruptly, her foot tapping the floor, a glint of annoyance in her eye.

"What are you talking about?" she attacked him.

"Your engagement ring, wasn't it?" he said.

"Are you by any chance serious?"

"Perfectly." Roger's schoolboy awkwardness, due to his encounter with an unexpectedly facetious jeweller, was wearing off.

"*My* engagement ring?"

"We'll change it, of course," he said, with maddening politeness, "if you really prefer pearls."

"Presupposing an engagement?" Alwynne was on her high horse.

"To me. That was the idea, I think. Elsbeth is delighted."

Alwynne dismounted hastily again, though she kept a hand on the bridle.

"Roger—this is beyond a joke. What have you been saying to Elsbeth?"

"Why, my dear," he said gently, "very much what I told you yesterday afternoon."

Alwynne grew scarlet.

"Roger—we were in fun yesterday. We were joking. I forget what it was all about. There was nothing to tell Elsbeth."

"Yes, you do forget," he said.

"Yes. I have. I want to," she answered unsteadily. "You know you weren't serious. Why, you were laughing at me—you know you were."

" Do you never laugh when you're serious ? "

" Never ! " said Alwynne earnestly.

" Well, then, we're like the Cheshire cat and dog. But I laugh when I'm most amazingly serious sometimes, Alwynne. I was yesterday, and I think you knew it."

" I didn't," said Alwynne stubbornly. " We only just talked nonsense. All about Holt Meadows—you know it was nonsense."

" I didn't," said Roger, with equal stubbornness.

" You did," said Alwynne.

" I didn't," said Roger.

" Oh, of course, if you're going to lose your temper——" cried Alwynne.

Roger shrugged his shoulders. It was deadlock.

Alwynne looked at him. He was grave enough now.

" I didn't mean to be rude," she said unhappily.

" Didn't you ? " He was all polite surprise.

" I expect I was——" she ventured.

" It all depends on what one's used to," he returned philosophically.

" Yes, I know I was. But you are so horrid to-day."

" Sorry," said Roger stiffly.

She turned to him impulsively.

" Roger—I've missed you awfully since I came back. It was quite absurd, when I'd got Clare all to myself. But I did. It was so nice seeing you. I was simply miserable yesterday, and then you turned up and were perfectly sweet. It cheered me up. And then you turned horrid. All the evening you were horrid. And now you're horrid, quarrelling and arguing. Why can't you be nice to me always ? "

She was very close to him. Her hand was on the arm of his chair. Her skirts swished against his knee.

" Alwynne, you're too illogical for a school-marm. Haven't you been bullying me since I came, on account of yesterday ? "

" Roger," she said unsteadily, " don't tease me. I do so want to be friends with you."

He put his arms about her as she stood beside him, and looked up at her, with laughing, tender eyes.

" And I do so want to marry you. Why not, Miss La Creevy ? *Let's be a comfortable couple.*"

She struggled away from him.

" No, Roger ! No. No. I don't want to get married. Why

aren't you content to be friends, as we were at Dene? Friendship's a lot. If I can see you very often, and write to you twice a week, and tell you everything—I should be awfully content. Wouldn't you?"

He looked at her with amusement.

"Your idea of friendship is pretty comprehensive. What's wrong with getting married, Alwynne?"

"Oh—I don't know."

"What's wrong with getting married, Alwynne?"

"How can I get married," cried Alwynne, in sudden exasperation, "when I'm not in love with you? You're silly sometimes, Roger."

"I suppose you're quite sure about it," he ventured cautiously.

"Oh, yes."

He looked entirely unconvinced.

"Why, I've hardly ever even dreamed about you," she remonstrated. "And I know all your faults."

"Oh, you do, do you? Out with the list."

"It would take too long." Alwynne dimpled.

"Love must be blind—is that the idea? Couldn't that be got over? One uses blinkers, you know, in double harness. I never dream, Alwynne, normally. Must I eat lobster salad every night?"

"There—you see!" Alwynne waved her hand complacently. "You're just as bad. You couldn't talk like that if——"

"If what?"

"Nothing!"

"If what?"

Alwynne looked at him.

"If what, Alwynne?" Roger's tone was a little stern.

She had taken a rose from the bowl at her elbow, and was slowly pulling off the petals. Her eyes were on her work.

He waited.

Her hands cupped the little pile of rose-leaves. She buried her face in them—watching him an instant, through her fingers.

"They are very sweet, Roger—are they from home—from Dene, I mean? Smell!"

She held out her hands to him.

He caught them in his own. The red petals fluttered noiselessly to the ground.

"If what, Alwynne?" he insisted.

"Oh, Roger! Do you really care—so much?"

" Yes, dear," he said soberly, " so much."

Alwynne looked up at him anxiously. She was very conscious of the big warm hands that held hers so firmly. She wished that he would not look so intent and grave; he made her feel frightened and unhappy. No—not frightened, exactly. There was something strong and serene about him, that upheld her, even when she opposed him; but certainly, unhappy. She realized suddenly how immensely she liked him—how entirely his nature satisfied hers.

" Oh, Roger ! " she said wistfully. " I do like you. It isn't that I wouldn't like to marry you."

His face lit up.

" Would—liking awfully—do, Roger ? Would it be fair ? Must one be in love like a book ? "

His face relaxed.

" I shall be content," he said. Then, impetuously, " Alwynne, I'll make you so happy. You shall do—nearly everything—you want to. Alwynne, if you only knew——"

She stopped him hurriedly, pulling away her hands.

" Don't, Roger ! Don't ! I didn't mean that. I only meant I'd like to. But I can't, of course. Of course, I can't. There's Clare."

" Clare ! " His tone abolished Clare.

Alwynne flushed.

" Why do you sneer at Clare ? You always sneer. I won't have it."

Her tone, in spite of her sudden anger, was unconsciously and comically proprietary. He repressed a smile as he answered her.

" All right, dear. But I wasn't sneering—not at Clare."

" At me, then ? "

" Not sneering—chuckling. My dear, what has Clare—oh, yes, she's your dearest friend—but what has any friend, any woman, got to say to us two ? We're going to get married."

" We're not. It's no good, Roger." Alwynne spoke slowly and emphatically, as one explaining things to a foreigner. " Why won't you understand ? Clare wants me. We've been friends for years."

" Two years ! " he interjected contemptuously.

" Well ! You needn't talk ! I've known you two months," she flashed out. " Do you think I'm going to desert Clare for you, even if—even if——" She stopped suddenly.

He beamed.

" You do. Don't you, darling ? " he said.

" I don't. I don't. I don't want to. I mustn't. I don't know why I'm even talking to you like this. It's ridiculous. Of course, there can never be any one but Clare."

" Yes, it is ridiculous," he said impatiently.

She faced him angrily.

" Yes, very ridiculous, isn't it ? Not to leave a person in the lurch—a person whom you love dearly, and who loves you. You can laugh. It's easy to laugh at women being friends. Men always do. They think it funny, to pretend women are always catty, and spiteful, and disloyal to each other."

" I've never said so or thought so," said Roger.

" You have ! You do ! Look at the way you've talked about Clare. That looks as if you thought me loyal and a good friend, doesn't it ? What would Clare think of me—when I've let her be sure she can have me always—when I've promised her——"

" At nineteen ! Miss Hartill's generous to allow you to sacrifice yourself——"

" It's no sacrifice ! Can't you understand that I care for her—awfully. Why—I owe her everything. I was a silly, ignorant schoolgirl, and she took me, and taught me—pictures, books, everything. She made me understand. Of course, I love my dear old Elsbeth—but Clare woke me up, Roger. You don't know how good she's been to me. I owe her—all my mind——"

" And your peace ? " he asked significantly.

She softened.

" You know I'm grateful. I don't forget. But she's such a dreadfully lonely person. You've got The Dears, at least. She's queer. She can't help it. She doesn't make friends, though every one adores her. She's only got me. She wants me. How could I go when she wants me—when she's so good to me ? "

" Is she ? " he said. " Yesterday——"

" I was a fool yesterday," said Alwynne quickly. " Of course, I get on her nerves sometimes. But it's always my fault—honestly. You don't know what she's like, Roger, or you wouldn't say such things. I hate you to misunderstand her. How could I care for her so, if she were what you and Elsbeth think ? "

He looked at her innocent, anxious face, and sighed.

" All right, my dear. Stick to your Clare. As long as you're happy, I suppose it's all right. Well, I'd better be off. Where's Elsbeth ? "

" Be off ? Where ? " Alwynne looked startled.

" To pack my traps. I'm going home."

" Oh, Roger, you're not angry with me ? "

" I am, rather," he said. " But you needn't mind me. You don't, do you ? "

She looked at him piteously.

" Good-bye," he said. He shook hands perfunctorily and turned away.

" You are angry—oh, you are ! " cried Alwynne, following him.

He laughed.

" You can't pay Clare without robbing Roger. Don't worry, Alwynne."

" Are you really going ? " she said wistfully.

" Yes. Any message ? "

" You'll write to me, won't you ? "

" Good Lord, no ! " said Roger, with immense decision.

Alwynne jumped. It was not the answer she had expected.

" But—but you must write to me," she stammered. " How shall I know about you, if you don't write to me ? "

He was silent.

A new idea struck Alwynne.

" D'you mean—you don't want to hear from me either ? " she asked incredulously.

" I think it would be better," he said.

" Oh, Roger—why ? Aren't you going to be friends ? "

Alwynne was looking alarmed.

" I wonder," he began, with elaborate patience, " if you could contrive, without straining yourself, to look at things from my point of view—for a moment—only a moment ? "

" That's mean. You make me feel a beast."

" That won't hurt you—— "

" Roger ! "

" Alwynne ? "

" You're being very rude."

" You kick at the privileges of friendship already ? I knew you would. Let's drop it, Alwynne. You've got your good lady : you're quite satisfied. I've not got you : I'm not.

So the best thing I can do is to go back to Dene and forget about you."

" If you can," said Alwynne's widening, indignant eyes.

" After all," he said meditatively, " you're a dear, but you aren't the only woman in the world, are you ? "

" Oh no," said Alwynne.

" I might go back to America," he said, " for a time. I've heaps of friends out there."

" Oh ? " said Alwynne.

" Yes, I shall get over it," he concluded comfortably. " You mustn't worry, my child. Well, good-bye again—wish me good luck, Alwynne."

" Good luck," said Alwynne.

He took up his hat—looked at her—smiled a little, and walked to the door.

But before he could open it, he felt a touch on his arm.

" Roger," said a soft and wheedling voice, " wouldn't you *like* to write to me ? Now and then, Roger ? "

He dissented with admirable gravity.

" All right ! Don't then ! " cried Alwynne wrathfully. She turned her back on him and sat down.

The luncheon-bell tinkled across the ensuing pause, like a peal of puckish laughter.

CHAPTER XLIII

ELSBETH'S voice, raised tactfully at the further end of the passage, warned them of her approach.

Said Alwynne over her shoulder—

"Anyhow, you must stay to lunch now, Elsbeth would be furious if you went. She'll say I've driven you away or something. Unless you want to get me into another row?"

She spoke ungraciously enough, for she disliked having to ask a favour of him at such a juncture; but she disliked even more the notion of a *tête-à-tête* lunch with Elsbeth. Elsbeth, by right of aunthood, would ask questions, demand confession. . . . Elsbeth, she knew instinctively, would be on Roger's side. . . . She told herself that she did not mind being bullied by Roger, because, after all, it was Roger's affair; but she would not be otherwise interfered with. . . . Elsbeth had a way of putting you in the wrong. . . . She would rather not talk with Elsbeth until she had seen Clare. . . . Clare would fortify her. . . . If only Roger would keep Elsbeth occupied till she got away to Clare. . . .

"You must stay, you know," she repeated uneasily.

"You made me forget about lunch," he said cheerfully. "Of course I must! You know, you're a terror, Alwynne. I never know which makes me hungrier, a football match or an argument with you. I'm ravenous."

Alwynne was speechless.

"Is no one coming in to lunch?" asked Elsbeth, entering She looked quickly from one to the other. Alwynne was at the glass, tidying her hair, and Roger seemed cheerful. Elsbeth smiled a significant smile : her eyebrows were question-marks.

Roger shook his head, but not before Elsbeth had caught sight of the scattered rose and disarranged vases. She was instantly engaged in restoring order, and missed the movement.

Suddenly she exclaimed, and pounced on a small object lying on the floor, half hidden in petals.

318

"Oh! Oh, how lovely! What an exquisite ring! Why, Roger—why, Alwynne—look! I might have trodden on it. How careless of you both."

But she beamed on them with immense satisfaction, as she held out the emerald ring.

"It's not mine," said Alwynne icily.

"Nothing to do with me," Roger assured her.

Elsbeth looked bewildered.

"One of you must have dropped it," she began.

"No!" said Alwynne.

"Oh no!" said Roger.

But there was a glimmer of fun in his eye, that enlightened Elsbeth, or she thought, at least, that it did.

"In my young days," she remarked severely, "young people didn't leave a valuable engagement ring lying about on the floor."

"A disengaged engagement ring," he corrected her sadly. "At least, it's disengaged at present."

"I think, Elsbeth," said Alwynne firmly, "that the lunch must be getting cold." And preceded them in all dignity to the dining-room.

Alwynne found the meal a trying one. Roger was talkative, and Elsbeth, though obviously puzzled, was too much occupied with him, to be critical of her niece. Alwynne was divided between gratitude to Roger for relieving the situation, and pique that he could be equal to so doing. A man in his position should be far too crushed by disappointment for social amenities. She would have been genuinely distressed, yet undeniably gratified, if his appetite had failed him; but she noticed that he was able to eat a hearty meal. He could laugh, too, with Elsbeth, and make ridiculous jokes, and draw Alwynne, silent and unwilling, into the conversation. He seemed to have no objection to catching her eye, though she found it difficult to meet his. He was a queer man. . . . She supposed he wasn't very much in love with her, really, that was the truth of it. . . . She found the idea depressing. She wondered if he were really going back to Dene at once, and was relieved to hear her aunt challenging his decision. Elsbeth was expostulating. She had plans for the next day . . . there was a concert that evening. . . . Roger appeared to waver. Alwynne, contemptuous that he could be so easily turned, annoyed that Elsbeth should sway him where she herself had failed, was yet conscious

of a feeling of relief. At least she should see him again, if only
to quarrel with him. . . . She was due to supper with Clare as
well as tea, though she had not told Elsbeth so. . . . It would
be quite simple—she would run round to Clare at once, and
spend a long afternoon, and get back for another peep at Roger
in the evening. . . . Clare wouldn't mind. . . .

She hesitated. Clare would be rather surprised if she didn't
stay. . . . She had never been known to curtail a visit to Clare
before. . . . But she would explain things to her. . . . Clare
would be as sorry for Roger as she herself . . . for, of course,
she must tell Clare all about it. . . . She hoped Clare would
not say she had been flirting. . . . But she must make her at
least understand what a dear Roger was. . . . She should like
Clare to appreciate Roger . . . she was afraid she would never
be able to make Roger appreciate Clare. . . . It was a great
pity ! . . . If it had. not been for Roger's unlucky prejudice,
she might have introduced them to each other, and it would
have all been so jolly. . . . She would have loved to show Clare
to Roger, if Clare had been in a good mood, and had worn her
new peacock-coloured frock and had looked and been as adorable
as she sometimes could be. They might have gone to-day—
and now Roger had spoiled everything. . . . But at least he
was not going till to-morrow. . . . She would slip away at once
while he and Elsbeth were talking—she would be back all the
sooner. . . .

She left the pair at their coffee, and hurried to her room to
put on her new coat and skirt and her prettiest hat. It was
Clare's birthday . . . and Clare liked her to be fine. . . . She
wondered, with a little skip of excitement, if Clare had got her
parcel yet ?

She was no sooner gone than Roger turned to Elsbeth, his
laughing manner dropped from him like a mask.

" It's all off, Elsbeth," he said. " You were right. It's
that woman. She's infatuated."

The pleasure died out of Elsbeth's face.

" I was afraid so," she said. " I saw something had happened.
But you were so comical, I couldn't be sure."

" I didn't want an explanation just then——"

" Of course not," she interpolated hastily.

" But I think I'll go straight back to Dene. Have you a
time-table ? "

" Have you quarrelled badly ? "

" Not exactly ! Alwynne's rather annoyed with me, though."

" Annoyed ? With you ? "

" Well, you see," he explained, with a touch of amusement, " I think she rather wants to retain me as a tame cat——"

" Oh, but Alwynne's not like that," Elsbeth protested.

" Don't you think every woman is, if she gets the chance ? She has to kow-tow to the Hartill woman, and it would be a relief to have some one to do the same to her—as well as an amusement. But she's had to understand that I won't be her friend's whipping-boy. I decline the post."

" Oh, well, if you put it that way—but it's hardly fair to Alwynne. Of course, you're angry and disappointed——"

" I'm not ! " he protested heatedly.

" Oh, but you are. Don't pretend you're not human. I don't blame you; I'm angry too. But you must be fair. Alwynne's motives are obvious enough. There's no cat-and-mouse business about it. She simply can't bear the idea of losing you."

" Yet she won't marry me."

" She would, if it weren't for Clare. Didn't you get that impression ? Roger, if you really care, wait here a little longer. Stay with us. Let her have a chance of contrasting you with Clare Hartill."

" No, I won't," he said obstinately.

" You care more for your own dignity than for Alwynne, I think," said Elsbeth, in her lowest voice.

" Cousin Elsbeth, I care more for Alwynne than for anything else in the world. You know that. Also, though you'll call me a conceited ass, I believe I know your ewe-lamb ten thousand times better than you do. And I've simply got to sit tight for a bit. The less she sees of me at present, the more she'll think of me—in two senses. If I can make her miss me, it'll be a profitable exile. Oh, you dear, worried woman," he cried, laughing at her intent face, " do you think I want to go away from Alwynne ? Nevertheless—where's the time-table ? "

She rose and fetched it, and gave it him, without a word.

He ran his finger down the page.

" There's a four o'clock," he announced.

" If only I could do something," mused Elsbeth.

He smiled at her gratefully.

" You're a pretty staunch friend," he said. " What more can one ask ? "

" Oh, but I ought to think of something," she said impatiently.
" I sit here and let you go—I see two people's lives being spoiled
—for the want of a——"

" What ? "

" That's it ! What ? What can I do ? Nothing, nothing,
nothing. Oh, Roger, it's hard. It's very hard to see people
you love unhappy, and not to be able to help them. It's the
hardest thing I know. It would be such happiness to be allowed
to bear things for them. But to watch. . . . It's harder for us
than for men, you know—we're such born meddlers. We think
it's our mission to put things to rights."

" When we've made a mess of 'em. I'm not sure that it
isn't ! "

" I've got to do something," she went on, without heeding
him. " There you'll be at Dene, miserable—you will be miserable, Roger ? " she interrupted herself, with a faint twinkle.

" Don't you worry," he reassured her. " It was bad enough
when she left. She's managed to make every nook and corner
of the place remind one of her. I don't know how she does it.
Oh, it will be rotten, all right."

" Then there will be Alwynne here," she continued, " pretending she doesn't care. Working herself into a fever each
time Clare is unkind to her—and pretending she doesn't care.
Watching the posts for a letter from you—I know her—and
pretending she doesn't care. Thoroughly miserable, and quite
satisfied that I see nothing, as long as she laughs and jokes at
meals. Oh, life's a comedy," cried Elsbeth. " You young folk
have your troubles, and think we are too old and blind to see
them; and we old folk have our troubles, and know you are too
young and blind to see them. Yes, Roger—I'm having a
grumble, and it's doing me good. One suffers vicariously as
one gets older, but one suffers just the same. You children
forget that."

" Do we ? " he said gently. " I won't again—we won't,
later on, Elsbeth—Alwynne and I."

" I want you two to be happy," she cried piteously. " I want
it so. Oh, Roger, what can I do ? "

" Nothing," he said.

She was silenced. But he was touched and a little amused
to see how entirely she was unconvinced. He admired her
persistence, and wondered if she had fought as vehemently
for her own happiness, as she now fought for Alwynne's. Failure

was instinct in her, in her faded colouring and eager, unassured manner. He thought it probable that the memory of failure was spurring her now.

He roused her gently.

"Elsbeth! It's past three o'clock. Will you come and see me off? I must go back to the White Horse for my bag first. Shall I call for you? I shan't be more than twenty minutes."

She nodded assent and promised to be ready.

Left to herself, she went to her room and dressed with mechanical care. Her mind tossed the while like an oarless boat in the sea of her restless thoughts.

What could she do? Wait—wait and hope, and watch things go wrong. . . . Roger was in love now, and prepared to be patient; but Roger was only a man. . . . He would get over it in time; and Alwynne, finally released from Clare's influence— that, too, surely, was only a question of time—would find out what she had lost. . . . She understood Alwynne well enough to know that if she cared, however unconsciously, for Roger, she would never be content to attach herself to any later comer. . . Alwynne was terribly tenacious. So she, too, would waste and spoil her life; and for the sake of an infatuation, a piece of girlish quixotry. . . . It was criminal of Clare Hartill to allow it. . . . She supposed that the situation amused Clare; at least, if Alwynne's version had allowed her to guess it. . . . She wondered exactly how much Alwynne would tell Clare. . .

Suddenly and wonderfully she was illumined by an idea.

Roger, returning punctually with his bag, found Elsbeth awaiting him on the step, in calling costume, pulling and patting at a new pair of gloves with extraordinary energy. Her cheeks were bright; she had the air of frightened bravery of a cornered sheep.

"Come away quickly, Roger," she whispered, with a glance at the windows. "I don't want Alwynne to catch me. I can't come with you to the station, Roger. I'm going to see Clare Hartill."

CHAPTER XLIV

ALWYNNE, for all her eagerness, took more than her usual breathless ten minutes in reaching Clare Hartill's flat. Underneath her pleasure at seeing Clare again ran a little current of uneasiness. There was so much to be told, not only in deference to the intimacy of their relationship, but in order to procure the proof that had never before seemed necessary, that Roger's, and incidentally Elsbeth's, view of that relationship was wrong. . . . Clare, of course, was reserved, undemonstrative, not, Alwynne was prepared to admit, so kindly or considerate a companion as—well, as Roger. . . . But why it should therefore follow that Roger loved her better, and was more worthy—preposterous word—of her own love, Alwynne could not see. . . Clare Hartill cared for her, had told her so, had—had not as yet proved it, because there had been no need of proof. . . Alwynne could love for two. . . . But to-day she felt only an aching desire that Clare should realize the importance of what she had just done; should reward her sacrifice with little softenings and intimacies, some such signs as she had shown her in the earlier days of their friendship, of affection and sympathy. . . . She did not ask much, she told herself; if Clare were only a little kind, she should not miss Roger. Even as she so decided, her cheek flushing at the idea of Clare's kindness, at the possibility of a return to their earlier relationship, she saw suddenly, with flashlight distinctness, how much, even then, she should miss Roger, how great her sacrifice would still be. . . . She saw, as in a vision, the man and woman drowning in waste seas, and she herself at rescue work with room for one and one only in the boat beside her. . . . She felt herself torn by the agony of choice, knowing the while, that a year ago it had not been so; that a year ago she would have outstretched arms for Clare alone; that even now, Elsbeth, The Dears, all alike might drown in that dream sea, so long as Clare were saved. . . . She acknowledged, she exulted in the narrowness of her affection. . .

Clare before the world ! But Clare before Roger ? Clare safe
and Roger drowning ? She chuckled as it occurred to her that
Roger would certainly be able to swim. . . . Yes, he would
swim comfortably alongside and spare her the fantastic trouble
of a choice. . . . Blessed old Roger !

As she passed the little kiosk at the corner of Friar's Lane,
where a red-haired girl sat behind branches of white and
mauve lilac, and high-piled mounds of violets, she hesitated
and turned back. It was a breaking of unwritten rules, and
Clare would give her no thanks, but to-day at least she would
not scold. . . . She would say nothing, but how big her dear
eyes would grow at sight of that armful of scented colour !
She bought lavishly, and forgot to stay for change, for she
was picturing her own arrival as she hurried on : the open door;
the pell-mell of flowers and sunlight; Clare's smile; Clare's kiss.
In spite of moods Clare could not do without her ! She tore up
the stairs and pealed the bell, with never another thought of
Roger.

Clare was at her writing-table and had but a bare nod for
Alwynne, as she stood in the doorway, flushed, smiling, expectant.
The girl was accustomed to finding her pre-occupied; there was
a time, indeed, when there had been subtle flattery in the cavalier
welcome, when the lack of ceremony had seemed but a proof
of intimacy, and she would bide her time happily enough, exploring book-shelves, darning stockings, tiptoeing from parlour to
pantry to refill vases and valet neglected plants, or, curled in
the big arm-chair, would sketch upon imaginary canvases Clare's
profile, dark against the sun-filled window, or stare half-hypno-
tized, at the twinkling diamond on her finger. But to-day, for
the first time, Clare's reception of her jarred.

She sat down quietly, the flowers in a heap at her feet, her
excitement subsiding and leaving her jaded and sore-hearted.
She felt herself disregarded, reduced to the level of an impor-
tunate schoolgirl. . . . She wondered how much longer Clare
intended to write, and told herself, with a little, petulant shrug,
that for two pins she would surprise Clare, wrench away her
pen, take her by the shoulders and anger her into attention.
Roger was right. . . . One could be too meek. . . . She rose
with a little quiver of excitement, her irrepressible phantasy
limning with lightning speed an imaginary Clare—a Clare be-
leaguered, with barriers down, a Clare with wide maternal arms,
enclosing, comforting, sufficing. . . .

The real Clare shifted in her seat and Alwynne sank back again. No, that was not the way to take Clare. . . . One must be patient, only patient, like Roger. . . . Clare would give all one needed, that was sure, but in her own time, her own way. . . . One must be patient. . . .

She loosed her coat. . . . How close the room was. . . . She would have liked to fling open the window, but Clare always protested. . . . She heard Elsbeth's voice : ' Fresh air ? Her idea of fresh air is an electric fan.' . . . Queer, how those two jarred ! But Elsbeth was not just. . . .

Her head throbbed. Listlessly she picked up a spray of lilac and crushed it against her face. It was deliciously cool. . . . She supposed that the lilacs were out by now at Dene. . . .

Tic, tac ! Tic, tac ! The tick of the clock would not keep time with the scratch of Clare's pen. . . . How stupid ! Stupid, stu—pid, stu—pid, stu——

" Clare ! " she cried desperately, " won't you even talk to me ? "

Clare wrote on for a moment as if she had not heard her, finished her letter, blotted it, stamped and addressed the cover and wiped her pen deliberately; then she rose, smiling a little. She had been perfectly conscious of Alwynne's unrest.

" What is it ? " she said. Alwynne flushed and gathered up her flowers.

" It's your birthday," she apologized. " Look, Clare, aren't they darlings ? I know you hate the school fusses, but your own birthday is important. Must you go on writing ? It ought to be a holiday. May I get vases ? Clare, I've such heaps to tell you, heaps and heaps, only I can't if you stand and look at me from such a long way off. Won't you sit down and smell your lilacs and let me talk to you comfortably ? "

With enormous daring she put her arm round Clare and drew her on to the sofa. Clare made no resistance, but she sat stiffly, unsupported, still smiling, her eyes glittering oddly. But the acquiescence was enough for Alwynne and she slid to the ground and sat there sorting her flowers, her face level with Clare's knee, radiant and fearless again.

" I wonder what you will say ? It's about Roger."

Clare raised her eyebrows.

" Oh, Clare, don't you know ? I wrote such a lot about him from Dene."

" I am to remember every detail of your epistles ? "

Alwynne looked up quaintly—

" I suppose there is a good deal to wade through. There always seems so much to say to you. Do you really mind ? "

" You remind me that I've letters to finish."

Alwynne looked at the clock in sudden alarm.

" Am I awfully early ? You did expect me to tea ? "

" And you're never on the late side, are you ? " Clare was still smiling, but her tone stung.

Alwynne got up quickly.

" I'm very sorry. Don't bother about me. I'll arrange these things while you finish. I didn't know you were really busy."

Clare put out her hand to the table behind her.

" I'm not busy. It seems one mayn't tease you since you've stayed at Dene."

Alwynne's eyes flashed.

" That's not fair. It's only that—that sometimes now you tease with needles—you used to tease with straws."

" So I had better not tease at all ? "

" You know I don't mean that."

Clare lifted an opened parcel from the table. Alwynne recognized it and beamed. So Clare was pleased !

" If I tease with needles," she smoothed the paper and began to straighten the little heap of knotted string, " it's because you annoy me so often. Why did you send me this, Alwynne ? "

She shrugged her shoulders.

" It was your birthday."

" I hate birthdays."

" I know." She spoke flatly, a lump in her throat. She might have known and saved herself her trouble and her pleasure. . . . She thought of the weeks of careful work and her delight in it; of the little sacrifices; the early rising; the walks with Roger curtailed and foregone. . . . Everybody had admired it, even Elsbeth had been sure that Clare would be charmed. . . . But Clare was angry. . . . Perhaps it was only that Clare did not understand. . . . She roused herself.

" Clare, it's different. Don't you remember ? "

Clare gave no sign. She had disentangled the string and was retying it with elaborate care. Alwynne spoke with eyes fixed upon the dexterous fingers—

" You challenged me, don't you remember, Clare ? When Marion showed us the things she was making for her sister's trousseau ? And you said, would I ever have the patience,

let alone my clumsy fingers? And I said I could, and you
said you would wear all I made. And you did laugh at me so.
So I thought I'd surprise you, and Elsbeth taught me the pillow-
lace, and I was frightfully careful. It's taken months and
months, and you love lace, and oh, Clare! I thought you would
be a little bit pleased."

Her lip quivered; she was very childlike in her eagerness and
disappointment.

"Did you think I should wear it?"

Alwynne dimpled.

"It's your size, Clare. Wouldn't you just try it?"

Clare looked at her inscrutably.

"You've taken great pains," she said. "I've been pleased
to see it. But you've shown it to me and I've told you that
you've learned to work well, so it has fulfilled its purpose, hasn't
it? And now you'd better take it back with you. I'm sure
you will be able to use it."

She held out the neatly fastened package.

Alwynne's face hardened. She put her hands behind her
back.

"I shall do nothing of the kind," she said.

Clare did not seem ruffled.

"Of course you will. And you'll look very pretty in it."
She smiled amiably.

But Alwynne's face did not relax.

"I won't take it back. I gave it to you. I made it to give
you pleasure. If you don't want it, burn it, give it to your
maid, throw it away. Do you think I care what becomes of
it? But I won't take it back. That is an insult. You say
that to hurt me."

"You'll take it back because I wish you to."

"I won't. You shouldn't wish me to."

"You know I dislike presents."

"I never labelled it a present in my mind. You talk as if
we were strangers."

"Perhaps, then," murmured Clare, still smiling, "I dislike
the hint that you consider my wardrobe inadequate."

Alwynne caught her breath. For the last ten minutes she
had been growing angry, not in her usual summer-tempest fashion,
but with a slow, cold anger that was pain. She felt Clare's
attitude an indelicacy—the discussion a degradation. She
sickened at its pettiness. She seemed to be defending, not

herself, but some shrinking, weaponless creature, from attack
and outrage. . . . The fight had been sudden, desperate; but
at Clare's last sentence she knew herself vanquished, knew that
the first love of her life had been most mortally wounded.

She turned blindly. She had no tears, no regret: her sensations were purely physical. She was numbed, breathless, choking, conscious only of an overpowering desire for fresh air, for
escape into the open. But first she must say good-bye, head
erect, betraying nothing . . . say good-bye to the dark figure
that was no longer Clare. . . . A sentence from a child's book
danced through her mind in endless repetition: *They rubbed
her eyes with the ointment, and she saw it was only a stock.*
Of course! And now she must go away quickly. . . . She
should choke if she could not get into the air. . . .

She heard her own voice, flat and tiny—

" Have you finished with me? May I go now? "

Clare's laugh was quite unforced.

" You're not to go yet! "

" Yes. Yes—I think so. May I go now, please? "

She had retreated to the door and clung to the handle looking
back with blank eyes.

" But, you foolish child, you've had no tea. Why are you
running away? Are you going to spoil my afternoon? "

She lied blunderingly, mad to escape.

" But I told you I couldn't stay long. Because—because of
Elsbeth. She's to meet me. I only ran up for a minute.
Really, I have to go." She made a tremendous effort: " I—I
can come back later."

Clare shrugged her shoulders.

" Oh, very well. Will you come to supper? "

Alwynne forced a smile.

" Yes." She crossed the threshold, Clare watching from the
doorway.

" I shall wait for you, we'll have a lazy evening. Supper at
eight."

There was no answer. Alwynne was stumbling down into the
darkness of the stairs and did not seem to hear. Clare turned
back into her flat, hesitated uneasily, and came out again.
She leaned far over the balustrade, peering down.

" Alwynne! " she cried. " Alwynne! Wait a moment,
Alwynne! "

But Alwynne was gone, gone beyond recall.

CHAPTER XLV

ALWYNNE fled down Friar's Lane in a mazement, conscious only of the need of escape. She had heard the outer door of the flat close behind her, yet she felt herself pursued. Clare's voice rang in her ears. Momently she awaited the touch of Clare's hand upon her shoulder. She felt herself exhausted; knew that, once overtaken, she would be powerless to resist; that she would be led back; would submit to reconciliation and caresses. And yet she was sure that she would never willingly see Clare again. She was free, and her terror of recapture taught her what liberty meant to her. There was the whole world before her, and Elsbeth—and Roger. . . . She must find Roger. . . . She was capable of no clear thought, but very sure that with him was safety.

She hurried along in the shadow of the overhanging lilac-hedge, ears a-prick, eyes glancing to right and left. Oblivious of probabilities she saw Clare in every passer-by. At the turn of the blind lane she ran into a woman, walking towards her. She bit back a cry.

But it was only Elsbeth—Elsbeth in her Sunday gown, very determined, gripping her card-case as if it were a dagger. She spoke between relief and distress.

" Alwynne ! Why did you disappear ? Where have you been ? "

" With Clare."

" It was more than rude. You could surely have foregone one afternoon. No one to see Roger off ! After all his kindness to you at Dene ! "

" See Roger off ? "

Elsbeth was pleased to see her concern.

" I should have gone myself, of course, but he would not allow it. The heat—as I have to pay a call. So he saw me on my way and then went off by himself, poor Roger ! "

" Where is he going ? Why is he going ? "

" Back to Dene. The four-five. I am afraid, Alwynne, he has been hurt and upset. Alwynne ! "

But Alwynne, tugging at her watch-chain, was already running down the road with undignified speed. The four-five ! Another ten minutes . . . no, nine and a half. . . . Cutting through the gardens she might do it yet. . . . She prayed for her watch to be fast—the train late. She ran steadily, doggedly, oblivious of the passers-by, oblivious of heat and dust and choking breathlessness, of everything but the idea that Roger was deserting her.

As she bent round the sweep of the station yard past the shelter with its nodding cabmen, and ran down the little wall-flower-bordered asphalt path, she heard the engine's valedictory puff. The platform was noisy and crowded, alive with shouting porters, crates of poultry and burdened women, but at the upper end was Roger, his foot on the step of the carriage, obviously bribing a guard.

She pushed past the outraged ticket collector, and darted up the platform.

Roger had disappeared when she reached the door of his compartment, and the whistle had sounded, but the door was still a-swing. The train began to move as she scrambled in. The door banged upon their privacy.

" Roger ! " cried Alwynne. " Roger ! "

She was shaking with breathlessness and relief.

" You were right. I was wrong. It's you I want. I will do everything you want, always. I've been simply miserable Oh, Roger—be good to me."

And for the rest of his life Roger was good to her.

CHAPTER XLVI

CLARE had paused a moment, half expecting Alwynne to return; but it was draughty on the landing and she did not wait long. Silly of Alwynne to dash off like that. . . . She had wanted to discuss Miss Marsham's letter with her before writing her answer. . . . Not that she was really undecided, of course. . . . The offer was an excellent one no doubt, and it was fitting that it should have been made. . . . But to accept the head mistress-ship was another matter. . . . Life was pleasant enough as it was. . . . She had plenty of money and Alwynne was hobby enough. . . . She wondered what Alwynne would say to it . . . urge her to accept, probably. . . . Alwynne was so terribly energetic. . . . Well, she would let Alwynne talk . . . (she picked up her pen) and when she had expended herself, Clare would produce her already written refusal. . . . Alwynne would pout and be annoyed. . . . Alwynne hated being made to look a fool. . . . Clare laughed as she bent over her letter.

She had achieved preliminary compliments and was hesitating as to how she should continue, when a violent rat-tat, hushing immediately to a tremulous tat-a-tat-tat, as if the success of the attack upon Clare's door had proved a little startling to the knocker, announced a visitor, and to their mutual astonishment, Elsbeth Loveday fluttered into the room. Though Elsbeth's naïve amazement at herself and her own courage was more apparent, it was scarcely greater than Clare's politely veiled surprise at the invasion, for since Alwynne's attempts to reconcile the oil and water of their reluctant personalities had ceased with her absence, there had been practically no intercourse between them. With a crooked smile for her first fleeting conviction of the imminence of a church bazaar or Sunday-school treat on gargantuan lines, Clare applied herself to the preparation of Elsbeth's tea, in no great hurry for the disclosure of the visit's object, but already slightly amused at her visitor's unease, and foreseeing a whimsical half-hour in watching her pant and stumble, unassisted, to her point.

Elsbeth was dimly aware of her hostess's attitude, and not a little nettled by it. She waved away cake and toast with a vague idea of breaking no bread in the enemy's house, but she was not the woman to resist tea, though Hecate's self brewed it. Fortified, she returned the empty cup; readjusted her veil, and opened fire.

"My dear Miss Hartill," she began, a shade too cordially, "I've come round—I do hope you're not too busy; I know how occupied you always are."

Clare was not at all busy; entirely at Miss Loveday's service.

"Ah, well, I confess I came round in the hope of finding you alone—in the hope of a quiet chat——"

Clare was expecting no visitors. But would not Miss Loveday take another cup of tea?

"Oh no, thank you. Though I enjoyed my cup immensely—delicious flavour. China, isn't it? Alwynne always quotes your tea. Poor Alwynne—she can't convert me. I've always drunk the other, you know. Not but that China tea is to be preferred for those who like it, of course. An acquired taste, perhaps—at least——" She finished with an indistinct murmur uncomfortably aware that she had not been particularly lucid in her compliments to Clare's tea.

Might Clare order a cup of Indian tea to be made for Miss Loveday? It would be no trouble; her maid drank it, she believed.

"Oh, please don't. I shouldn't dream—— You know, I didn't originally intend to come to tea. But you are so very kind. I am sure you are wondering what brings me."

Clare disclaimed civilly.

"Well, to tell you the truth—I am afraid you will think me extremely roundabout, Miss Hartill——"

Clare's mouth twitched.

"But it is not an easy subject to begin. I'm somewhat worried about Alwynne——"

"Again?" Clare had stiffened, but Elsbeth was too nervous to be observant.

"Oh, not her health. She is splendidly well again—Dene did wonders." Clare found Elsbeth's quick little unexplained smile irritating. "No, this is—well, it certainly has something to do with Dene, too!"

"Indeed," said Clare.

Elsbeth continued, delicately tactless : she was always at her worst with her former pupil.

"I daresay you are surprised that I consult you, for we need not pretend, need we, that we have ever quite agreed over Alwynne ?   You, I know, consider me old-fashioned——" She paused a moment for a disclaimer, but Clare was merely attentive. With a little less suavity she resumed : "And of course I've always thought that you—— But that, after all, has nothing to do with the matter."

"Nothing whatever," said Clare.

"Exactly. But knowing that you are fond of Alwynne, and realizing your great, your very great, influence with her, I felt— indeed we both felt—that if you once realized——"

"We ? "

"Roger. Mr. Lumsden."

"Oh, the gardener at Dene."

"My cousin, Miss Hartill."

"Oh. Oh, really. But what has he to do with Alwynne ? "

"My dear, he wants to marry her. Didn't she tell you ? " Elsbeth had the satisfaction of seeing Clare look startled. "Now I was sure Alwynne had confided the matter to you. Hasn't she just been here ? That is really why I came. I was so afraid that you, with the best of motives, of course, might incline her to refuse him. And you know, Miss Hartill, she mustn't. The very man for Alwynne ?   He suits her in every way.   Devoted to her, of course, but not in the least weak with her, and you know I always say that Alwynne needs a firm hand. And between ourselves, though I am the last person to consider such a thing, he is an extremely good match. I can't tell you, Miss Hartill, the joy it was to me, the engagement. I had been anxious—I quite foresaw that Alwynne would be difficult, though I am convinced she is attached to him—underneath, you know. So I made up my mind to come to you. I said to myself : ' I am sure—I am quite sure—Miss Hartill would not misunderstand the situation. I am quite sure Miss Hartill would not intend to stand in the child's light. She is far too fond of Alwynne to allow her personal feelings——' After all, feminine friendship is all very well, very delightful, of course, and I am only too sensible of your goodness to Alwynne—and taking her to Italy too—but when it is a question of Marriage—oh, Miss Hartill, surely you see what I mean ? "

Clare frowned.

" I think so. The gard—— This Mr. Lumpkin——"

" Lumsden."

" Of course. I was confusing him.—— Mr. Lumsden has pro-
posed to Alwynne. She has refused him, and you now wish
for my help in coercing her into an apparently distasteful
engagement ? "

" Oh no, Miss Hartill ! No question of coercion. I think
there is no possible doubt that she is fond of him, and if it were
not for you—— But Alwynne is so quixotic."

Clare lifted her eyebrows, politely blank.

" Oh, Miss Hartill—why beat about the bush ? You know
your influence with Alwynne. It is very difficult for me to talk
to you. Please believe that I intend nothing personal—but
Alwynne is so swayed by you, so entirely under your thumb; you
know what a loyal, affectionate child she is, and as far as I can
gather from what Roger let fall—for she is in one of her moods and
will not confide in me—she considers herself bound to you by—
by the terms of your friendship. All she would say to Roger was,
' Clare comes first. Clare must come first '—which, of course,
is perfectly ridiculous."

Clare reddened.

" You mean that I, or you, for that matter, who have known
Alwynne for years, must step aside, must dutifully foster this
liking for a comparative stranger."

Elsbeth smiled.

" Well, naturally. He's a man."

" I am sorry I can't agree. Alwynne is a free agent. If she
prefers my friendship to Mr. Lumsden's adorations——"

" But I've told you already, it's a question of Marriage, Miss
Hartill. Surely you see the difference ? How can you weigh
the most intimate, the most ideal friendship against the chance
of getting married ? " Elsbeth was wholly in earnest.

Clare mounted her high horse.

" I can—I do. There are better things in life than marriage."

" For the average woman ? Do you sincerely say so ? The
brilliant woman—the rich woman—I don't count them, and
there are other exceptions, of course; but when her youth is
over, what is the average single woman ? A derelict, drifting
aimlessly on the high seas of life. Oh—I'm not very clear; it's
easy to make fun of me; but I know what I mean and so do you.
We're not children. We both know that an unmated woman—
she's a failure—she's unfulfilled."

Clare was elaborately bored.

" Really, Miss Loveday, the subject does not interest me."

" It must, for Alwynne's sake.	Don't you realize your enor-
mous responsibility ?	Don't you realize that when you keep
Alwynne entangled in your apron strings, blind to other interests,
when you cram her with poetry and emotional literature, when
you allow her to attach herself passionately to you, you are
feeding, and at the same time deflecting from its natural channel,
the strongest impulse of her life—of any girl's life ? Alwynne
needs a good concrete husband to love, not a fantastic ideal that
she calls friendship and clothes in your face and figure. You
are doing her a deep injury, Miss Hartill—unconsciously, I know,
or I should not be here—but doing it, none the less. If you
will consider her happiness——"

Clare broke in angrily—

" I do consider her happiness. Alwynne tells you that I am
essential to her happiness."

" She may believe so. But she's not happy. She has not
been happy for a long time. But she believes herself to be so,
I grant you that. But consider the future. Shall she never
break away ? Shall she oscillate indefinitely between you and
me, spend her whole youth in sustaining two old maids ? Oh,
Miss Hartill, she must have her chance. We must give her
what we've missed ourselves."

Clare appeared to be occupied in stifling a yawn. Her eyes
were danger signals, but Elsbeth was not Alwynne to remark
them.

" In one thing, at least, I do thoroughly agree with you. I
don't think there is the faintest likelihood of Alwynne's wishing
to marry at all at present, but I do feel, with you, that it is unfair
to expect her to oscillate, as you rhetorically put it, between two
old maids. I agree, too, that I have responsibilities in connection
with her. In fact, I think she would be happier if she were
with me altogether, and I intend to ask her to come and live
here. I shall ask her to-night. Don't you think she will be
pleased ? "

Clare's aim was good. Elsbeth clutched at the arms of her
chair.

" You wouldn't do such a thing ? "

Clare laughed shrilly.

" I shall do exactly what your Mr. Lumsden wants to do. I'm
not poor. I can give her a home as well as he, if you are

so anxious to get her off your hands. She seems to be going begging."

Elsbeth rose.

"I'm wasting time. I'll say good-bye, Miss Hartill. I shouldn't have come. But it was for Alwynne's sake. I hoped to touch you, to persuade you to forego, for her future's sake, for the sake of her ultimate happiness, the hold you have on her. I sympathized with you. I knew it would be a sacrifice. I knew, because I made the same sacrifice two years ago, when you first began to attract her. I thought you would develop her. I am not a clever woman, Miss Hartill, and you are; so I made no stand against you; but it was hard for me. Alwynne did not make it easier. She was not always kind. But hearing you to-day, I understand. You made Alwynne suffer more than I guessed. I don't blame her if sometimes it recoiled on me. You were always cruel. I remember you. The others were always snails for you to throw salt upon. I might have known you'd never change. Do you think I don't know your effect on the children at the school? Oh, you are a good teacher! You force them successfully; but all the while you eat up their souls. Sneer if you like! Have you forgotten Louise? I tell you, it's vampirism. And now you are to take Alwynne. And when she is squeezed dry and flung aside, who will be the next victim be? And the next, and the next? You grow greedier as you grow older, I suppose. One day you'll be old. What will you do when your glamour's gone? I tell you, Clare Hartill, you'll die of hunger in the end."

The small relentless voice ceased. There was a silence. Clare, who had remained quiescent for sheer amaze at the attack from so negligible a quarter, pulled herself together. Rather white, she began to clap her hands gently, as a critic surprised into applause.

"My dear woman, you're magnificent! Really you are. I never thought you had it in you. The Law and the Prophets incarnate. How Alwynne will laugh when I tell her. I wish she'd been here. You ought to be on the stage, you know, or in the pulpit. Have you quite finished? Quite? Do unburden yourself completely, you won't be given another opportunity. You understand that, of course? If Alwynne wishes to see you, she must make arrangements to do so elsewhere. That is the one condition I shall make. This is the way out."

Elsbeth rose. She was furious with herself that her lips must

tremble and her hands shake, as she gathered up scarf and reti-
cule; but she followed her hostess with sufficient dignity.

Clare flung open the door with a gesture a shade too ample.

Elsbeth laughed tremulously as she passed her and crossed
the hall.

" Oh, you are not altered," she said, and bent to fumble at
the latch. ` " But it doesn't impress me. You've not won yet.
You count too much on Alwynne. And you have still to
reckon with Mr. Lumsden."

" And his three acres and a cow ! " Clare watched her contemptuously. It did not seem worth while to keep her dignity
with Elsbeth. She felt that it would be a relief to lose her
temper completely, to override this opponent by sheer, crude
invective. She let herself go.

" What a fool you are ! Do you flatter yourself that you
understand Alwynne ? Go back to your Cœlebs and tell him
from Alwynne—I tell you I speak for Alwynne—that he's wasting his time. Let him take his goods to another market :
Alwynne won't buy. I've other plans for her—she has other
plans for herself. She doesn't want a husband She doesn't
want a home. She doesn't want children. She wants me—and
all I stand for. She wants to use her talents—and she shall—
through me. She wants success—she shall have it—through
me. She wants friendship—can't I give it ? Affection ?
Haven't I given it ? What more can she want ? A home ? I'm
well-off. A brat to play with ? Let her adopt one, and I'll
house it. I'll give her anything she wants. What more can your
man offer ? But I won't let her go. I tell you, we suffice
each other. Thank God, there are some women who can do
without marriage—marriage—marriage ! "

Elsbeth, as if she heard nothing, tugged at the catch. The
door swung open, and she stepped quietly into the sunny passage.
Then she turned to Clare, a grey, angry shadow in the dusk of the
hall.

" Poor Clare ! " she said. " Are the grapes very sour ? "

She pulled-to the door behind her.

Later in the evening, as she sat, flushed, tremulous, utterly
joyful over Roger's telegram, she considered the manner of her
exit and was shocked at herself.

" I don't know what possessed me," said Elsbeth apologetically. " And if I had only known. It was unladylike—it was

unwomanly—it was unchristian." She shook her head at her mild self in the glass. "But she made me so angry! If I'd only known that this was coming!" She fingered the pink envelope. "She'll think I knew. She'll always think I knew. And then to say what I did! It was unpardonable."

"But I was right, all the same," cried Elsbeth incorrigibly; "and I don't care. I'm glad I said it—I'm glad—I'm glad!"

CHAPTER XLVII

The sun slid over the edge of the sweating earth. Its red-hot plunge into the sea behind the hills was almost audible. The black cloud, fuming up from its setting-place, was as the steam of the collision. In great clots and coils it rolled upwards, spreading as it thinned, till it was a pall of vapour that sheeted all the lemon-coloured sky. Suddenly a cold wind sprang up, raced down the silent heavens, and, by way of Eastern Europe and the North Sea and the straight Roman road that drives down England, tore along the Utterbridge byways, and into the open window of Clare Hartill's parlour. A touch of its cold lips on her hair, and brow, and breast, and it was out again, driving the dust before it.

Clare shivered. She was very tired of waiting. . . . It was inexplicable that Alwynne should be late; but Clare with a half laugh, promised Alwynne to forego her scolding if she would but come. . . . The dusk and the wind and the silence were getting on her nerves. . . . The tick of the hall clock, for instance, was aggressive, insistent, maddening in its precise monotony. . . . Oh, unbearable ! With a gesture that was hysterical in its abandonment, Clare rose suddenly and flung into the hall, plucked open the clock door, and removed the pendulum. The released wire waggled foolishly into silence, like an idiot, tongue a-loll.

As the quiet hunted Clare into her sitting-room again, a little silver wire flickered down the sky like a scared snake, and for an instant she saw herself reflected in a convex mirror, a Clare bleached and shining and askew, like a St. Michael in a stained-glass window. Dusk and the thunder followed. The storm was beginning.

Clare moved about restlessly. She disliked storms. Her eyes ached, and she was cramped with waiting, and Alwynne had not come. She would, of course. . . . That woman had detained her, purposely, no doubt, and now there was the storm to delay her. . . . But Alwynne would come. . . . Clare smiled securely.

Again the lightning whipped across the heavens, and thunder roared in its wake.

Clare went to the window and watched the sky. The pane of glass was grateful to her hot forehead. She was too tired, too bruised and shaken by her own recent anger to arrange her thoughts, to pose for the moment, even to herself—of all audiences the most critical. The interview with Elsbeth Loveday rehearsed itself incessantly, pricking, probing, bludgeoning, in crescendo of intonation, innuendo, open attack, to the final triumphant insult. Triumphant, because true. The insult could cut through her defences and strike at her very self, because it was true. Her pride agonized. She had thought herself shrouded, invulnerable. And yet Elsbeth, whom of all women she had reckoned negligible, had guessed, had pitied. . . . Yet even her enemy was forgotten, as she sat and shuddered at the wound dealt; plucked and shrank, and plucked again at the arrow-tip rankling in it still.

The hours had passed in an evil mazement. But Alwynne was to come. . . . She thought of Alwynne with shifting passions of relief and longing and sheer crude lust for revenge. Alwynne would come. . . . Alwynne would soothe and comfort, intuitive, never waiting for the cry for help.

And Alwynne should pay. . . . Oho! Alwynne should pay Elsbeth's debts . . . should wince, and shrink, and whiten. *Scientific vivisection of one nerve*—— Wait a little, Alwynne!

Ah, Alwynne—the dearest—the beloved—the light and laughter of one's life. . . . What fool is whispering that Clare can hurt her ? . . . Alwynne shall see when she comes, who loves her. . . . There shall be a welcome, the royalest welcome she has ever had. . . . For what in all the world has Clare but Alwynne, and having Alwynne, has not Clare the world ?

Ah, well. . . . Perhaps she had not been always good to Alwynne. . . . To-day, for instance, she might have been kinder. . . . But Alwynne always understood. . . . That was the comfort of Alwynne, that she always understood. . . . Why didn't she come ? Wasn't there an echo of a step far down the street ?

When Alwynne came, they would make plans. . . . It would not be easy to wean the girl from her aunt, at least while they lived in the same town, the same country. . . . But one could travel, could take Alwynne quite away. . . . Italy. . . . Greece. . . . Egypt . . . they would go round the world together, shake off the school and all it stood for. . . . In a new world, begin a new life. . . . Why not? She had money enough to burn. . . . It would not be hard to persuade Alwynne, adventurous, infatuate. . . . Once gone, Elsbeth might whistle for her niece. . . They would talk it over to-morrow . . . to-night . . . as soon as Alwynne came. . . .

Was that thunder or a knocking? Rat-tat! Rat-tat! She had not been mistaken after all. . . . Alwynne! Alwynne!

And Clare, with an appearance on her that even Alwynne had never seen, ran like a child to open the door.

On the threshold stood a messenger boy, proffering a telegram. She took it.

" Any answer, Miss? " for she had offered to close the door.

" Oh, of course! " She frowned, and pulled open the flimsy sheet.

The boy waited. He peered past her, interested in the odd pictures on the walls, and the glimpse of a table luxuriously set. The minutes sped. He had soon seen all he could, and began to fidget.

" Any answer, Miss? " he hinted.

" Oh! " said Clare vaguely. " Answer? No. No answer. No answer at all."

The boy knuckled his forehead and clattered away down the staircase.

Mechanically Clare shut the door, locked and bolted it and secured it with the chain. Then she returned to the sitting room and crossed to her former station by the open window.

The storm was ending in a downpour of furious tropical rain. It beat in unheeded upon her thin dress and bare neck and the open telegram in her hands, as, with lips parted and a faint, puzzled pucker between her brows, she conned over the message—

I cannot come to-night. I have gone to Dene. I am going to marry Roger.

She read it and re-read, twisting it this way and that, for it was barely visible in the wet dusk. It seemed an eternity before its full meaning dawned upon her. And yet she had known all there was to know when she confronted the messenger boy (Oh, Destiny is up to date) and took her sentence from his grimy hand.

I am going to marry Roger.

" Very well, Alwynne! " Clare flung up her head, up and back

Her face was drowned in the shadows of the crimson curtain, but her neck caught the last of the light, shone like old marble. The whole soul of her showed for an instant in its defiant outline, in the involuntary pulsation that quivered across its rigidity, in the uncontrollable flutter beneath the chin.

The thin, capable fingers twisted and clenched over the sodden paper.

She moved at last, spoke into space. Passion, anger, and the cool contempt of the school-mistress for a mutinous class, mingled grotesquely in her voice.

" Very well, Alwynne ! Just as you please, of course. There is no more to be said." She tossed away the little ball of paper as she spoke.

She wandered aimlessly about the room ; turned to her bookshelves after a while, and stood a long time, pulling out volume after volume, opening each at random, reading a page, closing the book again, letting it slide from her hand, never troubling to replace it. She was tired at last and turned to her writing-table.

It was piled high with exercise-books, and she corrected a couple before she swept them also aside.

The rain had not faltered in its swishing downfall. It beat against the panes, and on to the sill, and dripped down into a pool beneath the open window.

" She will have to come back on Monday," said Clare suddenly. " She can't go off like that. There's the school——" She broke off abruptly, as a gust of wind soughed by.

I cannot come. I have gone to Dene. I am going to marry Roger. She could hear Alwynne's voice in it, answering.

" But why ? " cried Clare piteously. " Why ? What is it ? What have I done ? "

" S'hush ! " sighed the rain. " S'hush ! "

"I loved her," cried Clare. " I loved her. What have I done ? "

" S'hush ! " sobbed the rain. " S'hush ! S'hush ! "

She turned to the darkening windows, and started, and shuddered away again, stricken dumb and shaking. A pool of something red and wet was spreading over the polished boards, and a thin trickle was stealing forward to her feet.

Blood ?

Fool. . . . The red of the curtains reflected, tingeing a pool of rain-water. . . . Blood, nevertheless. . . . She had forgotten Louise. . . .

What had Alwynne heard? A garbled version of that last interview? Fool again—unless the dead can speak. . . . But Alwynne knew. . . . Something had been revealed to her, suddenly, during their idle talk. . . . But when? But how? She had come as a lover . . . she had left as a stranger . . . what in any god's name, had she guessed? Clare's subconscious memory reproduced for her instantly, with photographic accuracy, details of the scene that she had not even known she had observed. Alwynne had changed, in an instant, between a word and a reply. . . . What was it that Clare had said—what trifling, teasing nothing, flung out in pure wantonness? But Alwynne's face, her dear face, had become, for an instant—Clare strained to the memory—as the face of Louise. . . . Louise had looked at her like that, that other day. . . . What had they seen then, both of them? Was she Gorgon to bring that look into their their faces? Louise—yes—she could understand Louise. . . . She did not care to think about Louise. . . . But Alwynne— what had she ever done to Alwynne? At least Alwynne might tell her what she had done. . . . She would not submit to it. . . . She would not be put aside. . . . She would at least have justice. . . .

I am going to marry Roger.

Useless! All useless! The struggle was over before she had known she was fighting. . . . She knew that in Alwynne's life there was no longer any part for her. And Clare had travelled far that evening, to phrase it thus. Sharing was a strange word for her to use. But she recognized dully that even sharing was out of her power. What had she to do with a husband, and housewifery, and the bearing of children? Alwynne married was Alwynne dead.

Alwynne in love. . . . Alwynne married. . . . Alwynne putting any living thing before Clare! She broke into bitter laughter at the idea. What had happened? What had Clare done or left undone? She realized grimly that of this at least she might be sure—it had been her own doing. . . . No influence could have wrought against her own. . . . Alwynne, at least, was where she was, because Clare had sent her, not because another had beckoned. . . . And that was the comfort she had stored up for herself, to last her in the lean years to come. . .

What was the use of regretting?

Alwynne was gone. . . . Then forget her. . . . There were other fish in the sea. . . . There was a promising class this term.

. . . That child in the Fourth. . . . She wondered if Alwynne had noticed her. . . . She must ask Alwynne. . . . Alwynne had gone away, had gone to Dene, was going to marry Roger. . . .

Well, there was always work. . . . Where was that letter to Miss Marsham ?

She moved stiffly in her seat, lit a candle, and drew towards her the half-written sheet that lay open on the blotter. She re-read it.

You will, I am sure, understand how much I appreciate your offer of the partnership, but after much consideration I have decided——

She hesitated, crossed out the *but* and wrote an *and* above it, and continued—

—to accept it. I will come to tea to-morrow, as you kindly suggest.

She finished the letter, signed it, stamped and addressed, and sat idle at last, staring down at it.

The neat handwriting danced, and flickered, and grew dim.

With an awkward gesture she put her hands to her eyes, and brought them away again, wet. She smiled at that, a twisted, mocking smile. She supposed she was crying. . . . She did not remember ever having done such a thing. . . .

So her future was decided. . . . It was to be work and loneliness—loneliness and work . . . because, it seemed, she had no friends left. . . . Yet Alwynne had promised many things. . . . What had she done to Alwynne ? What had she done ?

She turned within herself and reviewed her life as she remembered it, thought by thought, word by word, action by action. Faces rose about her, whispering reminders, forgotten faces of the many who had loved her : from her old nurse, dead long ago, to Louise, and Alwynne, and foolish Olivia Pring.

The candle at her elbow flared and dribbled, and died at last with a splutter and a gasp. She paid no heed.

When the dawn came, she was still sitting there, thinking—thinking.

March 1914—September 1915.